THE DIRTY TRUTH

SEAL OF THE PRESIDENT OF THE UNITED STATES

A NOVEL BY WILLIAM W. ANDREWS

Also by William Andrews

The Essential Truth

Daughters of the Dragon – A Comfort Woman's Story

THE DIRTY TRUTH © 2015 by William Andrews

Printed in the United States of America.

This is a work of fiction. Names, characters, places and incidents either are the product of the author's imagination or are used fictitiously, and any resemblance to any actual persons, living or dead, events, or locales is entirely coincidental.

Cover design by Doug Novak.

Library of Congress Control Number: 2014900030
ISBN: Print   978-0-9913958-3-5
                    EBook   978-0-9913958-2-8

MADhouse Press LLC
5904 Halifax Ave South
Minneapolis, MN 55424-1991
www.madhousepress.com
info@madhousepress.com

To order additional copies of this book, contact your on-line retailer or visit:

www.williamandrewsbooks.com
or
www.madhousepress.com

If we would learn what the human race really is at bottom, we need only observe it in election times.

                                                    - Mark Twain

ONE

Three weeks before the presidential election

The first election campaign Nan Smith managed was a massacre. That's what the Minneapolis paper called it the day after the election. In a one-word front-page headline. In one-hundred-fifty point type. Underneath the headline was a side-by-side photograph of the winner, the supposedly beatable incumbent U.S. Senator William Howard, next to Nan's supposedly unbeatable candidate, US Congresswoman Janice Theilen. A photo of a shaken Nan appeared on the second page with the caption: *Theilen campaign manager Nan Smith seemed overwhelmed in the last months of the election.*

Uh... yeah. Got that right.

Back then, Theilen had an eleven point lead two months before Election Day and it was looking like an easy victory and a big step up in Nan's political career. But Senator Howard was managed by billionaire communications mogul Sheldon Hanrahan who orchestrated a brilliant, brutal, and mostly illegal assault on Theilen's lead. Nan had expected the negative advertising, but then came the dirty tricks that she was completely unprepared for. Push polls, unaccredited mailers spreading lies about Theilen, misleading "research", hacking of their computers, and even sabotage of Theilen's campaign headquarters.

The coup de gras came the weekend before the election in what had then become a very close race. The media received newly discovered 'facts' claiming Senator Howard had once been the leader of a secret white supremacist group. The accusation was completely implausible, but since it appeared to have come from the Theilen campaign, the press ran with it. The accusation was so outrageous it made Howard a sympathetic victim of what looked like a desperate attempt to rescue Theilen's failing campaign. Nan immediately got Janice on the evening news to deny the story came from her office, but by then it was too late. Nan's campaign for Theilen was in a shambles and by the time she could get it together again, the election was over and so was Nan's political career.

It had been the first time Nan had seen the dirty side of politics. Before then, it was the only thing she'd ever wanted to do. She first got involved on campus, her sophomore year, in the campaign for U.S. president. She believed in her candidate and worked long hours for him. He lost, but instead of becoming disillusioned and walking away, she redoubled her efforts. She became addicted. The ideas, the debates, the long hours, the competitiveness, the *passion* of it thrilled her more than anything. She believed she was making a difference, changing people's lives, making the world a better place. And when she got married and gave birth to a beautiful baby girl, her passion grew. Then she was building a better world for her daughter Jenny.

But then she ran into Sheldon Hanrahan and it all came crashing down. She'd lost the election, the respect of her party, and her passion for politics.

So she was surprised when two years later, she got a call from the party asking her to run the state campaign for their nominee for president of the United States. Governor George Bloomfield of Massachusetts was running against the incumbent, Vice President Hal Marshall. Minnesota was one of the least important states in the national race. Nan had always admired Bloomfield, and it was a low-level, low-risk assignment so she accepted it even though the governor was a long shot to defeat the popular vice president. It was a chance for her to start over and maybe find her passion again.

Now, as Nan walked through the front door of Bloomfield's Minnesota campaign headquarters on a crisp October morning, she hoped nothing would knock the campaign off track this time. Minnesota was one of just four states where Bloomfield was leading and she was prepared for anything. But last night the evening news reported that Hal Marshall had another heart attack. Then, early this morning, Marshall's campaign manager announced that the vice president was dropping out of the race. This morning, there was an announcement coming from the president. Nan wanted to watch it from the office.

When she stepped into the lobby, Stephanie at the front desk nodded toward an elderly woman sitting in the reception area. "She's been waiting to see you for twenty minutes," Stephanie whispered. "She'll only talk to the campaign manager. She said it's important."

Nan studied the woman. She was sitting in one of the lobby chairs staring out the front window. She wore a coarse, brown overcoat and old tennis shoes. Her hair was greasy and tangled.

"Who is she?" Nan asked. After the Theilen campaign, she didn't like surprise visitors to her candidate's headquarters. Even non-threatening ones like this old woman.

"She wouldn't give me her name," Stephanie answered. "She seems kinda, you know, confused. By the way, did you hear about Vice President Marshall?"

Nan took off her overcoat and hung it in the closet. "Yeah," she said. "I'm not surprised. Running for president isn't good for anyone's health. What's the latest?"

"The president's about to make an announcement. They have the TV on in the back room."

Nan glanced at the woman in the reception area. The president's announcement was certainly going to be something about the election. After the announcement, Bob Hilton, Bloomfield's national campaign manager in Boston, would want to have a conference call with the state campaign managers to discuss who their new opponent might be and to formulate a new strategy. The announcement probably wouldn't affect Minnesota much, but there would still be things they'd have to do. She was going to be busy.

Nan went to the woman. "Ma'am," she said, "I'm Nan Smith, Bloomfield's Minnesota campaign manager. You wanted to see me?"

The woman's eyes widened. "Yes!" she said. "It's important."

"What is it?"

The woman looked around the reception area. "It has to be in private," she whispered.

Nan could hear the television in the other room. The president was going to make his announcement any minute.

"I understand, ma'am. I just have one thing to do. Then we'll talk. Do you want some coffee or water while you wait?"

"No," the woman said with a quick shake of her head. "I might not have much time."

"I'll only be a few minutes," Nan said. "Stephanie here will take care of you."

Nan locked eyes with Stephanie and pointed her chin at the woman. Stephanie understood and went to the woman.

Nan walked into the back of the campaign offices. Nearly the entire space of the one-story brick building was a bullpen area filled with old computer monitors resting on a mismatched collection of desks. Boxes with campaign literature were stacked everywhere. Against the back wall were two long tables set end-to-end supporting a bank of telephones for volunteers to make calls.

At night, there'd be two dozen people working in the office, but this early there were only three, all huddled around a small television. Jim Black, the assistant campaign manager, was working the remote. He spotted Nan as she walked in. "Nan, you're just in time. The president is holding a press conference about Marshall."

"CNN!" yelled Shelly Novak. Middle aged and overweight, Shelly was a permanent fixture at the campaign office ever since the party nominated Bloomfield. Nan had no idea what she did there. "CNN has the best coverage. Channel 3!"

"I want CNBC," Jim said. "I like their analysts. What channel is it?" He punched numbers on the remote.

Nan settled into a chair. "Sixty-two," she said. "CNBC is channel 62."

"Just turn on something!" Hank Mattson said pointing a finger at the TV. "You have it on the cartoon channel!"

Hank, an election campaign veteran, was in his early seventies. A retired carpenter, he always had a joke and a smile and was the hardest worker in the office. Nan had come to appreciate his work ethic and common sense since he'd volunteered after the party convention.

"I got it, I got it," Jim declared, pressing the remote again. CNBC came on the screen with their analysts talking seriously about the president's upcoming announcement.

"I watched channel 5 this morning," Shelly said excitedly. "They're saying Senator Howard could be the new candidate."

"If that's true," Jim said, "our little office will become very important since we're Howard's home state."

"That's just our local news talking," Hank interjected. "There's no way the national party will choose Howard. He's too radical. They have much better options."

"Well, that's what they said on the news this morning," Shelly said. She turned to Nan. "What do you think, Nan? Will it be Howard?"

Nan shook her head, but Jim interrupted before she could answer. "The president's coming on!" he said.

The small television blinked to a shot of the White House pressroom lectern with its blue and gold presidential seal. The press secretary and a clutch of assistants stood off to one side. After a few seconds, President Dougherty in a blue suit and red tie walked into the pressroom and stepped to the lectern.

"My fellow Americans," the president began, "I have a short announcement. As you already know, my good friend, Vice President Hal Marshall, has dropped out of the race for the presidency." As usual, President Phillip Dougherty, handsome with thick hair, penetrating eyes and an infectious smile, portrayed both a commanding presence and an aw shucks charm that had made him impossible to beat in the previous two elections. He explained that he had visited the vice president and that the doctors expected "Bulldog" to make a full recovery.

"We are losing an outstanding candidate who would have served our country well," Dougherty continued. "I'm sorry to see him drop out."

Then the president of the United States paused dramatically and stared directly into the camera. His charm was gone and only his commanding expression remained. "With only three weeks until Election Day," the president said, "it's crucial that voters have a clear choice of candidates. Therefore, I would like to announce that I, President Phillip Dougherty, personally endorse Minnesota Senator William Howard as the new presidential candidate for our party. Thank you."

The pressroom went into a stunned silence for a few seconds, and then erupted with reporters shouting questions at the president. He waved them off without answering and walked out of the pressroom followed by his entourage. The TV blinked to the stammering CNBC political analysts trying to make sense of the president's bombshell.

Nan and her colleagues looked at each other open-mouthed and said nothing. No one had expected the president to support anyone so soon after Hal Marshall bowed out of the race. And, in spite of what they said on the local news, no one seriously expected him to endorse William Howard. The president and Senator Howard had very different political views and were not personally close. But for some reason, the president had used the White House podium to preempt his party leadership and make Howard their new candidate. It was an incredible turn of events.

*

The phone rang in Nan's office. She quickly wound her way between boxes to her desk in the only enclosed workspace in the campaign headquarters. She swung herself into her chair and answered the phone, "Bloomfield campaign."

"Did you catch the president's speech?" It was Bob Hilton.

"Bob," Nan said pushing herself to the front of her chair. "Ah, yes, I saw it. Incredible. I can't believe he endorsed Howard."

"Total surprise. Came right out of the blue." Hilton talked as if his words were bullets from a machine gun.

"I'll say," Nan said nodding. "Why did he do it?"

"Don't know, but it doesn't matter. It's done. Now this race becomes veeery interesting. Dougherty is pressuring his party to make Howard their candidate. They'll have to comply. Only three weeks to go. No time to pussyfoot around. You know, of course, what this means for you?" Hilton asked.

"Um... yeah," Nan answered. "Howard's campaign headquarters will be here in Minnesota so this office will be directly in the line of fire, so to speak."

"Correctamundo," Hilton said. "Minnesota just became our second most important campaign office. And *you* just became a very important adviser. That's why I called you first." Nan could picture Bob's searing blue eyes and his Ivy League good looks. He was type-A from head to toe and Nan knew she had to be sharp to keep up with him. "You know Howard better than anyone," Hilton continued. "And you know who'll be his campaign manager."

Nan closed her eyes. "Sheldon Hanrahan," she said. She thought of the campaign from two years earlier and how it had ended her rise in the party. She remembered the humiliation she'd felt after the election. And now, she was running a campaign against Sheldon Hanrahan again. She shook her head.

In his rapid-fire style, Hilton told Nan that he was sending people to Minnesota who would work out of her offices but report to him. He said they'd have to dress up the Minnesota office. He told her they'd need her insights on Howard and Hanrahan. They had a ton to do, he said, and he wanted her in Boston as soon as possible for a strategy meeting.

"I can't tell you how exciting this is," Hilton continued. "Our guy just became the front-runner with only three weeks left until the election. We have a real shot at the presidency. And you'll be our person in Minnesota. If his party endorses Howard—and I think they have to—you'll be in the national spotlight."

Then Hilton's tone softened. "Nan," he said, "the Theilen campaign. It wasn't pleasant. This will be worse. Much worse. But I need you. The country needs you. Are you with us?"

Nan slid her fingers into her blonde hair and began twirling it. Until now, she was a minor player in this race. But suddenly she was an adviser to the man who would likely be the next president of the United States. It was a tremendous opportunity, one she wasn't sure she was ready for. But maybe this time it'd be different. This time, she had the entire party machine and the brilliant Bob Hilton behind her. Maybe this time she could win. Then again, they were against Sheldon Hanrahan.

There was a soft knock on her office door. The old woman from the reception area stood in the doorway clutching her coat around her. Her eyes were wild and focused on Nan. "They're coming to get me," the woman trembled.

"Excuse me, what? Hang on, hang on," Nan said, once to Hilton, once to the woman. Nan took a long look at the frightened woman in her doorway. "Bob, I'll have to call you back. There's someone here."

"What? Who?" Hilton demanded.

"I'll call you right back," Nan said and hung up.

Nan motioned the woman to come in to her office. The woman glanced over her shoulder toward the front door and quickly took a seat in front of Nan's desk. She continued to clutch her coat.

"Did you say someone's coming to get you?" Nan asked.

"Yes. they'll be here any second," the woman said. "I came to tell you something. You must help." The woman glanced over her shoulder again.

"What is it?" Nan asked.

"You can't let him win," she whispered, leaning over Nan's desk.

"Who?"

"Senator Howard!" she said. "He can't be the president. They said on television that Vice President Marshall has dropped out of the race and Howard might run for president!"

Nan smiled gently. "I think I understand, ma'am. I don't want Senator Howard to be the president either."

The phone rang. It was probably Hilton calling back demanding to know why Nan had hung up on him. She was about to answer it and tell Bob to give her a minute.

"No! You don't understand," the woman sobbed before Nan could grab the phone. "There's a reason. Something happened. You can't let him win because…"

There was a commotion outside Nan's office. Two men dressed in white barged into the bullpen. Stephanie was scrambling after them shouting, "Just a minute there. Hey! Wait just a minute!" The others, Jim, Shelly and Hank, looked up from their desks bewildered. The men quickly marched toward Nan's office. Nan's phone continued to ring.

Nan looked back at the woman who no longer clutched her coat. She'd stopped sobbing and her eyes were clear. "Ma'am," Nan said, "tell me why Senator Howard can't be president."

"Because," the woman hissed as the men in white reached the office door, "he murdered my daughter."

TWO

"IT DOESN'T MAKE SENSE," Silvia Mendoza said to the political editor at the *Washington Sentinel*. "Why would the president endorse Howard? And why would he do it without consulting his national committee? And on national television, no less?"

Looking ever the dapper English newspaperman, Ian Rutter sat across from Silvia at a plastic lunch table. Silvia, the paper's White House correspondent, had asked him to join her for an early lunch in the newspaper's basement cafeteria to talk about President Dougherty's endorsement of Senator Howard. Ian had told her he wasn't hungry—it was only eleven in the morning—but as usual, she was famished. So, he agreed to meet her in the cafeteria. He'd ordered a hamburger and fries but hadn't touched it.

"It is odd," Rutter replied in his delicate English accent. "I suppose the president thinks Howard is the best candidate."

"*No es cierto*," Silvia fired back. "Bullshit." She hovered over her plate of pasta salad and forked it into her mouth as they talked. "Howard isn't the best candidate and the president knows it. Bloomfield will bury him. What about Marshall's running mate? Why doesn't he support Masello?"

Ian twitched his carefully trimmed mustache. "That man is what you call a nut case. The only reason Congressman Masello was Marshall's running mate was to get California's fifty-five electoral votes. The president would never support him."

"No one expected him to support Howard either," Silvia replied. "There are plenty of other choices better than the senior senator from Minnesota."

"I believe the president wants to show everyone he is still in control. It's a case of lame duck resentment."

"Lame duck resentment?" Silvia asked, shoving another forkful of pasta into her mouth.

"Yes. Consider," Ian said folding his arms. "Phillip Dougherty has been the leader of the free world for the past eight years. He's been one of the country's most popular presidents. Everywhere he goes he's looked upon as practically a god. Women fall over themselves to get close to him. Men fear him. He gives orders and armies march. And in January, the poor man has to give it up to someone else."

"I see. It's a male thing. *Huevos*," Silvia said, reaching for her Coke. "The alpha male doesn't want to give up control, even though the twenty-second amendment says he has to."

"Indeed. And he wants to exercise his power while he still can. You see it all the time. Lame duck presidents do all sorts of preposterous things. Pardons, outrageous decrees. They sign bills they would never otherwise support." Ian picked up a french fry and examined it. "Mr. Dougherty doesn't have to worry about politics anymore so he just does as he pleases."

"Like endorse Senator Howard?" Silvia asked. "You'd think if he could do what he wanted to, he'd support anyone *except* Bill Howard. They're as far apart as two people in the same party can be."

Ian tossed the french fry back onto his plate. "As I said, lame duck presidents do preposterous things."

"To show they're still in control."

"Exactly, my dear girl."

Ian dabbed his mustache with his napkin, though he hadn't taken a bite of his food. He pushed his tray aside. He folded his arms and studied Silvia. "How can you eat so much and stay so thin?" he asked. "You eat like my teenage son."

"I burn it off. I'm not like the lazies sitting on their *colas* waiting for stories to drop in their laps. I *work*."

Ian chuckled and shook his head. "That you do, my dear. That you do."

Silvia had come to appreciate working for Ian. He wasn't like the other newspapermen in senior positions at the *Sentinel*. He was a true British journalist and enjoyed a bawdy story or juicy conspiracy. Over the past eight years, Washington newspapers had become little more than mouthpieces for the popular Dougherty Administration. Hard-nosed, investigative journalism had practically died. Silvia believed the press should do more and she found a sympathizer—albeit a cautious one—in Ian.

"I don't know," Silvia said eyeing Ian's untouched food. "It's as if Dougherty is handing the presidency to Bloomfield. It seems almost… desperate."

"Not everything that goes on in this town is a conspiracy, Silvia."

"True, but as reporters, we should assume it is," Silvia shot back. "Instead, we regurgitate what the White House gives us and not upset anyone," Silvia said. "All the media does these days is report what's given to us by the people we're supposed to watch. No one investigates anymore."

Ian let out a long sigh. "Silvia, I promise if you uncover something suspicious, we will investigate. Just be careful not to ruffle any feathers. Okay?"

Silvia had gotten what she wanted out of the meeting with Ian. He had just given her permission to probe the Dougherty endorsement of Senator William Howard. If there was something going on, she'd uncover it. She didn't become the paper's youngest female and first Hispanic White House correspondent for nothing. She had learned early on how to compensate for her gender, race, and petite stature in the male-dominated newspaper business. It was her ruthless determination. If there was a story somewhere, she'd dig it out and she didn't care what she had to do to get it.

"*Sí*," Silvia replied. "I promise I'll be careful, but if someone at the White House wants to slip a message to the media, I want to be the one they give it to. The best way to do that is to let people in the White House know I'm looking." Silvia pointed to Ian's untouched burger and fries. "Are you going to eat that?" she asked.

Ian waved his hand over the tray. "It's all yours."

She grabbed his tray and started in on the fries. "You know, you could help me with this," she said.

"I thought my advice was help enough. And I just gave you my lunch."

"Have someone cover for me at the White House so I can conduct a real investigation."

Ian studied Silvia carefully. "I can't do that. We need you at the White House. Anyway, we must be careful. Crusades like yours can get you and the paper in trouble. Be discreet or you will lose your White House press pass. Take it easy—at least until after the election."

Silvia took a bite of Ian's hamburger and glared at him. "Like I said, I need to burn off all this food."

Ian laughed and pushed away from the table. "Like *I* said, be careful. Talk to that mole of yours and see what she knows. If you discover something, tell me. If I think it points to a story, I'll see if we can get you some help so you can do your investigation. In the meantime, make sure you get your other work done."

"*Está bien.*"

"I must get back. Enjoy my lunch," Ian said and left the cafeteria.

*

Crusade. Hell yes, she was on a crusade. She'd been on one since she was a little girl, hiking the scorching Mexican desert with her family to get to the promised land of America. When they finally got to Los Angeles, her father worked two full time jobs and her mother cleaned the houses of rich Americans to give Silvia and her brother a respectable home so they could concentrate on their schoolwork. Her parents told them education was the key to success in America, so Silvia worked hard in school and brought home straight A's.

Her brother had gone the other direction. At fifteen, he became a foot soldier for the Vatos Locos and before he reached eighteen, he'd become a casualty of the south L.A. gang wars. After the priest issued the benediction at his funeral, Silvia's parents never talked about her brother again. But Silvia knew that from then on, they pinned their hopes of a better life entirely on her.

She finished Ian's hamburger and pushed the tray to the side. Why did she eat like that? Why couldn't she take it easy like Ian told her to? It must be habit from driving herself for all these years. Her drive had taken her far, and now she couldn't turn it off if she wanted to.

And she wouldn't be content until she uncovered the reason why the president endorsed William Howard.

THREE

THE MEN IN WHITE who came for the old woman were polite, but firm. "Mrs. Wilson escaped the hospital this morning," the tall one told Nan. "We don't know how she got out. She's..." he paused as the stocky one lead Mrs. Wilson toward the exit while the other campaign workers looked on, "...she's not all there, if you know what I mean. I'm terribly sorry for the inconvenience," he said backing away. "We'll take care of Mrs. Wilson now. Thank you. I'm sorry. Good day."

She wasn't all there? True, what she had said was preposterous. *He murdered my daughter.* Surely Senator Howard couldn't have possibly murdered anyone. As an important senator from Minnesota, he'd been in the spotlight for the past fourteen years. If he'd committed a murder, someone would surely know. But there was something in the way Mrs. Wilson—if that was her real name—looked at Nan as she uttered her accusation. It was her eyes. They were cold, lucid, sane.

A few minutes after they took the woman away, Bob Hilton called the main office number demanding to talk to Nan. She closed her office door and took the call at her desk. Bob asked who had interrupted his call. Nan apologized and thought for a second about telling him what the woman said. Instead, she told him it was a vagrant from the street causing a ruckus. Hilton seemed to accept the explanation and asked again if the party could depend on her. She said she was in and they spent the next few minutes talking about Nan's new role in Bloomfield's campaign. He repeated that it was a tremendous opportunity for her. She said she understood and was excited to take on the challenge. She agreed to fly to Boston the next day for a strategy meeting with the campaign's executive committee.

It would be exciting to work closely with Bob Hilton. He was smart, full of energy and enormously ambitious. He'd graduated at the top of his Yale law school class and had new ideas about elections and politics that he was determined to put into practice. After the party convention, he was on the cover of *Time* magazine with the headline, 'The New Political Wunderkind'. It was expected that if Bloomfield became president, Hilton would be his chief of staff.

*

After Nan hung up her phone, Hank knocked on her door. He was wearing jeans and a work shirt with the sleeves rolled halfway up his forearms. "Hey, Nan. Crazy morning."

"I'll say," Nan smiled. Hank was lean and strong from forty years of swinging a hammer.

He slid into the chair in front of Nan's desk. "What did that woman want?"

"She told me she didn't want Howard to be president."

Hank laughed out loud. "Yeah, me neither."

Nan chuckled, then turned serious. "Hank, I have to go to Boston tomorrow. I've suddenly become a valuable commodity to the Bloomfield campaign. I'll be the campaign spokesperson here in Minnesota. I'll have to handle all the media attention we'll be getting." Nan ran her fingers through her hair. "I just got a lot busier. I have to see if my mother can pick up Jenny from lacrosse practice. I hate it when I can't be home for Jenny."

"Nan," Hank said, "you don't often get a chance to be an important adviser on a national presidential campaign, and you don't often get a chance to work with someone like Bob Hilton. Don't worry about things here. You have your husband. Ben's a good man. And I can help. All my kids are grown," he said with a smile.

"I'm going to need it," Nan said. "No offense to him, but I'm afraid Jim isn't cut out for a campaign like this. I need someone with more experience."

"Yeah," Hank replied. "We'll be up against Sheldon Hanrahan again. We've never beaten a candidate managed by him. Looks like we won't beat him in Minnesota this time either running against our own senator. Nationally it'll be different though. Bloomfield should win."

Nan remembered the senate campaign from two years earlier. Sheldon Hanrahan had been ruthless. He'd gotten away with dirty, illegal tricks. Surely he wouldn't get away with it in a national campaign for the presidency of the United States, would he?

Nan studied Hank. He was a lifelong, card-carrying party member and had a stubborn pragmatism about politics. She'd need him in the next three weeks and was grateful he'd offered to step up.

"Hank," she said, after a pause, "that woman this morning said something else."

"Oh? What?"

"She said…" Nan shook her head, "…this sounds crazy." Nan looked directly at Hank. "She said Howard murdered her daughter."

"Huh?" Hank said cocking his head. "Howard? No way."

Nan shrugged. "That's what she said. 'He murdered my daughter.' Her exact words."

"That *is* crazy. Did they say who she was?"

"Those brutes called her 'Mrs. Wilson'. They were from the Rand Psychiatric Hospital. It was on their nametags. She must be a patient there. It's only eight blocks from here."

"Poor woman, she must be senile," Hank said shaking his head.

"That's what they said. But I don't know, Hank. There was something in her eyes…"

Stephanie poked her head in the office. "Nan, there's someone here to see you."

"What does he want?" Nan asked.

"I think it's about that woman earlier."

"You better talk to him," Hank said. "Jim and I have to re-do this week's mailing. I'll talk to you later."

*

Hank left and Stephanie showed the man to Nan's office. He was an African American, and wore a wrinkled overcoat over a sports coat and white shirt. He had pulled down his tie. Nan thought he looked like a cop. "Good mornin', ma'am," he said with a slight Alabama twang. "Your receptionist told me you're the manager here?"

"Yes. I'm Nan Smith. And you are?"

"I'm Mr. Woods," he answered extending a hand. "I'm in charge of security at the Rand Psychiatric Hospital. Terribly sorry about Mrs. Wilson this mornin'. Poor lady."

Nan shook his hand and pointed to a chair. "Do your patients escape often?" She asked.

"No, ma'am," Woods said, chuckling. "That's why I'm here. 'Fraid I have to ask you some questions. I need to complete a report for insurance purposes, you know. Standard procedure when somethin' like this happens."

"Of course. What do you want to know?"

Mr. Woods took a pad and pen from an inside pocket of his sports coat. "What time did Mrs. Wilson show up here?" he asked.

"She was here when I arrived at about 8:50. My receptionist said she'd been waiting twenty minutes, so I guess she was here at 8:30 or so."

"Eight thirty." He wrote the time on his pad. "And we caught her about 9:20 which means she was here for fifty minutes?"

"That sounds right."

"Who did she talk to while she was here?"

"Just me," Nan said.

"And what did she say?"

Nan cocked her head. "Why do you want to know what she said? I thought you were just filling out an insurance report?"

"Ah… it's routine, ma'am. The report needs to be very specific. Sorry for these questions but I have to ask 'em. Did you talk to Mrs. Wilson about anythin' in particular?"

"She told me she didn't want Howard to be president."

Mr. Woods smiled pleasantly. "Ah. So that's why she came here. I understand now. You see, Mrs. Wilson watches the news every morning without fail. She probably heard that Senator Howard might run in Vice President Marshall's place. Problem is, Mrs. Wilson suffers from dementia," Mr. Woods said, tapping his temple. "Loco, if you know what I mean. That's why she lives with us." He smiled and nodded. Then he looked straight at Nan. "So, did she say anythin' else?"

"No. Your men got to her before she could tell us she has proof that Senator Howard is a child molester and worships Satan." Nan offered a condescending smile. "Of course, we already know that about him," she said.

Mr. Woods let out a chuckle and nodded. "I'm sure you do, I'm sure you do." He closed his notepad and put it back into his coat pocket. "Ms. Smith, thank you for your time and I'm sorry for your trouble this mornin'. As I said, Mrs. Wilson is very sick. We'll keep a closer watch on her from now on. She won't bother you again, I promise."

As Mr. Woods rose to leave, Nan asked, "Mr. Woods, now I have a question for you. If Mrs. Wilson is as *loco* as you say," she tapped her head as Woods had done earlier, "why do you care what she said to me?"

For a split second, there was panic in Mr. Wood's eyes. But he quickly recovered and said, "The report... You know, for the insurance." He smiled weakly and nodded. "Thank you for your time, Ms. Smith." He turned on his heel and quickly left.

*

Nan closed her office door and returned to her desk. An insurance report? Really? It seemed like Mr. Woods was searching for something more than information for an insurance report. He asked too many questions. Perhaps she should call election headquarters and report the incident. Or maybe she should call the police. Or the FBI. But she remembered the senate race from two years earlier and the bogus report about Howard being a white supremacist that destroyed Theilen's campaign. She shook her head. She was letting the events of the morning get to her. After all, Mr. Woods' talking to her made sense—psychiatric hospitals were one of the most closely regulated institutions in the state.

Nan turned her attention to her work. She was now a senior adviser to the Bloomfield campaign and had to get ready for her trip to Boston in the morning. Bob Hilton would ask a thousand questions about Senator Howard and Sheldon Hanrahan and she had to be ready for him. She made a list of questions she thought he'd ask and wrote out her answers. But as she worked, she kept seeing the woman's eyes as she uttered the absurd accusation.

They were not the eyes of a crazy woman.

FOUR

"TELL ME EXACTLY what happened, Woods," Frank Pierce ordered. It was a cool October afternoon as Pierce sat on a Washington Mall park bench outside the Treasury building with his cell phone pressed to his ear. The phone was a field-hardened smart-phone transmitting over a private network programmed to handle clandestine calls. He'd used the same network for the past five years—ever since they gave him this fucked up assignment.

"I don't think there was any damage done," Woods said on the other end of the line. His Alabama twang was thicker than usual. "We got to her before she could say anythin'."

"I said tell me exactly what happened" Frank insisted. "Start at the beginning. How did she get away?"

"Well, apparently she's been flushin' her medicine. The damn nurse should-a noticed it. Yesterday, durin' breakfast, she escaped through the service door when no one was lookin'."

"A high security hospital and she just waltzes out?" Frank said, trying to stay calm. "It's your job to watch her, Woods."

"Yeah, but we've been on this assignment a long time, Frank, and this is the first time anythin's happened."

"I don't give a fuck," Pierce said. He could feel his blood start to boil. "I want her watched every fucking minute of every fucking day. Am I clear?"

"Yeah, you're clear."

"You said she went to the Bloomfield campaign office?"

"Yes."

"Who did she talk to there?" Frank demanded.

"Just the receptionist and Bloomfield's Minnesota campaign manager, Nan Smith. Nice looking woman, if you know what I mean."

"Nan Smith." Pierce burned the name into his memory. He didn't care that she was good looking. "What did the woman say to Ms. Smith?"

"She told her she didn't want Howard to be the next president. She didn't say anythin' more."

"Do you know that for sure?"

"It's what Ms. Smith said." Woods answered. "So, what do you want us to do?"

Pierce's blood boiled over. "I want you to do your goddamn job!" he hissed. "The woman is not to get away again. In fact, put a damn chip in her. And she must stay medicated. I don't care if you have to give her the fucking medicine yourself. Am I clear?"

"You want me to chip her? Seems kind of extreme."

"I said am I clear?" Pierce repeated.

"Yeah. You're clear," Woods replied.

"We'll also have to watch Ms. Smith now to see what she does," Frank said. "If the woman said something, we'll know by her actions. Put a tail on her."

"I already have."

Pierce let a long silence hang in the air. Then he said, "Woods, don't fuck up again or I'll see that you're assigned watching in Wyoming sheep for the rest of your life. It's not a place for a black man from Alabama. Am I clear?"

"Yes sir. You're clear."

"Keep me apprised," Pierce punched the 'End Call' button on his phone. He fumed. How could they have let the woman get away? Two full-time men and a frail, seventy-five year-old woman gave them the slip? And she went to Bloomfield's election offices for chrissake. What a fuck up. Hadn't Frank told Woods how important this operation was? Didn't he tell Woods nearly every week that the woman could never leave the nursing home? What a moron. After the election, he'd have Woods transferred to Wyoming anyway. It'd serve him right.

Special Agent Frank Pierce walked across the mall toward his small office in the bowels of the Treasury Building. A cold breeze blew some litter into a swirl in front of him. If they had only let him handle the woman the way he wanted to in the first place, shit like this wouldn't happen. Now he had to report the incident. It wouldn't be a pleasant call. A lot of very important people would be pissed off.

And after the call, he'd make sure he wouldn't have to make one like it again.

FIVE

ELECTIONS WERE DIFFERENT from what Nan thought they'd be when she got into politics. She'd thought it would be about ideas and character. But in elections this big, information was king. Data-miners produced mountains of information from voters' buying habits, credit card transactions, online searches, key words in e-mails and Facebook and Twitter—anywhere a voter left even the tiniest trace of information. They'd look at relationships, affinities, memberships, habits, places voters lived, places they visited, what they ate, what they drank, the clothes they bought, where they worked, their job titles and incomes, how they spent their free time, their donations, where their kids went to school, if they owned a dog versus a cat. Every tiny bit of data went into the formula that geeks crunched and sliced into tiny segments that they labeled and categorized according to how likely each one was to vote for their candidate.

When they were finally done, they handed their analysis to strategists who compared it to the information they got from pollsters on how voters perceived the candidates on issues they deemed were important. Then they divided the segments

they got from the data-miners into three broad categories—
those who would probably vote for their candidate, those
who would never vote for their candidate, and those who
were on the fence. They'd dismiss the voters who would
never vote for their candidate, and put those who supported
their candidate into a 'get out the vote' campaign.

It was the fence-sitters who got the real attention. The
strategists would craft messaging to try to get them on their
side of the fence. They'd try to guess how their opponents
would react to their messages and develop new ones to
respond to that. They looked several moves ahead like a high-
level chess match. Then, they'd hand it all to the media
people.

The media people would look at all the options for how to
reach the fence-sitters. Advertising, direct mail, fliers, e-mail,
online ads, telephone calls, door-to-door calls, social media,
events, speaking engagements, news media via a public
relations campaign. It was common for a campaign to have
several messages targeting each fence-sitting segment and use
dozens of media outlets.

And when the public's mood changed, when some big
news hit about the economy, foreign affairs, a Supreme Court
decision, a racially motivated shooting, or anything that
affected the voting public's mindset, the process would start
all over again. Strategies could change week-to-week and
sometimes, day-to-day.

And then there was the undercover campaign. The dirty
tricks, the clandestine maneuvers that didn't show up on a
budget line and often fell below the law. The things that
Sheldon Hanrahan was good at. It was a dirty little secret that
dirty tricks made up a big part of campaigns.

It all made Nan's head spin and she wished it could be about a candidate's character and position on the issues. But she had to admit, it was exciting. The energy of it, the game played with real people and real consequences. Everything had to be right. One small misstep or one inappropriate word could derail an entire campaign.

Elections. Nan was back in the thick of it.

She had to leave home before Jenny woke up to catch her flight to Boston. She hated it when she didn't see her daughter in the morning. Jenny was a happy, pleasant thirteen-year-old and Nan loved mornings with her. As she climbed into the cab for the airport, she realized there would be a lot more missed mornings with Jenny during the next three weeks. The thought made Nan ache with guilt. But to be in the inner circle of the man who would likely be the next president of the United States was a once-in-a-lifetime opportunity.

As the cab took her to the airport, Nan wondered what to do about the incident with Mrs. Wilson. Mr. Woods had said Mrs. Wilson was senile and he was probably right. But she didn't look senile and it seemed Mr. Woods asked a few too many questions. Was it possible the woman was telling the truth? The accusation sounded absurd and if Nan reported it, she'd look silly. Better not report it. She had to focus on the upcoming meeting and do what she could to get Bloomfield elected.

*

After the plane landed at Logan, Nan headed to the concourse bathroom. She wanted to look good so she studied herself in the mirror. She picked some lint from her suit coat and flattened her skirt. She brushed her shoulder-length blonde hair and reapplied just the right amount of makeup for a business meeting. In four months, she'd be thirty-six but she looked years younger. She worked out and ate right to keep her figure a size four and her skin smooth. She looked good. She was ready.

Outside the airport terminal a black Lincoln Town Car was waiting for her. The day was pleasant and it took less than fifteen minutes to get to Governor Bloomfield's red-white-and-blue festooned campaign headquarters in a two-story, South Boston renovated warehouse. There was a line of people outside waiting to get in, and a row of news trucks with satellite dishes on top were set up across the street. Nan walked in and pushed her way to the front desk. The reception area was filled with people waiting.

A man with a weary face stopped Nan at the reception desk. "You'll have to wait outside with the rest of the volunteers," he said.

"I'm Nan Smith, the Minnesota campaign manager. I'm here for a meeting with Bob Hilton."

"Yeah, you're on the list," he replied. He pointed to a door behind him. "That way."

Nan went to an entrance guarded by a uniformed security officer who asked for identification. Nan produced her driver's license and the guard studied it. He checked it against a list. "You're cleared," he said. He told her to give him her briefcase and go through the metal detector. As Nan stepped through the metal detector, the guard searched her briefcase. When he was done, he handed it to her. He told her they were waiting for her in the main conference room. "It's on the second floor," he said.

Nan walked through the door into a large, open, two-story brick and iron office space. It was abuzz with activity. Thirty people talked on phones or stared into computer monitors while others argued passionately between the desks.

Nan climbed a set of iron stairs to the second floor and walked around an iron-railed balcony to a conference room. As she stepped in, Bob Hilton stood and greeted her.

"Nan! Welcome to the ant colony. Crazy, isn't it?" Hilton was lean, blonde and dressed in a navy-blue suit, white shirt and no tie. He shook her hand as if he were the one running for president.

"Ant colony?" she asked.

"Yeah. That's what the governor calls it here. People running around working, just like an ant colony." Bob spoke in his trademark staccato. "We've had over a hundred people volunteer here in Boston since Dougherty endorsed Howard. Everyone's jumping on the bandwagon."

"I'm glad I can help," Nan said.

Hilton swept his hand across the room. "Our executive team. This is John Seligman, our pollster, Betty Morris our chief strategist, Jamal Brown the assistant campaign manager."

Nan raised a hand to the group. "It's very nice to meet you all," she said.

"The governor's on the campaign trail in Chicago," Hilton said. "He hates these meetings anyway. What can we get you, Nan? Coffee? Water?" He pointed to a credenza filled with beverages and finger food.

Nan took a bottle of water and sat in a chair facing the windows. The Boston harbor was visible several blocks away and she could smell the salt water in the air. In front of her was a four-inch thick stack of papers.

Hilton took a seat at the head of the table. "Those papers in front of you are what we've been able to pull on Howard since yesterday morning. We also have the overnight poll numbers. John was going over them when you came in. John, recap for Nan."

The pollster, tall and lanky, put on a pair of reading glasses and began reading numbers from a stack of papers. The overnight polls looked good for Bloomfield. The governor had a seven-point lead nationally and led in most of the critical states.

When John finished, Hilton stood and began pacing. "See what I mean? It's a whole new ballgame. We were five points behind and just like that, we're seven points ahead. I don't know what the president was thinking when he endorsed Howard but he just might've handed us the White House."

Jamal Brown, an intelligent-looking African American with wire-rim glasses, raised a palm to the air. "Maybe their party will endorse someone else."

"They won't," Betty Morris said. Betty, with her perfectly coiffed hair and dark red tailored suit, had the slick, practiced look of a D.C. insider. "They don't have time for an internal fight. It'd be suicide. They'll support Howard."

"I agree," Hilton said. "So, if Howard's their candidate, how do you think they'll come after us, Betty?"

Betty pushed herself forward. "First, they have to make Howard look like a legitimate candidate. He didn't last past Iowa in the primaries so people outside the Midwest don't know much about him. They have to grab hold of an issue and make it their own."

"What do you think it'll it be?" Hilton asked.

"Terrorism," Betty replied with her chin raised. "Howard is the vice chairman of the Armed Services Committee. He supports increases in military spending and a buildup of the CIA. He's voted in favor of every piece of terrorism legislation brought to the Senate for the past fourteen years and a majority of Americans agree with his position."

Seligman flipped to a page of the poll results. "She's right. He scores much higher on terrorism than Bloomfield. It could be a leverage issue for him."

Hilton slid back into his chair. "We'll have to formulate a response. Better yet, let's do something to pre-empt them. A position paper. Or how about a research report about the lessening threat of terrorism? Can we diminish the issue without dismissing it?"

"According to the polls," Seligman said, "terrorism is less important than four years ago, but it's still an important issue."

"Here's a question," Betty said. "Even if they can own an issue like terrorism, how do they get the message out? Howard has only a few hundred thousand left from the primaries. Marshall's supporters are not likely to hand over their funds. And a former dentist from northern Minnesota is not exactly a rich man."

"Good point," Hilton said. "Howard's starting from scratch with only a few weeks until the election. It's a big handicap."

Nan pushed herself to the edge of her chair. "I wouldn't be so sure." The group turned to her. Betty Morris looked sideways at Nan. "Sheldon Hanrahan can raise it," she said.

"But Hanrahan is only the campaign manager," Jamal said.

Nan paused and met the eyes of each person in the room. "My guess is you don't know much about Sheldon Hanrahan. You brought me here because I know about Howard. I do, but just as importantly, I know Sheldon Hanrahan." Betty looked away but the others stared at Nan. "Let me explain," she said.

She stood and began pacing the room. She explained that Sheldon Hanrahan was quietly one of the richest people in America. He and his communications companies manage the brands and the public image of dozens of *Fortune*-500 companies. He makes his clients very rich, she explained, so they put him on their boards and he's close friends with the CEOs, celebrities, and big investors.

"I guarantee Sheldon Hanrahan can raise money fast," Nan said. "He has connections and can call in favors. He'll create soft money channels, 527 organizations, PACs and financial schemes to raise all the money Howard needs. Howard will have a big war chest just in time for the last weeks of the campaign."

"Okay," Hilton said, "then how do we beat Mr. Hanrahan?"

"You won't," Nan said.

"Come on," Betty scoffed, turning toward Nan. "You don't think we can beat some ad guy who's never run a national campaign?"

Nan stopped pacing and grabbed the back of her chair. She leaned into the group. "He runs campaigns every day for products and companies worth billions," she said. "And he's very, very good at it."

"This is a different game," Betty sniffed. "This is politics."

"Really?" Nan said. "Remember, John Ehrlichman was an ad guy who was able to get Richard Nixon elected twice, even though Nixon was one of the most uncharismatic people to ever run for president."

"My dear," Betty said, "you might be overreacting because of the drubbing you took in the campaign two years ago. No offense, but I think we have better... resources on this one."

Nan remembered the heat she took from her party for the Theilen campaign. She took her seat and smiled at Betty. "No offense taken."

Bob Hilton stared at Nan. "Do you really think Howard could beat George Bloomfield?"

"No, I don't," Nan answered. "But I think the people in this room can be beaten by Sheldon Hanrahan."

Hilton shot a glance at Betty, then he looked back at Nan. "So what do you propose we do?"

"Push for debates," Nan said.

Betty folded her arms and Hilton raised an eyebrow. "Debates?" Hilton asked.

Nan leaned over the table. "Yes, debates. We should demand two nationally televised debates, one in each of the last two weeks. Howard isn't good at public speaking but more importantly, in a debate, he's on his own and it'd be one-on-one, Bloomfield against Howard instead of us against Sheldon Hanrahan. And it's a way to get the election to focus on the issues. They'll probably resist but it's our best strategy."

Hilton nodded. "George would do well against Howard in debates."

"What if they don't agree to your debates?" Betty asked.

Nan leaned back. "Then we do a campaign that asks the question, 'Why won't Howard debate Bloomfield? What does he have to hide?' The strategy was used years ago in Minnesota when Paul Wellstone ran against Senator Rudy Boschwitz. Wellstone was a huge underdog and won."

"That just might work," Hilton said.

"We'll take it under advisement," Betty responded. "I think we should move on. We have a full agenda. What's next?"

Hilton nodded at Nan then said, "The new advertising." He clasped his hands behind his head and wore an expression like he had gotten away with stealing the last cookie out of the jar. "People, I can't give you the details now, but I want you to know, Betty and I have been working on some very exciting plans. Let me just say, our campaign will be something America has never seen before in a presidential election. I'll be heading to Hollywood over the weekend to get it started. Let's move on with our agenda, but I want you all to feel the excitement of a new kind of campaign," Hilton grinned.

A new kind of campaign, Nan thought. They'd be running against Sheldon Hanrahan, a master of marketing and dirty tricks. They'd need more than a new kind of campaign.

They spent the rest of the morning going over more poll numbers and discussing direct mail messages, an e-mail campaign, telemarketing and fund-raising. They debated the get-out-the-vote strategy for Bloomfield supporters and then had a heated debate on how they were approaching the fence-sitters. Someone brought in sandwiches and the group worked through lunch. Nan contributed when she could and Hilton nodded at her approvingly. She sensed that she and Hilton were going to work well together.

The meeting went on until after six. They barely took time for bathroom breaks. Jamal and Hilton prepped Nan on the questions she'd get from the media. They went over the governor's platform with her. When they finally quit, Hilton told Nan he wanted to ride with her to the airport so they could talk alone. As the limousine wound its way to Logan, they talked about Nan's new responsibilities. Hilton pressed on the media briefing they gave her. "You need to be an expert on the governor's platform," he said. "Go over it again on your way back to Minnesota. Read our press reports every morning. And read the new reports we gave you. Call if you have questions. You're the face of the campaign in Minnesota, Nan. We're depending on you."

Nan said she understood her new role and would do her best. Hilton smiled. She had to admit, he was everything the media had said he was—movie star handsome, exceptionally intelligent—and he had more energy than a three-year-old. It would be interesting, to say the least, to work with Bob Hilton. She could tell from the way he looked at her that he felt the same about her.

Then he said, "I think I told you on the phone yesterday there'll be some new people in the Minnesota office. They flew to Minneapolis today while you were here. They report to me. You need to let them do their thing."

"What will they do?" Nan asked.

"Nothing you need to worry about," Hilton replied. "As I said, they report to me. I'm flying to Minnesota Friday night to check things out. Short visit on my way to California. We can talk Saturday morning. I want to learn more about Sheldon Hanrahan."

As the limo pulled up to the airport terminal, Nan wondered if she should tell Bob about Mrs. Wilson and Mr. Woods. But the day had gone so well that she decided against it.

The chauffeur opened the door and Nan turned to Hilton. "Bob, I hope you understand what we're up against with Sheldon Hanrahan. He doesn't play fair."

"You made your point in the meeting. We'll be sure to keep a close watch on Hanrahan and we'll talk about it on Saturday. And Nan, someday I want to talk to you about your role in the administration if we win this election. I have ideas."

Nan was surprised. "Really? Well… I look forward to discussing it."

"Let's win the election first," Hilton said, extending a hand.

Nan shook Bob's hand and climbed out of the limo. She caught the last flight back to Minneapolis with only five minutes to spare.

As the 767 roared west toward Minnesota, she wondered if Hilton, Betty Morris and the rest of Bloomfield's campaign staff really appreciated what kind of man they were facing in Sheldon Hanrahan. Maybe they did. Maybe Betty Morris was right—presidential campaigns are a different game. And maybe Hilton's new Hollywood advertising would offset anything Sheldon Hanrahan would do.

But Nan knew firsthand Hanrahan would not let Bloomfield and Bob Hilton win the presidency without a fight. She prayed they were prepared for it.

SIX

SHELDON HANRAHAN SAT in his corner office on the forty-seventh floor of the Wells Fargo Bank building in downtown Minneapolis listening to Peter Gray on the other end of the speakerphone. From the tone of the party chairman's voice, Sheldon could tell he was struggling to stay cool.

"If you expect our support, we must be involved," Gray insisted. "And I mean more than on a perfunctory level. Much more. I met with the party leadership this morning, and we aren't happy to have to support Howard. The only way we'll do it is if we run his campaign."

"I see," Sheldon said. The speakerphone rested on his glass desktop. Thin stripes of the afternoon sun poked between the slits of the Levolor blinds into his modern glass and steel office. The light, even dimmed as it was, hurt his eyes so Sheldon turned his chair to face the dark room. "Exactly how do you want to be involved, Peter?"

"First with your platform," the chairman replied. "I don't agree with your position on things. They're too extreme. We want you to adopt the party platform as written at the convention in Miami. Not a single word changed. We can't support Howard if you don't."

Sheldon didn't respond. He picked up his large, dark glasses—the ones he had worn every daylight hour for the past thirty years—and rolled them around his fingers like a magician with playing cards.

Peter's voice came on the speakerphone again. "Sheldon, are you still there?"

"Yes, I'm still here. You want us to adopt the party platform. What else?"

"We want Michael Masello to be Howard's running mate. He was Marshall's running mate throughout the primaries and the convention. He's put in a lot of work and he can deliver California. He thinks he should be our choice to run for president, but I can get him to agree to the VP spot instead."

"I see. You want Congressman Masello to be Senator Howard's running mate so we win California. Is that all?"

"No. Like I said, you also have to let us run the campaign. It's the only way we can win. I want my people at your national headquarters there in Minneapolis. And I personally want direct oversight of the entire campaign. That means daily briefings, my personal attendance in all important meetings and my approval on strategy."

"And for that we get...?"

"The Party endorsement."

Sheldon put his feet on the desktop and stretched out his long, lean frame. He continued to snake his dark glasses through his fingers. He was enjoying the repartee with the chairman. "The Party endorsement? It seems we already have it."

"All you have is Dougherty's endorsement. He doesn't speak for the Party. I do."

"Excuse me, Mr. Chairman," Sheldon said. "Phillip Dougherty is the most popular president since Eisenhower. His support means a lot."

"Look, Sheldon," the chairman was starting to lose it, "Howard won't win without the Party's endorsement. Period. This entire affair gives Bloomfield a big boost. The poll numbers don't look good and the only way we can keep the White House in November is if you cooperate with us."

Sheldon smiled at the picture in his mind of Peter Gray struggling to keep his composure on the other end of the line. He let a few seconds pass. "Okay," he said finally, "I agree to your terms. We will adopt the Party platform. Michael Masello is our running mate and you can run the campaign as you wish. For that, Bill Howard gets the Party endorsement."

"You agree?" Gray asked. "Just like that? Don't you have to talk to Howard first?"

"Senator Howard has cut short his visit to Japan and is on his way back as we speak. I sent my fastest jet for him. When I see him this afternoon, he will agree with my decision."

"Okay." Peter exclaimed. "We have a deal. My people will arrive in Minnesota tomorrow morning. You need to make accommodations for them. I'll get out there as soon as I can, probably late tomorrow. We'll make a joint announcement, just in time for the evening news. That won't give the press and the public much time to over-analyze everything before the weekend.

"And let's schedule my daily briefings," Peter continued. "I want them early. 7:30 A.M. here in D.C., 6:30 your time."

"That will work just fine," Sheldon replied.

"Are you sure you don't need to check with Howard on this?" Peter Gray asked.

"Mr. Chairman, I look forward to working with you. I'll call at 6:30 tomorrow morning for your briefing. Good day, sir."

Sheldon pressed the speakerphone button disconnecting the call. So the Party wanted to control Howard's campaign. Sheldon had expected that. With the Party in control, an inside-the-beltway collective of consultants, pollsters, media specialists and handlers would run the campaign. They all profited handsomely from elections. Sheldon didn't mind that they'd be in control, but only until it was time for him to take over.

Anyway, he didn't need the party. He already controlled several Super PACs through which he and his wealthy cohorts could donate large sums out from under the jurisdiction of the FEC. These funds, along with the small amount the party would raise would be more than enough to execute his plans. And it didn't matter that the Super PACs weren't allowed to coordinate their efforts with the candidate's campaign. Years earlier, Sheldon had set up a sophisticated organization with layers and buffers and a watertight communications system that the FEC and FBI would never penetrate.

And then there was the party platform. It was nothing more than platitudes and false promises. In spite of Sheldon's physical handicap—actually, because of it—he'd built one of the largest communications companies in the world. He sat on the boards of a half dozen *Fortune* 100 companies, helped clients make billions and was himself, one of the richest people in America. He knew that just having a platform didn't win important battles.

Anyway, the platform was wrong. America had been on the wrong track for fifty years and needed sweeping changes. It was quickly becoming a country of weak and weak-minded people and the government was coddling them. After all, no one coddled him when he was struck down. The people who he loved abandoned him, and it'd forced him to be strong.

All he had to do now was beat George Bloomfield in November and he and his colleagues could make the dramatic changes they believed the country needed. Of course, with less than three weeks until Election Day, it would demand an extraordinary campaign—not the typical, insipid campaigns the politicos were used to running. They needed the kind of campaign only he could give them.

He slipped on his dark glasses and the pain in his eyes eased. He opened the Levolor blinds a crack and gazed out the window. It was going to be bloody. People will get hurt—like he had been hurt.

But no one—especially not Peter Gray—would get in his way.

SEVEN

"WHAT'S THIS?" Nan asked as she walked into Bloomfield's Minnesota campaign office on Friday morning. There was a large tarp covering the entire reception area and two men in white painter's overalls were setting up ladders.

"They're redoing everything," Stephanie answered from the reception desk. "You won't believe what they've done in the bullpen."

Nan took off her coat and hung it in the closet. "Who?"

"The new guys from Massachusetts. They came in yesterday morning while you were in Boston and started moving in. This morning they said they were going to do the reception area and outside."

The new guys from Massachusetts? Hilton had said he was sending some people but Nan hadn't expected this. She wondered what else Hilton was going to do to her little office. "I better have a look," she said.

"Nan," Stephanie said coming out from behind her desk, "I have to talk to you about something. It's important."

"What is it?"

Stephanie leaned into Nan. "It has to be in private, in your office."

"Sure," Nan said. "Let me settle in first."

Nan headed through the door to the bullpen. After one step in, she stopped. Everything had changed. The dingy gray walls were now white and there was the clean, chemical smell of new paint. They'd replaced the ratty collection of desks and office furniture with new, Herman Miller desks, Aeron chairs and flat-screen monitors. In the middle of the room were two 60" TVs, each with split-screens running different news feeds. Three new cubicles with tall panel walls replaced the back tables where the bank of telephones had been. Nan could see one of the cubicles contained an impressive set of computer servers, flat-screen monitors and peripherals blinking red and green lights. Someone had organized boxes of campaign literature against the back wall.

Bob Hilton hadn't told her he would make changes in her office, but when she thought about it, they made sense. Minnesota would be in the limelight and apparently, like the extravagant Boston office, it would be a showcase for the media.

"Nan! Welcome back from Boston!" shouted Shelly Novak from a new desk in the middle of the bullpen. She smiled and swept her hand across the room. "We're in the big leagues now!"

"Well, it certainly looks that way," Nan said nodding her head. "Hi Hank."

Hank was at a desk next to Shelly. He waved. "Welcome back. How's the Ant Colony?"

Nan laughed. "How did you know that's what they call the Boston office?"

"You'd be surprised what I know," he replied with a grin.

"Where's Jim?" Nan asked.

"He's at the print shop," Shelly responded. "Now that we're up against Howard, our literature has to change. It was an order from Boston and he's taking care of it."

"They're changing the literature already?"

"That and a lot more," Shelly said.

Nan heard people coming through the front door. She went to the reception area where two men and a woman greeted Stephanie. Stephanie stood when Nan came in. "Nan," she said, "these are the new people from Massachusetts."

A thirty-five-ish man with dark hair and eyes to match stepped forward and stuck out his hand. "Hello Nan Smith," he said. "I've been looking forward to meeting you. I'm Rex Starkey, senior field manager. This is Sorrea Hosseni, our IT specialist, and this is Tom Dillon. We're the Massachusetts SWAT team," he said with a smile.

"Nice to meet you." Nan shook each person's hand. Sorrea was a middle-eastern beauty who looked as smart as a Silicon Valley billionaire. Dillon looked like a middleweight boxer with a square chin and steely eyes. He didn't smile as he shook Nan's hand. "So, Rex is in charge and Sorrea is the IT person. What do you do, Tom?" Nan asked.

"Tom is a field operative," Rex interjected. He pointed toward the door to the bullpen. "So, how do you like the changes? We had a crew here all day and night yesterday. Today we'll finish the reception area. We've learned our opponents will announce Howard as their candidate later today. This office will be a target for the press so we fixed it up. Don't worry. All this stuff is rented since we'll only use it for a month."

Rex led Nan to the bullpen and pointed to the cubicles. "Sorrea and I will be in those two cubicles. Tom will be out and about so he doesn't need a space. We've put a new desk and chair in your office, too."

"It looks great," Nan said. "Thank you."

Sorrea went to her office and Tom slipped to the back while Nan and Rex continued to look over the new bullpen. "You met with Bob Hilton yesterday," Rex said, eyeing Nan. "I trust he told you we'd be here."

"He did, although he didn't say anything about these changes."

"Well, I hope it's a pleasant surprise. Bob also told you that you shouldn't be concerned about us. You and I will work independently. We have our assignment and we'll stay out of your way."

"What is your assignment?"

"Mostly it's gathering intelligence on Howard. We're Boston's eyes and ears here in Minnesota."

"I think I understand," Nan said. "You're spies."

Rex shook his head and grinned. "Nothing like that. I assure you, it's all on the up-and-up."

There were voices in the reception area. The movers had come with the new furniture and were noisily removing the old furniture. The painters were yelling at them for moving their tarp. "We'll also hang new signs out front," Rex said. "Oh, and Nan, later there'll be a crew here to install a security system. You'll all need codes to get in."

"Seems like you've thought of everything."

"That's my job," Rex said. "I better make sure the movers and painters don't kill each other." He gave Nan the once over. "Perhaps we can catch a lunch later, just you and me, and we can talk more?"

"Thanks, but I have a lot to do today."

"Can I get a rain check?" Rex asked.

"Um, sure" Nan replied.

Rex went off to the reception area and Nan walked back to her office. Her new desk was matte black with chrome trim. A new Aeron chair sat behind it. On top was a large flat-screen computer monitor and a slick black desk phone. The contents of her old desk had been set up on the new desk exactly has she had left them.

In one day they'd transformed a shabby, backwater campaign office into a model of modern efficiency. It was just in time. The national press was already pouring into Minneapolis to cover Senator Howard and when they wanted to get the Bloomfield side of a story, they'd come here. They had to present the right image.

Nan would have to present a good image, too. As the spokesperson in Minnesota, the press would focus on her. She hadn't expected to be in the spotlight when Bloomfield was running against Marshall, but she was sure in it now and would have to be ready when the media called. She'd re-read Bloomfield's platform on the plane ride back to Minnesota and had studied the reports they gave her in Boston. She'd spend the rest of the day going over everything again and by the time the media showed up, she'd be ready for them.

As she read the morning press report from Boston, she looked over the bullpen and saw Sorrea staring intently into her computer monitor. It seemed overkill to have an IT specialist officed here in Minneapolis, but Hilton was the type who didn't leave anything to chance. Apparently, he thought Sorrea was necessary. What exactly she'd do, Nan didn't know.

Tom Dillon was another mystery. Rex had called him a field operative. What did that mean? Dillon didn't look like he'd be Rex's backup. He didn't look like a campaign worker at all. He looked like... a spy.

Nan smiled to herself at the thought. The sudden transformation of the office and all the new gadgets were playing with her imagination. It was all for show like Rex had said. And Tom? He was none of her concern.

Stephanie came to her office. "Nan, can we talk now?"

"Oh, yes," Nan said. "I'm sorry, I forgot. How can I help you?"

Stephanie closed the door and took a seat. Nan liked Stephanie. She was young, conscientious and a hard worker. A year earlier, Stephanie had graduated from the University of Minnesota with a degree in political science and took the receptionist job at minimum wage to get experience in political campaigns. At her interview, she'd said she wanted to be a campaign manager someday, just like Nan. She was still painfully naive but she was learning fast. This gig, now that it was in the national spotlight, would give her a great experience.

"Two things," Stephanie said. "First, these new guys. They came in here yesterday as if they owned the place, changing everything around, bringing in new furniture, installing their new equipment. It pissed me off how they just took control. And with you gone, Jim didn't know what to do so he just let them do what they wanted."

"Jim did the right thing," Nan said. "We have to let these people do their jobs. It's something we'll have to live with until Election Day. It's all for show, anyway."

"Not all of it," Stephanie said.

Nan cocked her head. "What do you mean?"

"Some guy showed up yesterday with a bunch of electronic equipment. It looked like cameras, those motion sensor thingies and little gray boxes. I couldn't tell what it was. That Tom guy quick took it and put it in the trunk of his car. It looked like, I don't know, surveillance equipment."

"Surveillance equipment?"

"That's what it looked like to me," Stephanie said. "And did you see those computers? I checked them out last night. They're huge. They look like they're running some sort of monitoring system or something. They brought in that ginormous shredder, too. I mean, what's that for? And Tom hasn't said a single word since he got here. He's creepy."

"Stephanie, you've been reading too many spy novels," Nan said. "I'm sure it's all legitimate. Don't worry about any of this. These new people won't bother us. We have to stay out of their way and run the Minnesota campaign."

Stephanie sighed. "I guess you're right. But there's one more thing. Something happened yesterday that totally creeped me out."

"Oh, what was it?"

Stephanie glanced over her shoulder, turned to Nan and said in a low voice, "You got a call on the answering machine. I took the tape out before the new guys took the machine away. You should hear it."

"A voice-mail message?"

Stephanie produced the ancient tape recorder they used for taking calls after hours. She plugged in the recorder and set it on Nan's desk. "This call came in at 5:23 yesterday morning," she said.

Stephanie punched 'Play' and the recorder came to life. There was a beep, then a faint woman's voice. "You must stop them," the voice said whispering. There was the sound of labored breathing and what sounded like a sob. "I have something to show you…"

A man's voice came on the tape in the background. "Hey, HEY! What are you doing?" The man's voice got louder. "SHIT! Give me that phone." There was a loud click and the phone went dead.

Stephanie turned off the recorder. "That's it," she said. "Who is it?"

Nan moved her eyes from the cassette recorder to Stephanie. "It's Mrs. Wilson," Nan said. "It's the woman who was here on Wednesday."

Stephanie returned Nan's stare. "Yeah, that's what I thought. What's she talking about—'you must stop them'?"

Nan looked out toward the bullpen. "No one else heard this?"

"Just me. I was the first one in yesterday. What should we do?"

Nan shook her head and produced a smile. "Nothing, Stephanie. The man who came here from the hospital said she was senile. I'm sure she is, poor woman."

"She said she had something to show you."

"I can't imagine what it would be," Nan said. "Look, Stephanie, I'm sure it's nothing. The woman is sick. Don't worry about it."

"Well, okay," Stephanie sad. "It's just so creepy. All of it—the new guys, their equipment. This call."

"Thanks for letting me hear the tape. Give it to me. I'll take care of it. And you shouldn't tell anyone about it. I don't want people to worry. Okay?"

Stephanie took the cassette tape out of the recorder and gave it to Nan. "Okay," she said. "I better get back to the front desk to see what they're doing out there."

"Thanks, Stephanie."

As Stephanie returned to the lobby, Nan looked at the tape in her hand. Just two days earlier, the woman had sat across from her and uttered her incredible accusation. Then Mr. Woods came with too many questions. Now there was this telephone call. Nan had been content to dismiss the woman but now she wasn't so sure.

She put the tape in her briefcase and stuck her head out her office door. "Hank," she said, "can I see you a minute."

Hank came to Nan's office and Nan pointed to the door. "You better close it."

Hank swung the door closed and took a seat. "What's up?"

Nan told Hank about Mrs. Wilson's message on the answering machine. And then she met Hank's eyes. "What are you doing for lunch?"

Hank smiled. "It looks like I just got lucky and scored a lunch date with you."

"Thanks," Nan said. "We'll go to Cassini's. We have a lot to talk about."

EIGHT

SILVIA MENDOZA PUSHED her mouth against her lover's breast and worked her hands between her lover's legs. She could feel the thrill of sex begin to captivate her. She hoped it would push aside her other thoughts.

Ellen Stein let out a moan and closed her eyes. Silvia looked up at Ellen's face as she worked her fingers. The senior aide to the White House press secretary was pretty when she let her brown hair down. Ellen could stand to lose a few pounds, but it was probably impossible for her to find time to exercise with her work schedule. Her time with Silvia was probably the only exercise the poor girl got.

Silvia didn't have to worry about exercise. She was naturally petite and burned off all the calories she took in without having to work out. And she was pretty, too. She knew it. She had fine facial features and with her thick, dark hair and olive skin, she was able to turn heads of men when she walked into a room.

She had turned Ellen's head, too, when on the first day of her new job, Silvia walked into the White House pressroom.

Silvia could see Ellen couldn't take her eyes off her. Later, Silvia had introduced herself and asked Ellen out for a drink. Ellen stammered and said it wasn't appropriate for her to talk to a reporter outside of her official White House duties.

A few days later at the *Sentinel*, Silvia saw a White House press release that listed Ellen as the contact. Even though she knew she wouldn't write a story about the release, Silvia called Ellen and asked for more information. They talked through the release and then Silvia said she needed someone at the White House like Ellen to show her the ropes. Ellen agreed as long as they kept their conversation on a 'professional level' as she said.

It took only two weeks for Silvia to get Ellen to agree to meet in a room at the Capitol Hilton. Ellen entered the room visibly nervous and excited. They kissed, took off each other's clothes and fell into bed.

Silvia was surprised at how much she enjoyed the sex. Until Ellen, she had only been with men who treated her like a little Mexican sex toy and didn't want to lie with her after sex. With Ellen it was different—long, gentle, sweet, and very passionate. Silvia never told Ellen she was her first woman and, as far as she could tell, Ellen never suspected it. Now that she had spent so much time with Ellen, Silvia worried that she might never want a man again.

Silvia continued to work her hand between Ellen's legs and Ellen moaned louder. She arched her back and shuddered in a long, hard orgasm. Silvia moved up and gave Ellen a tender kiss. They lay together without talking, but soon the trance of sex began to subside in Silvia and her questions rose in its place. She tried to push them away so she could enjoy the afterglow a little longer, but the questions won over as they always did.

She rolled over on her back on the cool satin sheets and stared at the coved ceiling of their hotel room. "I'm glad you could get away," she said. "It must not have been easy with everything going on at the White House."

Ellen rolled over, snuggled next to Silvia. "I'm glad too. It's been too long."

Silvia laughed. "Five days is too long?"

"You don't know what it's like for me."

"*Lo siento, comadre.* I've been busy. The president's endorsement of Howard took us all by surprise."

"It took everyone by surprise."

Silvia caught Ellen's eyes. "You mean you didn't know about it in advance?"

"The press secretary might have known minutes before the president's speech," Ellen said, "but no one else did. We didn't even have a release ready. We had to scramble afterward."

"Why did he do it?" Silvia asked.

"What, not tell anybody ahead of time about the endorsement?"

"No, why did he endorse Howard?"

Ellen rolled over onto her back. "You know I shouldn't talk to you about official White House matters."

Silvia pushed herself up on an elbow, faced Ellen and began to massage Ellen's breasts. "I know. I'm just curious, that's all."

Ellen closed her eyes again, sighed. "I don't think the president had a choice. He didn't seem happy with it. It seemed like he was forced into it."

Silvia continued to work on Ellen. She enjoyed touching her. "Forced into by whom?"

"I don't know." Ellen said. "There's a big hush-hush around the whole thing. No one is saying anything about it."

Silvia took her hand off Ellen and rolled over on her back again. "Seems strange. A big decision like that and neither the president nor his staff is trying to explain it. It sounds like someone has something on your boss."

"It's possible," Ellen said, her eyes still closed. "Powerful men like him often have something to hide."

"So do you think that's it? Do you think he was forced into it because of something he has to hide?"

"Like I said, it's possible. But I doubt it. It was probably part of some deal."

"A deal? Seems like a pretty big deal for the president to do something like that."

Ellen threw an arm around Silvia. "You know how Washington works. Things are never as they seem. Most of my job is putting a spin on a story to disguise what's really happening. And I don't even know the half of it. A lot of what the administration does is done in secret. Deals, agreements, trades. 'I'll give you this if you give me that.' It's all a big power grab. Everyone is angling for an advantage but no one wants it to appear that way. They all want it to look like they're doing something good for the country."

"But it doesn't make sense for the president," Silvia said. "He's already at the top and he's a lame duck. He has only three months left. What kind of deal would he make at this point? It must be something else—something personal."

Ellen pushed herself off the bed and began to get dressed. "I have to get back."

"You know something, don't you?" Silvia said.

Ellen turned and glared at Silvia. "I told you I don't know anything," she said.

"It's something personal, isn't it?"

Ellen turned away and hooked her bra. "Like I said, I don't know. All I know is no one is talking about it."

Silvia rolled onto her elbow again and watched Ellen dress. Ellen was usually willing to share inside information with Silvia as long as Silvia agreed not to reveal her source. She'd always been discreet and the *Sentinel* was becoming known for breaking stories about what was going on in the White House. Ellen often asked Silvia to leak information the Administration wanted to get out and Silvia was all too willing to do it. This time apparently, someone had ordered the White House staff to stay tight-lipped.

Silvia decided to try another strategy. "*Powerful men often have something to hide.*" she said, drawing a circle on the sheets with her finger. "That's what you just said. The president is the most powerful man on earth and he just might have something big to hide. Help me find out what it is, Ellen."

Ellen laughed as she pulled up her skirt and zipped it. "I'm supposed to work for the president, not you."

"Ellen, he's a powerful man with something to hide. I remember you told me you had experience with someone like that when you were young. That's why you became a lesbian."

Ellen's lip curled. "You know, I'd hate you if you weren't so beautiful. In three months when the new president takes over, I'll be out of a job and you'll drop me like a bad habit."

"Help me, Ellen. Help me get him."

Ellen took in a deep breath. "I'll tell you what, *señorita* Mendoza. I'll look into it and see what I can find. If something comes up, you'll be the first to know."

Silvia smiled. "Come kiss me before you leave."

Ellen's face turned soft. She came to the side of the bed and they gently kissed. Silvia felt a tingle of excitement. "When will I see you again?" Ellen asked.

"I don't know."

Ellen turned away and headed for the door. "Call me soon."

"I will. You call me if you get anything. Promise?"

Ellen walked out of the hotel room without answering.

Silvia pulled the sheets to her chin and pushed herself deep into the bed. She was alone again with her thoughts. A good Catholic girl shouldn't have sex with a woman and she especially shouldn't enjoy it. What would her parents think if they found out? And how could she—their only child since her brother was murdered—give them a grandchild if she never wanted to have sex with a man again? Her relationship with Ellen had given her inside information that made her a success at the *Sentinel* and after all, isn't that what her parents always wanted?

She was certain about one thing, though. Ian Rutter was wrong. He'd said Dougherty endorsed Howard to assert his power before he had to give it up. But something else was going on in the White House—something that required a gag order. Ellen's silence on the matter had said as much.

Silvia climbed out of bed and started to get dressed. She had to get back to the *Sentinel*. She'd arranged the rendezvous with Ellen to see what was going on at the White House and she was sure she was on to a big story. All she had to do was get Ellen to give it to her.

NINE

CASSINI'S WAS ONE of several new restaurants in Minneapolis whose owners named it to sound like a genuine Italian trattoria. It had a burnt Tuscan yellow stucco exterior and a white, green and red awning. Inside, the red and white checkered tablecloths and cheap paintings of Venice tried hard to give the impression Cassini's was the real deal.

Nan knew better. The food was not authentic Italian like she was used to growing up in Chicago. No one in the kitchen spoke Italian and there wasn't even a picture of the Pope anywhere. Still, it was clean and only one block away from the Bloomfield campaign offices.

When she and Hank arrived, the restaurant was less than half-full and they were able to take a seat at the window. A cold front had moved in bringing clouds with it. The leaves that remained on the trees were yellow and red, and in a few days they'd be gone and the bleakness of the long Minnesota winter would set in.

As Nan turned to the menu, she was grateful Hank had agreed to go to lunch with her. She had to talk to someone about the events of the past two days. She was excited about her change in status from one of fifty state campaign managers to an important senior adviser to the Bloomfield campaign. She'd have extra duties and she wanted to be sure that things were under control in Minnesota. She didn't know what to think about Rex Starkey and his people with their slick furniture and impressive electronics.

And of course, there was the ordeal with Mrs. Wilson.

Nan needed to sort it all out and knew Hank would help. He didn't have a prestigious degree like hers or her experience as a senior political analyst at a big Twin Cities public relations firm. But Hank had the knowledge and wisdom that came from decades of working in the political trenches. More importantly, over the previous twenty-five years, he'd worked for several campaigns opposing candidates managed by Sheldon Hanrahan. Each campaign was a loss but Hank kept volunteering. Maybe this was one Hank and his party could finally win.

A male waiter dressed in black came to take their order. He was showy and overly friendly and Nan guessed he was one of the restaurant's owners and that his act was an attempt to compensate for the empty tables. He took their food orders and Nan ordered a diet Coke and Hank, a glass of Chianti.

As the waiter left, Hank said, "The older I get, the more I like my wine. Two glasses a day, one at lunch, one at dinner. My doctor says it's good for my heart."

"It's working," Nan said. "You look great."

"Careful there, Nan. A young woman like you shouldn't flatter an old guy like me on our first date."

Nan laughed. "Thanks for joining me."

The drinks came and Hank wrapped his lean hands around the wine glass. They were the hands of a working man. As a carpenter, he'd spent a lifetime building things and in retirement, he was trying to build a better country. He had an air of quiet confidence and Nan knew he'd be a huge help in the weeks to come.

"How's your family, Nan," Hank asked. "Is Ben doing well?"

"Not really. Hanrahan Communications keeps taking their clients. His agency is losing money and he had to take another pay cut. He works so hard. My mother has had to help with Jenny during the campaign. It looks like she'll have to help even more."

"Jenny is what, twelve?"

"She just turned thirteen. She's a sweetheart. She loves school and sports. I'll miss seeing her now that I have to work all the time. Hilton's secretary called this morning and said Bob wants me in New York on Monday. She couldn't tell me why. I'll find out when he's in town tomorrow—I have to meet with him in the morning. I've suddenly gotten a lot busier."

"Don't worry, Nan," Hank said, taking a sip of his wine. "I can help. And this campaign will be over in three weeks. Then you'll have time to spend with your daughter."

Nan shook her head. "It's going to be crazy. Everything has changed. That's what I wanted to talk to you about."

"I'm all ears."

The waiter came to the table rubbing his hands together. "Your meals will be coming out soon," he said with a broad smile. "Chef Paul is creating them now. Can I get you anything in the meantime?"

"Ah, no," Hank said. "We're just fine."

"Excellent. Please let me know if you need anything," the waiter said with a bow as he backed away.

Hank rolled his eyes as the waiter returned to the kitchen. "You were saying?" he said.

Nan explained that her role had changed. She was now the face of the Bloomfield campaign in Minnesota. They'd get tons of media attention as soon as the other party endorsed Howard. She said that Hilton wanted her involved in strategy, too.

"The Ant Colony was a real treat," she continued. "Those D.C. people are something else. I get the feeling they'd switch sides for an extra buck."

"They probably would," Hank said.

"Do you realize how big the election business is today?" Nan asked. "There are research companies, consulting firms, media specialists, political analysts, all of whom make millions off an election like this. They don't really care who gets elected and they for sure don't care about the issues."

"Yeah," Hank said. "It's Election Incorporated. Running elections for profit instead of progress. Do you think it'll get negative?"

The waiter came and made a grand show of presenting their meals. After he bowed away, Nan started in on her caprese salad. "This election is for the presidency of the United States," she said. "Our opponents have to come out swinging to have any chance of keeping the White House. They're doing opposition research, just like I'm sure we are. They'll scrutinize every word both candidates said since they were in high school. If there's even a hint of something controversial, the other side will use it. When they do it, we'll accuse them of running attack ads. When we do it, we'll call it 'a hard contrast piece'."

"By any name, it'll be negative," Hank said. "It's too bad. I hate negative campaigns."

Nan nodded. "Maybe we'll avoid it. It sounds like Hilton has different ideas."

Hank took another sip of wine. He held the glass delicately as he slowly swirled the ruby liquid in the glass. "So, what're you worried about?"

"Negative is one thing," she said. "Dirty and illegal is a whole other thing"

Hank nodded. "Like the Theilen campaign."

Nan had taken a few bites of her salad. Chef Paul had used hard, unripe tomatoes and limp lettuce. His 'creation' was tasteless. She put her fork down. "I'm not naïve, Hank," she said. "Since John Adams ran against Thomas Jefferson, elections have been dirty to some extent. But it doesn't have to be that way. I got into politics because we need people in power who can solve this country's problems. When campaigns turn dirty, the right people don't get elected."

"Do you believe Bloomfield is the right person?"

"Of course I do," Nan said.

"Then help get him elected."

Nan picked up her fork and poked at her salad. "Don't forget, we're running against Sheldon Hanrahan. He probably has an attack all mapped out. I shudder to think what he'll do. Boston doesn't get it. I told them Sheldon was ruthless. They think since he's never run a national campaign he doesn't know what he's doing."

"I hope it won't cost Bloomfield the election," Hank said.

"Then again," Nan said, "maybe they already know. Maybe that's what the new guys are for. Did you see the electronics they brought in? Stephanie said she thought it was surveillance equipment."

"I didn't see anything like that," Hank said. "I'll tell you what, though. That Tom guy is a piece of work. I don't think I want to know what he's up to."

After a long pause, Hank put down his fork and met Nan's eyes. "What about the woman? You said she called."

Before Nan could answer, the waiter came sliding up to the table with a grin. "Madame, monsieur, Chef Paul would like to know if you are enjoying his creations."

Hank set his wine glass down. "Look, sir. I'm sorry if I'm being rude, but first of all, this is supposed to be an Italian restaurant, right? So it wouldn't be 'Madame' and 'Monsieur.' It would be 'Signora' and 'Signore.' Second, we're trying to have a conversation here so leave us be. Please?"

The waiter shrugged and quickly retreated into the kitchen.

Hank looked at Nan sheepishly. "Sorry. I just hate it when they're like that."

Nan chuckled. "I know what you mean."

Hank picked up his fork and started in on what was left of his pasta. "You were going to tell me about the woman."

"She called yesterday and left a message on the answering machine," Nan said. "She said she had something to show me."

"What is it?"

"I don't know. Before she could say anything, someone took the phone from her and hung up."

"Didn't you say she was senile?" Hank asked.

"That's what that guy from the hospital said. But I don't know. I'm bothered by it."

Hank finished the last of his pasta and wine. He wiped his mouth with the napkin and set it on the table. "I'll tell you what," he said. "I was supposed to take the afternoon off. I can go to the hospital and see what I can find out. I'll tell them I'm a relative or something. What is her name again?"

"Mrs. Wilson," Nan answered. "And the guy who came to talk to me was Mr. Woods. It wouldn't hurt to look into it, I suppose."

Hank nodded. "Mrs. Wilson and Mr. Woods. Right. I'll find out what Mrs. Wilson has to show us. Maybe she isn't so senile after all."

Nan pushed her uneaten salad aside. "Okay. But Hank, don't tell anybody about this. And be careful."

Hank put his hand over his heart and raised his other hand as if he were making a pledge. "I promise," he said.

The waiter came over and slapped a bill on the table without saying a word. Hank grabbed it. "I got it," he said.

Nan smiled at him. "Thanks. The next one's on me."

Hank pulled some bills from his wallet and laid them on the table. "It's a deal. I know an authentic Italian place in St. Paul I bet you've never even heard of. The waiters don't even speak English. And there's even a statue of the Virgin Mary above the stove."

"Sounds lovely," Nan said. "I better get back to the office and see what Rex and his people are up to."

"And you have to get ready for the media," Hank said. "You know they'll be at our offices after they endorse Howard this afternoon."

Nan sighed. "What have I gotten myself into?"

Hank just chuckled as they left the restaurant.

TEN

WHEN NAN GOT BACK to the campaign office, she and the campaign workers watched on the new sixty-inch television as Peter Gray, in front of a throng of reporters at Minnesota Army Reserve headquarters, announced his party's endorsement of Senator Howard. A rank of full-dress army reservists stood at attention behind Gray and Senator Howard. After Gray's announcement, Howard stated his hard line position on terrorism.

Fifteen minutes later, the press was at Nan's door and she was ready for them. She'd spent hours studying the governor's platform on topics ranging from abortion to Social Security. She'd read each of Boston's position reports and had even helped Hilton draft a paper on terrorism. The final terrorism position from Boston was a little misleading, but Bob reassured her it was just "spin". Anyway, he said, once the press started to look into it, they'd be on to something new. "Don't think about it too much," Bob had said.

The press arrived in television vans with satellite dishes on top. There were newspaper reporters with recorders ready to capture Nan's every word. Over the previous two days, they'd transformed Bloomfield's Minnesota campaign headquarters from a backwater office to a Norman Rockwell picture of American patriotism. They'd replaced the small, "Vote for Bloomfield" banner with a magnificent red, white and blue one, just like at Boston. Someone had washed the windows and six-foot posters of a smiling Governor Bloomfield hung in each one. Even the front door had been painted red, white and blue. Bob Hilton had thought of everything.

Nan stepped outside the building into the cool, gray October weather as Rex, Stephanie, Jim and the others watched from inside. The reporters descended on her, shouting questions and shoving their microphones at her. She stopped, raised a hand and issued a stern look that quieted the mob. "One moment please," she said. "Let's get set up properly and then I have a short statement. After that, I'll gladly answer questions."

Nan moved to a window and stood in front of a poster of Governor Bloomfield. She pointed to the cameramen. "You should back up to be sure to get the entire picture of the governor in the frame." She waited while the cameramen did as she said. "And please, reporters," she said, "don't ask questions unless I call on you. Let's keep this civilized."

When the cameras were pointed at the right angle and everyone was set, Nan spoke. "I'd like to make a short statement." She cleared her throat, raised her chin and looked directly into the cameras. She said her party wanted to congratulate Senator Howard on receiving his party's endorsement. She said that Bill Howard and Governor

Bloomfield had very different visions for America and that the governor was anxious to discuss those differences in a clean, informative campaign. For the sake of the citizens of Minnesota and the United States, she said, Governor Bloomfield hoped the campaign stayed focused on the important issues. "If we do," she said, "I'm confident Governor Bloomfield will be victorious in November.

"Now, I'll be glad to answer a few questions," she said.

The reporters all shouted questions at once and Nan raised a hand again. "People, remember what I said about being civilized? Please don't shout at me and don't speak all at once." She pointed to a local television reporter she remembered from when she ran Congresswoman Janice Theilen's campaign. "Susan, let's start with you."

"Thank you, Ms. Smith. You're running a campaign against Senator Howard again, just like two years ago. You lost by ten points back then. What will be different this time?"

Nan smiled. She knew she'd get this question and she was prepared for it. "Good question," she said. "The difference this time is that we'll keep the campaign focused on the issues. Two years ago, Bill Howard's campaign sunk to a level where a debate on important issues never happened. The American people deserve better and I encourage Mr. Howard and his campaign staff to keep it at that level." Nan pointed to another reporter.

"You're now running against Minnesota's senior senator. Do you think you can win the state?"

"I'd like to think we can win all fifty states," Nan replied with a smile, "but we'll be happy with enough states to win 271 electoral votes and send Governor Bloomfield to the White House."

She pointed to another reporter, a wolfish looking woman Nan had never seen before.

"You talk about issues," the reporter said. "One of the big differences between the two candidates is their position on terrorism. What's the governor's stand on terrorism?"

"He's against it," Nan replied. "Next question?" Several reporters laughed and Nan could see she had them right where she wanted them. She continued. "If you want a more detailed answer, Governor Bloomfield is releasing a statement on terrorism over the weekend which we will be sure you receive. I assure you his position will be tough yet balanced. Right now, I'm not at liberty to discuss the details."

Before the reporters could ask any more questions, Nan said, "Thank you everyone, that's all the time I have. I must get back to work to elect Governor Bloomfield as the next president of the United States." She waved off the reporters and squeezed her way through the red, white and blue door back into the campaign office.

"That was easy," Rex said as Nan walked in.

"You did great!" Stephanie said. "Those people are tough!"

"That's nothing," replied Nan. "Just wait a few days."

"Do you think we can keep it to the issues like you said?" Jim asked.

"I hope so," Nan answered. "Now, let's get back to work. We have a president to elect."

The group went back into the bullpen and Nan went to her office. Her first encounter with the press as an important spokesperson for the Bloomfield campaign had been a success. She stayed in control and delivered exactly the right image and message for her candidate. She was proud of herself and felt a surge of confidence. She was rocketing up the ranks of the campaign organization for the man who would probably be the next president of the United States. She was feeling the passion again.

ELEVEN

AT THE SUMMIT on Emerging Market Economics in the crystal-chandeliered White House East Room, the president of the United States leaned to his chief of staff, James Morrow, and told him he felt ill. "I need to lie down for an hour," he whispered. "Have Anne take over after the next break. We don't have much left on the agenda anyway."

"Do you need your physician, Mr. President?" Morrow asked.

"No, no. I'll be fine. The Secretary of State can handle the meeting."

"Yes, sir," Morrow said.

Ten minutes later, Phil Dougherty was in the president's residence on the second floor of the White House. His chief aide, Richard Craft, met him in the center hall. "You don't have much time, Mr. President," Craft said. The two men walked to the west wing into a small room off the president's sitting room. Craft pushed open a closet door revealing a hidden elevator. They rode the elevator to an underground parking garage where a Secret Service man held open the back door of a plain, unmarked GMC Yukon with tinted windows. The president climbed in.

"You shouldn't be gone more than forty-five minutes, Mr. President," Craft said, checking his watch. "That would bring you back here at two-thirty."

The Secret Service man got in behind the wheel and drove up the ramp out of the garage. The Yukon stopped at the guard gate where a Marine came up to the driver. "Key card," he said. The driver gave him a blue plastic key card. Before the Marine swiped it over a reader, he said. "Excuse me sir, I need to take a look in the car." The Marine opened the back door of the Yukon and stared squarely into the face of his Commander-in-Chief. He stepped back and clicked his heels together. "Sir," he said in a clipped staccato. "Sorry, sir. I wasn't told you were coming through."

"Let us go," the president ordered.

"Yes sir," replied the Marine as he swiped the card over the reader. The massive iron gates opened and he gave the card back to the driver.

"No report about the president leaving the premises," the driver said to the Marine.

"Yes sir," the Marine replied.

The Yukon drove northeast along New York Avenue for three blocks and turned north on Fourteenth Street. After four blocks, the driver turned into a parking ramp and went down two levels. A construction barricade sat at the entrance to the third level. The driver drove around it and pulled up to a black Mercedes limo waiting in the shadows at the far end of the empty ramp.

"Take a walk for a while Ron," the president said.

The driver got out and walked to the other end of the ramp. The back door of the Mercedes opened and a lanky man with gray hair got out, climbed in the back seat of the Yukon, and sat next to the president.

"You know, George," the president said, "it's not good form to be chauffeured in a foreign-made car when you're running for president."

Governor George Bloomfield flashed a broad, white smile. "I have to travel incognito to meet with you. It's a perfect disguise. No one would ever suspect a good American like me to be in a German car."

The president chuckled. "It's good to see you, George," he said. "You look tired."

"I *am* tired. You know how it is on the campaign trail. You can never let up until the election is over."

"And if you win," the president said, "you won't get any rest then, either. Why do you want this goddamn job?"

"To correct your eight years of government mismanagement."

The president laughed and shook his head. "Seriously, George. It's not all it's cracked up to be."

George Bloomfield pressed his head into the headrest. "I feel called, I guess. I want to do things, make a difference. I have ideas."

"Admit it, George. It's also an ego boost, being the most powerful man in the world."

"I'm sure it is and yes, I admit, it's appealing."

Phil Dougherty let out a sigh. "The responsibility grinds on you. Day after day, year after year. It changes you. I'm bone tired and ready to leave."

The governor nodded. "How's Hal, by the way? Is his heart as bad as the news says it is?"

The president nodded. "It was a bad one this time, but he'll recover. It was a blessing, actually. He needs to quit, too. Being president would have killed him."

"Assuming, of course, he would have beaten me."

The president grinned. "I believe it was a safe assumption."

Bloomfield chuckled and, after a moment of silence in the dark cab of the Yukon, he turned to the president. "What's on your mind, Phil? Why the secret meeting?"

"We can't let Howard win," the president said simply.

Bloomfield paused. "I see," he said finally. "Then why did you endorse him?"

"I didn't have a choice."

"You, Phil Dougherty, a lame duck president, didn't have a choice? Why?"

"Let's just say I was forced into it and leave it at that," the president said. "The point is you have to beat him in this race. I'm offering my help."

"Well, I'm ahead in the polls. Howard will get a boost now that your party has endorsed him, but I'll still have a comfortable lead. He's very beatable."

"It's not him I'm worried about."

"Oh?"

The president leaned forward and put his arms on his knees. "You know George, we have our differences, but at least we have ethics. I believe—actually I know—there are people in the Howard camp who do not. I have sworn an oath to protect the constitution of this country and that's why I'm here."

"That's why you're offering to help me win—to protect the constitution?"

"Ultimately, yes."

"What is it, Phil?" Bloomfield asked. "What's this really about? Level with me."

The president shook his head. "I can't tell you. Just watch yourself George, and remember you're running against people who don't play by the rules. In fact, they go way beyond dirty, if you know what I mean. You need to be careful. And I want you to know if it looks like you'll lose, I might be able to help. I won't do anything overt. It can't appear I'm going back on my endorsement. You just need to let me know if your campaign is in trouble. Okay? That's what I wanted to tell you."

"I have a big lead in the polls," the governor said. "My staff wants to push for two debates against Howard in the final two weeks of the campaign. I'll beat him in the debates. I should win the election."

The president leaned over the front seat and honked the horn for his driver to return. "Yeah, you should, George. Just be sure you do. And if something happens and it looks like you won't, get word to me."

"I will."

The president shook Governor Bloomfield's hand. "Get some rest, George," he said. "You're going to need it."

Bloomfield went back to his limo as the President's driver climbed behind the wheel. As the limo drove the president back to the White House, he wondered if Bloomfield really knew what he was up against. He doubted that the governor did. He himself hadn't known until it was too late and he'd had to pay the price.

He prayed that his country wouldn't have to pay the price, too.

TWELVE

"MOM, CAN I HAVE a cell phone?" Jenny asked. "*All* my friends have one. I'm the *only* one in the *whole* school who doesn't have a cell phone. Dad said I should ask you. *Please?*"

Nan examined her daughter and smiled to herself. Jenny stood at the kitchen counter in the Smith's two-story Cape Cod home in South Minneapolis wearing her lacrosse uniform. She was scarfing down a bowl of Cheerios and looking beseechingly at Nan.

Nan was surprised at how quickly Jenny was turning into a woman. She would be tall like her father and have his dark hair, but she had Nan's Nordic eyes and fine facial features. She already had breasts. When she grew out of her gangly stage, she'd be a beauty. She was a good student, too. She never had to be told to do her homework and always brought home straight A's. She was responsible, smart, cute, a good athlete and all she needed was a cell phone and her life would be complete.

Nan sat at the oak kitchen table and sipped her coffee while Ben sat across from her reading the morning paper.

Saturday mornings were her favorite time of the week when life slowed and she and Ben could sit back and watch their daughter grow up.

"Dad said you should ask me, huh?" Nan said shooting a look at Ben. "Is that true, Dad?"

Ben peeked from around the newspaper and shrugged. "I thought we could talk about it."

"Can I Mom?" Jenny said. "*Pleeease?*"

"I thought we said we'd wait until you're fourteen?"

"Fourteen? Marisa has had one since she was twelve! And Katie's had one for months now."

"What do you think, Ben?" Nan asked.

Ben folded the newspaper and put it on the table. "It wouldn't cost much. And it'd be handy for keeping in touch with her. Why not?"

"I'd need unlimited text messaging," Jenny interjected. "It would cost six dollars a month and I could pay for it out of my babysitting money."

Nan's heart ached for her daughter. In a few short years, she'd be off to college and Nan's mothering years would be over. Jenny had never disappointed them and maybe Nan shouldn't disappoint her daughter, either.

"I think we can pay the six dollars a month for text messaging," Nan said. "Sure, let's get you a cell phone."

Jenny ran to Nan and gave her a hug. "Thanks, Mom." Jenny hugged Ben and said, "Thanks, Dad. Marisa's mom is picking me up for practice. I'll be home at noon. Tonight I have to baby sit the Sundburg twins. Ugh, I hate that. Can we get the phone tomorrow?"

"Sure," Nan said.

"I gotta go. See ya later!" Jenny bounded off through the living room to the front door to wait for her ride.

"*Dad said I should ask you?*'" Nan said with a grin at Ben.

Ben laughed. "It's called passing the buck. Anyway, I knew you'd say yes."

Nan reached across the table, squeezed Ben's hand. "She's growing up fast. I wish I could spend more time with her."

"I'm proud of you for what you're doing. And now, you're an important adviser to the Bloomfield campaign. My beautiful wife is moving up in the world. And bringing home a paycheck, too!"

"Is my paycheck all you want me for?" Nan asked in mock disgust.

Ben gave Nan a long once-over. "That and other things."

Nan bit her lower lip and winked. "Anytime, big boy," she said affecting her best Mae West impression. "Anytime."

Ben laughed. "We better wait until our daughter leaves."

Nan slid onto Ben's lap. "So how's my handsome, hard-working husband? How are things at the ad agency?"

"They're fine."

"Right. I can see right through you. How are they really?"

"Profits are down. We need two or three new accounts to replace what we've lost to Hanrahan. Same old story."

"Well, I'm proud of you anyway. You've done well." They kissed and Nan jumped off Ben's lap and searched for her briefcase. "I have to meet Hilton at the Sofitel this morning. He promised I'd be home before noon. I'll have to go to the office later."

"So you're going to spend Saturday morning with Bob Hilton in his hotel room?" Ben said.

"Yes, discussing politics. I'd rather spend the morning with you in a hotel room doing something else, but as you said, we need my paycheck."

"I have to work this morning, too," Ben said. "Maybe we can do something with Jenny before you have to go to New York."

"I'd like that." Nan found her briefcase and car keys and headed to the door. "I'll see you in a few hours."

*

Bob Hilton had flown into Minneapolis late on Friday night and had taken a suite on the fifth floor of the 1960's style Sofitel Hotel in the southwest suburb of Edina. When Nan knocked on the door, Rex Starkey answered. He was dressed in a blue button-down shirt and jeans. "Hi, Nan, come in," he said. "We're just getting started. Bob's in the bedroom on the phone with Boston." Nan stepped into the small, modern suite and took a seat on the couch. Starkey sat in a chair eyeing her. There were dirty breakfast dishes on a tray next to the door.

"You handled yourself well with the media yesterday," Starkey said. "They can be rough."

"Thanks," Nan said. "I've handled the press before."

Rex continued eyeing her. "We could make a good team, you and I. I bet we can get a story on you—the state campaign manager who suddenly finds herself in the thick of the national campaign. In fact, I talked to Hilton about it yesterday. Perhaps you and I could go out for dinner and discuss it."

Nan shot Rex a look. "I don't think I want that kind of attention."

The door to the bedroom swung open and Bob Hilton came through wearing a Reebok jogging suit and a white towel around his neck. "Hey Nan, sorry about the outfit. I haven't had time to change." His words came fast. "I gotta find a hotel with a better gym next time. I had to wait ten minutes for a machine this morning."

Hilton sat on the edge of the chair next to Rex. "Just got off the phone with Boston. Howard picked up only one point with his party endorsement. That's less than we thought."

He flashed his Ivy League smile. "You won't believe what we've planned for our new ads, Nan. We've had to keep it a secret until now."

"What is it?" Nan asked.

Hilton leaned forward. "A new way of campaigning. Let's face it, most political ads stink. If they advertised consumer products as badly as they do most candidates, no one would ever buy anything. Well, we're changing that. Brent Springman has given us the rights to his song, *Road Home*. It's one of the biggest rock and roll hits of all time. And get this, he's changing the lyrics and will record a new cut just for us. Can you believe it? Brent Springman, 'The Man' for Christ's sake. And *Road Home*! It's perfect for us."

Hilton rubbed his hands together. "That's not all. Miles Jackson and Jocelyn Jones are starring in our new TV commercials and Jon Flesner will be directing them. They're at the very top of Hollywood's 'A' list and they're on our team."

"Who's Jon Flesner?" Rex asked.

"Jesus, Rex, you gotta get out more," Hilton said. "He is the director of *Daughters of the Dragon*. Top grossing movie last year."

"Sounds exciting," Nan said.

"It is," Hilton replied, "We'll be making history. Springman is a California guy, born and raised and with Hollywood icons Jackson and Jones, we might even steal

California. Like I said, it's a new way of campaigning—
Hollywood style. That's why I want you in New York on
Monday, Nan. I'm flying to L.A. this afternoon. Brent is
recording the new radio commercials there tomorrow. After
the recording session, I'm taking the redeye to New York.
We're shooting the ads with Miles and Jocelyn on Monday
and I want you there. We have you on a flight out tomorrow
night."

"You want me to help with the television commercials?"
Nan asked.

"I want you close to me during the final push of this
campaign, Nan. Your insights in our meeting in Boston were
very helpful. You can help with the script. And you'll get to
meet Miles Jackson and Jocelyn Jones," he said with a grin.

"I look forward to it," Nan said. She felt a surge of
excitement. She was indeed moving up in the party. Hilton
wanted her in New York to see his new ad campaign, and in
Boston, he'd mentioned he wanted to talk to her about a role
in the Administration if Bloomfield won.

"So, how can I help this morning?" she asked.

Hilton put his hands behind his head and leaned back.
"You can tell us what you know about Howard and Sheldon
Hanrahan. Now that he's officially our opponent, we need to
be all over him. That's why I stopped on my way to L.A. You
managed Theilen's campaign two years ago. Give us an
overview of that campaign."

Nan settled into the couch. "It was not pleasant," she
began. "Things turned ugly when Theilen took the lead. Let
me explain."

Nan spent the next forty-five minutes describing in detail
the negative campaign strategies, attack ads and dirty tricks
Sheldon Hanrahan used to win the senate race. She told them

how he flooded the entire state with pamphlets, mailers, e-mails, blogs, and press releases alleging Theilen supported illegal immigration because her maid was a Puerto Rican who, incidentally, was in the country legally. By the time they were able to react, Sheldon had come out with a new accusation that drowned out their response. They presented the new accusation through a massive push poll asking voters if they would vote for Theilen if they knew she was a lesbian. Lesbian? She'd been married twenty-seven years and had two kids. When the Theilen campaign objected, the push poll ended, but by then, the media was in a feeding frenzy and the damage was done. Then, yet another accusation surfaced, and another and another. Sheldon Hanrahan kept coming with allegations and slams all perfectly choreographed to keep the Theilen campaign on the defensive. The real issues were relegated to sound bites that, Nan explained, Sheldon Hanrahan and his writers were very good at. And there were dirty tricks, too. Banquet room reservations were mysteriously cancelled, calendars were altered causing people to miss important meetings, e-mail accounts were hacked, computer systems crashed. Then she told them about the improper smear letter that supposedly came from the Theilen camp that won the election for Howard. "We never did find out where that letter came from," she said.

"Sounds rough," Hilton said.

"It was," Nan replied. "Very rough."

Hilton folded his arms across his chest. "Was Howard's entire campaign choreographed by Sheldon Hanrahan?"

"Yep. Their party's national committee didn't get involved at all."

"We've been investigating your Mr. Hanrahan since you told us about him in Boston," Hilton said. "You're right, he's well connected. He knows how to win elections."

Nan pushed herself to the edge of the couch. "Bob, what we have to remember is that he doesn't play fair. It's not just the attack ads, the dirty tricks and the way he works the press to spin stories against his opponent. It's that he'll do anything to win. I mean, anything."

Hilton got out of his chair and started pacing the room. He grabbed the towel around his neck with both hands as he paced. "You've said that before. I'm hearing you, but I think it'll be different this time. He won't be able to get away with it. There's far too much media scrutiny in a presidential election. The media is like a gigantic microscope. Nothing escapes their attention."

"Sheldon Hanrahan is a very private person," Nan said. "He's good at avoiding the media."

Hilton shook his head. "He won't be able to on this," he said. "Especially if he steps out of line. We have some of our friends in the media watching him. I think we can keep this election on the up-and-up—for the most part."

"I wouldn't underestimate him, Bob," Nan said.

Hilton nodded. "We won't. It might not matter, anyway. Our sources say the national committee will run Howard's campaign, not Hanrahan."

Rex pushed to the front of his chair and turned to Nan, "What's with those glasses he wears?"

"He had a horrible, disfiguring accident decades ago," she answered. "The rumor is, he was betrayed by people. He turned bitter and set out to build a communication empire based on fashion and beauty. And he did. Let me be clear. Hanrahan Communications is one of the biggest, most skilled communications companies in the world. But no one knows much about Mr. Hanrahan and no one ever sees him without his glasses. Like I said, he's a very private person."

"By the way, Nan," Hilton said, "we took your advice and we're pushing for two debates. It looks like we're going to get them and then, as you said, it'll be Howard against Bloomfield, mano-a-mano. George will destroy him."

"That's good," Nan said. "It's the right strategy."

Hilton took a seat and grinned at Nan and Rex. "This is exciting, isn't it? Brent Springman singing *Road Home* for our new commercials. They'll be on the air next week, just in time for our final push. We're in the lead. All we have to do is stay there for the next two and a half weeks and we'll have the White House. Nan, I'm so glad you're on our team."

Nan could tell Hilton was flattering her but his praise was effective and his enthusiasm, contagious. "I'm glad too, Bob," she said. "I'll do everything I can."

After a pause, Hilton leaned toward Nan. "One more thing. We're going to have to cut the Minnesota budget. We can't win Minnesota against your senator so we need to reallocate funds to other mid-western states we have a chance to win—Ohio, Illinois, Michigan. You'll have to cut your mailings and advertising. You'll still get advertising from the national buy, but your office has a different purpose now. That's why I sent Rex. Of course, the office still needs to look legitimate, so you'll have to go on with your work."

"I understand," Nan said. "I was expecting it. I'll send you a new budget with cuts."

"By the way," Hilton said, "I saw a clip of your press conference yesterday. You were great."

"Thank you. I do my best."

Hilton stood and pointed at Nan and Rex. "Are you two going to get along here in Minneapolis?" he asked with mock concern.

"Oh, we'll get along just fine," Rex replied with a wink at Nan.

"I'm just going to stay out of Rex's way," Nan said.

"Good," Hilton said. "Thanks for your time, Nan. Rex and I have to talk about a few things."

Nan rose and gathered her briefcase. She shook hands with Hilton and left.

*

Nan drove the backstreets home instead of taking the freeway. She was a senior adviser to the national campaign but the office she managed would no longer try to win the state. It would be another losing campaign for her. At least there would be two debates as she suggested, and Minnesota would get the new national advertising.

A Hollywood campaign. That figured. Campaigns had been building to this for years—celebrity endorsements, jingles, logos and commercials created by Madison Avenue and big name Hollywood directors with a political agenda. It was exciting, to be sure.

But as she pointed her car toward her home, she wondered if they they were playing into Sheldon Hanrahan's hands. He was already a master of marketing and advertising who used these same strategies for his billion dollar clients. He knew better than anyone how to use Hollywood to sell to the public. And once again, Bob Hilton had dismissed what Nan was telling him about Sheldon.

Yes, she would be busy for the next two and a half weeks. She'd have to find time for Jenny and help Ben take his mind off of his problems at work. And she'd do her best not to worry about Sheldon Hanrahan.

THIRTEEN

SHELDON HANRAHAN WAS dressed in a white, loose-fitting cotton shirt and slacks. He was sitting in the lotus position on a simple granite bench gazing at his Zen garden. Through his dark glasses, he didn't see or wasn't even aware of anything outside the garden. At this moment, it was his entire world. The garden was the earth and the expanse of white stone, the sea. Inside the garden, the boulders were mountains and the carefully sculpted junipers were clouds floating over them. Sitting on his bench, Sheldon was the master of the entire world and his world was serene, beautiful... perfect.

Someday America would be perfect too. It wasn't now. No one had tended to it for decades. It would take more than the twenty-five years it took him to perfect his Zen garden, but once he got control of the White House, the pruning would begin.

His trance was broken by footsteps in the grass behind him. He stayed in the lotus position and the footsteps stopped behind him. "Senator," Sheldon said without turning around, "what do you want to talk to me about?"

"I don't like what we're doing in my campaign," the senator said in a clear, baritone voice. "I don't understand what you're doing and I want to know what you're thinking."

"What about my thinking don't you understand?" Sheldon said, still in a light trance.

"Why did you give in to the national committee? You gave them everything they asked for. We didn't have to. Once we got Dougherty's endorsement, they weren't going to endorse anyone else. We had leverage but you let them take over. Why?"

"The national committee will do what we need them to do," Sheldon answered, simply.

Howard stepped around the bench to face Sheldon. "I don't agree. They aren't going to run the kind of campaign we need to win. That pompous ass Peter Gray thinks he knows everything. Why do you kowtow to him? We've been waiting for this chance. We don't have much time. Why aren't you doing what we've done in the past?"

"We can't do what we've done in the past. The media is watching us."

"So we let Peter Gray run the campaign and give Bloomfield the presidency? He has a seven-point lead already! And Jesus, you agreed to two debates. That's a huge mistake. He's one of the best orators in Washington. Why'd you do it?"

"We had to. If we didn't agree to the debates, they would have used it against us."

Howard shook his head. "I won't let you make me look like a fool, Sheldon. Is that what you're trying to do? Because if it is, I won't let you."

Sheldon didn't respond right away. He continued to gaze at the garden through his dark glasses. The sun had come out from behind the clouds and it felt warm on his back. His trance was broken, but it wouldn't take long for it to return once the senator left. "You need to relax, Bill," he said finally. "Sit a while. Look at my garden. It's taken me decades to create. It's beautiful, don't you agree? Simple serenity. Sit. Let it calm you."

"I don't have time for your games," the senator said without sitting. "Let me know what you're planning or I'll have to find another campaign manager."

Sheldon turned his dark glasses on the senator. In his navy blue blazer and button-down shirt, the senator had the athletic good looks of the college hockey star he had once been. Over the years, Sheldon had coached him on what clothes to wear and helped him lose his northern Minnesota accent. He'd schooled him in high society etiquette and statesmanship. He had told him exactly what to say at every point of his political career. Bill Howard was going to make a good front man if he just toed the line for two and half more weeks.

"I'm surprised at you Bill," Sheldon said. "I've brought you this far. I was even able to take care of that incident you had years ago and you still doubt me?"

"Goddamn you. Why do you bring that up? That fucking incident."

"Yes, how unfortunate it was for you. I'm so glad I could help."

"Fuck you, Sheldon" Howard said.

Sheldon let the insult pass. He looked back out over his garden and started to work back into his trance. "Bill," he said, "in a little over two weeks, you will be elected president of the United States. That's all you need to know"

"Really? We're behind and you've done nothing."

"I'm doing what's needed," Sheldon said as his eyes half closed.

Howard faced the garden and shoved his hands into his pants pockets. "Okay, okay. Whatever you say. Two debates. Fine. I'll need help preparing for them. I'll do my best. I just hope you know what you're doing."

Sheldon said nothing and after a while, the senator walked back the way he came.

As the senator left, Sheldon's trance began to wash over him. Almost immediately, his world was perfect again. Simple serenity.

Of course the senator didn't understand. No one understood him and that was his great advantage. But someday, they would all understand and they would love him for it. Then, it wouldn't matter what was hidden behind his dark glasses. And perhaps he would know the love of a woman again.

FOURTEEN

Frank Pierce had his cell phone on vibrate so he could detect an incoming call above the sound of the gunfire. On Saturdays, the gunfire was louder than usual because the amateurs who used the basement firing range on the weekends brought in their heavy guns. Most of them couldn't hang on to anything bigger than a 9-millimeter. But they all wanted to show off their big pistols with their loud reports and it didn't matter that they sprayed their shots all over the place.

Frank didn't care about the size of his pistol. He only cared about his accuracy. His 9mm, Walther P88 was the most accurate handgun he'd ever used and he didn't need anything more powerful. The proof was in the grouping he had just made in the target. Not a single shot had landed outside the bull's-eye.

As Pierce reloaded the 14-round magazine, he felt the buzz of his special-issue cell phone in his back pocket. He grabbed his pistol and box of shells and made it up the concrete stairs, away from the noise, before the fourth ring. He punched the talk button. "Pierce," he said.

"Frank, it's Woods. Someone was here asking about the woman."

"Who? When?" Pierce asked as he holstered his pistol and shoved the box of shells in his coat pocket.

"Yesterday. I think it was one of the people from Bloomfield's campaign office."

"Yesterday... and you're telling me now?" Pierce could feel his jaw tighten. "Give me the details."

"It's probably nothing. Older gentleman. Wiry. I don't know exactly who he was, but I recognized him from when I talked to that Nan Smith woman. He's a campaign worker, I think. I'll find out his name."

"What did he do at the hospital?"

"He came in askin' to talk to the woman. He said he was a relative. She doesn't have any relatives so the guard desk got suspicious and turned him away. She's all drugged up now anyway. We had to double her dosage. He wouldn't have been able to talk to her even if he had been allowed to."

"Is that all that happened?" Frank walked through the gun shop past a bank of glass cases holding dozens of pistols for sale. He headed for the exit.

"No. The security cameras caught him in the parking lot talking to one of the orderlies. They were gone before we could get to them."

"Have you interrogated the orderly?"

"Not yet. He's off this weekend."

Pierce snorted as he pushed the gun shop door open and stepped out into the street. After having been in the dark basement for the past hour the low angle of the October sun made him squint. "Goddamn it, go to the orderly's home and talk to him now. Find out what he said to the man. And find out who the man from Bloomfield's campaign office is. Am I clear?"

"Yeah, you're clear."

"Have we kept a watch on Nan Smith?"

"Yes. She's not doing anything unusual. We don't need to worry about her."

Pierce closed his eyes and drew in a deep breath. "Woods, you are a fucking idiot. If we don't need to worry about her, why is someone poking around the hospital? She knows more than she told you."

"But it's this other guy who's askin' the questions, not her." Woods' Alabama accent was strong.

"I don't care. Keep a tail on her. And as soon as you know who was at the hospital, call me. I want this information today. Don't spoil my weekend by making me worry."

"Yeah, yeah. I'm on it, I'm on it."

"And Woods, if things keep getting fucked up out there, I'll have to send special help. Am I clear?"

"Yeah, you're clear."

"Good. Now do your damn job. Call me in two hours." Frank hung up. He climbed into his car and headed for home. Fucking Woods. He'd been an able field man when they assigned him to Minnesota, but over the past five years, he'd lost his edge. He was incompetent and a liability and Pierce could not let him fuck up this assignment. Not now. Not with the election a few weeks away and not with all the attention focused on Minnesota. Important people were depending on Pierce to keep the woman quiet.

As he climbed into his car and started the engine, he said aloud. "Woods, you fuck up. It's time to send you some special help."

FIFTEEN

The cell phone Jenny chose was tiny and pink and she was thrilled with it. She had her nose in it when they left the store and didn't come up for air for the entire drive home. Since it would take a few hours to activate, Nan suggested they pick up Ben and the dog and go for a walk around Lake Harriet. The sky was blue and the day was warm for mid-October. People out for a Sunday stroll filled the parkway around the lake. It was a glorious day and Nan was pleased to be spending some precious time with her family.

Jenny skipped ahead with the dog and Nan could see her daughter was excited that in a few hours her life would be complete with a cell phone that had unlimited text messaging. If only life were that simple, Nan thought.

Nan took Ben's hand and they walked a third of the way around the lake without talking. Her career was taking off again after the humiliating loss two years earlier. It would be a demanding few weeks and she hoped the results would be different this time. But whenever she daydreamed about winning, the image of Sheldon Hanrahan crushed it.

As they approached the Lake Harriet band shell with its towering gray spires, Ben said, "You never told me about your meeting with Bob Hilton. What did you discuss in his hotel room?"

"Oh, we didn't discuss anything," Nan said. "We had crazy sex all morning. Rex Starkey was there too. A three-way. It was amazing."

Ben laughed. "I thought you looked tired when you got home."

"If you only knew," Nan grinned.

"You're real funny. Seriously, what did Hilton want to talk to you about?"

"He wanted a brief on the Theilen campaign, and he told me about the new advertising. You won't believe what they're doing."

"I'm an ad man. Tell me and I'll give you a professional opinion, no charge."

Nan told Ben about Brent Springman doing a new version of *Road Home* for the campaign and that Hilton was in L.A. for the recording session. She explained that their new commercials would star Miles Jackson and Jocelyn Jones, and Jon Flesner was directing them. That's why she was going to New York.

"You're going to meet Miles Jackson and Jocelyn Jones?" Ben asked. "They're as big as they get."

"It's exciting, for sure," Nan said. "But this Hollywood strategy seems a little fake. So, mister professional ad man, what do you think?"

"It's expected," Ben replied, tossing a pebble into the lake. "Presidential elections are bigger than the Super Bowl, the Academy Awards and American Idol combined. Everyone wants in. They'll be pitting candidates against each other like

Coke versus Pepsi. It's been happening for decades. Lyndon Johnson used the best ad agency in the business to defeat Goldwater in 1964. Reagan fully understood the power of Hollywood and used it to his full advantage. Dougherty hangs out with Hollywood directors and movie stars. Every successive election has used Hollywood more and more. And it's just starting."

"It seems a little shallow. Like commercials for makeup or the latest gadget." Nan looked out over the lake. A few boats with brightly colored sails glided past for one last sail until the winds of winter locked the lake in ice.

"Exactly what it is." Ben said. "There's an adage in advertising: 'All advertising is ultimately fashion advertising,' and it's true. What we do is make people like our client's advertising first. If they like the commercial, they'll like the product no matter what it has to offer. It applies to presidential candidates too. People hate political advertising. It's one reason they hate politics so much. Hilton knows that and that's why he's connecting Bloomfield with Hollywood. It's the right strategy to get your man elected." A runner in a designer jogging suit ran past pushing a yellow stroller that looked like a Tour de France touring bicycle. Nan and Ben stepped out of the way to let it pass.

"It's a strategy that plays right into Sheldon's hands," Nan said. "He's better at it than anyone."

"True, but he got a late start. It takes time to crank up a Hollywood campaign, even for him."

"Then Sheldon will probably turn to attack ads right away," Nan said. "Remember what he did against Theilen?"

"Yeah," Ben replied. "If he does, Hilton might have to use attack ads, too. He'll use what we call a two-tier strategy. The Hollywood advertising will be the air cover and the attack ads will be the hand-to-hand combat. If one side starts a dirty fight, the other will counter with one."

Nan shook her head as they continued walking. "I really hope it doesn't come to that. I don't want to have to deal with that kind of slime again."

Ben put his arm around Nan. "It might not come to that. You said Howard's national committee is in charge. Sheldon may not have much say about how the campaign is run."

After a pause, Nan said, "They took my advice and agreed to two debates."

Ben nodded. "That's perfect. Bloomfield will destroy Howard in debates. You're smart for someone so good-looking."

Nan put an arm around Ben's waist and hugged him. Ben looked at her. "Don't worry, Nan. Your guy will win the election. Anyway, what does it matter? Jenny has her new cell phone so what could be wrong with the world?"

"We better get home. She'll be anxious to use it."

*

"Mom, my phone is working!" Jenny exclaimed an hour later. "I'm going to call Marisa."

As Ben went off to rake leaves, Nan tossed her jacket on the kitchen table and smiled as she watched Jenny trot off to her room with her new pink phone. Jenny was getting more and more independent. In three years she'd be driving and two years after that, she'd be off to college. Then, there'd be no more Sunday walks around the lake with Jenny.

How did it happen so quickly? It seemed like yesterday when Jenny burst into their lives. Nan had a morning-sickness-free pregnancy and an easy, quick delivery. Jenny had been a delightful child ever since. Nan and Ben had tried to have another child—Ben wanted three—but a second child never came. The infertility clinic said it had something to do with chemical incompatibility between Nan's eggs and Ben's sperm but in the end, Nan concluded the doctors didn't really know why she couldn't get pregnant again.

Perhaps it was meant to be. By then it had become clear that Jenny was a special child and she fulfilled Nan and Ben's parental needs, so they stopped trying to get pregnant. It was a decision they never regretted. Jenny was healthy and happy and well on her way to becoming a beautiful, successful young woman. And having only one child enabled Nan to pursue her career.

The way things were going in the Bloomfield campaign, she was getting excited about her career again. She'd helped put together the campaign's position paper on terrorism and had even been on television, talking about issues. It felt good.

The Hollywood advertising for the final two weeks of the campaign was also exciting. It was wild—the rock stars, movie stars and an A-list director. But, as Ben had said, it had been coming for years. Apparently, Bob Hilton knew what he was doing. He was as smart as they came, had tons of energy and, Nan had to admit, he was very good-looking. He was out to change the way elections were waged and it looked like he was on the right track—his man was leading the race.

Nan went into the kitchen to prepare dinner. Sunday was one of the few nights the family could eat together and Nan liked to cook something special. Tonight it was one of Jenny's favorites, lasagna. As she put the water on to boil, she heard voices coming from the front yard. A few seconds later, Ben called for Nan. She turned off the stove, went to the front yard, and saw Ben talking with Hank Mattson.

"Hello, Hank," she said. "What brings you here on a Sunday?"

"Sorry to bother you. I tried calling but your cell was off. And you said you'd be in New York tomorrow so I thought I'd see if you were home. I need to talk to you about something."

As Ben headed to the back yard with his rake, he said over his shoulder, "Later, Hank. I gotta get the back yard done before dinner."

"Come on in," Nan said.

"No, no," Hank waved. "I don't want to intrude. This won't take long. I learned something on Friday I thought I should tell you. It's about Mrs. Wilson."

"Oh?" Nan motioned for them to sit on the front step. She heard Ben raking again in the back yard.

"It might be nothing," Hank said, taking a seat next to Nan.

"Did you talk to her?"

"They wouldn't let me. I tell ya, that place is like a fortress. At the guard desk I told them I was Mrs. Wilson's nephew. They said it wasn't possible because she doesn't have any relatives. And they said contact with her was strictly limited. No one could see her without the permission of Mr. Woods."

"That doesn't seem unusual."

"No, it doesn't," Hank said, "but I was still curious. When I left, I saw this orderly—his nametag said 'Earl'. Anyway, I saw Earl going to catch the bus and I asked him about Mrs. Wilson. I got the impression he was a little slow, you know? Maybe mentally impaired. Well, he told me she's been a patient for five years, ever since the death of her daughter. I asked him how the daughter died and he said she killed herself."

"So she wasn't murdered by Senator Howard. That's good."

"Wait, there's more. I asked why she killed herself and suddenly big Earl goes quiet. He says he's told me too much and no one is supposed to talk about Mrs. Wilson or they'd get in trouble with Mr. Woods. Then he runs off to catch his bus."

Nan shrugged. "They're probably just trying to protect the privacy of their patients."

"Maybe. But it bothered me, Nan. Don't get me wrong, but there was something about that orderly. He looked like he wanted to say more."

"He was probably scared because he thought Mr. Woods would fire him or something."

"That's another thing, Nan. He can't fire him. I don't think Mr. Woods works for the hospital."

"What?" Nan said. "He told me he was in charge of security."

Hank turned to Nan. "Listen to this. They have their staff listed in the lobby—the managers, nurses, even the janitor. There was no Mr. Woods listed."

"Well," Nan said, "he could be new. Maybe they didn't post his name yet."

"It's possible. But you saw him when he came into the office the other day. Did he *look* like he worked for a hospital?"

"No, he didn't." Nan admitted. "I don't know, Hank. The poor woman lives in a psychiatric hospital. She lost her daughter and thinks Howard murdered her. It sounds like she's gone crazy about it."

"Then what's Mr. Woods doing there? And why don't they want anyone to say anything about Mrs. Wilson?"

Nan didn't have an answer. Hank was right; it didn't add up. After a few seconds Nan said, "When she left the phone message, she said she had something to show me. I wonder what it is."

"That's why I wanted to talk to you before you went to New York. I'd like to try to find out. I have a friend who works for the State Board of Examiners. I'll call him tomorrow to find out if Mr. Woods is an employee. Maybe I can find something out about Mrs. Wilson, too."

Nan shook her head. "I don't know, Hank. Is it worth it? Are you sure you want to do this?"

"You know, I've never worked on a campaign that beat Sheldon Hanrahan," Hank answered. "If there's something to it, maybe this is the one."

"I thought you didn't like dirty campaigns."

"It isn't dirty if it's true," Hank replied. "I mean, what would it hurt to look into it?"

"Okay. But be discreet." Nan motioned toward the house. "I have to get dinner on the table."

Hank stood to leave. "By the way," he said, "you never told me why Hilton is sending you to New York."

Nan grinned. "I'm going to meet Miles Jackson and Jocelyn Jones. They're starring in Bloomfield's new commercials. We're shooting them tomorrow."

"Miles Jackson and Jocelyn Jones?" Hank shook his head. "What ever happened to campaigning via whistle stops and town hall meetings? Ah, well. Have a good trip. I'll talk to you on Tuesday." Hank waved over his shoulder as he climbed into his car and drove off.

Nan went back into the kitchen and started cooking. It was indeed puzzling what Hank had found out at the hospital. He wanted to find out more and Nan had to admit she was curious, too.

She turned the stove on underneath the water. She had to be at the airport in less than three hours to catch her flight to New York where, tomorrow morning, she'd meet the two movie stars who had dominated the cover of *People* magazine for the past decade.

It was a new kind of campaign, Hilton had said.

That's for sure. It seemed almost surreal.

SIXTEEN

PRESIDENT PHILIP DOUGHERTY was at his best in photo ops and the White House invited Silvia to a good one. She watched as Dougherty positioned himself between the President of Turkey and the Malaysian Prime Minister. The weekend summit on Emerging Market Economics had been a huge success and the Administration had called in the press and brought out the president, secretary of state and the foreign dignitaries for a photo op on the north lawn of the White House. As the president postured and posed, the cameras clicked away. He was the most powerful man on earth and he looked it. But Silvia knew even powerful people kept secrets hidden behind their confident-looking façades. She wondered what he was hiding.

Silvia searched for Ellen Stein among the throng of the White House staff. She spotted her standing in the shade, talking to a reporter from CNN. She walked up to Ellen and listened in on the conversation. The reporter asked about the administration's budget commitment to the emerging market countries. Ellen carefully answered and kept referring to the information in the press packet. Eventually, the CNN reporter was satisfied and left Silvia and Ellen alone.

"Apparently," Silvia said, "the president wants to leave a legacy of helping emerging nations. I wonder what else will be in his legacy."

"Good morning, Ms. Mendoza," Ellen said. "May I answer any questions you have about the summit?"

"I think I have everything I need on that. I'm wondering if you have anything else for me."

"Everything is in the summit press release," Ellen said, "unless you need more detail or clarification which we would be glad to give you."

"You're cute, Ellen. I wasn't talking about the summit and you know it."

"Yes. I know." Ellen pressed her mouth into a professional smile. "When will I see you again?"

"I don't know. I'm very busy investigating a story about why the president endorsed William Howard. Would you care to comment on that?"

"When will I see you again?" Ellen repeated.

"I can't possibly get away until I have more done on this story."

Ellen held her smile and said, "You little Mexican whore. *Puta.*"

"I guess that means you don't have any information for me. In that case, I better get back to the *Sentinel.*"

Ellen looked out over the reporters and leaned ever so slightly toward Silvia. "It's big," she whispered, still holding her smile.

"Excuse me?"

"I said it's big. The story you are working on is bigger than you can imagine."

Silvia felt a surge of journalistic excitement. Ellen, a senior member of the White House press staff just told her she was onto a big story involving the president of the United States and she was on the verge of getting the scoop. It was the break she was hoping for, the one that would convince Ian Rutter to have someone fill in for her at the White House while she investigated the story. "Tell me more," she said.

"When will I see you again?" Ellen said, no longer smiling.

"I might be free on Wednesday night."

"Wednesday night," Ellen said. "That works for me."

"What about the story? You said it's big. How big?"

Ellen glanced at Silvia with mischievous eyes. She reached into her briefcase and pulled out an official White House press folder.

"Ms. Mendoza, I have prepared this briefing on the economic summit especially for you and the *Sentinel*. Now, I must talk to a few other reporters. If you'll excuse me please."

As Silvia took the briefing, she ran her fingers over Ellen's hand. "Thank you," she said. Ellen's eyes flashed and Silvia could sense Ellen's heart skip a beat at her touch. Silvia felt her own heart skip, too.

"Wednesday night." Ellen said, as she walked past Silvia into the crowd of reporters.

*

Silvia decided to walk back to the *Sentinel* instead of taking a cab. It was a short walk across the Mall and two blocks east to the *Sentinel* building. The weather was hot for late October and the humidity was high. It was the kind of weather she'd grown up with and she knew there wouldn't be many more days like this before the cold, dank D.C. winter set in. She hated the cold. A few high-profile stories for the *Sentinel* and maybe a Pulitzer Prize nomination and she could get a job anywhere in the world and it wouldn't matter what she'd done to get there.

Silvia took a seat on a Mall park bench and opened the folder. Inside was the release on the economic summit that covered the information the president had discussed in his press conference. In the back was a handwritten note clipped to an official White House memo. The handwriting was Ellen's and it read, "This is STRICTLY off the record. You did NOT get this from me." The words 'STRICTLY' and 'NOT' were underlined three times.

Silvia scanned the memo. On the top was printed, 'WHITE HOUSE PRESS CORPS ONLY' in red block letters. It was dated the day of the president's endorsement of Howard. The memo read:

> *To all press staff:*
>
> *The press will ask about the president's endorsement of Senator William Howard this morning. The official White House response is that the president personally feels William Howard is the best candidate to replace Vice President Marshall. Do not give any additional information or opinions on this matter. Report any persistent inquiries directly to the president's chief aide Richard Craft.*

Ellen had written a note on the bottom of the memo that read, "You were right. Someone made him do it. I can't tell you any more at this time."

Silvia read the memo again and Ellen's handwritten note. *Someone made him do it?* Phillip Dougherty was a lame duck president and lame duck presidents rarely did anything they didn't want to do. Who could have possibly forced him into endorsing a man he didn't like? And the internal White House memo said 'persistent inquiries' had to be reported to Dougherty's chief aide? Why? If it was a press matter, why wouldn't it be reported to the press secretary? It must be serious to get Richard Craft involved. He was the man in the White House closest to the president. He was the one who knew all of his darkest secrets.

Silvia shoved the memo into her briefcase and leaned back on the park bench. She'd been right; there was something fishy behind Phillip Dougherty's endorsement of Bill Howard. *Someone made him do it*, and Silvia had to find out who and why.

Silvia could tell Ellen knew more. Apparently, Silvia would have to spend time in bed with Ellen to get it out of her. That was fine. She looked forward to her next rendezvous with Ellen.

SEVENTEEN

Two weeks before the presidential election

"YOU SURE THIS is right address, lady?" asked the skinny Somali cabbie with an East African accent.

Nan had caught the cab outside her mid-town Manhattan hotel and had given the cabbie the address of the studio where they were shooting the television commercial. She assured the driver it was the right address—it was on an e-mail from Boston. The cabbie shook his head and merged into the New York City traffic.

The cab wound its way through the bumpy streets of Brooklyn into a neighborhood of dilapidated warehouses near the East River. The cabbie stopped in front of a large, three story yellow brick building. "This is it."

The cabbie had been right to question the address—it was a bad neighborhood. But when Nan saw a gaggle of black limos, a caterer's truck and two Secret Service SUVs parked in front of the building, she knew she had the right place.

She paid the cabbie and went through the front door into a musty entryway that was as rundown as the outside of the building. A Secret Service agent sat in a lawn chair next to a freight elevator door. He grabbed a list off the floor and stood as Nan approached. "ID, please." he asked. She showed it and he checked it against his list. "You're cleared, ma'am. They're on the third floor. Take this elevator."

The elevator was loud and slow and the doors rumbled when they opened on the third floor. Nan stepped into a studio that took up the entire third floor. Huge concrete pillars supported the twenty-five foot high ceiling. Lights, ropes and wires hung from the ceiling. There were reflector panels on aluminum stands and big black electrical cords crisscrossed the floor.

The studio was abuzz with activity. Two men wrestled a hooded light on a cantilevered boom over to a stage in the back of the studio. Several more of the crew tinkered with movie cameras. Even more sifted through new clothes lying on a table and hanging on racks. Off to one side was a long table with a banquet of food—cheeses, bagels, rolls, fruit, cakes, juices, pop and two silver tankards of coffee. In one corner, three makeup artists and their assistants busily worked on people sitting in front of lighted mirrors.

Nan saw Bob Hilton who was wearing jeans and a Yale sweatshirt. Even dressed casually, he looked like a model for GQ. She wound her way to him. He saw her before she got there. "Nan!" he said rushing up to her. "You made it. Welcome, welcome. Isn't it exciting? Check out this crew," he exclaimed with a sweep of his hand. "You'd think we were doing a full-length movie!"

"Good morning, Bob," Nan said. "Yeah, it sure is impressive."

Hilton took Nan's arm and led her to the makeup area. "I want you to meet some people. This is Jocelyn Jones and Miles Jackson," he said pointing to the people in the makeup chairs. "Lyn and Miles, meet one of our top campaign advisers, Nan Smith."

Jocelyn Jones had more hair than Nan had thought possible on a human being. And her facial features were more exaggerated than they looked in the movies. Her teeth were pure white. Nan extended a hand. "I'm pleased to meet you, Ms. Jones."

Jocelyn Jones smiled but didn't take Nan's hand. "Thank you so much and you can call me Lyn. Sorry, I can't shake your hand. Make up, you know. Jon even has our hands powdered. The man is a perfectionist."

Miles Jackson was smaller than Nan had expected but his smile was a stopper and his liquid eyes were full of sexual energy. He had the palpable air of a lady's man. He waived his hand at Nan and gave her the approving look a lady's man gives a good-looking woman. "The pleasure's all mine," he said pleasantly.

"And over here," Hilton said, "is Governor Bloomfield. George, this is Nan Smith from Minnesota whom I told you about."

Governor Bloomfield stood from his chair scattering the makeup artists and hair stylists who were working on him. He was tall, his hair was peppery gray and he looked like everyone's loving father. He put out a huge hand and Nan shook it. The governor clasped his free hand over Nan's. "So you're Nan Smith. It's a pleasure indeed to meet you. Thank you so much for coming today and for all your hard work on my campaign." He sounded as sincere as if he was telling his granddaughter he loved her.

"I'm honored to meet you, sir," Nan replied, honestly. Her heart beat fast being this close to the man who would probably be the next president of the United States.

"Governor Bloomfield," a tattooed makeup artist said, "we need to finish. They want to start shooting soon."

"One moment, Sheila." The governor continued holding Nan's hand with both of his own. He looked directly at her. "Nan, Bob has told me a lot about you. All good, I assure you. I'm very excited to have you working for us. We have a new commercial starring these two wonderful actors, music from Brent Springman and smart, dedicated people like you working for us. How can we lose?" he said with a warm smile.

"How can we indeed?" Nan replied. She felt flushed.

The governor let go of Nan's hand but held her eyes. "Excuse me Nan. I have to let these professionals do their jobs. I hear Mr. Flesner is a stickler about staying on schedule. Thanks again for being here. I look forward to working with you." The governor sat back in the chair and the makeup artists resumed their work. Nan realized her breathing had become shallow and she took a deep breath. She was surprised at how much the governor's legendary charisma had affected her.

Bob Hilton moved Nan to an area off to one side of the stage. The stage was a reproduction of a farmhouse kitchen. Everything was perfect and perfectly placed—pots and pans, a big iron stove, an oak table and cabinets. There was even a Chevrolet calendar on the refrigerator. It was a remarkable achievement of stage production and Nan could see they'd spared no expense.

"We're shooting the inside scene this morning," Hilton said like a child showing off a new toy. "Tomorrow at sunrise we're shooting the outside at a farm in Massachusetts. The ads will be on the air Wednesday and our opponents won't have time to react before the election.

"Nan, I want you to read the script," Hilton said. "You might have some input on it. You remember Betty?" Sitting in a tall director's chair was the governor's chief political strategist, Betty Morris, whom Nan had met in Boston.

"Someone get Nan a script and a chair," Hilton said to the crew. A crewmember placed a director's chair next to Betty. As Nan sat, someone pushed a two-page script at her. She took it and set it in her lap.

"Good to see you again, Betty" Nan said.

"Hello, Nan," Betty replied with a glance.

"Excuse me, I need to see to a few things," Hilton said. "Nan, look over the script and see what you think. Oh, and I want to talk to you after the shoot."

Nan turned to Betty who was studying a report. Betty's dark hair was coiffed short and professional and she wore a business dress. In Boston, Nan got the impression that Betty held anyone outside of the Washington, D.C. beltway in disdain. She only cared about the rest of the country based on how many electoral votes they had, and Minnesota only had ten. She was a top political consultant and it was obvious she knew her business. It was just as obvious that she believed her opinion was the only one that mattered.

Nan tried to break the ice. "Bob has pulled together quite a crew for this commercial," she said. "Have you read the script?"

"I helped write it," Betty said without looking from her report.

"In that case I'm sure there's no need for my input," Nan said.

Betty didn't respond, so Nan continued. "I heard our opponents agreed to two debates."

Betty set her report on her lap and shot a look at Nan. "Of course they did. Your suggestion that we get Howard into debates was obvious. You don't have a presidential election these days without debates."

"I'm sure you're right," Nan said. So much for breaking the ice.

Betty picked up her report and began reading it again. Nan waited a few seconds, then said, "I bet Sheldon Hanrahan will turn to attack ads. He doesn't have much time for anything else."

Betty set her report on her lap again and put on a condescending smile. "My dear, we've learned the national committee is controlling Howard's campaign, not your Mr. Hanrahan. He may be the campaign manager but he's taking orders from Peter Gray. I know Peter personally. He's a very smart man. Like I said in Boston, this is a different ballgame. It's for the Presidency of the United States. It's not a campaign for some breakfast cereal or laundry soap. So, I don't think you need to worry about Mr. Hanrahan. Now, if you please, I need to read this report."

"I wouldn't be so sure," Nan said.

Nan picked up the script and pretended to read it. Obviously Betty was a condescending egotist but she wouldn't work for Bob Hilton if she didn't know her stuff. And what Betty had just said was surprising. Sheldon Hanrahan would not take orders from the National Committee, especially with so much at stake. It'd be completely out of character. He always planned things in detail and far in advance. But this was, indeed, a different game, one Sheldon hadn't played before. Perhaps he was letting the national committee run the show because there wasn't time for anything else. Or, perhaps he had other plans no one knew about.

There was a shout from the stage. Jon Flesner stood with his hands on his hips yelling for everyone to take their positions. Flesner was a small man with a shaved head. His glasses were two circles of wire around lenses. He was one of the film industry's top directors and it was clear that on his set, he was the one in charge. The crew scrambled to take their places and the actors walked onto the set followed by the makeup artists fussing over last-second details. The sound crew moved microphones over the actors and the large, hooded light swung into place. Flesner barked orders at the crew who hustled to execute them. Even Betty put her report down and watched the action. Soon, everything was ready and the shooting began.

Nan took it all in. She'd never known it took so many people to create a thirty-second commercial, but everyone had a role. During the filming, everyone stood perfectly still while the actors moved around the set and delivered their lines. When Flesner yelled, "CUT!", the entire crew sprang into action again. The makeup artists and hair stylists ran on the set to fuss over the actors and Governor Bloomfield. The wardrobe crew brushed away lint and smoothed the actors' outfits. The scriptwriters made small changes to help the actors say their lines more smoothly. The lighting grips adjusted the angles of the lights. The sound crew listened to playbacks and the cameramen moved their cameras for a slightly different angle. And then, Flesner would call for everyone to be ready and the crew would stand silent while the cameras rolled and the actors delivered their lines again.

Nan was surprised at how professional Jocelyn Jones and Miles Jackson were. They had their lines memorized and listened carefully to Flesner's direction. They hit their marks and looked perfectly comfortable in front of the camera. Even Governor Bloomfield looked relaxed. He delivered his lines as if he'd been acting for years. Flesner kept calling him "Mr. President."

*

Two and a half hours later, Flesner declared the shoot a wrap and they'd finished that part of the commercial. Nan could tell the commercial would be a perfect complement to Brent Springman's folksy rock tune, *Road Home*. The shoot had been an exciting, fascinating experience.

But she wondered why Hilton had asked her here. Hilton told her to look at the script, but no one asked her about it during the shoot. While everyone worked, she sat in the director's chair next to Betty and just watched. He must have wanted her there for some other reason. He had said he wanted to talk to her after the shoot.

As the crew began to strike the set, Hilton approached Nan. "What do you think?" he asked.

Nan shook her head. "I think it's terrific. It will be a wonderful commercial."

"Of course," Betty said. She picked up her report and headed for the door.

"It's exciting, isn't it?" Hilton said. "It's a totally new political ad. The radio commercials will be on the air tomorrow and the TV commercials have a heavy schedule right up until Election Day. I'm telling you, Nan, we're making history here."

"I'm impressed, Bob. I didn't have anything to do, but thanks for having me here anyway."

"Speaking of being impressed, can I talk to you a minute. Alone?"

"Sure," Nan replied.

Bob led Nan to a dark corner of the studio away from the others. He looked her in the eye. "I wanted you here because I wanted you to meet the governor and see the big picture of what we're doing," he said. "I've been talking to George about you Nan. He and I think there's a job for you in the Administration when he's elected. I'm talking about an important job in the White House."

Nan felt her jaw drop. "You're kidding?"

"No I'm not. Nothing's firm, but we're thinking it'd be a senior adviser. Possibly even Communications Director."

"Communications Director? That's a huge job."

"Yes it is. We've been going over your track record and we think you're a good candidate. But don't get excited yet. We have to get the governor elected first. It's looking good, Nan. We have a seven-point lead and Howard's agreed to two debates. I'm optimistic." Hilton smiled boyishly. Nan noticed he had many of the same charismatic qualities as Miles Jackson.

"Well, I don't know what to say," Nan said.

"Just think about it. We'll talk more soon. You have a plane to catch."

"Yeah. Thanks Bob."

Nan left the studio and caught a cab back to LaGuardia. As the cabbie wound his way to the airport, Nan thought about what Hilton had said. White House Communications Director. It'd be a huge job—the pinnacle of her political career. It'd be exciting and important and would set her up for the rest of her life. She'd never even dreamed it would be possible, but apparently important people were discussing it.

Did she want it? She had a family in Minnesota and a husband with a career. But Ben's business was doing poorly and just last month he'd talked about selling out to his partners. Perhaps they could work it out. There was still Jenny to think about. She'd have to leave her school and friends and move to a new city. It'd be hard on Jenny most of all, but she was a resilient kid with good self-esteem. She'd be alright.

Nan Smith, White House Communications Director, working for Bob Hilton who was out to change the world. The thought gave her a shot of adrenaline. But as the cab pulled up to the airport, she knew she'd have to think it over very carefully.

And as Bob said, they had to get Governor Bloomfield elected first.

EIGHTEEN

POLITICS. NAN WAS EXCITED again like the heady days in college. The candidate she was working for had ideas about the country that she believed in. Bob Hilton had the energy, intelligence, and schemes to get Bloomfield's ideas implemented. She could be in the middle of it, an important player. Communications Director. The thought of it made her tingle.

When she got home, Jenny was already in bed and Ben was waiting for her. She and Ben sat at the kitchen table and she told him about the possibility of an important job in the Bloomfield Administration. He was thrilled.

"Maybe the Communications Director's job?" he asked.

"That's what Hilton said. He'll be the chief of staff so he'll have a lot of influence on who gets jobs."

Ben squeezed her hand. "Wow, I'm impressed."

"What about your job?" Nan asked.

"That's easy," he replied. "I'd sell the agency to my partners. Or maybe to Sheldon Hanrahan. He's wanted to buy us out for years. Maybe I should sell now while I can. I'm afraid if things get any worse, we might go under."

Nan felt sorry for her husband and she had a slight ache of guilt for her success. "I didn't know things were so bad," she said.

"We'll be all right for a while. If you get a White House job, I'll sell out. The money would help us move to D.C. I could find a new job or start a new career."

"You've always wanted to do that. You should someday." Nan said. "But what about Jenny?"

"Yeah," Ben said, nodding. "What about Jenny?"

They said nothing more and went to bed. Nan fell into a fitful sleep. In the middle of the night, she jerked awake from a nightmare where Mrs. Wilson was pointing at her and shouting, "Murderer! Murderer!" Ben continued to sleep and she crawled out of bed. She walked down the hallway to Jenny's room and looked in on her daughter who had her lanky frame spread-eagle on the bed. The sheet gently rose and fell with her breathing. Nan's heart ached for her daughter. She could only imagine the pain Mrs. Wilson felt at the loss of her own daughter. It would surely be enough to drive a mother crazy.

Nan went back to bed. When she woke in the morning, her nightmare about Mrs. Wilson haunted her. But it faded when she saw Jenny off to school. She headed to work. On the way, she heard Bloomfield's new commercial on the car radio. Brent Springfield, in his distinctive, gravelly voice, wailed *Road Hoooooome* while Governor Bloomfield talked about a new direction for America. It was both smooth and folksy and was immensely inspirational. Nan cranked up the volume and hummed along with the tune. At the end, the music came to a crescendo and the announcer said, "Bring

America back home. Vote Bloomfield for president." For a moment, she found herself imagining that Bloomfield had already won the election and she was the White House Communications Director. It brought a smile to her face.

Her daydream evaporated when she pulled up to the Minnesota campaign office. Across the street were two dozen demonstrators with signs that read, "Bloomfield Supports Terrorists," and "A Vote For Bloomfield Is A Vote For Terror." A television camera crew was interviewing one of the demonstrators. Two policemen sat in a squad car parked on the street between the protesters and the office.

Nan got out of her car and headed into the office. As she got to the door, the wolfish female reporter she'd first seen the week before ran to her and shoved a microphone into her face. "We have Nan Smith, Bloomfield's campaign manager here in Minnesota. Ms. Smith, can you comment on Governor Bloomfield's stand on terrorism?"

Nan kept her eyes forward and pushed past the reporter. "Read the statement we issued this weekend," she said over her shoulder. "I have no comment beyond that."

"I see," said the reporter keeping step with Nan. "Can you tell me why Governor Bloomfield supports negotiating with terrorists?"

Nan elbowed her way past the protesters to the door. "No comment," she said as she walked through the red, white and blue front door.

Stephanie stood as Nan walked toward the front desk. "They were out there when I got here," she said, wide-eyed. "We got an e-mail saying we should ignore them. Why are they doing it?"

"I got an e-mail from Boston this morning," Nan said. "They're at every campaign office in the country. Clearly it's been organized by Howard's party. They're trying to position Bloomfield as being soft on terrorism. It won't work if we don't let them bother us."

Stephanie wrung her hands. "I'm afraid they'll throw something through the window."

"They won't, Stephanie. Just ignore them and don't say anything to the reporters. We better get used to this." Nan hung up her coat and decided she had to change the subject to calm Stephanie. "Did you hear the new radio commercials?" she asked.

Stephanie eyes sparkled. "They're fantastic! I love that Springman song. How did it go in New York? I bet it was exciting."

"It was interesting, to say the least. You wouldn't believe how many people it takes to shoot a television commercial."

"I wish I could have met Miles Jackson."

Nan winked at Stephanie. "He is one... sexy... man."

Stephanie giggled. "I can't wait to see the new commercials. Oh, by the way, Jim said he wanted to talk to you as soon as you came in. I think it's important."

"Thanks Stephanie." Nan nodded at the protesters outside. "Don't worry about those people. They'll be gone in a few days."

"Okay," Stephanie said and turned her attention to her computer monitor.

Nan walked into the bullpen. Although the fresh paint smell had mostly gone, she still couldn't get over how dramatically the office had changed since the week before. Like the new commercials, it was slick without being pretentious. It had the feel of a winner.

As Nan walked to her office, Shelly sat at her desk reading the newspaper. What Shelly did for the campaign,

Nan still didn't know. Ah well, she was a volunteer so Nan couldn't expect much from her. Several new campaign workers assembled a mailer at a table in the back. Sorrea sat in her cubicle staring into a computer screen. Hank, Rex and Tom were not there. Nan glanced into Rex's cubicle and noticed the new shredder for the first time. It was big and looked powerful and Nan wondered what they could possibly need it for.

Jim saw Nan as soon as she walked in. "Nan, I need to talk to you."

"Sure Jim, give me a minute. I should meet our new people first." Nan introduced herself to the new volunteers. "I'm Nan Smith," she said. "Welcome to Governor Bloomfield's Minnesota campaign headquarters."

Each of the new workers introduced themselves. There was a college-age couple named Frank and Lora, a man in his thirties who called himself Will, and a short-haired woman named Jean who looked to be nearing retirement. After the introductions, Will said, "We joined because of Howard. None of us want to see him in the White House. He scares us."

"He scares me too," Nan said. "The good news is we have the lead in the weekend polls. I've been in New York shooting new commercials. They're great. If we all do our jobs, we have a very good chance of winning."

"I heard the Brent Springman commercials this morning," Frank said. "They rock!" Lora nodded in agreement.

"That they do," Nan said smiling. "Thank you for your help on our campaign. I look forward to working with all of you over the next two weeks."

As the new people went back to work, Nan walked to her office and Jim followed carrying a pad of paper. Jim had been a disaster as an assistant manager since he came to work for Nan by way of a recommendation from the state chairman's office. He had once run a successful campaign for an incumbent congressman in upstate Minnesota who hadn't lost in thirty years. Jim had said he wanted to "break into the major leagues" when Nan first interviewed him. He was affable and good at running errands, but Nan came to realize he'd never rise very far within the party. Until last week, she hadn't been concerned about him because she could handle the state campaign without his help. Since she'd gotten more responsibilities however, she wished Jim was more useful. Ah well, at least she had Hank.

Jim closed the door and gave Nan a solemn look as he sat.

"What is it, Jim?"

"I'm quitting," he said.

"What? You're quitting? Why?"

"This campaign is getting dirty and I don't want anything to do with it anymore."

"Jim, these protests are just part of the game," Nan said. "They'll go away after they figure out we aren't going to take their bait. This is a presidential campaign. It's bound to get a little nasty."

"It's not them. It's those new guys, Rex and Tom."

Nan crossed her arms. "Rex and Tom?"

Jim lowered his voice. "I think they're up to no good. I came in late on Sunday night and they were here. They had some Howard campaign letterhead."

Nan leaned forward. "*Howard* campaign letterhead?"

Jim pulled out a sheet of paper he had hidden between the pages of his pad and handed it to Nan. "I took this from their desk when they went out."

Nan examined it. "It sure looks legitimate. Is it the real thing?"

"Yeah it is. It's brand new. You can still smell the ink. The Howard people must've had it printed over the weekend after the endorsement. Tom had a whole box of it."

Nan brought the sheet to her nose and could smell that it had been recently printed.

"You have to ask yourself," Jim said, "what are we doing with Howard campaign letterhead? What would we use it for?"

"I don't know," Nan said. "Did you see anything else?"

Jim nodded. "Later they were hovering over Sorrea's computer, staring at something. Rex kept sneaking a look at me to make sure I didn't see what they were doing."

Nan looked up from the letterhead. "You think they're up to something?"

"Like writing an incriminating letter made to look like it came from Howard. Like intercepting e-mails or spying on people."

"That's illegal," Nan said. "Laws were passed after Watergate to prevent dirty tricks like that."

"That's why I'm quitting," Jim said. "If they're doing something illegal out of this office, we'll be held responsible. I don't want to go to prison."

"Prison?" Nan shook her head. "I doubt if it's anything like that. Bloomfield's in the lead. If anything, it's probably just for a political prank, something innocuous like canceling room reservations. Political opponents have been playing pranks on each other for over two hundred years."

"What if it's more than that?" Jim said. "Everyone's saying how this election will get dirty with Sheldon Hanrahan running Howard's campaign."

"Apparently, Mr. Hanrahan is letting the national committee run Howard's campaign," Nan said. She eyed Jim. "Look, you're overreacting. All we have is a sheet of letterhead. But I guess if you want to quit, I can't stop you."

"I have two kids. I don't want to go to jail like those Watergate guys," Jim said.

Nan sighed. "No one's going to jail. But, if you feel that way, you should go. Please keep this letterhead thing to yourself. I'll look into it." She slid the letterhead into her briefcase.

Jim left Nan's office and retrieved a few things from his desk as Shelly and the others looked on. Nan walked with him to the front door. She thanked him for his work on the Bloomfield campaign and wished him luck in the future. As she was shaking Jim's hand, Hank came in.

"Where is he going?" Hank asked Nan.

"He quit."

Stephanie asked, "Did he quit because of the protesters?"

"No, Stephanie." Nan sighed. She pulled Hank aside. "I need another consult."

"Sure," Hank said. Nan grabbed her coat and followed Hank out the door.

NINETEEN

THE PROTESTERS YELLED louder when they saw Nan and Hank leave the campaign office. "Bloomfield supports terror!" they shouted as they shook their protest signs. "Bloomfield supports terror!"

Nan noticed another television crew had arrived and was setting up next to the protesters. A reporter was doing a sound check. Nan would have to address the press before the five o'clock news, but for now, she wanted to talk to Hank about everything that was going on.

"This way," Hank said. Nan followed him east on Franklin Avenue toward the Mississippi River.

"This is getting a little crazy," Nan said.

"Yes it is," Hank said moving quickly.

They finally got away from the crowd and slowed their pace. "Why did Jim quit?" Hank asked.

"He quit because he thinks Rex and Tom are doing something illegal. He found some Howard letterhead and he thinks they're using it to write counterfeit letters."

"He might be right. I don't trust those guys."

"Me neither," Nan said. "But I'm not responsible for them. Anyway, Bloomfield is in the lead. As long as it isn't illegal, it flies under the radar."

"As long as it isn't illegal," Hank repeated. They made their way toward the river.

"So, what do you think we should do?" Nan asked.

Hank shrugged. "Right now, nothing. If we confront Rex, he'll know we suspect something. Tell him Jim quit because of the protesters, but let's keep our eyes open."

"I hope it's nothing. I won't be involved in a dirty campaign."

"You said they're not your responsibility."

"Yes, but I'm the Minnesota campaign manager," Nan said. "They're working in my office."

There was a pause, then Hank said, "Tell you what... I'll poke around to see if I can find out what they're doing. If I find something, I'll let you know."

"Speaking of poking around," Nan said, "what did you find out about Mrs. Wilson? You were going to contact your friend at the Health Department."

"Yeah, I did. I discovered two very interesting things. That's what I was coming in to tell you."

"Two things? Like what?"

Hank pointed Nan down a path that led to the Mississippi Parkway. "Well," he began, "first, everyone who works for a high-security hospital has to be listed with the state. It's the law. Your friend Mr. Woods is not listed."

"So you were right about him, he doesn't work for the hospital. Who is he, then? What's he doing there?"

"He might be a cop," Hank said. "Lord knows he looks like one. Or a private detective paid to watch Mrs. Wilson."

"That doesn't make sense. Why?"

"Maybe because her daughter was murdered by Senator Howard."

Nan let out a grunt. "Come on, Hank. You don't really believe that, do you?"

"Well, that's not all I found out."

They came to the Mississippi River Parkway, turned north toward the jumble of tall buildings downtown. A few joggers and bicyclists were on the pathway huffing along. In the distance, the University of Minnesota crew team cut a narrow wake in the middle of the river.

Hank continued. "I asked my friend to see if there was a Mrs. Wilson listed as a patient in the hospital. He confirmed there was but," Hank faced Nan, "there was no admitting physician. My friend said there has to be an admitting physician for them to lock up someone in a hospital like Rand. There wasn't one on her record. The line was blank."

"Could have been a clerical error."

"Right," Hank said. "A clerical error."

Nan slowed her pace. Until now, Nan hadn't really believed Mrs. Wilson's incredible accusation. But now she wasn't so sure. Too many things didn't add up. "She can't be telling the truth about Howard," she said half to herself and half to Hank. "Could she?"

Hank shook his head. "There's no way to tell. We don't know why she's there. We don't know if she is senile and we don't know if she's telling the truth. And there's Mr. Woods."

They walked a bit further and Nan stopped and pulled Hank's arm to make him stop with her. "Okay, Hank, here's how I see it. You're right, we don't know anything. So, if we think she's telling the truth, we should go to the police and let them investigate. If we don't believe her, we should forget the whole thing."

Hank shrugged. "We'd go to the police and say what, that a poor lady who happens to be a patient in a mental institution told us that the senator from Minnesota who happens to be our opponent in the election for the president of the United States killed her daughter? They'd laugh at us. Or worse, they'd accuse us of trying to smear Howard."

Nan remembered what had happened to her in the Theilen campaign. She motioned for them to head back toward the office. "You're right. So, then, we should forget about it."

Hank shook his head. "I can't just forget about it. I want to know what's going on. This whole thing stinks like Sheldon Hanrahan. I want to go back to the hospital and talk to the orderly. He wanted to say more, I could tell."

"I don't know, Hank. I can't believe Sheldon Hanrahan would be involved in a murder, if it's even true. Let's just concentrate on the election. Things are heating up."

"Remember Mrs. Wilson's phone call?" Hank asked. "She said she had something to show you. Aren't you curious what it is? I am."

Nan recalled her nightmare from the night before and Mrs. Wilson crying murder. A shiver went through her. Everything about the campaign was turning into a weird dream. Maybe it'd help if she knew the truth about Mrs. Wilson. At least it would be one less thing for her to worry about.

"I have to admit I'm curious about a lot of things right now, Hank," Nan said. "But I don't want you to get into trouble or do anything that might jeopardize the campaign. You're nosing around a high security hospital and now you'll be nosing around our offices to see what Rex and Tom are up to. It's risky. And we might not like what we find."

"Don't worry. I'll be careful."

They turned the corner at Franklin Avenue and headed back to the office. After a half block, Nan smiled openly. "What is it?" Hank asked. "You look like the Cheshire Cat."

"I want to tell you something, but you have to keep it a secret."

"Sure. What is it?"

"In New York, Bob Hilton talked to me about a job in the White House if Bloomfield gets elected. He said they're considering me for White House Communications Director."

Hank stopped and took Nan by the shoulders. "Nan, that's terrific! Communications Director? That's a big job!"

Nan smiled, shook her head. "Nothing is for sure, Hank. Let's see what happens before we get too excited."

"White House Communications Director," Hank said in amazement as they continued walking.

"Like I said, keep it to yourself. And Hank, be careful with your investigations, okay?"

Hank winked at Nan. "I will, Madame Communications Director."

TWENTY

VICTOR MIHAILOV WAS the only man in the world Sheldon Hanrahan was afraid of. He sat across from Sheldon in the cabin of Sheldon's personal jet—a Bombardier Global Express—as it cruised 35,000 feet above the western Nebraska prairie on its way to Minneapolis. Victor was large—not tall, but square and thick. He had short blonde hair, bushy eyebrows, and his gray eyes were hard as cold granite. He wore a black leather jacket and stared out the jet's window at the pale morning dawn. Other than the pilot and co-pilot, Sheldon and Victor were the aircraft's only passengers.

Sheldon had first seen Victor a dozen years earlier at an art auction in Paris. Sheldon could tell that Victor was one of the few people in the room who knew what he was doing. So when a seemingly unimportant celadon vase came up for auction that Sheldon knew was a Kangxi from the Seventeenth Century and worth ten times the catalog price, he thought Victor would be a bidder. But Victor stayed quiet and the bidding fell to Sheldon and a Chinese man. Clearly, the Chinese man knew the vase's value too, and bid far more than Sheldon was willing to pay.

After the auction, Victor introduced himself and said he too knew the vase was a Kangxi. He told Sheldon he could get the vase for him if Sheldon would pay him the amount of his last bid. Sheldon agreed and knew better than to ask how Victor would acquire the vase. A month later, the vase was in Sheldon's art collection, and a year after that, Victor was Sheldon's chief of security. Victor was smart, efficient and coldblooded. He had proven to be very effective at executing Sheldon's plans.

Sheldon unbuckled his seat belt. "Victor," he said, "I need to call Peter Gray."

Victor didn't turn away from the window. "Peter Gray, he is idiot," Victor replied in his thick Russian accent.

Sheldon walked to the back of the cabin to a wide leather seat facing the back of the aircraft. The hum of the jet engines was barely audible outside the windows. He dialed the phone on a burled walnut table in front of him. After a few seconds, he was connected to a satellite and heard a dial tone. He dialed Peter Gray's Washington, D.C. number.

"Office of the Chairman of the National Party," Gray's secretary answered.

"Good morning, Mary. This is Sheldon Hanrahan calling for Peter."

"Good morning Mr. Hanrahan. Mr. Gray just came in. I'll put you through."

There was a click and a few seconds later, Peter Gray's voice came on the line. "Hello, Sheldon." Gray's voice echoed telling Sheldon Peter had put him on his speakerphone.

"Good morning, Peter. I'm calling for our morning briefing."

"How did it go in California?" Peter said without a greeting.

"Senator Howard was in top form," Sheldon said. "I believe we have the state locked up."

"You should thank me for getting Masello to agree to be Howard's running mate. It wasn't easy. We need California's electoral votes."

"Yes, that was good, Peter. Thank you."

"Where are you now?"

"I'm on my way back to Minnesota," Sheldon answered. "The senator has a rally in Denver at noon and he'll be flying to Minnesota this afternoon for our meeting with you tomorrow morning."

"Good. We have a lot to do to get ready for the first debate. What have you done so far to prepare him?"

"Not much, I'm afraid. We haven't had time."

Peter Gray snorted. "What do you mean you haven't done anything? Goddamn it, Sheldon, you have to get Howard ready. The first debate is in three days. Bloomfield will bury him if he isn't prepared. That's your job. I expect you to do it."

Sheldon took off his dark glasses. Outside the jet, the morning sky wasn't bright enough yet to hurt his eyes. He twirled his glasses in his hand. "I'm not worried about the debates, Peter."

"How can you say that?" Peter said, his pitch rising. "Howard has to do well. He has to at least get a draw with Bloomfield."

"Howard will be prepared," Sheldon said. "You don't need to worry, Peter."

"Don't tell me I don't need to worry, you condescending prick!" the Chairman said. "It's my job to worry. You haven't done a goddamn thing."

"You insisted on running it. I'm letting you, per our agreement."

"Damn right I'm running it, but you have to help. We lost another point in the polls yesterday. We don't have much time to make up ground."

"I'm confident," Sheldon said. "I believe we will win."

"Look, when I get to Minneapolis, we need to work on the debates. I'm bringing two writers and our top speech coach. I expect your help. Shit, Sheldon, this sort of thing is how you built your business. You should be all over it!"

Sheldon continued to twirl his glasses. "Mr. Chairman, I'm not worried about the debates," he repeated.

"Goddamn it!" Gray shouted. "I guess I have to take this over too. You've been sitting on your ass for the past week while I've done everything."

"You've done a wonderful job, Peter. Senator Howard has lost only two points since you took over."

"Fuck you, Sheldon. Do you want to know what I've done? While you've been doing nothing, I got Travis Daniels to give us *I Love America* for our advertising. Travis Daniels! He's the biggest country western star in the country. He's sold way more records than that little shit, Brent Springman. *I Love America* is perfect for us. Daniels just might give us the south and no candidate has won the presidency without taking the south."

"Travis Daniels is a big star, Peter. Good job."

"Yeah, 'good job'. What are you and your firm doing about the TV commercials? You've heard the other side has Miles Jackson and Jocelyn Jones. Are you working on something?"

"We'll have new commercials soon." Sheldon could feel the jet begin a slow turn to the north toward Minnesota. He looked out the window to the golden Nebraska wheat fields. He was always taken aback at how colorful things were without his glasses on.

"And what about fundraising?" the chairman asked. "Where are we on it?"

"Senator Howard will have enough funds for the campaign," Sheldon said evenly.

"How much do we have in hard money contributions?"

"Forty-five million so far."

Sheldon could hear Gray cough over his speakerphone, "Forty-five million? That's it? Bloomfield has over two-hundred million for his campaign. What about political action committees and 527s? How much have they brought in?"

"As Senator Howard's campaign manager, I'm not allowed to coordinate the activities of PACs and 527s. We wouldn't want to get in trouble with the Federal Election Commission, Mr. Chairman, would we?"

"Don't give me that shit," Gray barked. "Since when are you worried about the FEC? You can find a way to get around the rules. Or just ignore them, for Christ's sake. The FEC won't do anything. They never do. We have to get PACs and 527s pushing the terrorism issue fast."

"You are right. Terrorism is the issue that will get Senator Howard elected." Sheldon continued to gaze out the jet's window at the early morning colors. The sky was getting brighter and his eye began to hurt.

"Christ, Sheldon. You aren't doing a goddamn thing, are you?"

"It's good you're coming to Minnesota to help, Peter."

"Damn right. I'll be there tonight. We'll start early tomorrow morning."

Sheldon put his glasses on easing the ache in his eyes, but the colors outside the jet window faded. "I'll see you then. And Peter," he said, "don't worry so much."

"Fuck you," the chairman said, and the phone went dead.

Sheldon gently replaced the phone in the cradle. Peter Gray was, indeed, an idiot. How could he have gained such prominence in the party? Surely he knew it would take much more than Travis Daniels and his banal song *I Love America* to win the election. Another hundred million dollars in campaign contributions wasn't going to help either. More extreme measures were required—the kind Sheldon had used to make his climb to the top of the business world. Tomorrow, Peter Gray would realize what Sheldon was willing to do to win elections.

He went to the front of the cabin and sat in the leather chair across from Victor again. Victor continued to stare out the window at the growing morning light.

"Are we ready?" Sheldon asked.

"Da," Victor replied.

"Tomorrow morning?"

"As we have planned."

Sheldon leaned back and pressed his head into the headrest. "Excellent," he said. "Make sure you don't kill him."

TWENTY-ONE

THE FIRST PERSON Frank Pierce killed was a woman. Her name was Muminah El Amin and she knew it was coming. Command had sent him to Saudi Arabia days before Desert Storm where, as a young captain in the Special Forces, he got the mission from a full-bird colonel and a somber CIA man. They dropped him into a remote area outside of the city of Basrah, hours before the coalition forces invaded Iraq. He'd gone to El Amin's house in the middle of the night to capture her and then hide in Basrah until the U.S. Twenty-eighth Airborne arrived. If he couldn't capture her, his orders were to kill her.

The second he saw her, he knew he'd have to kill her. He'd expected to find her wearing a chador and was surprised to see her with her raven hair down, wearing a t-shirt and khaki trousers. She was young, attractive and when she saw him, she wasn't afraid. Her eyes were filled with hate and he could see she'd been waiting for someone exactly like him. Inches away from where she sat at her kitchen table was an AK47. As El Amin made a cat-quick move for the rifle,

Pierce put a slug from his silenced 9mm Walther P88 into her forehead. She slumped onto the kitchen table. Pierce put two more slugs into her, one in her head, and another through her heart. Then he disappeared back into the desert night where, eight hours later, U.S. forces picked him up.

Since then, killing had become easy. He'd wanted to kill the woman in Minnesota five years earlier at the beginning of this mission. He told his employers he could make it look like an accident or a robbery attempt. They said, 'no' explaining that another body would only raise suspicions.

Normally, he would've done them a favor, ignored their order and killed the woman anyway. But the mission had come from somewhere high up so he placed the woman in the Rand Psychiatric Hospital and sent Woods to guard her.

His mission objective was containment, and outside of Minnesota, the mission had been uncomplicated. They had accomplished containment via simple clandestine operations and thinly-veiled threats. Only once did he have to hurt someone. Since then, there had been no trouble in Washington, D.C., but he'd always worried about the woman.

It didn't help that Woods was his man there. Woods didn't have the long-term focus to be effective in the field. He was easily distracted and had gotten lazy and sloppy. After the woman escaped, Pierce sent special help. The situation in Minnesota was out of control and he had to fix it fast.

The plan was simple but it needed to be executed perfectly. Pierce sent his best field operative to handle it and he needed to go over the details one more time to be sure everything was clearly understood. He left his office in the Treasury Building and took a seat on a park bench in the Mall. The previous evening, a front had moved through and the air was fall-like. Low gray clouds slid eastward over the white government buildings to the south. Pierce took out his secured cell phone and placed a call. After two rings, a man answered.

"I'm calling to check on the set up," Pierce said.

"We're ready to go," the man said. "It will happen soon, within a few hours."

"Exactly as planned?"

"Of course," the man said. "Don't worry."

"It's my job to worry. Minnesota is fucked up and I sent you to fix it. Am I clear?"

"It will be fixed soon."

Good," Pierce said. "And don't forget, our orders. Make sure our target isn't killed. Just… incapacitated for a while."

"The target won't be killed."

"Good. Call me when it's done."

Pierce pushed the 'End Call' button on his phone and shoved it in his pocket. He folded his arms against the cold and looked up at the graceful lines of the Washington Monument. Hopefully, this operation would end the troubles in Minnesota. It wouldn't have come to this if his employers had listened to him years earlier. Now, it was getting messy and it was threatening containment.

If things got worse, Pierce would have to go to Minnesota to take care of things himself.

And this time, he would do it his way.

TWENTY-TWO

WHEN NAN CLIMBED into her Camry to go to work on
Wednesday morning, there was a sealed envelope on the car
seat. On the front someone had written, "Read this ASAP!"
She tore it open. Inside on lined, yellow paper was a
handwritten note from Hank.

> *Nan:*
>
> *We're being watched. I don't know who it is or why. We must
> be careful about where we talk. DON'T CALL ME. I think
> they've tapped our phones and our e-mails, too.*
>
> *And don't talk to Rex. I learned some things last night that
> you need to know. I also found out who Mrs. Wilson is and what
> she has to show you.*
>
> *I'm looking into it and will be in the office later. We can go for
> a walk and talk then.*
>
> *Be careful.*
>
> *Hank*

Nan read the note twice, folded it and shoved it back in
the envelope. She sat behind the wheel without starting the
car. She was being watched? Was someone watching her now?
She scanned the street. The only cars parked on the street

belonged to her neighbors. Nothing looked out of the ordinary. Of course, that was the point. Whoever was watching her didn't want her to know.

If someone was watching, she shouldn't sit in her car and peer through the windows. She needed to act normally. She started the Camry and pulled out of the driveway onto the street. She looked in her rear view mirror but didn't see anyone following her.

Nan ran through the possibilities of who would want to watch her. Mr. Woods? Unlikely but possible. What about Rex and Tom with their surveillance equipment that Stephanie said she saw? She hadn't trusted Rex from the moment she met him and she hadn't exchanged a single word with Tom. Jim had said he thought they were intercepting e-mails. And she didn't have a clue what Sorrea did staring at her computer all day.

She turned the corner on Franklin Avenue a dozen blocks from the campaign office. Suddenly a homeless man pushing a grocery cart was in front of her. She slammed on the brakes and the man cursed at her as he pushed on across the street. As she pulled away, a thought hit her like a bullet.

Sheldon Hanrahan. Senator Howard had been in the presidential race nearly a week and there were no signs whatsoever of Sheldon's involvement in the campaign. In New York, Betty Morris said Sheldon was letting the national party run Howard's campaign, but Nan didn't believe it. Sheldon would get involved somehow and when he did, the campaign would get dirty, ugly and probably illegal. Perhaps he was having Nan watched.

Nan checked her rear view mirror again. She didn't see a car following her. She thought back over the past week. She didn't remember seeing anything suspicious.

There was another explanation. Maybe Hank was wrong. He hadn't liked Rex, Tom and Sorrea from the very beginning and he'd become a little too eager to investigate the situation with Mrs. Wilson. Maybe he'd become obsessed. Nan had suggested they forget about the woman and focus on the campaign. Now, apparently Hank was going to spend all day on his investigation. Maybe it was all in his imagination and no one was watching them.

Nan shook her head. Better to not speculate until she had more information. She pulled the car up to the campaign office. There were half as many demonstrators today and the police car was gone. There were no reporters. "Bloomfield is weak on terrorism!" the protesters chanted, uninspired. *It didn't take long for them to lose steam*, Nan thought.

She had arrived early and no one was at the office yet. She punched in the code on the new security system that unlocked the red, white and blue door. She went in, hung up her coat and went to the bullpen area. She snapped on the lights. She looked over at Rex and Sorrea's cubicles and remembered Hank's note. *We're being watched.* She glanced over her shoulder. She was alone. She went to Sorrea's cubicle. On her computer monitor was a series of scrolling ten digit numbers that appeared to be Internet addresses. Next to each was a string of unrecognizable computer characters. Nan didn't know what the characters represented, but they looked like encrypted e-mails.

On another monitor were dozens of folder icons. Nan clicked open a folder and then a file. On the top of the document was a ten-digit number in the form of a telephone number. Nan didn't recognize any of the area codes. Perhaps the numbers were in code. Below each number were paragraphs of encrypted type. The layout of the paragraphs looked like it could be a conversation between two people. Hank's note had said he thought someone had tapped their phones. Could it be Sorrea was running the program that was monitoring them right in their own office?

She closed the files and looked around the bullpen again. She moved to Rex's cubicle. She bumped into the big shredder and saw shredded pieces of paper on the floor next to it. *What could they possibly need to shred?* she wondered.

She went to Rex's desk and saw a few memos from Boston and some new Howard campaign literature. She picked up a memo. It was a standard communiqué from headquarters about how to respond to the demonstrators. Another memo gave Governor Bloomfield's schedule for the week. A third was a breakdown of the latest poll. Nothing unusual.

She pulled on a handle of the desk drawer. It was locked. She checked the drawer on the other side and it was locked too. She rolled the mouse on Rex's computer and the screen blinked to life. A dialog box from a security system she wasn't familiar with asked for a password. She didn't even try to get in.

She saw a manila file folder on the back corner of the desk with a red label that said "Issues." She opened it and inside was a list of items on Senator Howard's past. She studied it. There was a speech Howard had given during his first campaign for the Senate where he said public education "had seen its day" and should be replaced by private education. Another topic was Howard's driving record. It seemed the senator had a weakness for fast cars. He'd had over a dozen speeding tickets during the past five years. The entry questioned how Howard was able to get away with having so many tickets without having his license revoked.

Another entry named an intern who had worked for the senator and died from a drug overdose a few months after quitting her internship. Yet another entry chronicled his involvement in a fraternity when he was a student at the University of Minnesota in Duluth that reputedly had cruel and bizarre hazing practices.

All in all, it was typical opposition research and the list was nothing more than loose accusations and speculation. Although some items would certainly be embarrassing for the senator, there was nothing particularly damning. Nan replaced the folder and looked around the desk for the Howard campaign letterhead Jim had claimed he saw. She didn't see any.

A voice came from behind her. "What are you doing?"

Nan jumped out of the chair. She stood face to face with Rex Starkey. He hadn't taken off his coat and was glaring at her.

"I… I'm looking at these memos on your desk. I'm wondering what you're doing here in Minnesota."

Rex put a hand against the cubicle wall, blocking Nan's escape. "I thought we agreed we'd stay out of each other's way?"

Nan crossed her arms. "Why? Are you hiding something, Rex?"

Rex smiled condescendingly. "Of course not."

"Then why do you care if I see what's on your desk?"

"I don't." Rex kept his hand on the cubicle wall.

"Really? Then why are your desk draws locked? Why are all of Sorrea's computer files encrypted? And I heard that for some reason you have some Howard campaign letterhead."

Rex's smile faded. "We don't have any Howard letterhead."

Nan remembered the sheet of letterhead Jim had given her which was now in her briefcase. "Oh?" she said. "You better make sure you use that shredder of yours."

"Like I said, I thought we agreed to stay out of each other's business."

"This is my office," Nan said. "I'm responsible for what goes on here."

"You're not responsible for me."

"As long as you work in this building, I am."

The condescending smile returned to Rex's face. "I heard Jim quit. Why?"

"He said he didn't like the protesters," Nan said.

"That's a lame reason. Sounds like he can't take the heat. What will you do now?"

"It's not a problem. I'm making Hank our new assistant campaign manager. We'll be fine."

Rex moved closer to Nan. "We never had that date we talked about."

Nan held Rex's eyes as she removed his hand from the cubicle wall. "Ah, that date *you* talked about and you're right," she said, "we didn't have it. Excuse me, I have work to do." She could feel Rex leering at her as she walked to her office.

"Anytime," he said from behind her. "Anytime."

She went into her office and closed the door. She sat at her desk. *We're being watched*, Hank's note had said. The strange events over the past week made her believe it could be true. And maybe their own people were the ones watching them.

Be careful, Hank's note had said.

Absolutely, Nan thought.

TWENTY-THREE

SILVIA SAT IN HER CUBICLE at the *Sentinel* and was hungry again. She needed to get her story off the ground but the gnawing in her stomach made it difficult to concentrate. She and Ian had just gone over her story with Bradley Schwartzman, the *Sentinel's* editor-in-chief, in Brad's corner office. She'd shown Brad the White House internal memo she'd gotten from Ellen. "My source inside the White House is well placed," she had told Bradley and Ian. "My source said the president was forced to endorse Howard."

Brad Schwartzman was unimpressed. "Speculation," he kept saying from underneath his bushy gray eyebrows. "We need solid proof he was forced into it and we need to know why. Until you know why, you don't have a story."

Of course, the editor-in-chief was right. Silvia had researched all of the connections between Howard and President Dougherty over the past eight years. There were few areas where the president and senator had worked together. None of it was particularly controversial, and none of it gave Howard any leverage over Dougherty. So, even though Silvia was convinced someone forced the president to endorse Howard, she had no proof. If she didn't get some soon, the story would grow cold and Schwartzman wouldn't give her permission to do a thorough investigation.

She hoped to get something out of Ellen tomorrow. She'd reserved their room in the Capitol Hilton and got a message to Ellen via the shared personal e-mail account they set up for their clandestine communications. Ellen responded that she'd be there. In the year since their relationship began, Ellen had never missed a chance to be with Silvia. Ellen's information was getting less and less useful, but Silvia was beginning to crave the *amor* just like Ellen did. Hopefully, Ellen would come through this time and give Silvia the break she needed.

Silvia left the *Sentinel* and took a cab to Vidalias in Georgetown to get something to eat. At five-thirty, it was still too early for the political crowd—they usually showed after eight—so when she walked into the dark, below-street-level restaurant, it was nearly empty. She asked for a table in the back where she could be alone and go over her notes. Ian Rutter had agreed to meet her later, after he finished some work at the office.

The waiter came to the table and Silvia ordered two crab cakes, a Caesar salad and the Atlantic black bass with garlic red potatoes for an entrée. The waiter eyed her small physique and said, "That's a lot of food." Silvia waved him off with a cold stare, picked up her notes and began studying them for something that might signal why the president was forced to endorse Howard.

In the days since Howard entered the race, the campaign had been about terrorism. Could the president be supporting Howard because of something to do with that issue? Over the past eight years, the Dougherty administration had made terrorism a high priority. Then when Howard got in the race, his party had made an initial strike to leverage the president's policies and to try to make Bloomfield appear soft on terrorism. Bloomfield's team had been prepared. They trotted out statistics that showed how much the country had spent on terrorism since 9-11 and they had professional analyses on the actual threat posed to people in the United States. Their response was careful not to dismiss the issue and presented a well-balanced position designed to make Howard look like an extremist. So far, the issue was being fought to a draw.

The new advertising campaigns didn't provide any clues to the Dougherty—Howard connection either. Bloomfield had slick new ads starring Hollywood superstars Jocelyn Jones and Miles Jackson with music by Brent Springman. They were professionally produced and targeted the rock-and-roll generation who were most likely to vote. The ads had a decidedly upper-middle-class feel and it was rumored the Howard camp would soon counter with folksy ads featuring the country-western music of Travis Daniels which would appeal to voters in the south and to the middle and lower-middle classes. Each side was staking out its territory, but both ad campaigns were mostly fluff and didn't touch on issues or anything controversial.

The waiter brought the crab cakes and Caesar salad. Silvia devoured the first crab cake in a few bites. As she started in on the second, she forced herself to slow down to let the food pacify her. She scanned the restaurant. Only one table was occupied by a couple holding hands and giggling at each other. Silvia wondered if she would ever have a relationship like that with a man. Until Ellen, her relationships were out of convenience and mostly for sex. Silvia had tried living with a man for six months—Alex, was his name—and it'd failed miserably. He was handsome and good in bed but they were both more concerned about their careers than each other. Once the sex became routine, they started arguing and getting in each other's way and soon, they had a loud, ugly split.

Her relationship with Ellen was different. She'd begun the relationship to glean information about what was going on in the White House. But Silvia began to enjoy the intimacy and wondered if someday she could actually live with a woman. For Ellen, the relationship had been mostly about sex and Silvia worried that the sex was becoming routine for Ellen, just like it had with Alex. In three months, a new administration would come in, Ellen would move on, and their relationship would probably end. Then what would she do?

As she finished her second crab cake and started in on her salad, she saw the maître'd escorting Ian to her table. As Ian sat, he took his napkin off the table and put it in his lap. "You weren't happy with what Bradley said about your story, were you?"

"No I wasn't," Silvia said. "In so many words, he told me to drop it."

"That is an accurate summation." Ian signaled for the waiter.

"Sorry, I couldn't wait," Silvia said, pointing at her food. "I ordered the blackened bass."

"Not a problem. I'll be eating later. I just need a cocktail."

The waiter took Ian's martini order and left. Ian eyed Silvia. "Why do you want to pursue this story? You really don't have anything."

"I have the internal press release and my source's note," she said, shoving a forkful of romaine lettuce into her mouth.

"The press release indicates nothing more than the president's staff was surprised by his endorsement," Ian said. "And they needed to get control of the spin. Your source might be leading you on."

"Leading me on? Why?"

"Spite, my dear. Your mole has three months remaining on the job. Regardless of the face they present, the White House press staff loathes the press." Ian's martini came. After a sip, he ran a finger across both sides of his mustache.

"My source doesn't feel that way," Silvia replied. "Anyway, don't you think the press should ask why the president endorsed Howard? There were only a few superficial stories on it but no one did a real investigation. I'm not satisfied with the answers we got from the White House. Are you?"

"Maybe we should take the statement we got from the White House at face value. The president endorsed Howard because he felt Howard had the best chance to defeat Bloomfield."

"*No jodas*. You don't believe that and I don't believe that and Bradley doesn't believe it either. What's with the press today? Why are we so afraid of controversy?"

Ian pointed at Silvia's briefcase on the floor next to her. "That White House pass in your briefcase, that's why."

Silvia set her fork down and glared at Ian. "You're telling me we're so afraid of getting cut off by the Administration that we can't pursue stories that might offend them?"

"I'm telling you we are part of the system and we have to play our role."

"Which is what?" Silvia exclaimed, "Regurgitating the Administration's rhetoric? Whatever happened to the idea of the press as the fourth estate?"

Ian took a slow sip of his martini and wiped his mustache. "Silvia, there is always an ebb and flow of power. Over the past twenty years, the power has flowed away from the congress, judiciary and, yes, the press to the presidency. If we don't recognize that, we'll be crushed."

"We're already crushed and the only way we can regain power is through investigative journalism." Silvia's sea bass arrived and she dug into it. Her blood was boiling and her appetite along with it.

Ian watched her eat. After a while he said, "Silvia, you need to know after you left, I had a meeting with Brad. That's why I couldn't join you right away."

"And, what did he say?"

"He ordered me to order you to drop the investigation."

Silvia set her knife and fork on the plate and looked Ian in the eye. "An order? He gave an order? On what basis?"

"He doesn't think you have a story."

"How am I supposed to get a story if I'm not allowed to investigate?"

"That's the point. There is no story and therefore, investigation is not necessary."

Silvia folded her arms and glared at Ian. "*Cobarde.* Coward. You and your boss are afraid of the White House. I'm disappointed, Ian. I thought you had more guts."

Ian threw back the last of his martini, dabbed his mustache and pushed away from the table. "Silvia, I've always supported you, but now I'm ordering you to drop your investigation. Brad said if you don't, he will fire you. Please don't turn this into a problem. Now, if you excuse me, I have a dinner date."

As Ian left the restaurant, Silvia returned to her sea bass. She picked up her knife and fork and then set them down.

She'd lost her appetite. Perhaps Ian and Bradley were right. She didn't have much and the *Sentinel* needed to be careful to maintain a good relationship with the White House.

Well, she still had her rendezvous with Ellen tomorrow. But if Ellen didn't have anything concrete, she'd have to drop the story before it ever got off the ground.

TWENTY-FOUR

VICTOR KNEW THAT the hard part of committing a murder was the escape. The key was the planning—where the killing would be done, the time of day, the type of weapon used, the escape route. He had to think through every tiny detail. Even then the operation rarely went exactly as planned—a mark didn't show at the right time or place, or the mark had someone with them, or the primary escape route somehow got cut off. You had to know your options and choose the right one. It was the split-second decision that made all the difference in the world.

For Victor, pulling the trigger was simple. Someone living needed to stop living and it didn't matter what side of the argument the mark was on or if the mark had a loving wife or husband, children or elderly parents to take care of. The only two things that mattered were making sure the mark was dead and then making a clean escape.

As Victor sat in his sniper perch in the second story of a nightclub in downtown Minneapolis, he ran through his escape plans again. This one would be easier than most because he could do it at the right distance. He had carefully planned it days in advance. He'd take the shot at two hundred meters, and he'd use a suppressor on his rifle and a custom-packed, subsonic cartridge, which would make it impossible for anyone to hear exactly where the shot came from. It would give Victor valuable seconds.

There were a few variables that he had to account for. First, there was the rifle itself. Victor's Dragunov sniper rifle wasn't an item you could walk down the streets of Minneapolis carrying without someone noticing. Even carried in a case, it would be conspicuous, especially after all the tumult the shooting would cause. The solution was simple— the rifle had to be left at the scene. That created its own set of problems because a rifle left clues. It had to be clean. There could be no fingerprints or sweat or hairs or fibers of any kind. That's why Victor wore a leather coat, gloves and hat. A few hours earlier he had shaved his head and scrubbed himself down until his skin was raw. He knew he'd still leave small traces of evidence but there'd be very little for the authorities to use.

The rifle had to be untraceable, too. Years earlier, Victor had secured the Dragunov from an ice cold source in the Czech Republic for just such a job. It was expensive—over ten thousand Euros—but it was his favorite weapon from when he practiced his craft in Russia. It was perfect for this job.

Victor checked his watch. The mark was scheduled to arrive soon. His knees were getting sore from an hour of kneeling, but he ignored the pain. It would be only a few more minutes.

He kept running through his escape plan. The only thing that concerned him was his own physical stature. How did a

240-pound Russian dressed in black leather leave the scene of an assassination without someone noticing? Part of the solution was the location of the assassination. It had to be done at a place where there were no security cameras and few, if any, people. He had to be close to a car that would provide cover and a means of escape. There was also the timing. Done late at night or early in the morning, there'd be few people around to see a large Russian slinking away.

There was only one other thing. His orders were clear. He had to shoot the mark but not kill him. To accomplish this, Victor planned a shot in the right shoulder with a light, steel-core 54mm cartridge that would pass straight through the body, just below the clavicle and leave a minimal amount of tissue damage. The bullet would have to hit inside a two-inch diameter target to avoid the right subclavian artery or the mark would bleed to death. For Victor, two-hundred meters with a PSOP 8x magnification scope would be like shooting at point blank range.

The mark was supposed to arrive for a breakfast meeting at 7:00 in the morning at Butler Square in the warehouse district of Minneapolis. There would be others with him and people waiting inside. Victor had to make the shot as the mark got out of the car, but before he entered the building. Victor calculated that he had less than three seconds to make the shot. It would be plenty of time.

Victor crouched behind a window opened just enough for the muzzle of the rifle to poke through. He waited. He had a clear line of sight to the side of the building where they'd drop off the mark. The sky was cloudy and gray but there was no wind for him to compensate for. Morning rush hour hadn't begun yet so the traffic was light on the street below.

Victor checked his watch again. *6:56.* He scanned the street for signs of the limo carrying the target. He saw nothing. With the Dragunov resting on the windowsill, Victor went over his escape plan one last time. Take the shot, quickly wipe down the rifle and leave it. Place the letter next to it. Walk down the stairs, out the back door that he'd left ajar after picking it open in the dark three hours earlier. Casually walk to the stolen Toyota Celica in the parking lot next door and drive away. Ditch the Celica in an abandoned lot in North Minneapolis, walk two blocks to his Audi and drive home.

He went over the contingency plans. If there was someone in the building when he tried to leave, he would have to kill him. If the door was closed and locked, he would quickly pick it open again. If someone had moved the Celica, he would walk through the parking lot to downtown Minneapolis and move among the growing rush hour crowd until it was safe to retrieve his Audi. Yeah, he had it all thought through.

He was ready.

A limo drove underneath the window where Victor sat. It turned the corner, drove a half block and pulled up to the Butler Square entrance. Victor lifted the Dragunov scope to his eye. A familiar cool wave washed over him and time seemed to stop. He could hear his heart beat and feel the electricity flow through his nerves. Far away, he heard a church bell ring the seven o'clock hour. Out of the corner of his eye, he saw a pigeon glide onto a rooftop and a woman in a red hat get off a bus a block away.

Victor heard a noise in the first level of the club. Someone had discovered the unlocked door. He heard someone say, "Is anyone here?"

Victor continued to peer through the scope. A man in a dark gray sports coat got out of the limo and opened the back door. Another man, not the target, got out. Both men stood by the open car door and waited.

Victor heard the man inside the building again. "Hello?" the man said. "Is anyone in here?" The man was climbing the stairs to the second floor where Victor was.

Victor pressed the rifle butt into his shoulder. He placed his finger on the cold metal of the trigger. After a few seconds, the mark crawled out of the limo talking on his cell phone. The mark straightened and hesitated for a split second. Victor pulled the trigger and the Dragunov jumped against his shoulder.

Through the scope, Victor could see a red circle grow on the mark's right shoulder. It was a perfect shot, exactly where Victor had planned to put it. The mark took a half step forward and dropped his cell phone. One knee buckled and then the other and he slumped to the ground. One of the men in the gray sports coat threw himself over the mark. The other drew a pistol, crouched behind the limo and began to scan the area.

Victor heard footsteps coming from the hallway. The man's voice called out again, louder this time, "Hello? Who's here?" Victor took a cloth from his pocket and carefully wiped down the Dragunov. He set it on the floor. He took out the letter from the inside of his coat and laid it next to the rifle. The letter flopped open revealing writing in Arabic.

He walked to the other side of the room, peeked out the door. A man dressed in baggy clothes and dreadlocks was searching the second floor between Victor and the staircase. Victor drew a knife from an ankle sheath, opened the door and showed himself to the man. "In here," Victor pleaded. "Someone hurt. Help. Quick!"

The young man recoiled. Victor raised his empty palm and said in his thickest Russian accent, "I don't speak good English. Help. Please."

The young man hesitated, then approached. "Someone is hurt? Who?" he asked. When the dreadlocked man was two steps away, Victor lunged. He threw an arm around the man's neck and plunged the knife in the man's left kidney. The man's dreadlocks were wet and smelled like shampoo from a morning shower. He let out a short gasp and after a few seconds, went limp.

Victor left the knife in the man's back and dropped him to the floor. He walked down the flight of steps, through the door that was still ajar. As he took off his gloves and pushed them into his pocket, he casually walked across the parking lot to the Celica and with the rest of the morning traffic, drove down Hennepin Avenue toward north Minneapolis.

He had made another clean escape.

TWENTY-FIVE

STEPHANIE'S FRANTIC CALL came to Nan's cell phone as she was about to take Jenny to school. "Mrs. Mattson called," Stephanie said. "Hank is in the hospital!"

"In the hospital?" Nan said. "What happened? How serious is it?"

"Mrs. Mattson wouldn't tell me but it doesn't sound good. She told me he's at Methodist Hospital in the emergency room. He's asking for you."

Nan's mind raced. "Okay," she said. "Let's see. I have to drop Jenny off at school. Then I'll go to the hospital. I'll be late getting in. I was supposed to meet with the volunteer committee this morning to discuss the rally next week. Call everyone and tell them we'll have to push it back until this afternoon. Find an open slot later today."

"What'll we do without Hank?" Stephanie asked. Her voice quivered. "He was coordinating the mailings and cold calling. And he was doing Jim's job."

Nan looked for her car keys and briefcase. "Stephanie, listen to me. You're going to have to step up and do it. These things aren't hard and you're more than capable. You wanted to learn how to run a campaign? Here's your chance. I want you to help manage the mailings and cold calling. Do the best you can. I'll take over when I get back from the hospital."

"What about the printing? The new literature's being printed today."

"Tell Shelly to do it. Tell her I said I want her to take charge of the printing. And then, Stephanie, I want you to make sure she does it. Shelly's a volunteer so you'll have to treat her carefully, but get her to do it. Cajole her, tease her, appeal to her pride. I don't know. Do whatever it takes. Okay?"

"I'll do my best," Stephanie said weakly.

"Stephanie," Nan said, "if you do your best, you'll do great."

"Thanks. Okay. I'll get it done," Stephanie said.

Nan spotted her keys on the kitchen counter, pulled on her coat and grabbed her briefcase. She called upstairs for Jenny who came bounding down the stairs carrying an art project.

As they drove to Jenny's school, Jenny asked, "Who called?"

"The campaign office. One of our workers is in the hospital. I need to see him after I drop you off."

"How did he get hurt?"

"I don't know."

After a few minutes, Jenny asked, "Mom, are we going to move to Washington, D.C.?"

Nan glanced at Jenny. "What gave you that idea?"

"I heard you and Dad talking about it. I heard you say you might work for Governor Bloomfield in the White House."

"There's a possibility. He has to get elected first."

"Do you think he'll win?" Jenny asked.

"Well, he's leading in the polls with only two weeks left. It's looking good."

"So we might move to Washington, D.C.?"

"I wouldn't worry about it sweetie," Nan said. "If Governor Bloomfield is elected and he offers me a job, we'll have to decide as a family if we want to move."

"If you worked for the president, would I get to see the White House?" Jenny asked excitedly.

"You, my dear, would get a private tour," Nan said with a smile.

"Sweet!"

Nan pulled up to the school and Jenny climbed out of the car with her art project. "Love you, Mom," she shouted as she slammed the car door.

"I love you too," Nan said into the closed door.

Washington, D.C. It was a good question. Did Nan want to uproot her family for a position in the White House? It would be a once-in-a-lifetime opportunity. If she was the White House Communications Director, she'd be one of Washington's elite and she, Ben and Jenny would meet hundreds of important, interesting people. Jenny's world would expand well beyond her small circle of friends in Minnesota. She'd be exposed to privileges, people and places only a handful of thirteen-year-olds had ever known, and Nan would be a wonderful professional role model for Jenny.

But Jenny would lose a lot too. It would be difficult for her to make new friends at her age in the circus that's Washington, D.C. And Nan's mother, Jenny's grandmother, would be a thousand miles away.

Most importantly, Jenny would see a lot less of Nan. As Communications Director, Nan would put in 80-hour work weeks and Jenny would grow up quickly and head off to college while Nan spent most of her time working. It'd be a huge sacrifice for both of them.

Nan shook her thoughts away and turned her attention to Hank. Stephanie had said she didn't know what happened to him. Could it be something to do with the note he left in her car? *We're being watched,* it said. *Be careful.*

Nan checked her rear view mirror to see if a car was following her. She saw nothing. Ever since she got Hank's note, she'd become more aware of who was around her. She'd been more careful about what she said on the phone at work. She kept a close eye on Rex. She never saw Tom. She wondered if she was being paranoid.

She worried about Hank. His note had said he would be in the office yesterday afternoon to tell her what he'd discovered at the psychiatric hospital. She waited for him but he never showed up which was unusual. He always called if he was going to be late. She'd tried his cell but there was no answer. After work, she went home and didn't think much about Hank that night. Then this morning, she got the call from Stephanie.

Nan pulled into the Methodist Hospital parking lot and made her way to the Emergency room. She asked at the front desk where she could find Hank Mattson and the receptionist said they'd moved him to intensive care. Nan walked down the hallway to ICU. The nurse said Hank was in room 24 and pointed toward some doors.

The ICU was dimly lit and instead of walls, the rooms were divided by curtains hanging from metal rods attached to the ceiling. Nurses and doctors dressed in blue studied charts as they busily moved through the unit. There was expensive looking equipment everywhere. Nan saw Karen Mattson outside room 24 clutching her sweater around her. Standing next to her was a tall, slender man in his thirties. When Mrs. Mattson saw Nan, she started to cry.

"Karen," Nan said, "I came as quickly as I could. How's Hank?"

"He's not good," Karen Mattson said as she embraced Nan. "They hurt him so badly."

"Who hurt him?"

Karen moved away and clutched her sweater again. The man stepped forward and extended his hand. "Hi, I'm Eric, Hank's son. Thanks for coming. We don't know exactly what happened. The police are investigating."

"The police?"

"They think he got mugged. It happened last night."

Nan peeked around the curtain. The room was dark and she could see a bed surrounded by machines and monitors. A nurse sat in a chair next to the bed. "He was mugged?" Nan asked.

"That's what the police think, although I don't know. He wasn't in a neighborhood where that sort of thing happens— less than a mile from your offices. And it was 5:30 at night. Dad never carries much cash, and he's not the type of person to get into a fight. It just doesn't add up."

Nan nodded. "Can I see him?"

"Yes, of course, although he's unconscious. He lost a lot of blood." Eric's eyes began to well up and Nan could tell Hank's situation was serious.

She pushed aside the curtain and walked into the room. A nurse holding a chart looked up from a chair next to the bed. Nan approached and then took a step back. Over Hank's right eye was a purple knob the size of a golf ball and the purple had seeped into his eye socket. There was a white bandage around his head. He had a green oxygen mask over his mouth and nose, and his breathing was slow and deep. He had an IV in each arm and wires running from pads on his chest and head. Three monitors blinked graphs and numbers alongside the bed. One of them beeped softly.

Eric slid up next to Nan. "Who'd want to do this to him? It makes me so angry." His voice shook.

"Will he be all right?" Nan asked.

"He has a bad concussion, a broken arm and some internal injuries. They put him in a low-level coma to keep the swelling down in his head. The doctors say they'll take him out of it in the next day or two, but he might not remember much at first. They say there's a good chance he'll recover without any brain damage."

Nan stepped closer to Hank's side. "My office said he was asking for me," she said. "Do you know why?"

"You'll have to ask my mother," Eric replied.

Nan touched Hank's hand, the strong hand of a carpenter. His skin was leathery but warm. She could feel his strength and began to believe he'd be all right.

She went back outside the room and Eric followed. Karen Mattson stood with a tissue to her eye. "I can't go in there," Karen said. "I just can't bear to see him like that."

"I'm so sorry," Nan said. "It's awful. Why would anyone want to do that to him?"

Karen shook her head and dabbed her eyes.

"Karen, I have to ask you," Nan said. "Why did Hank want to talk to me?"

Karen sighed. "He was obsessed with that woman in the mental hospital," she said. "He went there again yesterday and learned something important. He wanted to tell you what it was. But he said he had to check one more thing first. That was about four o'clock. He never came back home." She began to cry again.

Nan put a hand on her shoulder. "Karen, I know this is difficult, but it might be important. Do you know specifically what he wanted to tell me?"

Karen shrugged. "It was something about the woman. He had something he wanted to show you. Some papers, I think. He said you'd finally beat Sheldon Hanrahan. What does he have to do with it?

"Do you know where the papers are?" Nan asked.

"You might find them in his briefcase."

"Did you tell the police what he was doing?"

"No," Karen said. "Should I have?"

Nan didn't answer. Eric put his arm around his mother. She rested her head on his shoulder and sobbed. "Mom, the doctors say dad will be okay. We just have to get through the next few days."

Nan looked at Karen Mattson and anger suddenly gripped her. Perhaps what had happened to Hank was a mugging as the police said. But maybe it was something else. Hank's note from yesterday had said they had to be careful. Perhaps he had discovered something and someone tried to kill him for it. It seemed insane, but with all the wild things going on, it seemed possible too. Perhaps she should tell the police about Hank's note. If she did, she'd have to tell them about Mrs. Wilson and her ludicrous accusation about Howard. And then it would be the Theilen campaign all over again. No. Better to wait to see what the police come up with. They said they thought it was a mugging. Best to leave it at that—at least for the time being.

Nan reached out and hugged Karen. "Please let me know if there's anything I can do." She turned to Eric. "And please tell me what the police say. I need to know."

"I will," Eric replied. "You should take his briefcase. He has some election stuff in it. It's over there." He pointed at Hank's briefcase on the floor next to a chair.

"Thanks," Nan said and took the briefcase.

*

As Nan left the ICU, her cell phone rang. She read the incoming number and saw it was the office. Nan punched the call answer button and said, "Hi, this is Nan."

It was Stephanie and she was hysterical. "You have to get into the office right now. Reporters are everywhere! No one knows what to do."

Nan hurried out the hospital exit into the parking lot. "You don't know what to do about what?"

"Haven't you heard?" Stephanie said. "It's all over the news!"

"What?" Nan asked as she reached her car. "What's all over the news? *What happened?*" She climbed into the car and tossed Hank's briefcase on the passenger seat.

"There's been an assassination attempt. It happened this morning."

Nan froze in her car seat. "An assassination attempt? My God. Who?"

"Senator Howard!" Stephanie said. "It happened this morning downtown. He's in critical condition. The media is outside looking for someone to talk to about it. Get in here as soon as you can. Please!"

"I'm on my way." Nan punched end call on her phone and roared out of the parking lot. As she sped to the

Bloomfield campaign office, her head spun. What had started with the president's shocking endorsement of Howard a week earlier had now taken an absurd turn. Hank was in the hospital brutally beaten and now there had been an assassination attempt on Senator Howard.

Had the world gone mad?

TWENTY-SIX

WHEN NAN APPROACHED Bloomfield's Minnesota campaign office, she could tell she was going to have a difficult time getting in. There were four news crews with at least a dozen people in front of the office. Two trucks with satellite dishes were parked across the street.

Nan drove down the street past the office and turned the corner at the end of the block. She parked her car, put on her sunglasses and started walking toward the office. As she got close to the door, one of the reporters—the wolfish woman in the red scarf who she saw days earlier—trotted toward her.

"Hey, it's Nan Smith!" the reporter said. Her cameraman struggled to keep up with her. "May I have a word with you Ms. Smith?"

Nan quickened her pace and was able to get to the front door one step ahead of the reporter. She slid inside the office and locked the door behind her. The reporter banged on the glass and said, "I have only a few questions. We want to know how you think the shooting will affect Governor Bloomfield's campaign. The public has the right to know." Nan shook her head and turned toward the reception desk.

"Thank God you're here," Stephanie said wide-eyed from behind her desk.

"I got here as quickly as I could," Nan said, catching her breath. "I didn't expect all those reporters."

Stephanie wrung her hands and didn't take her eyes off Nan. "They've been here for the past half hour, ever since the news about Senator Howard. They're ferocious! Rex had to threaten to call the police. And the phone is ringing off the hook. What should we do?"

Nan peeled off her overcoat and tossed it on a chair. "I listened to the radio on the way here but didn't get the full story. Tell me what happened."

"Someone tried to assassinate him in the warehouse district this morning. They think it might be terrorists. Someone got stabbed, too. He's dead."

"Terrorists? Why do they think it was terrorists?" Nan asked.

"I don't know," Stephanie said. "That's just what they said."

Nan paused. Then she said, "Stephanie, keep the door locked and don't answer the phone. I need to see what's going on before we decide what to do."

She walked to the bullpen area where Rex, Sorrea, Shelly and a half-dozen volunteers were huddled around the big screen television. When Rex saw Nan he said, "What a goddamn mess." He ran his hand through his hair and for the first time since she met him, Rex didn't wear his cocky smirk.

"What's the latest?" Nan asked, joining the group. The television screen showed reporters broadcasting live from downtown Minneapolis two blocks from the shooting.

"They didn't kill him," Rex said. "He's in surgery now. They say he'll live."

Nan pulled Rex aside. "Do they know who did it?"

"They think it was only one person. Doesn't sound like they have a lot of clues. There was a letter with the rifle. They think it might be from a militant faction taking a stand against Howard for his position on terrorism."

"What've we heard from Boston?"

"Nada," Rex answered. "I'm sure they are swamped."

"This is insane," Shelly said twirling her hair nervously. "Now what do we do?"

Everyone faced Nan. What do we do, indeed? During her career, Nan had handled difficult situations, but never anything like this. Not even close. She was in the center of an incredibly delicate situation and had no direction from Boston and probably wouldn't get any soon. She was on her own.

She looked at the people in the room who all had fear in their eyes. She thought of Governor Bloomfield, the good man from Massachusetts who she believed in and who was now depending on her. She thought of Ben and Jenny. Then, she nodded, picked up the remote and clicked off the television.

"This is what we do," Nan said meeting each person's eyes. "First, none of us says a single word to the reporters out there. Nothing. Not even you volunteers. The press is in a frenzy and they're looking for anything for a story. They'll take your comments out of context or twist them into something you didn't mean to say. This is their game. They gear up for this sort of thing and if we play with them, we'll lose. So say nothing, not a single word. Understand?"

Everyone nodded in agreement.

"Second," Nan continued, "put everything on hold. Everything has changed and until we hear from Boston, it's pointless to continue what we're doing. I expect we'll have our orders soon.

"That means the volunteers should go home. We'll call when we need you. Remember, not a word to the press about this. If a reporter calls, direct them to me. Rex, help escort everyone to their cars. Everyone except Rex, Sorrea and Stephanie should go home, now."

"What about me?" Shelly protested. "I can stay, can't I?"

"Sorry Shelly" Nan said. "Only the paid staff can stay."

Shelly looked disappointed but followed the other volunteers out of the office while Nan watched from the reception area. The reporters descended on the volunteers like starving hyenas, but with Rex's help they all made it to their cars. When the volunteers were gone, Rex came back and locked the door behind him. "Assholes!" he said. "I've never seen anything like it. I feel like hanging that bitch reporter with her fucking red scarf."

"Thanks," Nan said. "Now, I need to talk to the rest of you."

Rex, Sorrea, and Stephanie went back to the bullpen area. Nan addressed Stephanie first. "Stephanie, you need to get on the telephone and cancel our meeting this afternoon. Then, call the rest of the volunteers and anyone else connected to our office and reassure them we will be addressing this situation as soon as we can. Tell them to stay home and say nothing to the press. Nothing. They should refer all press inquiries to me. And they should wait to hear from us before they do anything. You need to strike the right tone—reassuring but serious. Okay?"

Stephanie nodded. Nan continued. "While you do that, I'll call our donors and do the same. When you're done with the volunteers, call the printers and anyone else doing work for us and tell them to put everything on hold. Okay?"

"I understand," Stephanie said.

"Start now. I need to talk to Rex and Sorrea in private."

Stephanie headed to the reception area and Nan returned the stares of Rex and Sorrea.

"Where's Tom?" Nan asked firmly.

"He's out," Rex answered. "I don't know when he'll be back."

Nan let a short silence fill the bullpen. "I don't know how to put this delicately, so I won't try. I don't know what you people are doing here but it has to stop, at least for the time being."

"I don't take orders from you," Rex said. He folded his arms across his chest, his dark eyes glared.

"That's true. But I'm telling you to do it anyway. Right now, our little office is in the spotlight because the assassination attempt happened in our city, and to our senator. The press will watch everything we do. If any of us gets caught doing something questionable, it will hurt us."

"What makes you think we're doing something questionable?" Rex asked.

"Like I said, I don't know. Just stop what you're doing, whatever it is."

"I have to talk to Hilton before I do anything."

"That's precisely my point. Stop what you're doing until you hear from Boston."

"I'll take it under advisement," Rex said.

"I suggest you take it under a strong advisement," Nan said.

"Is that all you have to say?" Rex asked.

"Yes. Now, if you'll excuse me, I have calls to make."

Nan went to her office and shut the door. She watched as Rex and Sorrea talked for a few minutes and then went to their separate cubicles. She was right to tell Rex what to do. Whatever he was doing—legal, illegal or just simple pranks—it had to stop. With Senator Howard in the hospital, the public would view any aggressiveness as kicking the other candidate while he was down.

She ran her hand over her head. The world had indeed gone mad—an assassination attempt on Senator Howard by a terrorist group and Hank was comatose in intensive care from a supposed mugging.

And there was still the issue of Mrs. Wilson.

She remembered Hank's briefcase sitting in the front seat of her car. Hank had said he had something to show her. Perhaps there was something in the briefcase. She pushed away from her desk and headed to the front door. Outside the media throng had grown by two teams of reporters and one truck. She unlocked the door and slipped out. The reporter with the red scarf descended on her followed by her cameraman pointing his big lens at Nan. "Nan Smith!" the reporter said. "Are you happy that Senator Howard has been shot?"

Nan recognized the reporter's ploy—say something inflammatory that Nan would want to respond to and once she was talking, the reporter would have an interview on film for the five o'clock news. Nan didn't take the bait. She pushed past the reporter, dodged two others and marched toward her car as they followed, shouting questions.

When she got to the car, she retrieved Hank's briefcase, and faced the gauntlet of reporters again. They'd apparently gotten the message that she wasn't going to talk and only the reporter in the red scarf pursued her. She shoved a microphone in Nan's face. "Do you think the terrorism issue will propel Senator Howard into the White House?" the reporter asked. Nan didn't respond as she marched through the red, white and blue door and locked it behind her.

Nan took Hank's briefcase to her office and shut her door. She placed the briefcase on her desk and opened it. Inside were several folders about mailings for the Bloomfield campaign and a receipt for postage. There was nothing about Mrs. Wilson. She looked in the top pocket of the briefcase and found a folder of information about the Rand Psychiatric Hospital Hank got from his friend at the Department of Health. There was a list of the employees and another list of residents. She flipped through the list of residents and on the second page saw a name circled. Edith Wilson. Below her name was a note in Hank's handwriting that said, *She has proof!*

Proof? The woman has proof that Howard murdered her daughter? Senator Howard, a *murderer?* Hank had to be wrong. What had Karen Mattson said? Hank had become obsessed with the woman. He'd also become obsessed with beating Sheldon Hanrahan and wasn't thinking clearly.

She remembered that she and Hank agreed to go to the police if they discovered something. But Nan couldn't go to the police, not now with Senator Howard in the hospital. It'd look like a very poorly timed smear tactic. It would be the Theilen campaign all over again.

If Mrs. Wilson had proof like Hank's note said, Nan would have to find it herself.

TWENTY-SEVEN

THE MOUNTAINS OF THE Apache National Forest in eastern Arizona was a difficult place to land a helicopter. Nevertheless, President Phil Dougherty and his riding party had to find a landing place fast. The president had hoped for a quiet four days in his home state, most of it spent on the back of Ike, his favorite horse. His day had gone as planned until the radio had interrupted him with news about the assassination attempt on Senator Howard.

Matt, the lead Secret Service man riding with the president, suggested they head a few miles north through rugged terrain to a bald where a helicopter could pick up the president and carry him to Tucson where Air Force One was waiting to take him to Washington. The president was impressed the Secret Service could provide him with such specialized help as Matt. He was a skilled rider and he knew the area almost as well as the president himself who had grown up nearby. Dougherty agreed with Matt's suggestion and the riding party pointed their horses northward.

Ike, whom the president nicknamed, 'The General,' was small, even for an Arabian. But the horse was strong and had a steadfast heart. He instinctively knew he was the favorite ride of the most powerful man in the world, so they made good time. As they rode through a heavily forested valley and up a long ridge, they heard helicopters overhead.

At the top of the ridge, they came to an opening where a black unmarked helicopter perched surrounded by three marines with M-14 rifles at the ready. The president dismounted from Ike and handed the reins and his riding gloves to Matt. He put his hand over his Stetson hat as two Secret Service men ushered him into the helicopter. The helicopter lifted off and as soon as it cleared the treetops, two AH-64A Apache attack helicopters pulled alongside. The triangle of helicopters thumped their way west toward Tucson.

Thirty minutes later, the president's helicopter landed thirty yards from Air Force One on the tarmac of the Davis Monthan Air Force Base. Marines with M-14 rifles surrounded Air Force One. Two Secret Service men escorted the president up the stairs into the belly of the 747.

Richard Craft and John Hodges, the chief Secret Service man on site in Arizona, met him in the main cabin as the airplane revved its jet engines and began taxiing toward the runway. "Mr. President," Hodges said, "you need to buckle in. We're taking off immediately."

The president sat and pulled the seat belt around him while Craft and Hodges sat in the seats across from him. "You have all the security forces out this morning, Mr. Hodges," the president said. "What's going on?"

"We're approaching this situation as a level one security threat, sir," answered Hodges. "We have reason to believe

Senator Howard's assassins are linked to terrorists and we're taking every precaution to keep you safe."

"Terrorists?" The president tossed his Stetson on the seat next to him. He ran his hand through his hair.

Craft looked at the president from under his blonde eyebrows. "There was a letter…"

Hodges leaned forward. "We're thinking you shouldn't go back to Washington until we know exactly what the situation is, sir. I've been on the phone to the security chief in Washington and we're evaluating alternatives."

The president looked Hodges in the eyes. "Get me to the White House."

"But sir," Hodges replied, "it's a level one threat. The Secret Service is authorized to take charge in situations…"

"I don't give a damn what level security threat it is or what you're authorized to do. Get me to the White House. Now."

"Sir, it's my job to make sure you…"

"John, it's my job to run this country at times like this and I can do that best from the White House. It's now your job to get me safely there in three hours or less. If you aren't able to do it, I'll find someone who can."

Hodges stared blankly at the president, then at Craft who smiled and said, "Excuse us please, John. I need to brief the president and you need to get us safely to the White House in three hours or less. Thank you."

Hodges got out of his seat and disappeared into the back of the aircraft. Craft clicked his seat belt around his lap as the aircraft rumbled down the runway. Soon it was in the air jetting toward Washington, D.C.

"What's this about terrorists?" Dougherty asked.

"As I said, there was a letter left at the assassin's perch. It claimed the assassination was part of a Jihad against the United States. It looks legit. The paper is from a mill in Iran. There was a claim on a Jihadist website well before word got out in the press. And there've been e-mails from Islamic factions claiming credit for it. The rifle was a Dragunov—the kind the Russians left behind in Afghanistan when they bailed out."

"How's Senator Howard?"

"He'll live. He was hit in the right shoulder. The bullet passed through his torso and didn't hit anything vital. He'll be in the hospital a few days and after that, he could be back on the campaign trail."

"What happened to security? Where was Howard's Secret Service protection?"

"They didn't do anything wrong. Howard was in the open only a few seconds. He was surrounded by two men."

Dougherty gazed out the window at the eastern Arizona mountains where only a short time ago, he was enjoying a peaceful ride on The General. He longed for the day when he could stay in the mountains as long as he wanted and no one would force him away for a national emergency. "So the shooter was in exactly the right place at exactly the right time?"

"Yes, sir."

"Sounds like he was lucky."

"Very lucky," Craft said. "Maybe too lucky."

The president turned back to Craft. "Let's see what the FBI and CIA uncover before we start cogitating."

"Yes sir. Of course, there's something we don't have to speculate on."

"What's that?"

Craft leaned forward, clasped his hands in front of him. He was all business as usual. "This incident has the potential to propel Howard into the White House."

The president picked up his Stetson, ran his fingers along the rim. "Explain."

"Two things. First, there's the sympathy vote. Howard will come out of the hospital looking like a hero. He'll be back on the campaign trail during the last week of the campaign just in time to milk the sympathy vote for all it's worth. Imagine, his arm in a sling, bravely defying death and the enemies of America to boldly campaign for the presidency. The press will eat it up and the American public will love him for it.

"But more importantly," Craft continued, "it's the issue he's known for, the issue they've been hitting hard since Howard became their candidate. Terrorism. It's once again the concern of every American. Voters will think America is under attack, just like the extremists in our party have been saying all along. Bloomfield and his people will look like fools for trying to downplay the issue. They'll take a huge hit and Howard will make big gains right before the election. It could win it for him."

Dougherty closed his eyes. He let Craft's analysis sink in. Craft was right. Howard had just become the favorite to win the election and his endorsement had made it possible. "Good God," he said, "what have I done?"

The president opened his eyes and gazed out the window at the high plains thirty-thousand feet below. Events were spinning out of his control and Sheldon Hanrahan and his extremist friends might soon take control of the country. He couldn't let it happen. It'd destroy America, the country he loved so much. The country he had sworn to protect.

There was one way to stop them. Until now, he'd never considered taking such drastic action. It'd ruin him, of course. It would destroy his legacy. But he was a lame duck president and in a few months, none of it would matter. He could withdraw to his Arizona ranch, write a few books and spend more time in the mountains riding The General.

For the time being, he'd wait to see what happened in the election. But if Craft was right, if Howard was going to ride the sympathy vote to the presidency, he would have to make his move.

TWENTY-EIGHT

MRS. WILSON HAD PROOF, and Nan wanted to know what it was. But she remembered the warning in Hank's note. *We're being watched. Be careful.* So she sat at her desk making calls to major donors to reassure them they'd soon have a new strategy for the campaign after the shocking events of the morning.

How were they watching her? Who was watching her? Hank's note also said their phones might be tapped. If someone was watching her, how could she find out what Mrs. Wilson had that proved Senator Howard was a murderer? With both Hank and Senator Howard laying wounded in the hospital, she was determined to find out, but she had to be careful.

She had an idea. She picked up her phone and dialed Ben's work number. The ad agency's receptionist answered. "Julie," Nan said, "this is Nan Smith. Is Ben available?"

"Yes, Mrs. Smith. Let me get him for you."

A few seconds later Ben came on the line. "Hi, hon. You must be dealing with a huge mess. Are you alright?"

"Yes, I'm fine. I need to talk to you. I'm wondering if I can see you for lunch."

"I have a lunch meeting but I can cancel it. Where do you want to meet? We should stay away from downtown. Half the streets are blocked off by the police."

"Can you meet me at Jasmine's?"

"Jasmine's? That's kinda out of the way."

"It's where I want to go."

"Okay, whatever you say. What time?"

"12:30."

"I'll have Julie make the reservations. I'll see you then."

Nan hung up and resumed calling donors. After a few hours, she went to the bullpen and watched the TV for the latest news on Senator Howard. The reporters said he was out of surgery and was recovering in the ICU. A surgeon from the Hennepin County Medical Center explained that Senator Howard was expected to leave the hospital in a few days and could be back on the campaign trail in a week, "if everything goes well."

They brought in a few Washington, D.C. analysts to talk about the terrorists behind the assassination attempt. They talked about how Islamic terrorists would not want Howard to be president because of his stand on terror. They used as evidence a letter discovered by CBS News apparently written by Howard on his campaign letterhead. It was addressed to the president of the American Conservative Union and listed a number of actions Senator Howard was committed to if elected president. The list revealed an extremist stance that would have done severe damage to the Howard candidacy prior to the assassination attempt. Not anymore. With the Senator recuperating in the Hospital from an apparent terrorist's bullet, the analysts were saying the letter made Howard look prophetic.

Nan remembered the Howard campaign letterhead Jim found and wondered if the letter was the work of Rex and Tom. No, it couldn't be. Bob Hilton wouldn't go to that extreme to get Bloomfield elected. Would he?

She returned to her desk and called the rest of the people on her list. Rex had been talking on the phone nearly the entire morning and Sorrea stared like a zombie into her computer monitor.

At noon, she reached into Hank's briefcase and pulled out the list of residents at the Rand Psychiatric Hospital. Edith Wilson was in room number 235. Nan scanned the list and saw that the person in room 234 was a Mr. Gordon Peterson. She shoved the list back in Hank's briefcase, grabbed her car keys and headed to her car.

As she walked past the front desk, she asked Stephanie, "How are the calls going?"

"I'm over half done."

"Good job, Stephanie. Make sure you leave messages for those you don't get through to. And then get an e-mail to everyone, including our suppliers, saying we have no official position as yet on the Howard situation. Have Rex go out and get lunch for you. I'll be out for a while. I should be back later this afternoon. I'll have my phone with me."

"Will do. And Nan," Stephanie said with a smile, "thanks."

Nan ran the gauntlet of reporters to her car and drove to the west suburb of Golden Valley where Jasmine's was on the first floor of the International Tech office complex. She'd chosen the ferny Jasmine's for one simple reason—it was attached to an underground parking ramp. She pulled her

Camry into an empty space on the second level of the parking ramp and headed to the restaurant. Ben was already seated at the table when she got there. "Hello, beautiful," he said as she took a seat. "I didn't think you liked Jasmine's."

"I didn't choose it for the food and especially not for the ambiance."

"Oh?"

"I need to swap cars with you," she said, "and I didn't want anyone to see."

"Who would see?" Ben asked with a raised eyebrow. "And why do you care?"

"I have a few things to tell you." Nan felt a pang of guilt. She hadn't told Ben about Hank's note or what Hank had found out about Mrs. Wilson at the psychiatric hospital. Last week, Ben had dismissed Mrs. Wilson's accusation as the ranting of a crazy woman. It did seem absurd and Nan hadn't raised the topic again. Besides, Ben had his own problems. His agency was continuing to lose money and he was losing sleep over it. She thought it best to keep her work problems to herself.

Until now. Hank lay comatose in a hospital bed and it was possible he was there because he'd learned something about Mrs. Wilson. She wanted answers and needed Ben's help.

The waiter took their order, brought their food and while they ate, Nan told Ben the entire story about Mrs. Wilson and Hank's discoveries. She told him that someone beat up Hank.

"Whoa," Ben said setting his fork down. "Do you think he got beat up because he was asking questions about Mrs. Wilson?"

Nan poked at her chicken dijon. "I don't know. It sounds preposterous, but it's possible."

"If you think it's even remotely possible, you should go to the police, Nan."

"I can't. Think about it. The police would never believe me. It'd look like I was trying to smear Howard while he's in the hospital, for goodness sake. No, I have to find out about this on my own."

"*Find out on your own?*" Ben said leaning in. "Are you serious?"

Nan nodded. "Yeah," she answered. "I am."

"So what're you going to do?"

"I'm going to the hospital to see what the woman has as proof."

"Nan," Ben said, "think this through. It's not a good idea."

"I have thought it through," Nan stated. "I don't see a better option. I need to do this."

Ben stared at Nan for a moment. "I'm not going to be able to talk you out of it, am I?"

"All I need are your car keys."

Ben shook his head. "Maybe I should do it instead. No one's watching me."

"Mrs. Wilson won't recognize you. She'll only recognize me. Maybe she'll tell me what I need to know."

"Yeah," said Ben. "That Woods guy will recognize you, too. What then."

"If he's there, I'll just tell him I wanted to see if Mrs. Wilson was okay. I mean, what could he do?"

First Ben shook his head, then he sighed and nodded slowly. He reached into his coat pocket and retrieved his car keys. He slid them across the table. "My car's on the first level. Promise you'll be careful."

Nan pushed aside her dijon chicken and grabbed the keys. She gave her keys to Ben. "I promise. I'll be home for supper," she said and headed to the parking ramp.

TWENTY-NINE

NAN HAD REMEMBERED to take her sunglasses out of her car before swapping cars with Ben. It was a cloudy, gray day, but she wore them anyway. She felt silly thinking the glasses would somehow conceal her identity, but she left them on just in case. She shoved her hair underneath her hat and drove out of the ramp. She pointed the car to the Rand Psychiatric Hospital. She looked in the rear view mirror to see if anyone was following—it was becoming a habit. She saw no cars behind her.

As she drove, she worried that she was being foolish. It wasn't like her to be impulsive like this. She should probably let go of the whole matter with Mrs. Wilson. The chances of her accusations being true were remote at best. And if Hank's beating had anything to do with his activities at the hospital, she should let the police do their investigation and bring Hank's assailants to justice. But everything had turned so strange over the past week. Ever since President Dougherty's endorsement of Senator Howard for president and Mrs. Wilson's absurd accusation, nothing seemed normal. Perhaps she was letting herself get caught up in everything and was becoming obsessed with Mrs. Wilson just like Hank had. And maybe, a small part of her wanted Mrs. Wilson's accusation to be true so Bloomfield would win the election and Nan would become the White House Communications Director.

Nan pulled Ben's old Land Cruiser into one of the Rand Psychiatric Hospital visitor's parking spaces. The hospital was a square, one-story building with small, dark windows ten feet above ground. The stark, concrete walls made the place look like something out of cold war Russia.

Nan got out of the car and walked through the front doors. An imposing guard desk dominated the austere reception area. A security camera mounted in the ceiling eyed her. She kept her sunglasses on. She didn't see Mr. Woods.

A bored-looking, middle-aged man glanced up from the guard desk. "Can I help you?"

"Why yes," Nan replied. She put a lilt in her voice. "I'm Betsy Peterson from Malibu, California. I'm visiting relatives here in Minnesota and want to visit my dear Uncle Gordon. Gordon Peterson?"

"Gordy?" the man said surprised. "You wanna visit Gordy?"

"Why, yes. Is there a problem?"

"No, I guess not. You have to sign in." The guard reached for a clipboard and handed it to Nan. "I gotta see your I.D."

Nan felt her pulse quicken. She put a hand to the top of her breasts. "Oh, goodness me, I left my purse at the hotel. You're not going to make me find my way back to the hotel to get my purse, are you? You wouldn't make me do that."

The man stared at Nan's hand on her breasts. "Ah… we have to check I.D.s."

Nan leaned toward the man keeping her hand on her chest. She smiled. "I won't cause any trouble for you sir," she said. "I promise. I came all the way from Malibu…"

The guard eyed her. "I ain't supposed to let visitors in without I.D. but I guess I can let you through seeing as you came all the way from California. Next time, you gotta bring your I.D. Gordy's in room 234. That's the door to your left, halfway down the hall. I'll buzz you in."

Nan signed her name in the visitor's log as Betsy Peterson and handed the log back to the man. "Thank you so much, dear," she said. "I won't be long."

The guard buzzed the big metal door open and Nan walked in. The hallway was beige and devoid of warmth. The moans of patients floated like howls of ghosts in a haunted house. Human odors invaded Nan's nostrils. A patient shuffled along the hallway clutching the handrail. There was an unoccupied nurse's station at the end of the hallway. Nan did not see Mr. Woods.

She stepped into room 234 and lying on the bed was a gaunt man staring hollowly with his mouth agape. His cheeks were sunken and his hair was strings of gray sticking out at angles. The tiny room smelled like stale urine and the walls felt like they were closing in. Nan took a step into the room; the man didn't blink.

She went back to the hallway and peeked out. The nurse's station was still unoccupied. She sneaked down the hallway and slid inside room 235. A woman in a faded flowered robe with her back to the door sat in a chair gazing out the tiny window at the gray day. Nan could only see the back of her head but she recognized her as Mrs. Wilson. Nan quietly approached. She stopped at a laminated dresser where a photograph in a cheap frame rested. Nan picked it up and examined it. The photo was of a pretty, intelligent-looking woman in her early twenties standing in front of the U.S. Capitol building in Washington, D.C. The young woman wasn't smiling and Nan could see in her eyes, a cold cynicism for someone so young. Nan stared at the photo and the girl stared back. For a split second, Nan had the sensation that the girl was asking Nan to help her.

Nan set the photo back on the dresser and moved to Mrs. Wilson's side. The woman looked up at her and greeted Nan with a slow, sad smile. Nan crouched next to the woman and took off her sunglasses.

The woman's smile slowly dropped. Her eyes grew wide and her mouth opened. She grasped Nan's hand and stared wide-eyed into her face. "I'm Nan Smith from Governor Bloomfield's campaign office," Nan said softly. "You came to see me last week. Do you remember?"

The woman moaned and her eyes grew sadder.

"You called our office and said you have something to show me. What is it?"

The woman's breathing became shallow. Her expression was a combination of hopelessness, desperation and fear. She glanced at the door and then back at Nan. She opened her mouth as if to talk but only squeaks and moans came out. She continued to clutch Nan's hand. She let out a long, low moan and eased back into her chair. She looked out the window again.

Nan glanced over her shoulder at the door and saw no one in the hall. She left the woman's side, went to the door and closed it. She moved to a crouch in front of the woman. "Don't try to talk. Just nod your head 'yes' or 'no'. Okay?"

The woman's breathing eased as she stared beseechingly at Nan.

Nan looked into her face and took her hands. "Do you have something that proves Senator Howard murdered your daughter?"

The woman let out a soft moan. Her head moved but Nan couldn't tell if she had nodded. The woman gazed pitifully into her lap.

Nan moved closer to the woman and tenderly pulled the woman's chin up so their eyes met. "Mrs. Wilson, are you being held here against your will?"

The woman appeared to nod. Then, her face contorted and she began to sob. Nan felt a wave of pity for this poor woman. Anger welled up in her chest.

A man's voice came from the door. "You ain't 'posed to be in here."

Nan jumped to her feet startled and saw that a huge black man dressed in white had opened the door half way and was peering in. He was holding a stack of folded blue bed sheets. "I'm sorry," she said. "I'm just visiting."

"No one 'posed to visit Mrs. Wilson," the man said. He talked slowly with a slight slur.

Nan patted Mrs. Wilson's shoulder and approached the orderly. He recoiled.

"It's okay," she said. "I won't say anything."

"You better leave," the orderly said. "They's comin' back."

Nan pushed the door open and looked out to the hallway. A nurse in a white uniform had taken a seat at the nurse's station and was talking on the phone. Nan slid back into the room, looked at the orderly's nametag. It was big Earl that Hank had mentioned. She smiled at him and asked, "Earl, are you the man who talked to my friend about Mrs. Wilson?"

Earl relaxed a bit. "That skinny guy who was here on Tuesday?"

"Yes, that was him. He said you told him Mrs. Wilson had something. What was it?"

Earl recoiled again. "I ain't 'posed to talk to no one 'bout Mrs. Wilson. I got me in big trouble for that."

"I won't get you in trouble."

"That what your friend say, too. You best be goin', ma'am. They's coming back any minute now."

"Who?" Nan asked. "Mr. Woods?"

Earl's eyes widened as he backed out into the hallway. "I gotta go. Don't talk to me no more. Go away." He scurried down the hall with his stack of sheets and disappeared through a door.

Nan heard a man's voice at the nurse's station. A man in a dark sports coat carrying a Starbuck's coffee cup was joking with the nurse. It was not Mr. Woods. Nan glanced back at Mrs. Wilson who sat slumped in her chair. She stepped out into the hallway, slipped on her dark glasses and walked toward the exit.

The man in the dark sports coat waved at the nurse and headed down the hallway toward Nan. As Nan reached the door to the reception area, the man gave her a long look and then hesitated. She didn't stop as she walked past the guard area and pushed out the front door. She quickened her step, got to Ben's Land Cruiser and climbed in.

As she pulled out of the hospital parking lot, she saw the man watching her from the front door.

THIRTY

"YOUR GUY WAS getting *coffee* and she just waltzed in and talked to the woman?" Frank Pierce asked. "I can't believe it, Woods. I CAN'T FUCKING BELIEVE IT!"

Frank Pierce sat on a Washington, D.C. Mall park bench barely able to contain his anger. Woods was lucky he was a thousand miles away in Minnesota instead of with him in person or Pierce would have inflicted serious bodily harm on the man.

"Are you sure it was Nan Smith?" Pierce asked, trying to keep his composure. "How do you know?"

"We saw her on the security camera. It was her." Woods said. His Alabama accent was thick.

"Weren't you tailing her like I'd told you?" Pierce could feel himself losing control. At any moment, he would go off like a rocket.

"She was driving her husband's car. We got the license plate number when she left and traced it to Ben Smith. He's her husband. She must have swapped cars with him at lunch.

We tailed her Camry to a building in downtown Minneapolis and didn't see she wasn't driving it."

Pierce closed his eyes and the fire in him burned. "You fuckup, Woods. I'm having your neck for this. Do you hear me?"

"We were only gone for five minutes, Frank. She got lucky or we'd have been there. At least we know she was there."

Pierce stared at the top of the Washington Monument in front of him and imagined dropping Woods on top of it skewering him with the point. It would be a mercy killing compared to what Frank was going to do to him.

"Where are you now?" Pierce asked.

"I'm in our room across the hall from Mrs. Wilson." Pierce could hear Woods' voice shake. Good. He should be scared.

Pierce got to his feet and began to pace. "Woods, listen to me very carefully. Do not—I repeat, *do not* let Mrs. Wilson out of your sight and do not—I repeat *do not* lose Nan Smith again either. I am coming to Minnesota to manage the situation myself. I'll be there early tomorrow. Until then, make sure no one talks to Mrs. Wilson. I want you to feed her yourself and change her diapers, tuck her into bed and read her a goddamn bedtime story if you have to. Do not leave her side until I get there. Am I clear?"

"Yeah, Frank. You're clear."

"And, Woods, make sure you know exactly where Nan Smith is at all times. Do not let her give you the slip again. Am I clear?"

"Yeah, Frank. You're clear."

"Good. Now, I need to make what will be a very unpleasant call. I'll probably be asked to meet with our employers in person and they will *not* be happy. All the time I'm doing this, I want you to know I'll be thinking of you."

"I'm really sorry, Frank."

Pierce pressed the 'End Call' button on his phone and marched back to his office. If Nan Smith visited the woman, she knew something. And Pierce had worked for years to prevent anyone from knowing anything about Mrs. Wilson. He was losing containment because of that fuck-up Woods. He should have relieved him years ago. He'd do it tomorrow and send him somewhere Woods would hate and never be able to leave. If Woods quit, Pierce would use his influence to guarantee the best job he'd ever have would be as a low-level, poorly paid security guard.

If only his employers had let him do his job the way he wanted to in the first place, none of this would've happened. Now Pierce would go to Minnesota and take care of Mrs. Wilson like he'd wanted to at the very beginning.

Then, he would turn his attention to Nan Smith.

THIRTY-ONE

NAN DIDN'T HEAR from Boston until she got home from the office late. Jenny was getting ready for bed and Ben had cooked stir-fry that was waiting for Nan in the wok. Before she could eat, Bob Hilton's assistant called her on her cell phone and said Governor Bloomfield and Hilton were coming to Minnesota the next day so the governor could have breakfast with Senator Howard in the hospital to show unity against the terrorist. "It plays into Howard's hand," the assistant said, "but we have no choice." The assistant told Nan that they'd scheduled a press conference after the breakfast and Hilton wanted Nan to attend. Nan agreed to be there.

After the call, Nan ate and tried to relax. But she couldn't force out of her mind the picture of Mrs. Wilson's daughter standing in front of the Capitol building. Mrs. Wilson clearly wanted to tell Nan something but she wasn't able to. And it looked like she was being held against her will. Why? And what about Earl? It felt like he knew something.

Nan shook her head to try to clear her thoughts. She'd have to put it all out of her mind until after Bloomfield's press conference. She spent some time with Jenny and saw her to bed. With Jenny in bed, Ben asked Nan how it went at the hospital. Nan told him that Mrs. Wilson was unable to talk and she learned nothing. However, she didn't tell him her suspicions. After a while, she and Ben went to bed.

*

The next morning, she rose early, showered and put on her best business dress. She was careful to get just the right professional look with her hair and makeup. She said goodbye to Ben and Jenny and drove to the IDS center in downtown Minneapolis. She made her way inside to the Crystal Court atrium. Hilton's assistant had said she should wait there for a call, so Nan sat on a white bench next to the seven-story waterfall and waited. The waterfall splashed noisily behind her and business people with briefcases hurriedly crossed the court in front of her.

She saw reporters and some paparazzi hovering outside the entrance to the Marquette hotel inside the atrium. They were ready to pounce on anyone who could give them even the tiniest bit of information about the assassination attempt on Senator Howard. Nan knew they were just doing their jobs, but it was important to handle them correctly. They could break a candidate by twisting a story or publishing an innocuous phrase out of context. Handling the media was part of the game and she'd better get used to it. If she became the White House Communications Director, it'd be a game she'd have to play every day.

Her phone rang and she answered. It was Bob Hilton. "Nan, where are you?" He spoke faster than usual.

"I'm in the atrium outside the hotel."

"Good. We are on our way back from the hospital. We've set up a press conference in the St. Croix conference room. Third floor. I've cleared you. Give your name to the Secret Service agent in the lobby. He'll let you through. See you in five minutes." Hilton hung up.

Nan pushed her way through the paparazzi to the hotel lobby and approached two Secret Service agents guarding the elevators. She gave them her name, showed her driver's license and one of the guards escorted her into the elevator. He took an elevator security key out of his pocket and put it in the control panel. He punched the button for the third floor and stepped off the elevator leaving Nan alone. "You'll need to show your I.D. to the agent on the third floor, ma'am," the agent said. The elevator doors closed and when they opened again, two more agents stopped her. She showed her I.D. to an agent with close-cropped hair and a serious expression as the other waved a metal-detecting wand over her. When they were satisfied, the short-haired agent escorted her to the St. Croix meeting room. "Sorry for the extra precautions, ma'am," the agent said as they walked. "The assassination attempt has us on high alert." He pointed to a door, guarded by yet another agent. "Please don't exit this room until after the governor leaves. Understand?"

"Yes," Nan replied and stepped into the room.

The St. Croix meeting room was packed. It appeared that the press corps from every major news organization in the country was there. Facing the podium at one end of the room, fifty people tinkered with cameras, video cameras, recorders and lights. Reporters holding notepads and pens huddled together, talking seriously. Secret Service agents with busy eyes lined the room.

Nan spotted Bloomfield's assistant campaign manager Jamal Brown standing against a wall trying to look inconspicuous. She walked over to him as the reporters sized her up to see if she was someone they might want to talk to later. She put out a hand for Jamal.

"Nan," he said with a sigh as he shook her hand. "Glad you could make it through the mob. What a circus, eh?"

"That's for sure."

"The governor and Hilton will be here soon. George will give a short speech. Then we'll head to the governor's suite and talk in private."

"What's the latest on Howard?" Nan asked.

"He'll be released from the hospital over the weekend, maybe even tomorrow. He'll be confined to his home for a few days and will be campaigning by midweek. That's one week before the election," Jamal said, shaking his head. "Just enough time to make a heroic tour of the country."

"You sound cynical," Nan said.

Jamal looked askance at Nan. "I am."

Before he could say anything more, the door to the meeting room flung open and Governor Bloomfield's entourage, led by Bob Hilton, barged in. The governor stood inches higher than the rest. Two Secret Service men stood on either side of him.

The media mobbed the entourage and shouted questions at the governor. Bloomfield waved them off and stepped to the lectern. Hilton spotted Nan and Jamal and motioned them to join him on the podium. Nan moved over and stood next to Hilton in front of a dozen television cameras pointed at the governor. Bloomfield cleared his throat and made a short speech about his breakfast with Senator Howard. He said he thought Senator Howard looked good for a man who had been shot the day before and was looking forward to doing battle with him when he recovered. He said despite political differences, Americans needed to stand together against enemies of the country. "And I hope," the governor concluded, "that when Senator Howard fully recovers, we can still have at least one debate to discuss the issues important to America. Thank you."

Nan watched from behind and could see the governor no longer had the stature of a front-runner. He couldn't overcome the fact Howard had taken a bullet for the country and everyone's attention was now firmly on the senator, not him. Bloomfield could not take the offensive on a single issue and he had no good defense for his moderate stand on terrorism. He looked like a man who had been checkmated just when he thought he would win the match.

As the governor stepped away from the lectern, the reporters shouted questions about his stand on terrorism. The governor refused to answer. He and the entourage, including Nan, marched out of the meeting room. They shoved into an elevator guarded by a Secret Service man. The elevator doors closed leaving the shouting reporters behind. Someone pushed the button for the 18th floor. In the quiet of the elevator, Hilton said, "Good job, Governor."

After a moment of silence the governor said, "It was a mistake to mention the debate. As soon as I said it, I knew it was a mistake."

He was right. Nan had thought so during the speech. Pushing for a debate was like challenging a wounded soldier to a fight. All he needed to do was show up, wince in pain a little, and he'd win no matter how well he did. Nan felt a pang of guilt for suggesting the debates the week before in Boston.

The elevator doors opened and the group followed Bloomfield to his suite. The governor made a beeline for the bathroom and Hilton took Nan aside and pointed her to the couch. "Once I clear the rest of these people out of here, you, the governor and I need to talk about what we do now," he said gravely. "I'm especially interested in what you've been telling us about Sheldon Hanrahan."

Sheldon Hanrahan. Nan took a seat on the couch. She hadn't heard much about Sheldon since Betty Morris told her the national committee was running Howard's campaign.

Apparently, Sheldon Hanrahan was more involved than Betty Morris thought.

THIRTY-TWO

SOMETHING HAD JUST CHANGED between Silvia and Ellen. For the first time in nine months, Ellen had taken charge of the sex. Until now, Silvia had always been in control and Ellen was the submissive one. Not today. As soon as Ellen came in the room at the Capitol Hilton, she pushed Silvia onto the bed and took over.

At first, Silvia wasn't sure she liked what Ellen was doing to her, but eventually she let go and was surprised how much she enjoyed it. But she was uncomfortable with what the change might mean to their relationship. She needed Ellen for inside information about what was happening at the White House and she needed to be in control.

After Silvia's shuddering orgasm, she lay on her back in the silky sheets while Ellen leaned on an elbow facing her. They didn't say anything for a long time. Finally, Silvia said, "That was different."

"You seemed to like it—a lot," Ellen cooed.

Silvia slowly broke into a broad smile. "I wouldn't mind doing it again sometime."

Ellen flopped back onto her pillow and giggled.

"I'm glad you could get away," Silvia said, trying not think about how much she enjoyed what Ellen had just done to her. "With everything going on, it must have been hard."

"I'll say there's a lot going on," Ellen said. "The assassination attempt sure has made things exciting."

"What does the White House make of it? Are there any theories?"

Ellen pulled the sheet around her neck. "The FBI is backing the terrorist angle."

"Really? Because the big question everyone's asking is how the shooter knew Howard would be at that place at that time. He'd have to be tipped off."

Ellen smiled at the ceiling. "I'll tell you what, my little Mexican girlfriend, do you want a scoop? I'll give you one strictly off the record."

Silvia quickly rolled over to Ellen. "What is it? Tell me."

Ellen faced Silvia and they were like two teenage girls about to share juicy gossip about the head cheerleader. "The shooter knew because Howard's detailed schedule was on the Internet."

"¡No me digas!" Silvia exclaimed. "On the Internet?"

"On Howard's website. It was buried deep in the site but it was there. Can you believe it?"

"What an incredible screw up. Are you sure?"

"I saw the FBI report this morning," Ellen said. "It'll be released later this afternoon. We're trying to formulate a position for the press."

"So the terrorist just needed to jump on Howard's *website* to see where he would be? Mother Mary."

Ellen rolled onto her back. "You can bet heads will roll in Howard's national party when the report comes out."

"Why them?"

"Because, they're managing Howard's website. Ever since Howard came into the race, Peter Gray has been running the show. And for some inexplicable reason, they thought it'd be a good idea to put Howard's schedule on his website."

"*Idiotas*. They're lucky he wasn't killed. The report will come out this afternoon? This isn't much of a scoop."

"I'll tell you what isn't in the report, my dear. Again, off the record."

"Understood. Off the record."

"The person who had the brilliant idea to post Howard's schedule was none other than Peter Gray himself."

Silvia sat up on the bed with her legs crossed under her. "You're kidding? The chairman is responsible?"

Ellen flashed a devious grin. "Yep. Peter Gray sent an e-mail to the webmaster telling him to publish Howard's itinerary on the website. He thought voters would find it interesting to see what a presidential candidate's schedule looks like. The Secret Service would have squashed the idea if they had known about it, but they didn't think to ask. They probably thought no one would be so stupid to do it in the first place."

"What a screw-up. Do you think it will hurt Howard's chances?"

"No. The party will take the hit. Howard wasn't their candidate coming out of the primaries so it'll look like he's a victim of the party's stupidity. He won't be blamed."

"And now he'll probably win the election," Silvia said shaking her head. "I wonder if President Dougherty really thought he'd win when he endorsed him."

Ellen looked up at Silvia who was kneeling on the bed. Silvia could see her naked body had an effect on the senior aide to the White House press secretary. Silvia moved her hands between her own legs. She met Ellen's eyes and smiled suggestively. Ellen's mouth opened slightly.

"You never told me why President Dougherty endorsed Howard," Silvia said. "You told me someone made him do it but I haven't found out who. Do you know?"

Ellen held her gaze on Silvia. "I know some things."

Silvia moved her hands further between her legs as Ellen watched. "What can you tell me?"

"I shouldn't tell you anything."

"Come on, Ellen. You won't be sorry, *mamacita*. Powerful men with powerful secrets—you have history with that. Tell me what the president is hiding."

"I can't."

Silvia stopped what she was doing to herself and turned away. "Damn it Ellen, quit leading me on. You've as much told me something is going on and I need to know what it is. I don't have any other leads and my editor wants me to drop the story. You're my only chance."

"Listen to me, Silvia," Ellen said. "I don't know the whole story and I don't want to know because if I did and if I told you, it'd put both of us in danger. I have only a few months left on this job and I'd just as soon not get in any trouble, understand?"

"Like you said, you'll be out of a job at the White House soon. What do you care?"

"Because it involves more than the White House."

"Really?" Silvia said. "So it must be big. Just tell me what you know and leave the rest to me."

"And then what? You'll start digging around and they'll start investigating you and they'll find out about our little liaisons here. Then, I won't be able to get a job anywhere."

Silvia said, "I'll be discreet. I always have been."

Ellen shook her head. "You don't know what you're up against."

"Then tell me. Let me handle it. I promise I won't get you in trouble."

"I can't," Ellen said.

Silvia left the bed and started to dress. "I have to get back," she said, angrily. "Thanks for the scoop on Gray. I'll be discreet about that, as always."

Ellen sighed and lay back on the pillow. She looked sad, almost as if she was about to cry and Silvia's anger cooled. She stopped dressing and sat on the bed again. After a long silence, Silvia said, "In January, after you leave the White House, I still want to see you." She was surprised at her words and even more surprised that she meant what she said.

Ellen didn't respond and Silvia stood up and pulled on her dress. She went to the mirror and brushed her hair.

Ellen lay on the bed watching her. "There's a big cover-up," she said finally.

"What? What are you talking about?"

"I'm talking about why Dougherty endorsed Howard. It involves sex and a big cover-up."

Silvia stood at the end of the bed and stared at Ellen. "What do you mean?"

"Sex. You know, sex, like what you and I do in this hotel room. Dougherty was having sex with someone he shouldn't have and someone found out and that's why the president endorsed Senator Howard."

"How do you know?"

"Because of the way the whole affair was handled. It happened five years ago, and all of us in the White House knew it involved something personal with the president.

Richard Craft held a bunch of closed-door meetings and there was that cold, nervousness you see in a situation like that. Months later, through the grapevine, we learned it was about an affair the president had."

"An affair?" Silvia said. "Dougherty?"

"I don't know who it was with or what happened but it went away and never resurfaced until last week. Craft was at it again and the feel around the White House was the same as back then. The other night I was working late and I overheard Craft talking to someone about 'the girl and the president'. I heard the word 'blackmail'. I hurried away because I didn't want to know anything more. And frankly, I don't think you do either."

"Who's involved?"

Ellen returned Silvia's stare. "I got the sense that the cover-up involves more than just the president."

Silvia raised her palm. "This is huge, Ellen. I need to do something with it."

Ellen shook her head. "What will you do? Do you think you can crack the secrecy? They've covered up the whole affair for five years. There are a lot of people working to keep it quiet. Forget it, Silvia. You're in over your head. You'll never learn anything."

"You know about it, and now I do too."

"We don't know anything," Ellen said with a flash of her eyes. "And we never will." Ellen nodded toward the door. "You better get back."

Silvia slipped on her shoes and said no more. Ellen lay on her back and pulled the sheets up over her shoulders. She was expressionless and for the first time since they'd been seeing each other, Ellen didn't ask Silvia when she would see her again. It made Silvia sad and she wondered if she'd fallen in love with Ellen.

As Silvia walked back to the *Sentinel,* she wondered how big the cover-up really was. *'I got the sense that the cover-up involves more than just the president,'* Ellen had said. If it was true, it'd be a huge story, the one that would set Silvia up for life. But Ellen was probably right that she wouldn't be able to penetrate a cover-up like this. And Ian and Brad Schwartzman gave her clear orders to drop the story.

But this, this was a cover-up involving the president of the United States. She knew she couldn't let it go.

THIRTY-THREE

IT TOOK ONLY a few minutes for Hilton to clear the suite.
Bob Hilton was in charge and when he gave an order, people
obeyed. Nan sat on the couch and watched the governor's
election staff leave. They shot looks at her, wondering why
she'd been invited to stay.

When the room was empty, Governor Bloomfield came
out of the bathroom with his tie pulled loose. In New York,
at the television commercial shoot, the governor was leading
the election race by seven points and was genial and happy.
Now, he was solemn. He took a chair from the table, turned it
backward and sat facing Nan with his arms folded on the
back of the chair. He towered over her. Hilton took off his
suit coat, grabbed a notepad and pen and sat in an
upholstered chair.

Hilton spoke first in his rapid-fire staccato. He told Nan
that they were losing the race. The overnight poll showed that
Howard was now leading by seven points. The experts were
telling them that Howard's numbers would go up when they
started hammering away on the terrorism issue, and then

they'd go up again when he got back on the campaign trail.
They'd been in planning meetings all night, Hilton said, and
they were getting conflicting advice from their pollsters,
consultants, their own party—everyone. It was no longer
politics as usual and they wanted Nan's opinion on how
Sheldon Hanrahan might respond to their new plans.

Nan looked from Hilton to the governor. "I thought the
national party was running Howard's campaign. Why do you
care about Sheldon Hanrahan?"

The governor didn't take his eyes off Nan. "We believe
Mr. Hanrahan is more involved than we thought," he said,
simply.

"Everything's changed, Nan," Hilton said. "The debates
are off. Too bad because they'd have iced it for us. Betty
Morris recommended we push to reschedule one the week
before the election, but we couldn't win it, not now. If
George won the debate—and he would—it'd look like he was
beating up on Howard while he's down. It'd be a disaster.

"We also have to pull our commercials off the air,"
Hilton continued. "The message is all wrong now. Even
Springfield's *Coming Home*, doesn't work anymore. Basically,
we're starting from scratch with one week left."

"And we're behind," Bloomfield said.

Hilton pushed himself to the edge of his chair. "Nan, last
Saturday you briefed me about the senate campaign you ran
for Janice Theilen. You told me about the negative ads and
dirty tricks. We have to use those tactics now that we're
behind. We want to know how you think Hanrahan will
react."

"Negative ads?" Nan asked. "Dirty tricks?"

"Yes," Hilton said. "Attack ads, push polls, scare tactics,
half-truths if we have to."

Nan leaned forward. "We're not going to do anything illegal, are we?"

Hilton stood, tossed his pad and pen on the coffee table and began pacing the room. "Illegal? What's illegal? There are a lot of gray areas in the election laws, Nan. You bet we'll take advantage of them. Anyway, what does it matter? The Federal Election Commission is a bunch of self-important bureaucrats sitting on their butts in Washington. They're toothless. Candidates get away with anything. The FEC rarely prosecutes, and when they do, it's after the election. Convictions, if they happen, usually result in small fines. The FEC has never forced a major candidate from office for a violation. Ever."

"So, you're saying we're ignoring the FEC regulations?"

"I'm saying we're going to do what it takes to win."

"Including things that are illegal," Nan said.

Hilton stopped pacing and glared at Nan. "As I said, there's that gray area."

Nan recalled the letterhead that Jim had found and the letter discovered by CBS News exposing Howard's extremism. On the news last night, Howard's election staff had denied ever sending the letter. She reached into her briefcase and pulled out the Howard campaign letterhead that Jim had found. She showed it to Hilton and the governor. "What was Rex Starkey doing with this in our offices last week?" she asked.

Hilton looked at the letterhead and said, "I don't know anything about this. But if that's what it takes."

It was Nan's turn to glare at Hilton. "So it's going to be Watergate all over again?"

"Look, Nan," Hilton said firmly, "dirty tricks and smear campaigns have been part of presidential elections for over two hundred years. You know that. And the Watergate laws didn't stop it. They're still done in every election. We'll do them too."

"I don't like it," Nan said, folding her arms. "I don't want to work for that kind of campaign."

Bloomfield hadn't taken his eyes off Nan. Before Hilton could continue, he put up a hand to stop him. "I understand," the governor said softly. "I didn't want to run that kind of campaign either but what choice do we have? Ask yourself, Nan, what's best for the country. Do you really want William Howard to be president? Would you feel you'd done the right thing if Sheldon Hanrahan and his mob ran the country? It would destroy this great nation and I, for one, am willing to do anything to prevent that from happening. What about you?"

Nan sunk back into the couch. She envisioned America run by Sheldon Hanrahan and the prospect disgusted her. Governor Bloomfield was right; they had to prevent Howard from winning. And if it took a dirty campaign....

She looked at Hilton and then the governor. "Let's not trash the U.S. Constitution in the process."

"Let's save the country from people who we know would," Hilton said, picking up his pad and pen and returning to his chair. "Now, please, how do you think Sheldon Hanrahan will respond?"

Nan nodded. Then she reminded them that Sheldon Hanrahan was the most skilled marketer she'd ever seen, and that he is ruthless. She told them that he has vast resources and a very strong will.

Nan raised a palm. "So, what will he do when we go negative? If we hook onto something that threatens Howard, he'll come after us hard. And I mean, he'll hit you harder than you've ever been hit, Governor. If you smear Howard, Sheldon Hanrahan will smear you worse. It'll be like a boxing match. If you want to win, you have to be willing to take some heavy punches."

"I'm willing," the governor said.

"As I've said before," Nan said, "Sheldon has played this game in the corporate world for decades. He's buried many of his client's *Fortune* 500 competitors with much bigger budgets and lower ethics than we apparently have. If we start a negative, dirty campaign, I believe he'll bury us, too."

Hilton hunched forward, looking defeated. Bloomfield sat motionless watching Nan.

Nan continued. "But when you think about it, he doesn't have to use a negative campaign or dirty tricks. He can stay on the high road with Howard looking like a hero. If we come at him with attack ads, his best option would be to play the martyr and make us look like bullies."

"We know," Hilton said. "We have to be very careful."

"So you want to know how I think Sheldon Hanrahan will respond to a negative campaign." Nan asked. "He'll leverage the public's distaste for negative campaigns against us and make us look bad. Which leaves us with very few good options."

"That is correct," Hilton replied. "We have very few options."

Nan looked at Hilton and then at the governor again. What a difference a few days made. In New York, they were sitting on a seven-point lead and hobnobbing with movie stars and Hollywood directors. Now they were underdogs without answers to how to win the race. It was a recipe for defeat by a landslide.

She thought for a second about telling Hilton and Bloomfield about Mrs. Wilson's accusation and what she and Hank had learned. But there were too many questions and if Nan brought it up, it would put her on the dirty side. She decided to keep it to herself.

"Thanks, Nan," Hilton said. "We have to get the governor back to Boston. We'll have new campaign plans to you soon."

Hilton and the governor rose but Nan stayed seated. All the talk about dirty tricks and smear campaigns made her remember Sorrea's encrypted computer files, Rex's locked desk drawers and Hank's note warning her they were being watched. "I have to ask a question," she said. "Is anyone doing anything illegal in my office?"

"Illegal?" Hilton responded "Like what?"

"You know what I mean, Bob. Are they bugging our phones? Are you reading our e-mails, opening our letters? Am I being followed? What are those three doing in my office that has to be kept such a big secret?"

The governor glanced at Hilton. "Ah, I have to wash up before we leave. Thanks for your help, Nan." He quickly disappeared into the bedroom.

Hilton glowered at Nan. "This is a presidential election, Nan. There's a lot going on that you don't know about. As I've said, Rex, Tom and Sorrea report to me."

"You're not answering my question," Nan said.

"I'm not obliged to answer your question," Hilton replied.

"Okay, then let me put it this way. If you are bugging my phones or reading my e-mail or doing anything illegal in my office, stop it immediately if you want my support."

Hilton's face softened. He sat again. "Nan, look, we need you. We can't afford to lose any of our senior staff or it will look like people are jumping ship. You're visible here in Minnesota. If you leave, the press would get a hold of it and it'd hurt us."

Nan rose, picked up her purse and headed to the door. "I'm still with you, Bob," she said as she left the room. "Just don't do anything illegal in my office."

As Nan left the room and walked back to her car, she felt unclean. She hated the dirty campaign Sheldon Hanrahan ran two years ago to defeat Janice Theilen. Now, the roles were reversed and she'd be the one helping to run the dirty campaign. She'd told Hilton she was with him but if the campaign got too ugly, she'd have to reconsider.

And then she would have to worry about a country under the control of Sheldon Hanrahan.

THIRTY-FOUR

"WHAT'S THE PROBLEM, PETER?" Sheldon Hanrahan asked from behind the desk of his glass and steel office. The midday sun poured through the floor-to-ceiling windows and Sheldon wore his dark glasses to protect his eyes. "We've had a fourteen point jump overnight. There's never been anything like it in U.S. election history. Ever."

"I don't understand. I never sent this e-mail," Peter Gray said, shaking his head.

"It appears that you did. It's addressed from you and they traced it to your laptop. You must have written it. There's no other explanation."

"But I didn't," The Chairman moaned. "I wouldn't."

Hapless. That was the word that Sheldon had for Peter. He was an incompetent fool that Sheldon might have pitied if The Chairman wasn't such a pompous ass. As is, Sheldon felt it was his duty to make sure this weak, arrogant man would never hold a position of power. The human race depended on it. The strong must survive. The hapless, destroyed.

The Chairman sat on Sheldon's couch holding a printout of an e-mail that the *Washington, D.C. Sentinel* had discovered the day before. The e-mail from Gray ordered the webmaster to post Howard's detailed itinerary on the website. Apparently, the webmaster had complied which explained how the terrorists knew exactly where Senator Howard would be when they tried to assassinate him.

"I'm telling you, Sheldon. I never sent it. It has to be a setup. That fucking prick webmaster is in on it, too. He leaked this goddamn e-mail and then resigned. Last I heard, he's in Barbados or something."

"Saint Lucia," Sheldon said. "I suppose it's possible that it's a setup. The FBI has established that the Mohamed Fazul faction of Al-Qaeda attempted the assassination. Do you think they sent the e-mail to set you up?"

Gray shook his head. "I don't know. Maybe. But it doesn't explain how it came from my computer. They would've had to have access to it."

Sheldon nodded. "Yes, that is a mystery. Are you sure you didn't send it? You've been very busy running the campaign. Perhaps you were tired and don't remember."

"Look, Sheldon," Peter said, slapping the e-mail on the coffee table, "I wouldn't do such a stupid thing. The idea never even crossed my mind."

"I see," said Sheldon. "Well, the good news is Bill Howard is going to win the election. The debates have been called off so all we have to do is manage him properly and we should win by a landslide."

Gray jumped to his feet and started pacing the room. "I don't care about the goddamn election. I need to get to the bottom of this fucking e-mail to clear my name."

"Yes you do. You work on that while I take over the campaign." Sheldon said.

"You'll take over? No, no. I have the team in D.C. We can still run Howard's campaign."

"You're not hearing me, Peter," Sheldon replied. "I said I'm taking over the campaign. I already have plans in place. We have new commercials ready to shoot. Newspaper ads and an online campaign ready to go. I have a new public relations plan and have rescheduled the senator's travels to accommodate his recovery."

Gray glanced at Sheldon from the couch. "You've done all of that in one day? How could you so soon after Howard was shot? It's been only two days."

Sheldon smiled. "It's my job, Peter. We change plans quickly for my business clients. This is no different. In fact, we've already begun to implement the new plans."

"You can't do that," Gray said. "You can't change things without my approval. You should've told me. You have to go through my staff in Washington, D.C."

"I don't need your staff in Washington D.C."

"Sheldon, damn it, we have the best pollsters, media analysts, online experts and consultants—everybody—already under contract. You have to use them. You agreed."

Sheldon glowered through his thick, dark glasses and his blood turned cold. He despised the man sitting in front of him telling him what to do. Gray had no idea how he'd had to suffer and how it had prepared him for this very moment.

It was time for Sheldon to take over.

"Your pollsters, Peter?" Sheldon said. "Your consultants? You want me to use your people—the ones who have done nothing since you took over except watch as Howard's numbers plummeted?" Sheldon rose from his desk and paced the room. His six foot four inch frame towered over Peter Gray.

"Why would I want to use your people, Peter? You and the party force candidates to use your so-called experts. To get your endorsement, a candidate has to hire your consultants and use your pollsters. To tap into your funds they have to use your media analysts, direct mail and marketing people. You and the rest of Election Incorporated don't care if your candidates win. You'd rather lose an election than give up control. You're only concerned about your own self-preservation and taking money from candidates and the people who contribute to them. You're all craven and narrow-minded and would be miserable failures in nearly any other field."

Sheldon stopped in front of Peter Gray. "No, Peter. I refuse to use your people. I refuse to use people who don't care about winning and who wouldn't have enough skill to land even a junior position in any one of my firms."

Peter pushed himself to the edge of the couch and tapped his finger on the coffee table. "We get people elected," he protested. "We have a high-winning percentage."

"A high winning percentage?" Sheldon scoffed. "With only two candidates in each election, someone flipping a coin can do as well. In the business world, your winning percentage would put you in bankruptcy very quickly. Besides, the incumbent wins over ninety percent of elections. You re-elect incumbents because it's easy and they're already obligated to you. It's a sham, Peter. You and the election system are nothing more than an inside-the-beltway collection of fakes, racketeers and false scientists. It's a colossal scam and I will not be scammed by you. I'm taking over the campaign and, if you stick with me, you and your party will be winners in November. But you will not run this campaign."

"You agreed to let me run it, Sheldon," Peter said.

Sheldon returned to his desk, leaned back in his chair. "I don't agree anymore. And you're not in a position to fight me on this, Peter. Not now. Not with this e-mail scandal hanging over your head."

The chairman drew a deep breath. "That goddamn e-mail. I just don't understand how it could have come from my computer. It's dated a week ago last Friday. Let's see... I was here in Minneapolis to announce the Party endorsement. As a matter of fact, I was right here in these offices with my laptop. I couldn't have possibly sent it. I was in meetings with you all day."

Sheldon gazed down upon Peter from his desk. "Yes," he said, "you were."

"I just don't get it." Peter shook his head. Then he looked at Sheldon. Slowly, his expression changed to shock. "You. *You!*" Peter pointed a finger at Sheldon. "*You* sent the e-mail from my computer."

"Really, Peter. Why would I do such a thing?"

"To set me up, that's why! You set me up!"

Sheldon shrugged. "Set you up? How? How could I have anticipated an assassination attempt by terrorists?"

Peter thought a moment and sat back. "I don't know. You couldn't, of course. Unless..." Peter sat motionless on the couch while his mind worked. After a few seconds, his eyes grew wide and he stared at Sheldon. "My god... Oh *my god!* You did it. You planned this whole thing and you set me up to take the fall! You orchestrated the assassination attempt, didn't you?"

Sheldon folded his arms across his chest, fixed his eyes on the chairman through his dark glasses. He didn't answer.

Peter jumped to his feet. His breathing was fast. "Tell me you didn't do it. Tell me, Sheldon, that you did not do it!"

"Peter," Sheldon replied evenly, "get a hold of yourself. Think about what you're saying—how it would appear to the public. The FBI has already concluded the assassination was attempted by Al-Qaeda. If you come out with this... this unbelievable accusation, people would think you'd gone completely mad. You, the esteemed party chairman, certainly don't want that."

"I have to clear my name and if that means I have to bring you down with me, I will."

Sheldon let a few seconds pass. "I see. Well, Peter, now that I think about it, I remember you mentioned putting Senator Howard's itinerary on the website. I tried to talk you out of it but you insisted. Yes, that's what I'll have to tell the press if they ask. Maybe I should volunteer the information to keep my own name clean."

"You son-of-a-bitch! Don't you dare! I didn't say that and you know it."

"Perhaps you're right. Perhaps I am mistaken. But the important question is, what will people believe? It would be your word against mine."

Gray stood in front of the couch and blinked at Sheldon.

"Sit down, Mr. Chairman," Sheldon said softly. "Take a deep breath and listen to me." Peter did as he was told.

"I will help you with your e-mail problem. My people can spin your response so it will go away quickly with the least amount of damage to your reputation. You will be able to retain your chairmanship and you'll be just fine. And, in less than two weeks, you and your party will have retained control of the White House. And you will continue to be a very important person in Washington."

Peter Gray didn't respond for some time. Finally he said, "This is insane."

"It's the right thing to do, Mr. Chairman," Sheldon said.

After another long pause, Peter looked up. "Is there any way we can make it look like I didn't send the e-mail?"

Sheldon left his desk and took a seat in the chair next to Peter. "We can certainly cast doubt about it. You should continue to deny sending the e-mail. Be evasive. My people have already drawn up a formal statement for you. You'll come away from this relatively unscathed. You just need to let me handle everything. Understand?"

Peter looked at his feet and nodded.

"Good, good." Sheldon placed a hand on the chairman's shoulder and smiled. "Just think. In two weeks, we'll celebrate William Howard's victory together and you will be the hero of your party."

"Yes, that will be good," Peter said without looking up.

Sheldon glanced at his watch. "Mr. Chairman, you're running late for your flight back to Washington. I'll have my driver take you."

Peter Gray quietly rose from the couch, collected his briefcase and headed to the door while Sheldon followed. "Get that statement to me right away," Gray said.

"Absolutely. You'll have it the moment you land in Washington, Mr. Chairman."

Peter paused at the office door and looked at Sheldon. Sheldon looked at him without emotion. Then Chairman Peter Gray turned and said nothing as he made his way toward the elevators.

THIRTY-FIVE

NAN DIDN'T GO to her car from the IDS parking ramp after her meeting with Bob Hilton and Governor Bloomfield. Instead, she walked from the Marquette Hotel to the warehouse district and Ben's office on the eighth floor of a renovated warehouse building. She hoped Ben didn't have a meeting so they could go for a walk and talk.

When Nan stepped into the wood-beamed lobby of the Jacob and Marin Advertising agency, Julie, sitting behind a black marble reception desk, greeted her with a warm smile. "Mrs. Smith! Ben didn't tell me to expect you."

"He didn't know," Nan replied. "Is he available?"

"I'll see. Just a minute." Julie pressed some buttons on her telephone console and after a few seconds, said, "Your wife is here to see you.... Five minutes...? I'll tell her."

Julie smiled again. "He's in a meeting but he said he can wrap it up in five minutes." Julie pointed to a lobby chair. "Have a seat. Can I get you some coffee or water?"

"No thank you, Julie," Nan answered.

Nan pretended to read a magazine while she waited. She kept running over the meeting she'd just had with Bob Hilton and Governor Bloomfield. She'd agreed to help with the campaign, but wondered about her decision. She agreed because the prospects of a country led by Sheldon Hanrahan and his cronies through their puppet president Bill Howard was more troubling than being involved in a negative, dirty campaign. Still, it was a choice between two evils. The type of campaign Bob Hilton was about to run was politics at its very worst and it reflected badly on Bloomfield and the country as a whole.

As she sat in the lobby of Ben's agency, she wondered if she had agreed to help Hilton for selfish reasons, too. Over the past two months, her modest paycheck had enabled her and Ben to make ends meet and stop dipping into Jenny's college savings. And if Hilton found a way to win the election, she might become the White House Director of Communications. Then she and Ben would be set for life. Ben could sell the agency and his troubles would be over. They would have a status and privilege most Americans only dreamed of.

After a few minutes, Ben came into the reception area. He wore a white, cotton shirt and an artsy tie she'd given him for his birthday. He looked both professional and creative. "Nan," he said, "imagine my joy at having my lovely wife here to brighten my day."

"You're full of it," Nan smiled. "I'm intruding and you know it. I do like the flattery, however."

"You're never an intrusion. Anyway, I could use a break. What's up?"

Nan stood and nodded toward the elevators. "Can you take a walk with me? I need to talk."

"Of course. Julie," Ben said over his shoulder, "I'll be back in an hour."

They left the warehouse and walked a block to the nearest building connected to the skyway system. The lunch hour rush had just begun and people stood in lines at fast food counters or sat on benches reading newspapers. People wearing running shoes power-walked, talking loudly to companions as they huffed through the skyways.

"So, what's on your mind?" Ben asked. "How did the press conference go this morning?"

"It went well. It was the meeting after that I'm concerned about."

"Oh?" Ben said, looking sideways at Nan. "Tell me about it."

Nan stepped aside to let a power-walker by. "Maybe we should find a quiet place."

"Good idea. I know where. The Midwest Savings atrium."

The Midwest Savings atrium was a seven-block walk and Ben and Nan said little on the way. The skyway ended at the Midwest Savings building and there were only a few people in the atrium. The atrium was three stories high with a shallow pond in the center surrounded by granite benches and tropical plants and trees. There were small private spaces with a single bench where people could read or eat lunch. It was quiet and smelled slightly musty, like a greenhouse.

They took a seat on one of the granite benches. "Sorry to take you away from work," Nan said.

"It was a blessing. We were going over projections for the fourth quarter. We'll have to make more layoffs if things don't turn around soon."

"I'm sorry, Hon. You have troubles at work and I'm creating more problems because of this damn election."

Ben took Nan's hand. "Nan, stop apologizing. It's all good. So tell me, what's going on?"

Nan squeezed Ben's hand. Then she told him about her meeting with Hilton and Governor Bloomfield and how they were taking the campaign negative with attack ads, dirty tricks—anything they think they could get away with. She said she wondered if they planted the letter to the American Conservative Union about Howard's extremist stand on terrorism.

"You think *they* did that?" Ben asked with a raised eyebrow. "Aren't there laws against those sorts of things?"

"Yes there are, but they aren't enforced," Nan said. "The Federal Election Commission is woefully ineffective. Hilton will be able to do most anything and I agreed to help."

"Why?"

Nan paused for a few seconds. "For us. For Jenny."

Ben looked out at the atrium. "I see," he said.

Nan faced him. "Can you imagine what would happen if Sheldon Hanrahan and his gang ran America? Democracy would be gone. We'd be a country run by a few extremists who don't care about the Constitution. And the more power they get, the harder it will be to break their grip. I don't want Jenny to come into adulthood in a world like that."

"Me neither," Ben said.

"There's something else. I suppose I'm being selfish, but if Hilton figures out a way to win, I'd probably be the new White House Communications Director."

Ben folded his arms and leaned back on the bench. "And I'd sell the agency and we'd be set. But you're opposed to dirty campaigns. You refused to go negative two years ago in the Theilen campaign."

"Yeah, I did. And we lost."

"Okay, then what're you going to do?"

Nan shook her head. "I don't know. What do you think?"

Ben paused, took in a deep breath. "I think things have a way of working out. I don't believe that Sheldon will get away with hijacking the country. And if the system is broken like you say, it's up to ordinary citizens like us to fix it."

Between the greenery of the atrium, Nan watched a couple on a bench making out. Nan sidled up to Ben and he threw an arm around her. "You're right. The system is broken. I should help fix it."

"It seems to me it's your highest priority."

"My highest priority," Nan sighed. "My highest priority is you and Jenny. If I quit, we'll have to borrow against our savings and the pressure will be on you again."

"Nan, don't worry about it. We'll figure something out. And, if you quit your job, you can stay home and cook."

Nan laughed. "I suppose you want me in a dress and heels when you get home, too."

"That short, low-cut black thing I like. Wear that one."

"We have a daughter at home, remember."

"Yes, we do. And the best thing for her is to do what we can to fix the system, Nan. Standing up against a dirty election could be a first step."

"You might be right," Nan said.

"Is there anything else I can do for you Mrs. Smith?"

Nan smiled, then looked at her feet. "There is one more thing. I'm haunted by Mrs. Wilson. What if she's being held against her will?"

Ben glared at Nan. "Nan, I've said it before. If you think there's something illegal going on, you should go to the police."

"Yeah, right again. But, I can't do it now. Not with Howard in the hospital and the election less than two weeks away. I should let it rest and look into it after the election."

"You mean go to the police after the election."

She faced Ben and smiled at him. She was right to seek his advice. He was a good man and she was grateful they had each other. She leaned in to kiss him. They held the kiss for a long time and Nan felt the stress of the morning lift from her. They left the atrium and headed back to Ben's office holding hands. Ben was right about everything. She should keep her professional ethics high, and that meant she should resign from the Bloomfield campaign.

And Ben was right about Mrs. Wilson, too. She should forget about her until after the election and then, she'd go to the police with what she knew.

Halfway back to Ben's office, her cell phone rang. She took it out of her purse and answered it.

"Mrs. Smith," a man's voice said, "this is Eric Mattson, Hank's son."

"Eric," Nan said. "What's going on?"

"Dad came out of his coma," Eric said, "and he's obsessed about talking to you. I don't think he'll calm down until he does. Can you come to the hospital soon?"

"Sure. Of course. I was planning to see him later, but I can get there right away."

"Great, thanks. I'll see you soon."

Nan pushed the end call button. "That was Hank's son Eric. Hank wants to talk to me."

"About Mrs. Wilson?"

"Probably."

"I thought you were going to drop it until after the election," Ben said with a glance.

"Yes, dear, I will," Nan said. "But I have to visit Hank anyway. Let me see what he says. I'll see you at home. Thanks honey. I love you."

Nan peeled away and headed toward her car in the IDS garage. She planned to drive to the hospital to talk to Hank and after that, she'd go back to her office and write Bob Hilton a letter of resignation. And then, she'd go home, forget about the election and Mrs. Wilson and try not to worry about how her family would make ends meet.

THIRTY-SIX

THEY'D MOVED HANK from intensive care to a regular hospital room on the 4th floor of Methodist Hospital. When Nan got to the room, Eric was at the door waiting for her. He motioned for her to stay out in the hall and pulled the door half-closed as he stepped out into the hall with her.

"Thanks for coming," Eric said. "I'm sure it wasn't easy to get away."

"It's okay. How's your father?"

Eric nodded. "He's better. He came out of the coma last night. He was groggy and disoriented until early this morning when he started asking for you."

"Have the police found his attackers?"

"No, but they tell us they're looking for two vagrants in their twenties someone saw in the neighborhood around the time Dad was mugged. Dad gave the police a description that matched that of the vagrants. They also found his billfold in the trash a few blocks away. There were no prints and the police don't have much to go on. It doesn't sound like they'll catch them."

"Why does your dad want to talk to me?"

Eric glanced over his shoulder into the room and turned back to Nan. "He says he has something to tell you," he whispered. "He won't say what it is. He says he wants to talk to you in person, alone. I think it's about that woman."

"I guess I better talk to him." Nan made a move for the door.

Eric put his hand up. "Just a warning, he's still in a bit of an ICU psychosis. I don't know what he's so riled up about, but it might be nothing. We're hoping he'll get some rest after he talks to you."

"I understand. Let me see what he wants."

Nan followed Eric into the room. Hank's wife Karen sat in a chair beside the bed. When she saw Nan, she stood and took Hank's hand. "Hank," she said softly, leaning over the bed, "Nan Smith is here to see you. You wanted to talk to her."

Karen moved aside and Nan stepped forward. Hank's face was still a battered mess. The purple around his eyes had become black and the knob above his right eye had not shrunk since Nan had seen him yesterday morning. They'd removed the oxygen mask but there was still an IV in his arm and a machine next to his bed monitored his vital signs.

When Hank saw Nan, his breathing quickened and his good eye widened. "Nan," he rasped. "Come here."

Nan sidled up to the bed. Karen and Eric moved out to the hallway and shut the door behind them.

"Hi, Hank," Nan said. "Looks like you lost the fight."

Hank smiled weakly. "Yeah. There were two of them."

"Ahh, that explains it," Nan said with a smile. "Seriously, how are you feeling?"

"I'll be okay. I'm tough." He looked at Nan with his good eye. "Did we win the election?" he asked.

"No. It's still over a week away."

"Oh, yeah, that's right. I get confused." Then, Hank took two deep breaths. "Nan, I learned something about that woman. Remember her?"

"The woman in the psychiatric hospital. Yes, I remember."

He raised his head off the pillow and his good eye went wide. "She has letters."

"Letters? What do you mean?"

Hank's breathing quickened. "She said she wanted to show you something," he said. "Didn't she? I think she has letters to show you. We can use them to beat Sheldon Hanrahan!"

"Letters about what?"

Hank dropped his head back on to the pillow. "I don't know. The only thing I remember is I had to tell you about the letters. I think someone at the hospital told me about them. Was his name Earl? I can't remember exactly. I'm sorry."

"It's okay, Hank. I'll look into it."

Hank rose up again. "There's something else. I think that guy from Boston... I think he might be spying on us."

Nan nodded. "You might be right. Don't worry about it. You relax now."

Hank closed his good eye and eased into his bed. "Yeah, I'm tired." He drew a few long breaths and soon his breathing returned to normal. He opened his eye and looked at Nan. "Hey Nan," he said, "did we win the election?"

Nan shook her head. "We'll know in a less than two weeks, Hank. Get some sleep. I'll see you again in a few days."

Nan left the room and stepped out in the corridor. "He's a little out of it," she said to Karen and Eric. "What do the doctors say?"

"They're not sure," Eric answered. "They won't know if he has any brain damage until they run some tests and they won't do that until he's better."

Karen placed a hand on Nan's arm. "Why is he so obsessed about that woman? He needs to sleep but all he does is talk about her. Do you think she has anything to do with his attack?"

Nan paused a few seconds. "I think we should trust the police, Karen. As for the woman, she's senile and said some things a few weeks ago when she came to the office. I'm convinced it's nothing. I think he'll sleep now that he's talked to me."

"Thanks for coming," Eric said. He looked into the room at his father. "Yeah, he's already asleep. I hope he stops obsessing about that woman."

"Take care of him," Nan replied. "Call me if there is anything I can do. If he asks about the woman, tell him I have it under control."

"We will," Eric said.

Nan hugged Karen, squeezed Eric's arm and headed toward the exit. *I have it under control.* Right. Nothing was under control in her life right now. Later that day, she'd resign her position in the Bloomfield campaign and her career as a campaign manager would be over forever. After running a losing campaign two years earlier and resigning less than two weeks before the election on this campaign, they'd cast her out of the party and would never ask her to be a campaign manager again.

But there were other things she could do. Perhaps she could work for campaign reform as Ben suggested. Or maybe an independent candidate would hire her to run a campaign. She didn't know what the future held for her and for the time being, she really didn't care.

As for Mrs. Wilson and her absurd accusation, she was done with that, too. Sure, there were unanswered questions. Sure, it there was any truth to it, it would throw the election to Bloomfield. But the fact was there was no proof and the chances of the woman's accusation being true was slim at best. And how could she possibly have letters as Hank had said? She had nowhere to hide them. No, it wasn't possible.

It was time for Nan to let it all go. She'd go home after writing her letter of resignation, cook a great meal for Ben and Jenny. And someday, maybe she'd find another way to help her country.

THIRTY-SEVEN

"I've MADE A huge mistake, Hal," President Phil Dougherty said. "And the only way to fix it will ruin me."

"It will ruin many others, too," replied the vice president.

The president sat in a Queen Anne chair in the first floor library of the vice president's residence in the Naval Observatory in Georgetown. Across from him was Hal 'Bulldog' Marshall wearing a U.S. Army sweatshirt and sweatpants. The Vice President, recuperating from his near fatal heart attack, had been restricted to light deskwork and no meetings so the president had labeled his meeting a social visit to check on Bulldog's recovery. But it wasn't going to be a social visit. The president needed Hal's advice on how to handle the mess he'd created.

It wasn't supposed to have worked out this way. Had it not been for the vice president's bad heart, Bulldog would have succeeded him in the White House and Dougherty's legacy as president would've been secured. Then, he would have been able to retire a hero and ride out his days at his ranch in Arizona.

Dougherty only agreed to endorse Howard because he didn't believe the senator had a chance to win. Howard was a huge underdog and a poor debater and all the political pundits had predicted a landslide victory for Bloomfield. All that changed with a bullet to Howard's right shoulder. The assassination attempt had canceled the debates and propelled the Minnesota senator into the lead with a little over a week remaining in the race. The pundits had changed their predictions.

Of course, the president could still protect his reputation. He could let the election run its course and hand over the president's office to William Howard in January. But then he'd have to watch as Sheldon Hanrahan and his inner circle destroyed the country, and he would go down in history as the person who endorsed Senator Howard and set the country on the road to destruction. Whichever way he went, it would ruin his reputation.

"You should have come clean years ago," Hal said, crossing his legs. "It'll be much worse because of the cover-up."

The president pulled his chair closer to his vice president. "Yeah. I know," he said, looking at his hands. "I need your advice."

The vice president had served three decades as an influential congressman from Illinois before Phil, a two-term governor from Arizona with no experience in Washington, had chosen him as his running mate. Hal's political acumen had been critical in winning the presidency and the re-election four years later. And unlike most presidents, Dougherty depended on his vice president for advice.

The president felt the strong gaze of the vice president on him. Bulldog had been uncomfortable with the entire affair from the very beginning, but like a good soldier, he obeyed his orders and went along with the cover-up. Now, the president was asking what to do about his mistake.

"The first thing you need to remember," said Bulldog, "is this is bigger than just you. It's not about your legacy or what will happen to you personally. A lot of people are entangled in this mess and you have to ask yourself what's best for the country."

"Yes. The public can't lose confidence in the government," the president said.

"It'll hurt but it won't destroy us," Bulldog continued. "The country has gone through crises like this before. It will hurt much more if this mess stays buried and someone discovers it years from now. And you know it'll be discovered eventually. Too many people know too much."

Dougherty frowned. "You're suggesting I come clean, aren't you?"

"I'm not telling you what to do," Hal said shaking his head. "You're the president, not me. I'm saying you should be careful and think of the country first and foremost. Then, make your decision based on what's best in the long run. If that means your reputation must be sacrificed, so be it."

Sacrifice my reputation, the president thought. He'd been careful to build a sterling reputation his entire life and now he might have to throw it all away.

After a few seconds, the president said, "What do you make of this assassination attempt on Howard?"

"I've seen the FBI report but haven't gotten the 'between the lines' from headquarters. They haven't let me do anything since my damn heart attack. What are they telling you?"

"Everything points to terrorists. But there are questions. It was just a little too slick for Al-Qaeda. They're good but they aren't that good. The FBI brass says it was professionally done."

"That rules out the average nut case," Bulldog said, clasping his hands behind his head. "So who'd hire a professional of that caliber to kill Howard? Who'd benefit by having him dead?"

"Maybe they didn't want him dead," replied the president.

Bulldog dropped his hands and cocked his head. "What are you saying?"

"It was a two-hundred yard shot, Hal. Anyone with that kind of skill wouldn't miss a kill from that close. So, you have to ask, who'd want him shot but not killed? I can think of someone."

Bulldog paused. "Surely Hanrahan wouldn't do something that extreme. You can't believe he'd shoot his own candidate."

Dougherty raised his palms. "Why not? You know what he's capable of."

"Is the FBI investigating that angle?"

"Of course, but they're doing it quietly. If they find something—anything—I'll be sure a report gets out."

"Good. So, what about your situation, what we were talking about before?"

The president paused for a few seconds. Then he said, "You say I should be concerned about the country and I am. I have to be very careful how I handle this."

Bulldog raised an eyebrow. "So you're sticking with the cover-up."

"For the time being," the president answered. "I want to see what the assassination investigation turns up. If they find something, maybe we can keep my thing buried."

Bulldog glared at the president. Dougherty shifted his weight in his chair. He looked at his hands again.

"It certainly is a conundrum, Phil," the vice president finally said. "I remember in your first inauguration speech you said our system of government is an exercise in sacrifice. You were right. Throughout history, our greatest leaders were the ones who, when given a choice between their own well-being and that of the country, chose the country. George Washington and the founding fathers, all wealthy men with everything to lose, risked being hung for treason. Abraham Lincoln chose to make his presidency the one that ended slavery and gave his life to preserve the Union. Even Richard Nixon, reviled as he was, made a personal sacrifice when he chose to resign."

Hal leaned back and continued to stare at the president. "So my friend, what are you willing to sacrifice?" he asked.

It was a question the president had been asking himself for days. Had it really come to this? Did he really need to destroy his legacy to save the country?

The president of the United States stood and placed a hand on the shoulder of his vice president. "Thank you," he said. "By the way, I might have to tell your doctors that you insisted on talking business. They won't be happy with you."

"Fuck 'em," Bulldog said. "I've never been good at taking orders. Not even from you."

The president chuckled as he walked out of the vice president's residence toward his limo. As usual, Hal hadn't answered his questions directly. Rather, Bulldog put things in perspective and let his boss know exactly what was at stake.

One thing was clear: whatever choice the president made, it would be unpleasant. It would be, as Hal had said, an exercise in sacrifice.

THIRTY-EIGHT

AH, JENNY. Over the previous months while Nan was working on the Bloomfield campaign, she'd forgotten how delightful it was to be a mother, especially to her sweet, talented, intelligent daughter Jenny. Jenny was a good athlete too. She had just scored a goal in her lacrosse game, tying the score late in the second half, sending the game into sudden death overtime. As Nan sat on the sidelines of the lacrosse field under an October sky waiting for the overtime period to start, Jenny trotted past, shot a look at her mother and pumped her fist with the confidence of an athlete who knew she was able to win a game for her team. Nan had been the same way when she was young—confident and in control.

But she'd changed. She wasn't so confident anymore and she certainly didn't feel in control. Yesterday, after she returned to the office from her talk with Ben, she'd written an e-mail to Bob Hilton tendering her resignation saying she objected to the direction the campaign was taking. She never sent it. She realized she was making a career-defining decision and, she thought she should take the weekend to think about it.

But the more she thought, the more conflicted she became. She could see both sides. If she stayed, she'd be making a stand against Sheldon Hanrahan and his cohorts and their radical vision for America. And if Hilton's dirty campaign worked, she'd become the White House Communications Director and the family's financial woes would be over. On the other hand, if she left, she'd be making a stand against a badly broken election system. But with Sheldon Hanrahan and his cronies in power, the system would never get fixed. And how could she—a pawn in the election game—help fix a system that had been broken for decades? Wouldn't it be better to do everything she could to defeat Sheldon Hanrahan and work on fixing the system after the election?

At this moment, the only thing she knew for sure was how much she loved her daughter. Nan had taken a break to watch Jenny's lacrosse match and clear her mind. It was working. She'd watched with pride as Jenny cut across the field to block the opposing team's forward from advancing on her team's net. She beamed when Jenny led the charge toward the opponent's goal. And when Jenny scored the tying goal, she jumped from the grass and cheered like the parents she always thought were a little too caught up in their child's sports. The presidential campaign and Sheldon Hanrahan and Mrs. Wilson and the position of White House Communications Director were fading from her mind.

The excitement of the sudden death overtime buried Nan's thoughts about the election completely. Jenny's team got the ball and Jenny led the charge on the opponent's net once again. Nan hugged the sideline as Jenny ran down the field and flung the ball across the field to the opposite side wing. She was surprised to see Jenny bend over and grab her knees gasping for air. Jenny's defender saw it too and left Jenny to move toward the action on the other side of the field. When her defender was a few yards away, Jenny grinned and took off with a burst of speed Nan didn't think was possible. In an instant, she was in front of the opponent's net. The winger flung the ball toward her and Jenny made a lunge for it. She caught it in her 'crosse' and in mid-air, she flung the ball toward the net. The back of the net bulged and the goalie slumped to the ground. The referee blew his whistle, raised his arm and the game was over. Jenny had scored the winning goal.

As Jenny's teammates mobbed her, Nan yelled and jumped like a junior high school cheerleader. She burst with pride for her daughter and a lump grew in her throat. She continued to clap as the teams shook hands and when Jenny ran to the sideline to embrace her, Nan shamelessly cheered again. "I'm so proud of you! What a great goal!"

"Did you see me fake out my defender?" Jenny asked, laughing. "She thought I bonked."

Nan laughed with Jenny. "You fooled me, too."

"No way!" Jenny protested. "I could go another hour!"

Nan hugged her daughter under the cobalt blue sky and her world was perfect. At that moment, she knew what her decision about the election should be.

Jenny pushed away. "I'm going with Marisa and some other girls to D.Q.," Jenny shouted, trotting toward the parking lot. "Marisa's dad'll drop me off later. Bye!"

"Have fun!" Nan waved. "Proud of you!" She smiled and marveled at her daughter's zeal. She fished her keys from her purse and walked to her car. She decided to go to the grocery store to buy the ingredients for Jenny's favorite meal—chicken tetrazzini.

But first, she planned to stop at the office. Bob Hilton should know as soon as possible that she was resigning.

*

As she pointed the Camry toward the office, her cell phone rang. She ignored it. She was out of the game—in twenty minutes, it would be official, and she didn't want to talk to anyone. The phone continued to ring. Perhaps it was Ben calling from his office to check on the plans for the evening or maybe Jenny's plans had changed. She fished the phone from her purse and looked at the number. It had a '202' area code. Washington, D.C. Who'd be calling from Washington? Before the call rolled into voicemail, Nan answered it.

An unfamiliar woman's voice responded. "Good afternoon Mrs. Smith. I hope I'm not bothering you. I just want to ask a few questions." Nan regretted answering the call, but it was too late now.

"Who's calling please?" Nan asked.

"My name is Silvia Mendoza. I'm the White House correspondent for the Washington *Sentinel.*"

Another reporter. Nan thought she detected a slight Spanish accent. "I see. How can I help you?"

"I'd like to ask about Senator Howard and President Dougherty."

"You want to ask me questions about the president?"

"More specifically about Senator Howard. I'm investigating why the president endorsed Senator Howard and frankly, I don't have much to go on. You ran the campaign for Congresswoman Janice Theilen against Howard two years ago. I was hoping you had some insights you'd be willing to share."

Nan had come to a stoplight and was waiting for it to turn green. "I'm sorry, Ms… Mendoza, is it? I was as surprised by the president's endorsement as everyone else. I'm not sure I can help."

"I understand. I was just wondering, is there anything you know about Senator Howard that would shed some light on my investigation? Anything he might have done?"

The image of Mrs. Wilson at the psychiatric hospital flashed across Nan's mind. The words, *'he murdered my daughter'* echoed in her ears.

"Hello? Ms. Smith? Are you still there?"

"Yes… yes, I'm still here." The light turned green and Nan pressed the accelerator.

Ms. Mendoza continued. "I read that the campaign for Howard's senate seat was dirty, and I was just wondering what you discovered about him in your opposition research."

"Ms. Mendoza, Senator Howard ran a dirty campaign, not us. We chose to stay on the high ground. We ran a clean campaign." Nan turned a corner eight blocks from the office.

"I see. Can you think of any reason President Dougherty would have to endorse the senator?"

"No I can't. I'm sorry."

"Okay. Thank you for your time. If you think of anything, will you give me a call? Again, my name is Silvia Mendoza with the Washington *Sentinel*. I'd appreciate anything you can give me. Anything at all."

"I will." Nan said.

"Thank you."

"Just a minute, Ms. Mendoza," Nan said quickly. "May I ask you a question?"

"Um… sure. What is it?"

"In your investigations of Senator Howard, have you come across the name Wilson?"

"Why do you ask?"

"Ms. Mendoza, I am a seasoned campaign manager and I know how to handle the press. I'm asking the questions now. Please answer."

"I haven't run across anyone with the last name Wilson," Silvia said.

"Are you sure?"

"Yes, I'm sure. Trust me, I've looked into everything."

Nan shook her head. "Ah, well. I guess it's nothing. Thanks." She went to hang up the phone. "Wait," she said. "Was there a young woman who died while working for or even being associated with Howard?"

"Not that I know of." Silvia replied. "Maybe you better tell me why you're asking."

"No." Nan said. "I'm sure it's nothing."

"There was an intern, however," Silvia said, "who killed herself with prescription pills four months after leaving Howard's staff. But her name wasn't Wilson. It was Elizabeth Czerwinski."

Nan was still blocks from the office but pulled over to the curb and put her car in park. "Excuse me, but how is it that you remember one of Senator Howard's interns out of the thousands of interns in Washington, D.C.?"

Another pause. "I'll tell you what," said Silvia Mendoza, finally, "I'll tell you what I know about it if you tell me why you're asking. Deal?"

"Ms. Mendoza, honestly, I don't know anything for sure and, as a senior staff member of Governor Bloomfield's campaign, I must be careful about what I say. But I'll tell you what, if I find anything that helps you with your story, you'll be the reporter I call about it. In the meantime, I've given you a lead simply by asking about this. Now, please, tell me what you know about her."

There was a short pause. Then, "Okay. I was a new beat reporter for the *Sentinel* five years ago when I was sent to investigate a suicide. A young woman named Elizabeth Czerwinski took a bunch of prescription drugs. She'd resigned from Senator Howard's staff four months earlier."

"That's terrible. Was there an investigation?"

"No," Ms. Mendoza said. "The police ruled it a suicide. It wasn't much of a story. But..."

Nan switched the phone to her other ear. "But?" she said.

"Elizabeth was apparently very bright. She was planning to go to Stanford, I recall. And she was beautiful—strikingly beautiful. She had everything going for her but evidently she was troubled. She'd been seeing a psychiatrist who prescribed the pills she took. But what puzzled me the most was her lifestyle. She drove a Mercedes, SL 600—a one-hundred sixty-five thousand dollar car. And she lived in a six-thousand dollar per month condo in Georgetown. I mean, how does a 20 year-old intern from a poor family get that kind of money? Someone must have been paying for it. Anyway, I wrote the story and moved on to the next one and didn't think there was anything more to it—until now."

"Are you sure her name wasn't Wilson?" Nan asked.

"Positive."

"And she was from Minnesota?"

"All senators get their interns from their home state," Silvia said. "So, who is Wilson?"

"Ah... Someone I know named Wilson said she had a daughter that knew Senator Howard."

"Well, it wouldn't be this girl. She didn't have a family. No living parents, no relatives, no one. It was sad. In fact, the county in Maryland where she died was looking for someone—anyone—to claim the body.

"So, who is Wilson?" Silvia asked again.

"It's nothing," Nan said. "Seriously, I'm sorry I asked."

"Ms. Smith," Silvia said, "If you want to tell me anything about this Wilson person, please call. Anytime. You should have my number on your cell phone from this call."

"I will," Nan said.

"I mean it. Anytime," Silvia said, "Day or night."

"Okay," Nan replied. "Goodbye."

Nan pressed end call button and sat in her idling car. Wilson. Czerwinski. Maybe Elizabeth Czerwinski was Mrs. Wilson's daughter. Maybe someone changed Mrs. Wilson's name when they admitted her to the Rand Psychiatric Hospital.

Or not. Maybe—in fact probably—Elizabeth Czerwinski wasn't related to Mrs. Wilson at all.

THIRTY-NINE

NAN SAT AT HER DESK and reread her e-mail letter of resignation. It was succinct and clear—she was quitting because she didn't agree with what Bob Hilton was doing to win the election. Slander, dirty tricks, push polls, character assassinations, half-truths and outright lies—they disgusted her and she wanted no part of it, even if by resigning, she was helping Senator Howard's campaign and would never be the White House Communications Director. She had to stand up for what she believed in.

But what would she do for work after she resigned? The family needed her paycheck so she'd have to get a new job right away. Perhaps she could find a job working for campaign reform. Since the McCain/Feingold Act, there was a growing movement for what was called 'clean elections' where the primary financing of elections came from the government. Clean election bills that provided public financing had passed in Maine and Arizona and both politicians and voters welcomed the reform. Minnesota was considering a clean elections bill as were many other states.

But campaign finance reform didn't solve a core problem with the election process. Nan's concern was not just with finance, but with the way the parties conducted campaigns. Elections had been hijacked by pollsters, political consultants, and direct marketers. It was less and less about ideas and more and more about how to gain and keep power. Candidates no longer debated the issues. Negative campaigns had become the norm and Nan, like most Americans, had had enough.

She read her e-mail again but couldn't bring herself to hit the 'send' button. Something was wrong. She looked out over the bullpen. It was Saturday afternoon and Stephanie had come in on her day off to help get a mailing out. Some of the new volunteers—Frank, Lora, Jean and Will—were there too. Shelly sat at her desk doing who knows what. This was her staff. These people were her responsibility. If she resigned now, she'd be running out on them ten days before Election Day. She was going to resign, but she should wait until Monday when Bob Hilton could send someone to replace her. Yes, that would be the right thing to do.

*

As she picked up her coat to leave, she spotted Hank's briefcase leaning against a wall. She remembered that inside was the list Hank got of the Rand Psychiatric Hospital residents and employees. Hank had said that Mrs. Wilson had letters that proved that Howard murdered her daughter. Was it possible?

She retrieved the folder from Hank's briefcase and scanned the list of employees. She tried to remember the orderly's name who she had talked to. Was it Earl? She spotted the named Earl Sampson on the list. She grabbed the Minneapolis telephone book from her desk drawer and scanned through the 'Sampsons'. There were two 'Earls'— one who lived in the swanky suburb of Orono, the other lived in a poor, near-north side neighborhood of Minneapolis. Nan wrote down the north side address and headed for her car.

*

The apartment building Earl Sampson called home was a run-down, two-story stucco building in a neighborhood where broken windows stayed broken. Nan parked her car and checked the rearview mirror—it was starting to become a habit. She didn't notice anyone following her. As she got out of her car, she saw Earl in the front yard lazily raking leaves. His huge frame loomed over the rake. Nan walked toward him and he looked up. He pointed a finger at her. "Hey! You the lady who was at the hospital the otha' day," he said. "You was talking to Mrs. Wilson."

"Yes," Nan replied. "That was me. I didn't have a chance to introduce myself. I'm Nan Smith." She extended a hand.

Earl recoiled. "I got me fired for talkin' to you. I don' work there no more."

"They fired you? I'm so sorry. I didn't know."

"S'okay," Earl said shaking his massive head and looking down at his rake. "I didn't like it there anyways. Them guys was mean to me."

Nan smiled at him. "Earl, that's your name, right?"

"Yeah, that me. I's Earl. Earl Sampson."

"Well, Earl, I was wondering if I could ask you some questions about Mrs. Wilson. Do you mind?"

"It don't matter, I guess. Mrs. Wilson ain't there no more."

"What?" Nan said. "Not there? Where did she go?"

"Don' know fo' sure. The day they fired me I saw she gone. Her room cleared out. Poor lady." Earl leaned on his rake.

"Where was she moved to?"

Earl shook his head again. "Don' know. Maybe she died and they buried her next to her daughter."

"Buried next to her daughter?"

"Yeah. Mrs. Wilson used to visit the cemet'ry every Sunday before she weren't allowed to go out no more."

Nan nodded. "I see. Earl, did Mrs. Wilson ever mention something about letters from her daughter?"

Earl smiled sweetly, "Hey, I forgot about them letters! Mrs. Wilson tol' me about 'em and say I shouldn't be tellin' them guys. How'd you know about 'em?"

"Remember my friend who talked to you about Mrs. Wilson?"

Earl grinned. "Yeah, that skinny guy. That's right, I told him about them letters." His grin fell from his face. "Them guys at the hospital saw me talkin' to your friend and they got real mad. They tol' your friend go away and say I shouldn't talk to no one no more." Earl looked at his shoes and scuffed at the ground.

Nan paused a moment. "Earl, listen carefully. This is very important. Do you know where the letters are?"

"Don' know, ma'am. They wasn't in her room. No place to hide 'em there. And Mrs. Wilson she never say where they's at."

Nan smiled and put a hand on Earl's massive, black arm. "Thank you. I hope you find another job soon."

"Yeah," Earl replied. "You a nice lady, not like them guys. They was mean to me. Real mean." He went back to raking his leaves.

Nan climbed into her Camry and headed to the grocery store to buy the ingredients for Jenny's chicken tetrazzini. Mrs. Wilson was gone from the Rand Psychiatric Hospital and any hope Nan had of finding the letters had gone with her. Where they'd taken her, she could only guess. Certainly it was far from Minneapolis. Hopefully, she was still alive.

Nan felt a pang of guilt that perhaps she could have done more to help the poor woman when she first came to the campaign office. She hoped her inaction hadn't cost Mrs. Wilson her life.

It was out of her hands, now. The woman was gone and Nan would soon be out of the political game. She had to go home, make Jenny's chicken tetrazzini and think about what to do next with her career.

FORTY

FRANK PIERCE WAS NOT happy to have to be in Minnesota. He didn't like the cold weather and he certainly didn't like being away from his base in Washington, D.C. He felt more comfortable in D.C. where he could keep an eye on everything. But Woods had fucked up here and Pierce had to fix things. His job was containment and if that meant he had to spend a few weeks in Minnesota to mop up Woods' mess, well, he had to do it.

Pierce had made sure Woods was gone by the time his airplane landed. If Pierce had seen Woods in person, he'd have punched him out—or worse. Pierce found a position for Woods in Eastern Montana in the middle of the Crow Indian reservation. He'd be the only African American within a hundred miles. There was no cable TV and nothing for a city boy like Woods to do. He'd go nuts in less than a year. Then he'd resign five years short of qualifying for his pension. And Pierce would see to it he would not get good references. The incompetent bastard deserved it.

The woman was gone now, too. They should've let him handle her the way he had wanted to years ago—as he'd done now. As long as there were no problems in Minnesota, no one would care about what he'd done with the woman. After all, what were they going to do, arrest him and expose the entire affair? He'd done the right thing and they should thank him for it.

Good thing they'd wiped the woman's records clean five years earlier. Good thing the woman had no relatives to worry about. And good thing the hospital director had a taste for high-priced prostitutes and a healthy fear that his wife would discover his habit. It would take only a few thousand dollars to keep the lid on things at the hospital.

It was also a good thing Minneapolis was only a few hours from Lake Superior. Bodies didn't rot in the forty-five degree water and stayed on the deep lake bottom forever.

Yeah, Mrs. Wilson was gone for good.

As Pierce drove from the Rand Psychiatric Hospital back to his hotel room, he was satisfied that everything at the hospital was secure. The only loose end left was the person the woman talked to—Nan Smith. Shortly after that fuck up, they'd caught one of Bloomfield's campaign workers snooping around, asking questions. Pierce's people had taken care of him, but then Nan Smith visited the hospital, too. Taking care of her would be more difficult. She was a senior campaign adviser to Governor Bloomfield and it was a little over a week before the presidential election. Containment for Nan Smith was going to be tricky.

Halfway to his hotel, his cell phone rang. It was the field man in charge of watching Nan Smith. Pierce hit the "talk" button. "What's the problem?"

"She visited the orderly," the operative said. "They talked for about five minutes and then she left. It looks like she's heading home."

"She visited the orderly? Goddamn it. Tell me again, he doesn't know anything."

"We interrogated him thoroughly, Frank. I guarantee he doesn't know a thing."

The men Pierce had brought to Minnesota with him were the very best. If they interrogated the orderly and said he didn't know anything, Pierce probably didn't need to worry about him. He'd have been more comfortable, however, if he had conducted the interrogation himself.

"Alright," Pierce said. "But Ms. Smith is becoming a problem. I'm heading your way. Stay on her. Am I clear?"

"We're on her."

Pierce punched his phone off and pointed his Escalade toward the Smith home. Nan Smith was indeed becoming a problem. Now that he'd taken care of Mrs. Wilson, Pierce would turn his attention to solving that problem, too.

FORTY-ONE

One week before the presidential election

As Sheldon Hanrahan's limo approached Senator William Howard's two-story brick home in the posh St. Paul suburb of Sunfish Lake, it looked like a fortress under siege. Secret Service men, some with Dobermans, ringed the house and there was a black Suburban with dark windows parked across the front of the long driveway. Sheldon spotted an agent with a sniper rifle on the roof of the house. They'd spared no expense to keep the senator safe from the people who'd tried to assassinate him. *A little late*, Sheldon said to himself.

Sheldon's limo driver pulled up to the Suburban and showed his I.D. After the Secret Service man did a thorough search of the car, he backed the Suburban away to let the limo through. The driver stopped at the front door and Sheldon got out. Yet another Secret Service man escorted him through the foyer to the den, a cozy, oak-paneled room with soft leather furniture. Senator Howard sat in a big leather chair wearing corduroy slacks, a gray sweater and loafers. His right arm was in a sling. The senator smiled as Sheldon came in. "I'd shake your hand but I have to keep my arm still."

Sheldon sat across from the senator and crossed his legs. "Are you in pain?" he asked.

Howard shook his head. "Only when I move my arm too much. I still get a little tired but I feel great. We have an eight-point lead with one week left. The doctors say I can start campaigning again tomorrow."

"You shouldn't look like you feel well," Sheldon said. "I want you to appear to struggle."

The senator raised the palm of his good hand. "But I feel fine. I can handle anything. I'm ready to go!"

"Bill, listen to me," Sheldon said. "You need to look like it's an effort to campaign. Understand? You start campaigning again tomorrow. On Wednesday, you'll be in Florida and in the afternoon you'll be in Orlando at a rally. I want you to stop halfway through your speech and sit down. Someone will escort to your room and call a doctor. Later in the afternoon, we'll have a news conference to tell the public you're okay. In the evening, you'll make a brief appearance at another rally. All the press will be there. I have it all planned."

"But, Sheldon," the senator said, "we don't need these theatrics. The people who shot me have given us an extraordinary platform. The public loves me now and they'll listen to what I have to say, especially about terrorism. America is ready for our message and I'm ready to deliver it. It's a golden opportunity."

Sheldon leaned his head back and stared at the senator through his dark glasses. "Bill, if you do as I tell you, in eight days you'll be the president-elect of the United States. If you do not, if you try to do things your way, you risk losing this election. We've been working at this for two decades and I'll not let you ruin our chances. Do you understand?"

The senator jutted his jaw at Sheldon. "You're not the one running for president. I am."

Sheldon continued to stare. "And you'll make a fine president, Bill, as long as you do exactly as I say. If you don't, I will ruin you and you'll have to go back to drilling teeth in Duluth."

The senator recoiled at Sheldon's rebuke. "Why do you have to be like that? Why do you make threats? I'm just making a suggestion, that's all. I should have a say."

Sheldon softened his gaze. "What are you concerned about, Bill? You'll be the president of the United States soon. The entire world will think you are the most important, most powerful person on earth and all you need to do is pose for the cameras, read the speeches I write for you, sign the bills I tell you to sign and keep your thoughts and opinions to yourself. You get to be the one everyone loves. And you don't need to do anything except show up. In eight years, you can leave the White House an American hero and the history books will write a glowing chapter on the William Howard presidency.

"Or..." Sheldon hardened his stare again, "you can fight us and history will write an entirely different account of Bill Howard. It's your choice."

Senator William Howard slumped in his chair and didn't respond. Sheldon uncrossed his legs and leaned forward. "Cheer up, Bill," he said. "We'll be able to fulfill our dreams once you're in the White House. I've brought you to the brink. Just do as I say for one more week. We have new campaign plans."

"We don't have to use the party machine? You've taken over the campaign now, right?"

"I have," Sheldon answered. "They were never going to win the election for us."

"Then... why did you agree to what they said? Why did you..." Senator Howard cocked his head to the side and Sheldon could see his mind working. Finally, the senator shook his head and sighed.

Sheldon stood and the senator stayed seated. "I must check on the details for the last week of the campaign. We have you in Florida, Illinois, Ohio, Michigan and New York. Congressman Masello is campaigning in California and the rest of the west. I'm predicting victory by a landslide."

The senator looked up at Sheldon Hanrahan and flashed a grin. "You know," he said, rubbing his wounded shoulder, "I am feeling a little tired. This last week will be more of a struggle than I thought."

Sheldon smiled. "Get some rest, Mr. President. It will be a long eight years."

Howard continued to grin.

*

Sheldon returned to his limo and instructed his driver to take him to his office. Howard was a lucky man, indeed. Sheldon had taught him how to act presidential and, unlike Sheldon with his scarred eye, Howard had the good looks that got people elected. The public would indeed grow to love President William Howard, the man Sheldon had created.

As the driver pointed the car toward Minneapolis the driver said, "Mr. Hanrahan, there was a call for you while you were talking to the senator."

"Who was it?"

"It was Victor, sir. He asked me to give you a message. He said I should tell you Frank Pierce is in Minneapolis and he doesn't know why. He also said they are following Mr. Pierce and will keep you informed. He didn't say anything more, sir."

"Thank you, Jeffrey," Sheldon said.

Sheldon slid the privacy glass closed. He took off his tinted glasses and rubbed his bad eye. If Frank Pierce was in Minnesota, something was wrong. Sheldon had never been concerned about Pierce because he was supposedly the best in the business. Sheldon was content to let the others manage Pierce. So far, they'd done just fine.

But with one week left until he had his hands on the White House, Sheldon was not going to leave anything to chance.

FORTY-TWO

ON MONDAY MORNING after Nan had sent her e-mail letter
of resignation, she gathered her campaign staff and told them
about her decision. She hadn't anticipated the effect her
resignation would have on Stephanie. Since Stephanie began,
she'd watched Nan's every move and practically worshipped
her. Now, as Stephanie stood in the doorway watching her
mentor pack her office, she looked lost.

"I don't understand," Stephanie said. "I thought you
believed in what Governor Bloomfield stood for. You
certainly don't want Senator Howard to win the election, do
you?"

"Of course not, Stephanie. It's just there are other things
to consider. There are bigger issues are at stake. Like I said,
I'm making a stand against dirty campaigns. If we don't clean
up our election system, we'll never elect good candidates like
George Bloomfield."

"But Governor Bloomfield is already a good candidate
and we're seven points behind. Shelly said if you leave, the
press will make an issue out of it. It could hurt us."

Nan put books in her box. "Maybe that will happen, I don't know. All I know is this is the right thing for me to do. I'm sorry Stephanie."

"What should I do? Should I quit too?"

"I can't answer that," Nan said. "You have to decide what's right for you. If you want my advice, I'd stay until after the election if I were you. You aren't involved in this mess so if you stick it out, you'll be fine."

"Okay," Stephanie said, looking at her hands. "But I wish you were staying, too."

Nan stopped packing and looked at Stephanie. "I'll tell you what," she said. "Once this election is over and the smoke has cleared, let's you and I have a long lunch on me. We can talk about elections and why I chose to quit. And we'll talk about your career. You're a good worker, Stephanie. You have a bright future and I want to help you. I know some people who would be interested in hiring you."

Stephanie's eyes brightened a little. "I'd like that," she said.

Nan smiled at Stephanie and went back to packing. "What are you going to do for the next week?" Stephanie asked.

"Well, first I'm going to the hospital to visit Hank. I talked to his son who said he's much better. They're discharging him tomorrow. I need to explain my decision to him. Then, I'll watch the campaign, vote for Governor Bloomfield on Election Day and decide what I'm going to do next."

"Okay," said Stephanie. "Can I call you if I have any questions?"

Nan slid out from behind her desk and gave Stephanie a hug. It felt like she was hugging her adult daughter who was moving to another city. "Of course you can," she said. She released the embrace and smiled at Stephanie. "We'll have that lunch soon."

Stephanie managed a smile, nodded and went back to the reception area. Nan quickly finished packing, put on her coat, and picked up the box. She turned toward her door.

Rex Starkey was blocking her exit. "So, you can't hack it, can you?" he said with a smirk.

Nan set the box down and faced Rex directly. "Can't hack what?"

"A tough campaign."

"A tough campaign?" Nan said, leaning against the desk. "I can handle a tough campaign, Rex. It's a dirty campaign I don't want anything to do with. The kind of campaign you're here to conduct."

"I get people elected," he said.

"No, Rex. What you do undermines the integrity of our election system. And since the election process is central to our system of government, you're helping destroy our country."

Rex's smirk spread to his entire face. "Aw, come on. I'm not that bad, am I?"

Nan picked up the box and pushed her way out the door. "Yes, Rex," she said, "you are."

"I guess we'll never have that candle-light dinner now," he said as she left. "Too bad."

She didn't bother to respond as she headed out of the campaign offices.

*

When she got to her Camry, she tossed the box in the back and climbed into the driver's seat. She headed to Methodist Hospital to visit Hank and tell him about her decision. He was a traditionalist, like her, and believed campaigns should be about issues, not about character assassination, slander and which candidate had the slickest commercials or the biggest stars on their side. He'd be disappointed that the Bloomfield campaign had turned dirty and would worry about how a Howard presidency would change the country. But he'd understand.

As she drove from the campaign office, she was sure she'd made the right decision. Something had been wrong ever since President Dougherty endorsed Senator Howard. In two short weeks, she'd gone from a simple state manager running a straightforward campaign to rubbing elbows with Jocelyn Jones and Miles Jackson and being told the new administration might offer her the position of White House Communications Director. Then when Hank got beat up and Senator Howard was shot, she felt like she was in a surreal play where moral and ethical laws bent like the laws of physics in a Salvador Dali painting. She had to step away so that her grasp on reality would return.

She'd give herself a week, watch the election from home and then turn her attention to finding a new job. It would be a grind. She'd be on the outs with the state party and it wouldn't look good that she'd resigned from the Bloomfield campaign one week before the election. But the family needed her paycheck. Hopefully, she'd find something fast.

As she drove through south Minneapolis, the only regret she had was that she hadn't done more about Mrs. Wilson. The poor woman had come to Nan for help and she had failed her. Nan had tried, but now it was too late. The woman was gone and even if she had letters that proved Howard had murdered her daughter, Nan would never find them. There was nothing she could do about it anymore.

She turned the corner on Lake Street and headed west toward Methodist Hospital. It was a beautiful late October day in Minnesota. Wispy white clouds slid across the blue sky and the city was busy at work. Most of the leaves had fallen but a few still clung to branches. She drove her car through the Lake Street and Hiawatha Avenue area where people waited to catch the light rail for downtown. She drove under a bridge. To her left were old buildings that'd been renovated and turned into funky clothing and music stores. To her right was the Pioneers and Soldier's Memorial Cemetery.

She thought about Mrs. Wilson's daughter buried in a cemetery just like this. Earl had said the woman visited the grave every week before they didn't allow her out anymore. Nan remembered the picture she'd seen at the hospital of Mrs. Wilson's daughter standing in front of the Capitol Building in Washington, D.C. A beautiful young woman who had become cynical at such a young age. As Nan drove past the cemetery she tried to imagine how she'd feel if Jenny died and was buried in a cemetery like this. She'd want to visit Jenny's gravesite every week too, just like Mrs. Wilson. Every week for the rest of her life.

Nan slammed on the brakes. The Camry's tires squealed and the driver in the car behind her honked his horn and roared past in the outside lane. He flipped her off as he drove by. Nan didn't care. She peered through the passenger window of her car. There, spread before her were rows and rows of gravesites marked by cold gray monuments. She looked out over the cemetery and said out loud, "It can't be that easy."

But she knew it was. Mrs. Wilson's entire life and all her possessions were confined to her tiny room in the Rand Psychiatric Hospital. If she was hiding letters, the only place they could be, the only place she could hide them from Mr. Woods and the men who guarded her was at her daughter's gravesite.

Another car came up behind her and honked. Nan pulled the car to the curb and turned off the motor. She'd been ready to put Mrs. Wilson behind her and move on with her life. Now, as she stared out over Soldiers Memorial Cemetery, she knew what she could do for Mrs. Wilson. She'd find her daughter's gravesite and, if the letters were there—the letters that proved Senator Howard murdered her daughter—she would take them and give them to the FBI.

FORTY-THREE

ACCORDING TO GOOGLE there were seventy-nine cemeteries in the Twin Cities and Nan had no idea how to go about finding out which one held the body of Mrs. Wilson's daughter. She thought about calling the cemeteries closest to the Rand Psychiatric Hospital but she knew they would not give out names of the interred over the phone.

Nan sat at her kitchen table and scanned the listings again. Certainly she couldn't visit each cemetery and ask to look at their plot list to try to find the gravesite. She had to find another way.

She Googled 'Wilson obituary Minnesota.' She got 400 hits. She scanned the list but found nothing about a young woman named Wilson who died five years earlier. Nan thought about going back to the psychiatric hospital and asking someone where they took Mrs. Wilson each week. But she knew no one would talk to her there. Earl wouldn't know either. The big orderly most likely never left the hospital and would have no idea where they took Mrs. Wilson on her outings.

When Nan had driven past Soldiers Memorial Cemetery, she thought she knew where to find the letters. But did she really? Did the letters even exist? As she sat at her kitchen table, she realized she was going on information from a mentally slow orderly. She was probably on a wild goose chase.

Nan shut down her laptop. A few hours earlier, she'd resolved to get on with her life. It felt good letting it all go. It was time to put the questions about Mrs. Wilson behind her once and for all.

She looked at the kitchen clock. Ben was picking up Jenny from lacrosse practice and they'd be home soon. Nan put some water on the stove for red potatoes. She turned on the oven to warm the ham she'd bought the day before. She dug through her recipe box and found the recipe for fudge pie, one of Jenny's favorites. As she dug out the mixing bowl, butter, flour, eggs and cocoa, the back door opened with a crash followed by the thud of a backpack of books being dumped on the floor. "Hi, Mom. I'm home," Jenny shouted.

Nan smiled. "Hi sweetie. Guess what? I'm making fudge pie. You up for it?"

"Sure!" Jenny said bounding through the kitchen with an armful of books. "I gotta get some homework done before dinner. Later." She disappeared to her room.

"I'm up for fudge pie too," said a voice. Ben was taking off his coat and hanging it behind the door. He grinned at Nan. "Do I get some?"

"Only if you give me a kiss," Nan answered. Ben gave her a long, tender kiss and Nan felt the joy of being a wife and mother fill her again. "So tell me, my handsome, hardworking husband, how was work today?"

"Okay," Ben said grabbing the mail off the counter and taking a seat at the kitchen table. "We've been invited to pitch Right Electronics. It's a pretty big account. We need it."

Nan returned to her mixing bowl. "Well, I hope you get it because you're our sole breadwinner now."

Ben looked up from the mail and smiled. "So, you did it? You resigned?"

"I sent the e-mail this morning. Hilton's been calling my phone ever since but I'm not taking his calls. Not for a while, anyway. I'll have to talk to him eventually, I suppose."

Nan cracked two eggs into the mixing bowl and measured out the flour. "You were telling me about work. Things are picking up?"

"Yeah, Right Electronics. We might have a shot at it, knock on wood." Ben rapped his knuckles on the kitchen table. "The problem is, we're probably pitching against Hanrahan Communications again. I tell you, Nan, it won't be long before he runs all other agencies out of business."

"How about the rest of your clients?"

"They're okay. Katch Financial is raising its IRA budget and most everyone else is holding steady. If no one cuts budgets like they normally do in the fourth quarter, we won't have to make many layoffs."

Ben's clients, Nan thought. She stopped mixing the fudge pie. The photograph of Mrs. Wilson's daughter standing in front of the Capitol building flashed in her mind. She turned to Ben. "Do you still have Adams Mortuary Service as a client?"

"Yeah. They've been a client forever. Why?"

Nan crossed her arms. "I bet they can find where someone is buried in the Twin Cities, can't they?"

"Sure. There's an online service that lets them look up all the gravesites in the five-state region. I've seen it work. It's slick. They just type a name and a date of death and up pops the cemetery and a plot number. It even gives them a map. Takes only a few seconds."

Nan placed a hand on her hip. "Do you think you could call and ask them to find where someone is buried?"

"Now?"

"Yes, if you could."

Ben dropped his hands from behind his head and leaned forward. "Ooo-kay," he said slowly. "Cecil's daughter Monica answers the phones until eight. I just need a name and date of death. But tell me, who do you want to find? And why?"

"Someone named Wilson. She'd have been in her early twenties. Died about five years ago."

"Wilson? Is she the daughter of...?"

"Yes she is."

"Nan, you better tell me what you're thinking."

Nan sat at the table and told Ben about Earl and the letters that supposedly proved Howard murdered Mrs. Wilson's daughter. She told him about the weekly visits Mrs. Wilson made to her daughter's gravesite and her theory that the letters were hidden there.

Ben glared at Nan. "Nan, you resigned this morning. None of this is your business. And, as I've said before, if you think there's something to Mrs. Wilson's accusation, you should go to the police."

"What if there isn't anything to it?" Nan asked with a palm raised. "What then? I'd look like a fool. It'd be the Theilen fiasco all over again. You're right, Ben. I should forget about it. Problem is I can't. Maybe if I saw for myself that there wasn't anything at the gravesite I could forget about it."

Ben nodded. "Alright," he said. "So if I do this, and you don't find anything, you promise to let it go?"

"Yes, my dear. I promise."

"Okay, I'll make the call. When did you say Mrs. Wilson's daughter died?"

"I don't know the exact date but it was about five years ago. Thanks."

Before Ben could reach for the kitchen phone, it rang. "You answer it," he said, "and I'll call Monica from my cell phone." He retrieved his phone from his coat pocket and headed to the den.

Nan answered the kitchen phone. "Hello?"

"Nan, this is Bob Hilton. Sorry for calling you at home but you aren't answering your cell. We need to talk."

Nan eyed the half-assembled fudge pie on the counter top next to the hot oven. "Bob, this isn't a good time. I promise I'll talk to you about it tomorrow."

"That's fine. That's why I'm calling. I'm in Chicago with Bloomfield. I'm making a special trip to Minneapolis tomorrow morning to talk to you in person. There've been developments you should know about. I was hoping you'd meet me for breakfast. The Sofitel. 7:30. Already made reservations. Please, Nan. It's important."

Nan paused to think. She was going to have to talk to Hilton anyway and it wouldn't hurt to hear what he had to say. So she agreed to meet him. He thanked her and hung up. Nan went back to the mixing bowl and stirred the batter again.

Ben came back into the kitchen. "Who called?" he asked.

"Hilton. He says he has something to tell me before he accepts my resignation. Apparently there are some new developments."

"He's going to try to talk you out of it."

Nan nodded. "I'm sure but I should at least hear what he has to say. Anyway, I'm meeting him for breakfast tomorrow."

Nan stopped mixing the fudge pie. "What did you find out?" she asked.

"Bad news," Ben said. "There was no one named Wilson under the age of forty buried in Minnesota five years ago."

"Positive?" she asked.

"Sorry, Nan. It appears your theory is falling apart. And if I may say, the entire affair about Senator Howard murdering someone sounds a little shaky, too—like it was made up by a senile woman and mentally-retarded orderly."

Nan shook her head. "Yeah, I guess you're right."

Ben came to Nan and gave her a long hug. He pushed away and smiled at her. "So, when's my fudge pie going to be ready?"

Nan smiled back at him and picked up the mixing bowl. "Yes sir. One fudge pie, coming up."

As Ben walked back toward the den, Nan dropped the spoon into the mixing bowl. "Wait," she blurted. "Call Monica Adams back and ask her to look up a different name." She turned to Ben. "Tell her to look for the gravesite of Elizabeth Czerwinski."

FORTY-FOUR

"I THOUGHT WE TOLD YOU to drop the investigation," Bradley Schwartzman said from behind his desk. "Weren't we clear about that?" The *Sentinel's* editor-in-chief's eyes peered angrily at Silvia from beneath his bushy eyebrows. He'd rolled the sleeves of his shirt halfway up his arm.

Silvia looked over at Ian Rutter sitting next to her. He didn't look back. She pushed herself to the edge of her chair and straightened to make her 4'11" frame as large as possible. "Yes, you were clear, but I got a tip and thought I should pursue it."

"You got a tip…"

"My source at the White House told me President Dougherty endorsed Senator Howard because he was being blackmailed. I think it might have something to do with a woman named Elizabeth Czerwinski who'd been an intern for Senator Howard. She committed suicide five years ago. I got a lead from someone in Minnesota who might have more for me soon. I believe there's a cover-up involving not only the president but other high-ranking officials, too."

"That's a pretty bold accusation. Do you have proof? Anything we can hang a story on?" Bradley asked.

"No, I don't. That's why I was investigating."

"So, you've been asking embarrassing questions about the president without anything more than a tip from your source in the White House."

Silvia returned Bradley's stare. "My source is impeccable. I won't tell you who it is, but, if my source says there's a cover-up, there is. And we should do a story on it. Come on, Brad. What's wrong with a little controversy?"

Bradley glanced at Ian, then back at Silvia. He sighed, rose from his desk and swung the door to his office closed. It was now a closed-door meeting and Silvia felt her stomach jump.

Bradley sat back at his desk. Silvia saw a glint of pity in his eyes, but then Brad was all business. "We know about your source at the White House, Silvia," he said. "We know who it is and we know about the nature of your relationship with Ellen Stein."

Silvia stiffened. "You know... everything?"

"Yes. And, unfortunately, so do others."

Silvia's heart stopped. The gray walls of the room seemed to close in and the lights in the office seemed to be focused on her. Her secret was out. "The White House knows, too?" she heard herself ask.

Bradley glanced at Ian again who sat expressionless in his chair. The editor-in-chief opened a manila folder sitting in front of him. He took out several glossy photographs. "I got these late last night. We don't know who sent them. There was no note attached—only the photos in a White House envelope." Bradley pushed the photos across the desk at Silvia. She picked them up and examined each one. They showed Silvia and Ellen in various stages of sexual embrace during their last liaison at the Capitol Hilton. One showed Silvia completely naked and in the throes of an orgasm. Silvia's face grew hot and her throat tightened. She carefully set the photos back on Bradley's desk. She wanted to say something, but the words didn't come.

Bradley slipped the photos back in the manila folder and tossed the folder onto his desk toward Silvia. "You take them."

Silvia slid the folder off the desk and clutched it to her chest. Her heart thumped and she wondered how her proud parents would feel if they ever saw these photographs.

Bradley folded his arms and looked at Silvia like a father talking to his son who had just been charged with a felony. "These photos are a message, Silvia. A message that you're no longer invited inside the White House or anywhere else near the Administration."

Silvia didn't respond. Ian shifted his chair and finally spoke up. "How do you know that if there was no note attached?"

Bradley kept his eyes on Silvia. "Because the photos were sent to me, that's how. If they wanted to just scare you off, Silvia, they'd have sent them to you. If they wanted to get you suspended or in trouble with the *Sentinel,* they would have sent them to Ian. But they sent them to me, the editor-in-chief, and the message is crystal clear—they want you out. And, given the rather dramatic nature of this warning, I have to comply."

Silvia's shame grew into anger. Everything she and her parents had worked so hard for was about to be destroyed. She'd only had the affair with Ellen to get inside information about the White House, and affairs in over-sexed Washington were as common as pigeons in the city's parks. Perhaps she'd gotten too caught up in the affair with Ellen, but she was only trying to get leads. Now they were firing her for it.

Her blood boiled. She tossed the manila folder on the floor spilling its contents. She rose from her seat and leaned toward Bradley. "This is bullshit, Brad, and you know it," she said. "Reporters have been working sources like this for centuries. To get stories, you hire female reporters to get in bed with powerful men. Well, I happened to attract a woman—a well-placed woman at that. Ellen gave me a lot of information including the scoop on Peter Gray's e-mail about Howard's itinerary. You loved that scoop when you got it. You should be praising me instead of firing me. And we should be pursuing this story too. What the hell happened to this newspaper? It made its name on investigatory journalism and now you just fold at the first challenge from the White House."

"Silvia, sit down," Brad demanded. His bushy eyebrows were furrowed. Silvia took a few short breaths and sat on the edge of her chair. "You're not an investigative reporter, understand?" Brad said. "You are... were the White House correspondent. It's different. The job needs to be handled with a high level of diplomacy and you blew it. You betrayed the trust the White House gave you when you jumped in bed with Ellen Stein. Now this newspaper is on the White House shit list and I have to get us off it."

"Ellen is the one who betrayed the White House," Silvia snapped. "I was just doing my job."

"You got caught having sex with a senior White House aide. I'm sure Ms. Stein has lost her job too and will never work in Washington, D.C. again. You might be able to escape the same fate, although I'm sure you'll never get close to the White House. That means you can no longer be this newspaper's White House correspondent and to placate the people who sent these photographs, I must fire you."

Silvia looked at Ian who returned a pained expression and then looked away. "So, you're not going to do anything about the story?" Silvia asked both of them. "Doesn't this 'message', as you call it, prove someone is trying to hide something? Why would they come down so hard on me if I wasn't onto something big?"

"It doesn't prove a thing," replied Bradley, shaking his head. "For all we know, they're coming down on you because you're sleeping with a senior White House aide, not because you're onto a story. Anyway, even if there was a story, we couldn't do anything about it. Not now. We'd run the risk of your affair being exposed. Then we'd be blackballed by the entire D.C. establishment."

Silvia crossed her arms and slumped into her chair. "So I'm out?" she asked.

The editor-in-chief nodded. "I have no choice. As of right now, you're through here. Ian will help you pack your office. You'll get five months' severance and we'll pay six months of medical insurance. Frankly, given the reason for your dismissal, it's a generous package."

Silvia took a deep breath and gathered the photos back into the manila folder. She tried to resist an urge to tell Bradley what she really felt about him and the newspaper. But as she went to the door, her emotions boiled over. "*Tú eres un cobarde, mi amigo,*" she said. You're a coward. You have an opportunity. "You're only risking a three-month relationship with a lame duck Administration. All you need is courage—*huevos*—but you don't have it. You and the rest of the newspapers in this city—in this country—have become nothing more than shills for the government. It's sad."

Silvia burst out of the editor-in-chief's office with the photographs and marched toward her cubicle. Ian followed her. "I'm sorry, Silvia," Ian said, his British accent thick. "Bradley didn't have a choice."

"Bradley doesn't have a spine, Ian," she snarled over her shoulder. "I can understand why I can no longer be the White House correspondent, but he shouldn't give up on this story. He should let me run with it instead."

"I'm afraid you don't have enough evidence," Ian replied.

They got to Silvia's cubicle and Ian watched as Silvia threw her personal belongings into a cardboard box. When she was done, she thrust out her chin and marched through the hall to the elevators. Other *Sentinel* employees tried not to stare as she walked by. When she got to the elevators, Ian took her security card and press pass. He smiled at her sheepishly and said, "Let me know if I can help. Take some time, then give me a call."

Silvia didn't respond as the elevator doors closed and took her to the ground floor.

FORTY-FIVE

When Nan arrived at the Chez Colette restaurant in the Sofitel Hotel, Bob Hilton was waiting for her at a table in the corner. As Nan approached the bistro-style table, Hilton stood and extended a hand. "Thanks for meeting me, Nan," he said with a sincere smile. She had to admit Bob Hilton had a magnetic charm. He was, as usual, impeccably groomed and dressed in a conservative, yet sharp navy blue suit. He had an obvious intelligence about him and an Ivy League look like he had never lost at anything in his life. Apparently he didn't want to lose Nan, either.

Nan shook his hand and they sat. A waiter angled over, skillfully poured coffee in their cups and took their orders. After he left, Hilton leaned his elbows on the table and cradled his coffee in both hands. "I wasn't surprised to get your resignation," he began. "Believe it or not, I sympathize with your position."

"Then you know I can't change my mind if you go forward with your plans," Nan said.

Hilton nodded. "I have some things to tell you. If after you hear what I say you feel the same way, I won't try to change your mind. But hear me out first."

"That's why I'm here," Nan said, taking a sip of coffee.

Hilton admitted that his people were monitoring her staff in Minnesota. He didn't give details, but he reassured Nan he did nothing illegal.

Nan shot Hilton a look. "It might be legal but it isn't right, Bob. Is that what Rex, Tom and Sorrea are doing?"

"Among other things, yes." Hilton folded his hands in his lap. He told Nan that he'd sent his people to Minnesota to do opposition research and keep an eye on Senator Howard and his staff. Since they didn't know Nan's people in the Minneapolis office, Rex had the idea that they should monitor their staff, too. At first he disagreed, Hilton explained. "But after what you told us about Sheldon Hanrahan and his dirty tricks, I told Rex to go ahead."

"So you spied on me, too?"

Hilton looked at his hands. 'Spied' is a strong word, Nan. Let's just say we checked out everyone. I trusted you, but since we were checking on the others…"

Anger welled up inside her. So that was what Hank had discovered when he left the note in Nan's car that said, *We're being watched'*. He was right; they were being watched—by their own people. "That stinks, Bob," Nan said.

"Yeah," Hilton replied, "it does. But understand, you made an impression regarding Hanrahan. 'He doesn't play fair,' you said. Today, they play dirty tricks via the Internet. Hacking, stealing information, hijacking e-mail accounts and sending harmful e-mails. Even crashing an opponent's entire system. So yeah, I sent Sorrea to keep an eye on things, including the people in your office. As it turns out, it was a good thing we did. We discovered one of your campaign workers is feeding information to our opponents."

"You're kidding? Who?"

Before Hilton could answer, the waiter came and served their meals—for Nan, a croissant with black currant jam and freshly squeezed orange juice. Eggs Benedict for Hilton.

Hilton began to slice off a section of his eggs.

"Who is it?" Nan asked again.

"Shelly Novak," Hilton replied without looking up. "We don't think she's working directly for Hanrahan, but she's been working for the other party since well before Marshall bowed out."

"Are you sure? Shelly Novak?"

"Positive. We have evidence."

Nan hadn't touched her croissant. She tried to remember the talks she'd had with Shelly and what she might have slipped to their opponents. She realized she'd trusted Shelly with some sensitive information. She couldn't believe Shelly Novak had fooled her.

Hilton swallowed another mouthful of his breakfast and washed it down with coffee. He looked at Nan and said, "So you see, maybe we were justified in checking on your people.

"Still," Hilton continued, "it was a bad decision. Please understand I make hundreds of decisions every day, and I don't always make the right ones. One of the reasons I'm here is to apologize and to tell you, we've pulled Rex, Tom and Sorrea from the Minneapolis office. They're gone. I'm sorry. I hope you'll forgive me."

Nan took a bite of her croissant and mulled over what Hilton had just said. One of the reasons she'd resigned was because she wasn't sure she could trust Hilton anymore. But he was admitting his mistake and asking her to forgive him.

He seemed sincere and for the first time since Nan started working with him, he showed some humility. And maybe he was justified in monitoring the Minnesota staff.

"Thanks for your apology, Bob," she said. "This doesn't change the campaign, however. The main reason I resigned is because I don't agree with your plans. I won't support them, even if it means I'm helping Senator Howard in some small way."

"When the press learns about your resignation, they'll write about it." Hilton said. "It won't kill us, but with one week left, anything negative hurts."

"Sorry, Bob. If the press calls me, I'll do what I can to keep the damage to a minimum."

"If you decide to resign, that is." Hilton set his fork on the marble table and stared at Nan. "You might not want to after you hear what I'm about to say."

"Like I said, I doubt it. But go ahead."

Hilton told Nan that they had learned the FBI has a theory that someone inside the Howard camp arranged the assassination attempt to get him elected via the sympathy vote. Specifically, he explained, the theory is Sheldon Hanrahan choreographed the assassination attempt.

Nan set her croissant down and returned Hilton's stare. "You can't be serious," she said.

Hilton leaned forward. "Think about it. The shot was two hundred yards away with a sniper rifle and high-powered scope. It didn't kill him. And, there was only one shot taken. After the first shot, Howard was on the ground so if the assassin wanted to kill him, he could have taken several more shots to be sure he was dead. Furthermore, the assassin knew where Howard would be. They supposedly posted his itinerary on his website. But it's hard to believe Gray is that stupid. Maybe, but doubtful."

"What about the terrorist letter? And the claims made by Al Queda? They admitted to it."

"Of course they did," Hilton nodded. "They'd take credit even if they had nothing to do with it. And the letter could easily have been a forgery."

"It's unbelievable," Nan said.

"Right now it's only a theory, but it's a good one. The FBI is taking it seriously."

"I don't know, Bob," Nan said shaking her head. "Not even Sheldon Hanrahan would go to that extreme."

Hilton cocked his head. "Really? You, yourself, told me Sheldon didn't follow the rules. You said he'd do anything to win."

Hilton was right. She had said that about Sheldon Hanrahan. But this? Would he really go to these extremes? Maybe. Deception was Sheldon Hanrahan's game, and he was the game's grand master. And this, if he got away with it, would be his *magnum opus*.

Hilton held his coffee in both hands again. "Nan, there's one more thing. You say you can't work with us if we conduct a dirty campaign. Well, we've decided not to. We've determined the best chance we have to win this election is to run a clean campaign and let the press report the FBI investigation. Once word gets out, it'll throw the election to Bloomfield."

Hilton eyed Nan from over his coffee cup. He took a long sip and set the cup down. "So, your reason for quitting our campaign is no longer valid. Now you have to ask yourself a question. If you want to make a statement against dirty campaigns, wouldn't it be better to stay with the

Bloomfield campaign to take a stand against what could be the biggest con in election history?"

Nan ran her hand through her hair. Everything Hilton said made sense but it was crazy, too. A half hour earlier, she knew exactly what she had to do. Now, she wasn't so sure. She had to take time to think things through. "Can I have some time, Bob?" she asked.

Hilton took his napkin from his lap and placed it on the table. "I'll be working from my hotel room all morning and then I'm leaving for San Francisco this afternoon. My flight is at 2:35. Why don't you pick me up at 1:00 and take me to the airport. You can give me your final decision then. That's all the time I can give you. Okay?"

"That's fair," Nan answered. "I have something to do this morning but I can be back at 1:00." She tossed him a smile.

Hilton nodded and motioned for the waiter to bring the check. When it came, he wrote his room number on it and they both rose to leave. When they got to the hotel lobby, Hilton said, "Nan, I hope you decide to stay. You should know, I talked with George, and if you stay and we win, the position of White House Communications Director is yours—if you want it."

Nan gave Hilton a nod. "I'll see you at 1:00, Bob."

FORTY-SIX

As Nan drove to the Crystal Lake Cemetery among the small, blue-collar homes of Minneapolis' northwest side, she didn't keep checking her rearview mirror for the first time since getting Hank's note warning her they were being watched. Hilton confessed to spying on her and he promised it had stopped. She believed him and sensed he was genuinely sorry for having done it in the first place.

She was also pleased that Hilton and Governor Bloomfield decided to drop their plans for a negative campaign. Nan could not be part of a something like that. She'd refused to do it when she ran Theilen's campaign and she wouldn't do it now, either.

Of course, she was not so naïve to believe that Hilton had changed strategies for ethical reasons. If what he said was true, if the FBI was investigating Sheldon Hanrahan for the attempted assassination of Senator Howard, then a clean campaign was, in fact, their best strategy. Once the story got out about the FBI's investigation, the entire election would be in turmoil again and this time Bloomfield would be the beneficiary. It just might get him elected the next president of the United States.

Then there was the job of White House Communications Director. Two weeks earlier, when the possibility first came up, she was flattered and excited about it. She could picture herself in the West Wing of the White House working among some of the most brilliant people in the world. She'd have power and influence and could make a real difference. Naturally, she was concerned about how her busy job and the move to D.C. would affect Jenny. But she genuinely believed that, with effort, she could make it work. Nan would be a wonderful role model for Jenny and would earn an income that would make the family finances healthy again.

She still needed to decide if she wanted to withdraw her resignation. She had less than three hours to make up her mind and as she drove up to the cemetery, she had no idea what her answer would be. She decided to put the question aside until after she had searched the gravesite of Elizabeth Czerwinski.

As Nan drove through the gates of the Crystal Lake Cemetery, she reached in her briefcase and pulled out the plot map Ben had gotten in an e-mail from Monica Adams. The gravesite for Elizabeth Czerwinski was in section 16, lot 5. Nan stopped her car to study the map. When she saw where she should go, she drove the narrow, winding roads to the back of the cemetery and found a small, sad sign for section 16. She parked her car. She glanced at the map again, got out of the car and began to search for lot 5.

A wind with the promise of winter blew dead leaves in a swirl among the low, gray gravestones. This section of the cemetery was for recent burials and had none of the marble monoliths that graced the entrance. Here, it felt like death—sad and final. Nan pulled her coat tight around her.

She located lot 5 and began to search for Elizabeth Czerwinski's grave. She read the names and dates engraved on the cold headstones. Most showed people who had lead long lives. Some, were for younger people—people like Elizabeth. Nan was looking for just such a grave site—the grave of a young woman who, like these young people, died before she could know many of life's joys and mysteries; a daughter whose mother's heart had been broken and who wanted answers to why her precious girl had been taken from her at such a young age.

At least she could see if Mrs. Wilson was telling the truth about how her daughter died. If there were letters that proved Senator Howard murdered her daughter, Nan was convinced they'd be here. If there were no letters, then Nan would know that the grief Mrs. Wilson bore for her dead child had driven her mad.

Nan spotted the grave for Elizabeth Czerwinski and walked over to it. There was a low, cheap gravestone with the words 'Beloved Daughter' engraved below the name. To the left was a green, metal flower vase tilting on its side. Nan looked inside the vase. It was empty. Nan noticed several other graves had the same type of vase but that some had only a metal base where the vase should be. Nan examined the vase more closely. It was secured to a metal ring in the ground. She knelt next to the vase and with both hands, twisted the vase until it released from the base exposing a cavity below.

She saw that when it wasn't being used, the vase was designed to be stored upside down inside the hole. The hole had to be at least as deep as the vase was tall—deep enough to hide letters.

Nan looked inside the hole. It was dark and she couldn't see to the bottom. She glanced over her shoulder to see if someone was watching her. A car was parked on the other side of section 16 and two people carried flowers toward a gravesite. No one else was near. The wind blew and dead leaves rustled nervously where they'd been trapped against a gravestone.

Nan tried to reach inside the hole but the opening was too small for her hand. She looked inside again. There was something at the bottom.

Nan pushed her hand into the hole again. The edge of the base scraped her but she pushed it through. She reached to the bottom and felt a plastic package. She grabbed it and tried to pull her hand out but now her fist was too wide. She loosened her grip on the package and pulled. The package dropped back to the bottom.

She thought about what she might have in her car to grip it. She couldn't think of anything. Perhaps she could go home and grab tongs from the kitchen. No, there wasn't enough time.

She looked in the hole again. She could see the plastic bag had landed with the zip-lock top facing her, almost as if it was begging to be taken. Nan thought of Mrs. Wilson. The woman had come to her for help, and so far, Nan had done nothing for her. Nan clenched her teeth and pushed her hand in the hole again. She held the plastic bag with the tips of her fingers and pulled her hand out. This time, the base cut into her hand and a strip of skin peeled off. She winced as she squeezed her hand through the opening. Blood oozed where the skin was scraped away, but in her hand was a zip-lock plastic bag with red yarn around it.

Inside were letters.

FORTY-SEVEN

FRANK PIERCE WAS PISSED. Containment had been breached and the person who had breached it was Nan Smith.

From inside his Escalade, Pierce peered through 10X powered Ziess field binoculars as Nan Smith's silver Toyota Camry pulled out of the Crystal Lake Cemetery. Since he had taken care of Mrs. Wilson, he'd been watching Nan Smith's every move. She knew something and he wanted to know what it was. The tap on her phones, the bug in her office and the transcripts of her e-mails didn't reveal anything. Her movements hadn't been suspicious either.

Until now. She was digging around the girl's grave for Christ's sake. Goddamn it, how did she find it, anyway? What made her come here and what had she found underneath the vase? She was carrying something as she walked back to her car. A package.

Pierce cursed at himself for letting Woods handle the operation in Minnesota. If Pierce had been here, they'd have searched the gravesite and there would have been nothing to find. Now, it was clear Nan Smith suspected something and was digging around for clues. Apparently, she had found one.

Pierce started the Escalade and threw it into gear. He followed the Camry back to the Smith house, careful to stay well back. He had to know what she had found and, if it was something important, he had to take it from her. They paid him a lot to keep things under control and five years of work would go up in smoke if this nosy woman knew too much.

He had come to hate this job. Five years earlier when they tapped him for it, the nature of it, the angles and twists had intrigued him. And the job had come from high up, he could tell. A job like this, with its secrecy and money, was one that would put him in good standing. If he did it well—and Frank always did his job well—he would move to the top.

But they hadn't told him everything and mistakes were made. Now it was getting messy and it was up to Frank to clean the mess up.

The orderly. Nan Smith had talked to the orderly just yesterday and today she was poking around the girl's grave. The fucking orderly must know more than he'd said. The men Pierce had sent to Minnesota said they interrogated him and were convinced he didn't know anything. But the orderly was stupid and slow and may have forgotten something. They had to interrogate him again, and this time they'd use the dogs.

After that, he would take care of Nan Smith once and for all.

FORTY-EIGHT

NAN SPREAD OUT the letters on the kitchen table. She'd dressed the scrape on her hand with Neosporin and a large Band-Aid. The wound throbbed and she could tell it would soon form an ugly scab.

She examined the letters. There were three short, single page letters, handwritten, on baby-blue stationery with a cursive 'EC' etched on the top. A fourth, longer letter was also handwritten but this one was on three pages of Howard's Senate office letterhead. The letters were all dated from the spring and summer of five years earlier.

The handwriting was flawless—almost as if Elizabeth was recording an historical event. *Perhaps she was*, thought Nan.

The words were clear and to the point and reflected an intelligent, thoughtful mind. The photograph of the beautiful, cynical young woman Nan had seen at the Rand Psychiatric Hospital floated in her mind as Nan picked up the first letter and carefully read it.

Dear Mother:

As I write this letter, the cherry blossoms are in full bloom in Washington, D.C. and the air is thick with their fragrance. They are magnificent. Yet when I walk through the city, I wonder if they planted them to cover the stench of what goes on here. The games these people play stink. They don't care about anyone but themselves.

But I'm no better than they are, I guess. I know why I'm here...

Sorry for being such a downer. I am fine and looking forward to starting Stanford in the fall. I've decided I want to go into law after I graduate. I have to keep my focus on that.

I'm glad to hear the money I've sent has enabled you to finally get the medicine you need. Is it helping? Is the pain less?

I'm sorry I can't be there with you. I think of Daddy every day. Please don't worry about me.

Love,

Elizabeth

Nan folded the letter into its envelope and opened the second one. It was in the same precise handwriting as the first.

Dearest Mother,

I'm so glad your medicine is helping. I'll send more money.

I need to tell you something that you must keep to yourself. I've been introduced to some very important people and my job is to get information from them for Senator Howard. I hope what I'm doing isn't illegal – I don't think it is. If these idiots want to show off by blabbing to some intern with a cute smile and big boobs, it's their fault, right?

Anyway, it's exciting to mix with the people you see on the news every day. I just feel sleazy sometimes.

It's getting hot here. That reminds me, I've been invited to a pool party with some VIPs and I really want to wear my yellow bikini. Will you send it? ☺

Love,

Elizabeth

P.S. I'm going to the White House tomorrow. Maybe I'll meet the president!

Nan opened the third letter dated a month after the last.

Dear Mother,

I think I've made a huge mistake. Today, Daniel Rabkin, Howard's assistant chief of staff, told me Stanford would revoke my admission if they knew what I did here. He said I'd never get into law school, either. It seems like a veiled threat to embarrass me if I don't do what they ask.

I may have gone too far. I thought I could handle this. I'm not sure what to do.

Don't worry. I'll think of something.

Elizabeth

Nan unfolded the last letter—the one written on Senator Howard's letterhead. It was dated a full two months after the last one and was three pages long. It began with the cryptic sentence: *Save this letter in case something happens to me.* The letter went on to explain Elizabeth's activities since she'd come to Washington, D.C. to work for Senator Howard. In words painful and hard for Nan to read, Elizabeth admitted to her mother that she was a prostitute hired to blackmail powerful men in the government for Sheldon Hanrahan. Before she came to Washington, Sheldon had trained her personally and offered to pay her college expenses and help her get into Stanford. She said it was the only way she could think of to break out of the poverty they'd known all their lives. But it hadn't worked. They'd used her.

The last two pages listed in graphic detail Elizabeth's crimes and who she had done them to. It was an impressive list. There was an influential congressman who she had gotten drunk and who, while she stroked him under the table, gave her the details of a covert, sensitive arms agreement being worked out with Iran. Someone hired by Howard's Chief of Staff, Daniel Rabkin, secretly filmed the entire scene. Then there was the head of the Senate banking committee with whom she'd had an ongoing affair and had recorded giving her advance information on banking legislation that would affect stock prices. There was another incident, the letter said, where someone had taken photos of her at a stag party sitting topless on the lap of a married, front-running presidential hopeful. Nan recalled that, four years earlier, the candidate had unexpectedly bowed out of the race.

The list went on and on. Finally, at the end, was a short reference to a "brief affair" with someone in the White House. The letter didn't name who the affair was with.

At the end of the letter, Elizabeth wrote she feared for her life because she knew too much. It'd all gotten out of control so quickly, she wrote, and she wasn't sure if she could escape. "But I have a plan," the letter concluded, "and I'll be home soon. I'm so sorry, Mother. I love you."

I'll be home soon, Nan thought. Indeed, she was home soon afterward—to be buried in the Crystal Lake Cemetery.

Nan folded the letters into their envelopes and tucked them back in the plastic bag. She was stunned at what they revealed. They incriminated more than a dozen high-ranking government officials and if they got out, it would force many important people from office. It would be the biggest scandal

Washington had ever seen. And who was the affair in the White House with? Could it be it President Dougherty? Is that why he endorsed Senator Howard?

The letters would also destroy Senator Howard's presidential bid. There was no conclusive evidence that Senator Howard had killed Elizabeth Czerwinski, but there was certainly enough evidence to open an investigation. Even if no homicide was committed, the letters proved Senator Howard, the man who in less than a week could be the next president of the United States, was part of a conspiracy to blackmail officials at the very highest levels of the United States government.

Nan stared at the packet of letters and wondered what to do with them. She'd promised Ben that if she found evidence of foul play in the girl's death, she'd take it to the police. But the gravity of the information seemed far too important to just hand over to the local police. This was a scandal of national proportions.

Nan checked the clock on the kitchen wall. She had less than twenty minutes to pick up Bob Hilton at the Sofitel and take him to the airport. She'd promised to give him a decision about her resignation but she hadn't had time to think about it. She looked at the letters again and a wave of disgust for everything about politics rose in the pit of her stomach. How could they have destroyed this beautiful young woman by luring her into their game with the promise of the American dream—the very dream they had the responsibility to protect?

Then a new emotion gripped her. She had in her hands one of the most important pieces of incriminating evidence in American history. A lot of people would want these letters— the people being blackmailed, Senator Howard, Sheldon Hanrahan and maybe even the president of the United States.

Some of them might even kill for it.

Nan fished her phone out of her purse. She hit the buttons to look at her call history. She saw she still had the number with the 202 area code for Silvia Mendoza at the *Sentinel*. She hit the call button and the phone rang. The call rolled into voice-mail. Before Nan could listen to the voice-mail greeting, she ended the call. She looked at the letters again. She took them out of the plastic bag, pulled some aluminum foil out of a drawer and wrapped them in the foil. She opened the freezer and tucked the letters behind a bag of frozen peas.

Then she grabbed her car keys and headed out the door to pick up Bob Hilton and give him her decision.

FORTY-NINE

As HE SAT IN a black leather chair in his office, Sheldon Hanrahan asked to watch the video for a third time. Victor, sitting next to him on the couch, pressed the 'Play' button on the DVD player and the giant screen built into the wall blinked to life again. The grainy, shaky video showed Nan Smith in the Crystal Lake Cemetery carrying a small package away from the grave of Elizabeth Czerwinski. When the video ended, Sheldon sat quietly for some time. Then he asked, "Frank Pierce was watching her, too?"

Victor nodded. "Da. He watched from car and followed her to house."

"Do we know which one of Frank's employers sent him?"

"No. Maybe is no one. Maybe he is here on his own."

"Do we know what Ms. Smith took from the grave site?"

"No. We should search house and car."

Sheldon stood from the chair and went back to his glass desk. "I'm more concerned about Pierce. There's no telling what he'll do. You say the mother has disappeared from the hospital?"

"Da. She is gone. No trace."

"Don't waste your time looking," Sheldon said. He folded his hands and set them on his desk. "I don't want him to hurt Nan Smith. Understand? We'll find out what she took from the grave ourselves. In the meantime, I'll see who sent Pierce and get them to call him off. Just in case, keep a tail on him and let me know if something comes up."

Victor moved to the office door. As he reached the door Sheldon said, "Victor, remember, protect Nan Smith at all costs."

"I will do," Victor replied and disappeared through the door.

Sheldon closed the Levolour blinds to dim the light. He took off his dark glasses and rubbed his tender eye. Sheldon had never completely trusted Frank Pierce. He'd proven to be the Hollywood stereotype of the undercover government operative who didn't think things through. Sheldon had had to clean up the mess five years earlier on his own. Then they brought in Pierce. The people who employed him said he was their very best and they wanted him in charge of the cover-up. Sheldon had agreed to let them use the former CIA operative. After all, they were the ones who had the most to lose. And during the last five years, Pierce had done an adequate job— until now.

Pierce had let things get out of hand just as Sheldon was in reach of the White House. And now Nan Smith was Peirce's target. Nan Smith. Beautiful, intelligent... someone Sheldon could love.

Yes. It was time to take control.

FIFTY

W̲ʜᴇɴ N̲ᴀɴ ᴅʀᴏᴠᴇ ᴜᴘ to the front of the Sofitel Hotel, Bob Hilton was standing at the door talking on his cell phone. Resting on the sidewalk next to him was a black suit bag and a large, cube-shaped briefcase. He continued to talk into his phone while he tossed the bags into the trunk of the Camry and climbed into the passenger seat. Nan drove out of the parking lot and pointed the car toward the airport.

As Hilton continued on the phone, Nan thought about her decision. Bloomfield was right that it would be dangerous to let Howard win and have Sheldon Hanrahan run the country. And she was relieved that Hilton decided not to run a dirty campaign. But Elizabeth Czerwinski's letters had moved her. Politicians who wanted nothing more than power, mone,y and fame destroyed the poor girl. It made Nan's stomach turn.

Hilton didn't hang up from his call until they were nearly to the airport. "Sorry about that," he said, stuffing the phone in his coat pocket. "I was talking to Betty Morris. The FBI is coming out with a report on the assassination attempt this afternoon. All hell will break loose and we need to be ready. George will be the front-runner again tomorrow."

"That's great," Nan said, keeping her eyes on the road.

"What happened to your hand?" Hilton asked.

"I, ah, cut myself in the kitchen." Nan answered.

"That's a strange place for a cut," Hilton said, eyeing her.

Nan didn't respond. She thought about the letters and tried to imagine what Hilton would do if he knew about them.

After a pause, Hilton said. "Sorry I don't have much time, Nan. I need your decision."

Nan sighed. "To be honest, I haven't had time to think about it, but I know what my decision is. I'm sorry, Bob. I'm sticking with my resignation."

Hilton nodded. "Okay. I have to say I'm disappointed. We could've worked well together. I was hoping to talk you out of it. But, frankly, with the FBI report coming out, it won't hurt us much."

"I'm glad, Bob," Nan replied as she turned onto the airport road. "I really hope Bloomfield wins. In fact," she said, thinking of the letters in her freezer, "I know he will."

"You're missing a great opportunity, Nan. I can't imagine why you wouldn't take it. White House Communications Director. It's a very important job."

"I'll tell you why, Bob. You've been planning a dirty campaign since you sent your people to Minnesota. You only abandoned it because you felt it wasn't the right strategy anymore. If this FBI report wasn't coming out, you'd run a negative, dirty campaign. Your decision doesn't have anything to do with right and wrong. It's all about taking advantage of a broken election system to get your guy elected."

"You're right, Nan," Hilton said. "The system is broken. But you can't change things unless you're in power."

Nan pulled the car in front of the drop off area and put it in park. "I'm not so sure," she said, turning to Hilton. "You know, I like you, Bob. I think you'll make an outstanding Chief of Staff. And I wish you and Governor Bloomfield well. I just hope that putting success ahead of ethics doesn't get you in trouble someday."

Hilton got out of the car and extended a hand to Nan who shook it. "Good luck to you, Nan. Look me up when you're in Washington and we'll have a proper debate on the subject."

"You'll be too busy to see me and you know it," Nan said.

Hilton shut the car door, waved and retrieved his bags from the trunk. He was on his cell phone again as he disappeared through the sliding airport terminal doors.

And then Nan knew once and for all, her career in politics was over. She'd never again run a political campaign and she certainly would never have a job in the White House. But she'd done the right thing. She'd stood up for what she believed in. Perhaps, in some small way, the country was better, too.

She had just one more thing to do.

*

As she drove back home, she thought about Elizabeth Czerwinski's letters. She still couldn't believe they existed. It was outrageous that something so terribly important was wrapped in aluminum foil behind a package of peas in her freezer. Out of habit, she checked her rear-view mirror to see if anyone was following her. She thought she recognized an Escalade she'd seen on the way to pick up Hilton. Of course, there were hundreds, maybe thousands of black Escalades in a big city like Minneapolis, but, to ease her mind, she took her foot off the accelerator and let the Camry slow to fifty, then forty. A driver in a yellow cab behind her abruptly changed lanes and roared past honking his horn. As the Camry slowed, the Escalade maintained its speed and soon was passing her. Nan glanced at the driver, a man in his late thirties who did not look back. After a few seconds, the Escalade was well ahead, and she continued to drive at a normal speed.

She grabbed her cell phone and redialed the number for Silvia Mendoza. She got Silvia's voice-mail again. This time, Nan listened to the voice-mail greeting intending to leave a message. The greeting said Silvia was no longer with the *Sentinel* and that her editor, Ian Rutter was taking her calls. The greeting gave the editor's number but Nan didn't listen to it. She pressed 'zero' on her phone and the call was transferred to the operator. A woman answered. "Washington, D.C. *Sentinel.* How may I direct your call?"

"Hello. I need to talk to the person taking calls for Silvia Mendoza."

"Yes, ma'am. I'll transfer you." There was a click and pulsing static and then a man with a slight British accent came on the line. "This is Ian Rutter."

"Hello, Mr. Rutter. My name is Nan Smith. I talked with Silvia Mendoza a few days ago about a story she was working on and, well, I have something. Something important."

"Ms. Mendoza was working on several stories when she left," Rutter said. "Which one was she talking to you about, specifically?"

Nan told the newspaperman that she was the Minnesota state campaign manager for Governor Bloomfield and that Silvia called to see if Nan knew why President Dougherty endorsed Senator Howard. Nan explained that she ran the campaign for Congresswoman Janice Theilen for Howard's senate seat two years earlier and Silvia thought she might have insights.

"Ah, that story," Rutter said. "What did you say your name was?"

"Nan Smith. I'm calling from Minnesota."

"Yes, I think I remember hearing about you," Rutter said. "When Howard entered the race, you became a senior adviser to Governor Bloomfield. Am I correct?"

"Actually, I'm not an adviser anymore."

"Oh?"

"I'm sorry, Mr. Rutter. That's not why I'm calling. I have something important you should know about."

"Yes, you said that. Do tell me, what do you have?"

"It's a long story. Let me just say I have in my possession letters written by a former intern for Senator Howard to her mother that proves Senator Howard and Sheldon Hanrahan ran a conspiracy to blackmail highly placed government officials. There is even a reference to the White House."

There was silence at the other end of the line. Nan looked at her cell phone to see if the call had been dropped. It had not.

"I, ah…" Rutter stammered finally. "I mean… Are you sure?"

"Positive." Nan's exit off the freeway was coming up. She checked her rear-view mirror before changing lanes and thought she spotted the black Escalade again, this time much further back. She looked in the mirror more closely. The Camry's right front tire skidded off the pavement with a loud thumping noise. Nan quickly jerked the car back onto the exit ramp. She checked her mirror again but the angle of the car going up the ramp pointed the mirror too high.

She heard Ian's voice through her cell phone. "Ms. Smith. Are you still there?"

"Yes, yes. I'm still here. Sorry," Nan said.

"Ms. Smith, please forgive me, but what you are telling me is really unbelievable," Rutter said. "I'm sure you are a reliable source, but you say you have letters that prove a candidate for president of the United States is a criminal? And you work for Governor Bloomfield. Do you see where I'm going?"

"Yes. I know how it looks, Mr. Rutter." Nan had turned onto Portland Avenue and checked her mirror again. She saw no sign of the black Escalade. "First of all," she continued, "I no longer work for George Bloomfield. I've resigned. Second, I've had information about this for weeks and have held off telling anyone because I was afraid of how it would look. But I found the letters this morning and they're far too important for me to wait to give them to someone until after the election. I've chosen to give them to you. Do you want them or shall I call someone else? The *Washington Post* perhaps. Or maybe the *New York Times?*"

"No, no. I understand. Give me a little more information. Who wrote the letters again?"

Nan gave Rutter Elizabeth Czerwinski's entire story. She explained that Elizabeth's mother thought that Elizabeth was murdered and that someone might have murdered the mother, too.

"Senator Howard? Murder?" Rutter said. "It's unbelievable."

"Yes. That's what I thought, too. But now, I have these letters, Mr. Rutter."

"What else?" Rutter asked. "Tell me everything."

Nan's cell phone beeped and she looked at the readout. The screen flashed a warning that her battery was low. "Mr. Rutter, my phone is running out of power. I can't tell you the entire story now. And you should have these letters, not me."

After a pause, Rutter said, "Ms. Smith, I want to hear your story and get the letters as soon as I can. I can be in Minneapolis first thing in the morning. Can I meet you then?"

"It would be well worth your time."

As Nan pulled into her driveway, she gave Ian Rutter her cell phone number and arranged a time and place for them to meet the next morning. She hung up from the call and walked into her house. She threw her keys on the kitchen table and stared at the freezer. She resisted the urge to retrieve the letters and read them again.

She opened the refrigerator and grabbed a pound of hamburger. It was going to be a nice evening and Jenny would be home from school soon. She decided they would grill one last time before winter came to Minnesota.

As she pressed the meat into patties, the presence of the letters in the freezer loomed over the kitchen. It felt odd doing something as mundane as making hamburgers when the future of the nation was in her hands. Tomorrow, she'd turn the letters over to Ian Rutter and the ordeal that began over two weeks before when Mrs. Wilson came to her office would be over.

She only needed to make it through the night.

FIFTY-ONE

WHEN HE WAS DONE here, he'd go to Montana and kill Woods, Pierce thought as he shivered inside his Escalade waiting for the sun to rise. It would serve him right, the incompetent asshole. He'd make it look like a race crime. A black man killed by a Montana redneck. He'd torture him a bit first. Maybe break his knees or cut off his dick. Might be a bit extreme, but Pierce didn't care. Woods should have checked the goddamn gravesite.

There'd been a pain in Pierce's stomach ever since the retarded orderly finally remembered to tell them about the letters. Pierce knew the Dobermans would jog the retard's memory. He'd never seen anyone as scared as when they sicced the snarling dogs on him. As the dogs tore at his ankles, the orderly screamed and sobbed like a baby and then remembered he and 'that lady' had talked about Mrs. Wilson's weekly trips to her daughter's grave. And then he remembered the letters.

Nan Smith. Nan... fucking... Smith. He had to get the letters and take care of her or she'd blow containment. She knew too much. And if she talked, the whole thing would fall apart. They'd convict him of the mother's murder and he'd spend the rest of his life in prison.

This was his last operation on this goddamn job. It'd been fucked up since the day they said they'd take care of Mrs. Wilson their way. He'd do what he had to do, then go back to Washington and demand another assignment. He'd earned it. Five years on this one was more than anyone should be expected to do. Anyway, after the election there'd be new people coming in. They'd have different priorities and new assignments. Australia. That's where he wanted to go. Never been to that part of the world. He'd heard that the men liked to fight and the women liked to fuck. Yeah, Australia. Just one more thing to do.

He'd considered breaking into the house late at night, but there was no reason to think she'd done anything with the letters. Not yet, anyway. So he hatched a plan as he waited in the cold inside his SUV a block from the Smith home. Soon, it would be morning and Nan's daughter would go to school.

The daughter was the key.

First, he'd have to shake the people who were tailing him. He knew who they were. When he first saw them, he cursed them for not trusting him. If they'd just let him do his job, they wouldn't need to worry about a thing.

Losing them would be easy enough. His people had their instructions and when the Smith daughter was in the right place, he'd be able to slip away and execute his plan.

Then he'd be off to Australia and no one would have to worry about letters—or Nan Smith—anymore.

FIFTY-TWO

"JENNY!" NAN SHOUTED from the kitchen. "Remember, you're not taking the bus this morning. I'm taking you to school. We should get going."

"One minute, Mom," yelled Jenny from the upstairs bathroom.

"So," Ben said, standing at the counter, sipping his coffee, "you're going to turn the letters over to the reporter this morning?"

"Yeah," Nan replied. "I'm meeting him at Starbucks on 48th and Lyndale. He's flying in from D.C. His plane lands at nine."

"Then, you'll be done with this, once and for all?" Ben asked with an eyebrow raised.

"Yeah. I hope so."

"Good," Ben said as he put on his coat and gathered his briefcase. "Call me after your meeting. We can go out to lunch. I'll want to know how it went with the reporter."

"Ben," Nan said as he headed for the door. "Thanks for understanding. I'll get another job soon."

"We'll be alright, babe," he said as he pushed his way out the back door.

A minute later, the staircase rumbled as Jenny bounded down from her room. "I'm ready," she said.

"Put on your coat, sweetie," Nan said pulling on her own. "It's cold this morning."

Jenny put on her coat, squeezed past Nan out the back door and headed to the car. Nan followed carrying her briefcase. Inside were the letters, still wrapped in aluminum foil. The briefcase felt like it weighed a ton.

As Nan drove to Jenny's school, she checked for the black Escalade she'd seen yesterday. She saw nothing. Perhaps it was her imagination and she wasn't being followed at all. When Hilton said that he'd called off Rex and Tom, she was relieved and quit worrying about being followed. But then she found the incriminating letters and thought she'd seen the black Escalade. She'd be glad when she gave the letters to Ian Rutter and wouldn't have to worry anymore. In the meantime, she'd have to act as normally as possible, just in case.

"Mom," Jenny said, looking out the window, "why did you resign?"

"I resigned because I didn't like what they are doing in the campaign. I believe it's wrong."

"What are they doing that's wrong?"

"It's kinda hard to explain. Let's just say, they aren't following the rules."

"Won't they get in trouble for not following the rules?" Jenny asked.

"Not necessarily. The people who are supposed to enforce the rules don't do a very good job."

"Why not?"

"Well," Nan said, "I think it's because they're appointed by the people they're supposed to watch."

Jenny paused to think. "I see. It's kinda like if the lacrosse referee owed you a favor."

Nan smiled. "It's exactly like that."

"So will Senator Howard be the next president?"

Nan felt the presence of the letters in her briefcase sitting behind her in the backseat. "No, I don't think so," she replied.

"So you could have gone to work in the White House. Now you won't."

"No I won't, sweetie. Sorry." Nan pulled the Camry to the school drop-off zone. "There are some things more important than a job in the White House."

"I guess," Jenny said grabbing her backpack. "I'd still like to see the White House someday."

Nan smiled at her daughter. "I think we can arrange that. Have a great day. Call me if you need anything, okay? Anything."

"I will. Love you, Mom," she shouted as she slammed the car door.

"I love you too," Nan said into the closed door.

*

As Nan drove away heading for her meeting with Ian Rutter, she thought about what she had just said to Jenny. *There are some things more important than a job.* She'd made a sacrifice for her principles but for some reason, she didn't feel ennobled by it. There were consequences of giving up a lucrative position in the White House. Jenny would be heading off to college in a few years and she and Ben would be saddled with the expense of tuition. And Ben's business was taking a toll on him—she could see it in his face. He wanted out and Nan wanted to help. Now, she was out of work and it would be months before she could find a new job. She certainly wouldn't find anything with the pay, prestige and future earning power of the White House Director of Communications.

She'd made a huge sacrifice, indeed. Was it worth it? Would the stand she had made against a broken election system really make a difference? Perhaps not. But it had to start somewhere. Revolutions always started small. Maybe her action would—like the butterfly's wings that start a chain of events that ultimately causes a tornado—start something that would help fix the election system.

Nan pulled into the Starbucks parking lot and retrieved her briefcase from the back seat. She was forty-five minutes early and decided to spend the time sipping coffee and reading the newspaper. She hoped Ian would be there early. She prayed that this meeting would be the end of her crazy ordeal.

As she walked across parking lot toward the coffee shop, her cell phone rang. The ring tone, '*You Are My Sunshine*,' told her it was a call from Jenny's cell phone. *Why was Jenny calling while she was in school?* Nan wondered. Perhaps she forgot something at home and wanted Nan to get it for her. Or maybe she'd had an accident or was sick. Nan retrieved her phone from her briefcase and answered the call. "Jenny?" she queried.

A man's voice answered. "I have your daughter," he said evenly. "You must do exactly as I tell you if you want to see her again."

Nan felt her knees buckle. She groped for something to hold on to. Her hand found the brick wall of the Starbucks. Bile rose in the back of her throat and her breathing stopped. It felt like everything around her had changed to a thick liquid. "Who are you?" she gasped. "Where's Jenny? Why do you have her phone?"

"I have your daughter. You don't need to know who I am. Just do as I say. This will be all over quickly and Jenny will be fine."

"I... I understand," Nan heard herself say.

"I want the letters," the voice demanded, coldly. "Do you have them?"

"Yes. Please don't hurt Jenny. Please." Nan willed her way back to her car through her liquid world.

"Just do as I say. First, do not—I repeat, do not—hang up until we meet in person. If you hang up and I have to call you back, I will cut off your daughter's hand. If you hang up again, I will cut off her other hand. After that... I'll leave it up to your imagination. Am I clear?"

"Yes, yes, you are clear. Please don't hurt her. Please." Nan sat in her car shaking uncontrollably. The air inside the car was thick and she could only draw it into her lungs in big gulps. Her heart felt like it was about to burst. She squeezed her eyes closed and tried to regain control so she could do as this man said. She opened her eyes and pulled herself straight. She forced herself to take a deep breath. "What do you want me to do?" she asked.

"I have your daughter at Minnehaha Creek under the Nicollet Avenue bridge. Bring the letters and you can have her back unharmed. But on the way here, do not hang up. Talk to me the entire time until you get here. Am I clear?"

"Yes. The Nicollet Avenue bridge at Minnehaha Creek. I'm less than ten minutes away. I'll be there as soon as I can."

"Good. Remember, do not hang up. I have a few questions for you that will keep you on the phone while you drive."

As Nan started the Camry, her phone beeped. Another call was coming through. She glanced at the readout and saw it was a Washington, D.C. number. Ian Rutter said he would call when his plane landed. She ignored the call. She glanced back at the readout and her breathing stopped again. The readout said, "Low Battery." She had forgotten to recharge her phone.

Nan floored the accelerator and the Camry roared out of the parking lot. She screeched into the street and pointed the car toward Minnehaha Creek.

"Are you still there, Ms. Smith?" the voice asked.

"Yes, I'm still here," Nan answered quickly, swerving around a corner. "My phone's battery is low. I'm not sure it will make it until I get to you. I'm hurrying. Please don't hurt Jenny."

"Slow down," the voice demanded. "Don't do anything to attract the police."

He was right. She shouldn't attract the police or this man would kill Jenny. Nan eased up on the accelerator and the Camry slowed to a more reasonable speed. "Okay," she said. "But my battery is low."

"That's a problem. Now, I said I have some questions for you. First, tell me what you know about Elizabeth Czerwinski."

Nan's mind raced. Her phone beeped again telling her Rutter had left a voice-mail message. The low battery message still flashed its warning. "I..., I know she was an intern for Senator Howard. She killed herself with a drug overdose."

"What else?"

"I don't know. What do you want me to tell you?" Nan pulled up to a stop light. She was tempted to plow through it, but thought better of it. She waited for the light to change.

"Do you know what she did while she was an intern? What do the letters say?"

Nan struggled to think what she should tell him. If she said something wrong, if she told him what she learned in the letters, he would have to kill her and Jenny. "The letters didn't really say anything," she said quickly. "They just said she was disillusioned about everything in Washington. I can't imagine why they're important to you."

"I'll have to see for myself when I get them. How far away are you?"

The light changed, Nan accelerated through the intersection. "I'm still five minutes away. I'm going as fast as I can without attracting attention."

"Good. Now tell me what you know about Mrs. Wilson. She visited you at the campaign headquarters. You visited her at the hospital. What did she tell you?"

"How do you know about that? Who are you?"

"I'm asking the questions, Mrs. Smith. Answer them."

Nan's phone beeped with a different sound than before. She looked at the readout that said, 'Battery Critically Low. Phone will turn off in ten seconds.' Nan's stomach jumped and bile rose in her throat again.

"Sir," she blurted, "my phone is about to run out of power. I'm still a few minutes away. Please don't hurt Jenny. Please!"

"You better not hang up," the man replied angrily. "If you do, I'll…"

The phone went dead.

"No!" Nan cried. She threw the phone on the passenger seat and jammed the accelerator to the floor. As the car careened through stoplights and squealed around corners toward the Nicollet Avenue bridge, she prayed Jenny would still be alive when she got there.

FIFTY-THREE

"PHIL, YOU HAVE to tell me everything," Governor Bloomfield said as he sat in the back of President Dougherty's Yukon. They were meeting again in the closed-off basement parking garage five blocks from the White House and this time, the governor had called the meeting. Bloomfield's people had gotten a message to Richard Craft saying the governor needed the president's help to win the election. They arranged another secret meeting and now, as their drivers chatted at the other end of the parking lot, the president had to tell Bloomfield what all the intrigue was about. "I need to know," Bloomfield said.

The president eyed the governor and nodded. He knew Bloomfield was right. If he wanted to help the governor prevent Sheldon Hanrahan from taking over the country, he had to tell George everything. Maybe it would make him feel better, too.

"It's not easy to admit this, George" the president began. "But you're right. You need to know."

Bloomfield folded his arms and settled into his seat in the dark Yukon. His face was in shadows and Dougherty was glad he didn't have to look him in the eye. "I told you before, this job takes everything out of you," The president said. "It requires tremendous courage. I didn't have it when it was most needed."

The president studied his hands. "I had an affair, George, with an intern from Howard's office."

"I see," Bloomfield said from the shadows. "You aren't the first president to have had an affair in office, Phil. It surely wasn't ethical, but it shouldn't cause all this. You didn't fall in love with her, did you?"

"No, although I could have. I confessed the affair to Margaret and we struggled to get through it. I hurt her terribly, but she's strong—stronger than I am. I love her very much and would never leave her."

"Then what was it, Phil? What required so much courage?"

The president told Bloomfield about Elizabeth Czerwinski, that she was beautiful and intelligent. He explained that she was from a poor family in Minnesota and didn't understand what she'd gotten into. Her father died years earlier and all she had was dreams of going to Stanford and on to law school. He went on to say that one day, she confessed that she'd set him up. Sheldon Hanrahan was using her to blackmail some of the very highest officials in government. It was an elaborate conspiracy. She'd tried to get out but they threatened to ruin her. So she turned to him. He explained that Elizabeth had information that would've exposed the entire conspiracy, but she was only a small part of it. There was extortion, payoffs, illegal deals, bribery, perverse sex—everything and anything. Elizabeth had them cold and was willing to come forward and confess to put an end to it all. But she needed the president's help. She knew no one would believe a poor, young girl like her. And her employers were very powerful. So she handed him the files— everything needed to bury Sheldon Hanrahan and his mob.

President Dougherty stopped and inspected his hands again. Finally, Governor Bloomfield leaned out of the shadows and put a hand on the president's shoulder. "You didn't do anything with it," the governor said. "You didn't help her, did you?"

The president looked at George Bloomfield and nodded. "I didn't have the courage, George. I wasn't willing to make the sacrifice. At that moment, I could've stopped Hanrahan. But I knew if I did, it'd expose my affair with Elizabeth. So I ended the affair and all contact with her. I sat on the files and did nothing. I let him off the hook. I swore an oath to protect and uphold the Constitution of the United States. I broke that promise to protect my own reputation."

Bloomfield removed his hand from the president's shoulder and fell back into the shadow. "You still have the files, don't you?"

"No," Dougherty replied, "I don't." The president leaned on his elbows and slowly rocked back and forth. He started to say something and then stopped. Bloomfield remained silent in the shadow.

Finally, the president said, "Four months after I broke off our affair, she killed herself, George. The day she died, she got a note to me saying she'd lost all hope. Sheldon turned her into a whore, she said, and her dreams had died. They were holding her mother hostage, too. She planned her suicide to expose the grand plan. Her only hope was that I would find the courage to come forward with the documents she gave me.

"Do you know what I did instead?" the president asked. "At two-thirty in the morning, I shredded the files in the Oval Office. I was so afraid of ruining my reputation, I destroyed everything. I betrayed my oath of office and cut a deal with Sheldon Hanrahan. Then I arranged a cover-up using the Secret Service and CIA. All of us who were being blackmailed came together to save our necks but we did nothing to save Elizabeth Czerwinski. I made sure there was no investigation into her death. I let her die for nothing, George. She sacrificed her life for her country and I wasn't even willing to sacrifice my goddamn reputation."

The inside of the Yukon stayed silent for a long time. In the darkness, the air didn't move. Finally, the president took a handkerchief from his back pocket and wiped his eyes.

As the president held the handkerchief in his lap, he said, "You heard about the FBI report that came out today about the assassination attempt on Howard? I was behind the report getting out. I believe Hanrahan orchestrated it to get Howard elected on a sympathy vote. The problem is we can't prove it. I'm afraid they'll spin the report as a smear tactic and use it to Howard's advantage. He'll get elected anyway."

Bloomfield looked hard at the president. "There's something you can do to save the situation, isn't there?"

Dougherty blew his nose and stuffed his handkerchief back in his pocket. "Yeah," he replied.

After a while, Bloomfield moved from the shadows and reached for the door handle. Before he opened it, he said, "Phil, if I'm elected I'll remember what you said—it takes courage to be the president of the United States. I'm sure it does, my friend. I'm sure it does. Thanks for meeting me."

Bloomfield got out of the Yukon and slipped into his limo. The big black car drove out of the parking ramp leaving the president alone.

Dougherty sat in the quiet darkness of the Yukon for a long time. Yes, he could do something. He just needed to find the courage to do it. He had to make the sacrifice.

He reached over to the front of the car and honked the horn for his driver to return. As the driver climbed into the car, President Dougherty said, "Get me back to the White House. I have something important to do."

FIFTY-FOUR

THE CAMRY'S TIRES SQUEALED as Nan turned the last corner before coming to the Nicollet Avenue bridge. The one-hundred-yard long, forty-foot high bridge spanned Minnehaha Creek and a tree-lined parkway that ran along both banks. She wasn't sure where she should go. She didn't remember if the man had said to meet him on Nicollet Avenue itself or under the bridge at the creek or on the north side or south side of the parkway. She guessed he was on the secluded parkway under the south side of the bridge. She punched the accelerator and headed for it.

For Jenny's sake, she hoped she had guessed right. She spotted a black Escalade parked underneath the great white arches of the bridge. It looked like the same car she'd seen following her the day before. Nan pulled up behind the Escalade and came to a halt with a screech. She threw the Camry door open, ran to the back of the Escalade and peered in. There was nothing in the back. She looked in the back seat, then the front. The car was empty.

She scanned the area around the creek. "Jenny?" she cried out. "Jenny! Where are you?" She couldn't see Jenny anywhere. The creek rolled along its low banks and a cold breeze made the leafless trees sway. The cars on the bridge forty feet above, made a rhythmic thumping sound as they drove over the bridge.

"Over here," she heard a man say. She spun around and saw a man standing in the shadows ninety feet away leaning against one of the massive arches. Jenny was not with him.

"Where's Jenny?" Nan demanded, shouting over the distance. "Where's my daughter?"

"Do you have the letters?"

"Yes."

"Bring them to me."

Nan ran to the Camry and grabbed the package of letters from her briefcase. She held the silver package out as she approached the man. "Where's Jenny," she demanded again, her voice shaking.

"Keep coming," the man said. As Nan got near, she could see he had dark hair and a lean build. He was dressed in a black overcoat with a dark green turtleneck sweater underneath. His eyes were intense. Along the side of his leg, he gripped a pistol with a long silencer. Nan's heart sank.

When Nan was a few feet away, she pulled the package of letters back. "Where's my daughter?" she shouted. "Did you kill her, you bastard? You'll have to kill me to get these letters unless you tell me where Jenny is."

The man grinned. "That won't be a problem. But there's no need right now. Your daughter's fine. She's probably in her second class of the day at school, wondering where she left her cell phone. She's cute, but I wouldn't bother with a kidnapping when a simple burglary would do." He reached into his pocket and pulled out Jenny's pink cell phone. "I'll have to make sure I get this back to her. You know how teenage girls are about their cell phones."

Nan felt a wave of relief. This man hadn't kidnapped Jenny after all. He'd used her phone to lure Nan to this secluded place. But now, a new fear gripped her. She was standing only a few feet from a man with a gun who would surely have to kill her once he discovered what she had learned from the letters.

The man slipped Jenny's phone into his pocket and held his hand out. "The letters," he demanded.

As another car thumped across the bridge overhead, Nan slowly raised the letters. Then, quick as a snake, the man grabbed Nan's wrist and snatched the letters from her. His grip was strong and she let out a shout.

"Shut up," the man said. "I need to see what's in these. You and I are going for a drive. If you try to get away, I'll kill you. Am I clear?" He put the gun to her head.

Nan nodded. She wasn't breathing again and everything around her had lost its shape. The only thing she could see was the man's face and the only thing she could feel was the cold barrel of the pistol pressed against her head.

"Walk to the car, slowly." The man pointed Nan toward the Escalade and they began to walk. Nan knew if he got her in the car, this man would kill her. The letters revealed too much. She was equally sure that if she ran, he'd shoot her in the back. So she did neither. Instead, she bent her knees and let herself slump to the ground.

"What are you doing?" the man shouted. He kicked her. "Get up, bitch!"

Nan didn't move. He'd have to drag her kicking and screaming to the Escalade and he surely didn't want to do that. If Nan had to die, she'd do it when and where she wanted to. At least if she died here, she wouldn't just disappear and leave Ben and Jenny with a lifetime of anguish over what happened to her.

"I said get up!" The man pulled Nan's arm but she stayed on the ground. He brought the pistol to her head again and pushed the cold steel into her temple. "Okay," he hissed. "If this is what you want, you got it. You have until the count of three to get up and walk to that car or I *will* kill you. Am I clear?"

Nan stayed on the ground and the man said, "One."

As she sat on the ground with the pistol to her head, Nan's breathing returned to normal and everything around her grew clear again. Minnehaha Creek gurgled and rolled in front of her and the great white arches of the bridge loomed overhead. She thought of Ben and wondered how he'd cope with her death. He had been a good, true husband and they had always been deeply in love. His heart would be broken, but he would find the strength to go on.

The man said, "Two."

Nan thought of Jenny and tears welled up in her eyes. She knew she had given her daughter a great start in life. Jenny was strong and Ben was loving and supportive. Nan's death would be difficult for Jenny, but she would cope, too.

Then Nan realized she'd never know the pride for Jenny when she graduated from high school or the sweet sorrow the day she went off to college. She would never share Jenny's joy on her wedding day and she'd never hold her grandchildren in her arms. And she would never make love to Ben again.

But Nan had known a great love with Ben and a mother's special love for Jenny and she realized she had been enormously blessed. She closed her eyes and tears rolled down her cheeks.

Then she heard the man say, "Three."

FIFTY-FIVE

Nan didn't know what death should feel like. She expected to hear a muffled gunshot and feel the heavy thud of a bullet as it struck her skull and tore into her brain. After that she expected to be at peace—no pain, no worries, none of the constraints of time and space. Free at last from everything.

But peace never came. Instead, she was trapped in a bizarre nightmare and couldn't tell what was dream and what was real or even if she was alive or dead. At first, she didn't recognize the shouts of the man far away. Then eventually she realized what she was hearing. "Pierce!" she heard the voice say. "Don't do it."

As she sat on the ground, she opened her eyes and tried to locate where the voice was coming from. She looked to her right and thought she saw two men running toward her from underneath the arched bridge. One of the men was tall, well dressed in a suit and a wool overcoat. The other was a large man in a black leather jacket. He was pointing a gun at the man behind her.

"This is none of your business," she heard the man behind her say. "Let me handle it."

"If you shoot her, Victor will kill you," the well-dressed man said. Nan thought she recognized his voice. "Just holster your pistol and let's not make a scene. Do as I say, Frank."

Nan wiped the tears from her eyes with the back of her sleeve. She looked at the well-dressed man with the familiar voice. He was closer now and she could see he was wearing large dark glasses. It was Sheldon Hanrahan.

She felt the man behind her step back as Sheldon and the large man stopped feet away. "Holster your pistol, Frank," Sheldon repeated.

"She's read letters from the girl to her mother," the man behind her said. "She knows too much."

"Do you have the letters?" Sheldon asked.

"Yes," the man answered.

"Take them and go. I've talked to Richard Craft. He's ordering you to back off. Before you murder Ms. Smith, I suggest you call him to verify your orders."

After a long pause, the man said, "This isn't over." Then Nan heard footsteps go around her and saw the man who almost killed her walk to the black Escalade and drive off.

Nan sat on the cool, damp ground. She couldn't wrap her mind around what had just happened. She thought she might be dead and in a bizarre alternative reality. She noticed a hand extended to her. She looked up and saw dark glasses and the face of Sheldon Hanrahan looking back. She took his hand and pulled herself up.

"Are you okay?" Sheldon asked.

She took a deep breath, forced a few hard blinks and looked around. Minnehaha Creek still gurgled and rolled under the great white arches of the Nicollet Avenue bridge.

Yes, she was still alive. Then she began to sob. Sheldon put an arm around her. "I won't hurt you," he said softly. "You're safe now, Nan. It's over."

Nan leaned into Sheldon and cried. But as she cried, she realized she was in the embrace of the man who ultimately caused what had just happened to her. She pushed away and wiped away her tears. Sheldon offered a white handkerchief. She refused it. She glowered at him, "You're responsible for this," she said. "You and your damn games. The way you use people, what you did to that poor girl. You made her kill herself and you almost got me murdered."

Sheldon carefully tucked his handkerchief inside his pocket and looked out over the creek. "Come, let's go for a walk," he said, "You're upset and shouldn't drive for a while. A walk will calm you and give us a chance to talk." He took her arm and gently pointed her toward the pathway along Minnehaha Creek.

Nan shook him off with a jerk. "No," she said.

Sheldon took her arm again. "I want to talk to you, Nan. And I won't let you drive yet. A walk will help. Come. Victor will escort us."

Nan knew Sheldon was right. She shouldn't drive. She was shaking and didn't have full control of movements. She glanced over at the huge man named Victor and knew she'd have to take a walk with Sheldon. She let him lead her to the pathway along the creek and they began to walk together. Victor followed a few paces behind.

Sheldon walked slowly with his hands behind his back. "That was a close call. I believe Mr. Pierce would have killed you if Victor and I hadn't showed up. I didn't want that, Nan."

Nan's legs felt strange making it an effort to walk. She pushed herself to keep going. "How did you know I was here?"

"Victor has been following you for the past several days. We've been following Mr. Pierce, too, but he gave us the slip this morning. When he did, we thought he might go after you. So I got in my car and joined Victor watching you. We lost you when you started speeding. But we found you again, here. Just in time."

Nan's legs still weren't working and her mind was racing. She looked out over Minnehaha Creek. The tidy parkway along the banks was a place she and Ben used to walk when they bought their first home less than a half mile away. It was a special place for her but after what had just happened, it wouldn't be special any more. She wished she didn't have to walk here with Sheldon Hanrahan, but she felt the presence of the large man behind her.

"Minnehaha Creek," Sheldon said casually. "Laughing water. Minnehaha of course was the lover of Hiawatha in the Longfellow poem, *The Song of Hiawatha*. I memorized the entire poem once—all five thousand lines. It's true, I really did. My literature professor at Harvard—Dr. Tobias was his name—didn't believe I could do it. He said he'd give me an 'A' if I did. It wasn't easy. It took over a month and the recital, in front of the entire Harvard literature department, took over two hours. It would have been much easier to study for the class," Sheldon said with a smile.

"Have you ever read the poem, Nan?"

"No," she answered.

"It's about the life of Hiawatha and tells how he lived in the wilderness of eighteenth century America. The poem is a tribute to survival. The Indians had an innate understanding of survival that we've forgotten today. Survival is not a guarantee."

"Is that why you're trying to take over the government through blackmail?" Nan asked. She felt her strength starting to return.

Sheldon looked over at Nan. "So, the letters revealed everything. It's a good thing Mr. Pierce got them from you. There was no need to kill you, though. Pierce is overzealous. You know of course, that if you go to the police or the press without evidence, I'm afraid they won't believe you."

"We'll see," Nan replied.

"I'm sorry if you don't agree with my tactics, Nan, but frankly, it's the only way to acquire power in Washington today. The two-party oligarchy prevents anyone from ever making a run at national office except for the people under their control. The Republicans and Democrats insist on taking over campaigns and they milk candidates and their financial supporters dry. Until we have better candidates, until we break the two-party grip on U.S. politics, we'll never do anything important."

Nan tried to keep her attention on what Sheldon was saying. "Is that why you break the election laws—to beat the system?"

"Can you think of another way? And don't be naïve, Nan. Everyone breaks the election laws."

Sheldon continued to walk casually with his hands still behind his back. "My guess is you and I aren't very far apart on our beliefs regarding the election system in our country. I heard you resigned from Bloomfield's campaign. I bet I know why. They're planning a dirty campaign and you don't want to be a part of it, right?"

Walking was finally easier but Nan's mind still wasn't completely right. "I... I didn't want to be involved in a campaign like you ran two years ago, Mr. Hanrahan."

Sheldon smiled. "I'd be pleased if you called me Sheldon. Yes, I should apologize for that. I wasn't very nice. But my tactics were tame compared to some."

"Tame, Mr. Hanrahan? That was tame?"

"What I did two years ago was nothing. Anyway, when you have a higher cause as I have, election laws mean very little."

"A higher cause?" Nan said. "Just what is your cause? You have everything a person could ever want. Why do you want control of the government, too?"

Sheldon turned his dark glasses to Nan and frowned. "Do you really believe I have everything I want?"

Nan didn't answer.

Sheldon faced forward again. "There are some of us, who believe the democratic system of government is designed to support the weak. It's threatening our country and ultimately, the human race. The most fundamental law of nature is that the strong must survive for the species to survive. Hiawatha understood that principle. But today, we've forgotten it. Our government has built massive programs to help the weak. The way we're going, the human race is heading for extinction."

They'd come to a footbridge over the creek and Sheldon motioned for them to turn around and head back toward the cars. Victor let them pass and stayed behind them as they walked.

Sheldon continued. "Some of us believe we can do more than simply survive. Do you realize our understanding of the human genome puts within our reach the ability to develop humans who could live productive lives for hundreds of years? If we put our resources behind that, can you imagine the advancements we could make? In a mere few hundred years, we'd solve all of our problems. We could turn the world into utopia."

"The problem with your philosophy," Nan replied, "is someone must choose who survives."

Sheldon nodded. "The question isn't who makes the choices, rather what the choices are based on. Today we choose to support the weak and therefore we choose extinction. I believe the choice should be to support the strong. Think about it, Nan. Utopia, Eden, Arcadia, Xanadu, Shangri-La. Isn't that the kind of world you want your daughter Jenny to have?"

Nan was beginning to understand the man behind the dark glasses. There was something wrong with what he was saying but her mind wasn't clear and she couldn't think of what it was. And she really didn't care. "Fine, Mr. Hanrahan," she said. "You work for your Utopia or whatever you want to call it. I just want to go home."

"Of course," Sheldon said. "You appear to be feeling better."

As they walked back to the car, Sheldon's words echoed in her mind but Nan could only think of Jenny and Ben. A few minutes earlier, the thought of her daughter being murdered had been almost too much to bear. Then, when she faced her own death, she realized the only thing real in her life—the only thing that mattered—was the love she had for Ben and Jenny.

And then she knew what was wrong with Sheldon's vision. As they walked along Minnehaha Creek toward their cars, Nan said, "Mr. Hanrahan, you talk about creating a human Utopia. But do you know what you don't see behind those dark glasses of yours?" Sheldon looked at Nan. His face was expressionless.

"What ultimately makes us human isn't whether we are survivors or not," Nan said. "It's that we have the capacity to love each other. And that's where your concept falls apart. It's based on a loveless view of the human race. If you've ever known true love, you'd know what I'm saying is right."

Sheldon didn't respond right away and Nan could tell her words had hit home. Finally he said, "That's an interesting point of view, Nan. I'll have to give it some thought."

As they took the last few steps to Nan's car, she said, "Thank you for saving my life, Mr. Hanrahan. I hope you find what you're searching for someday."

"Do take care, Ms. Smith," Sheldon replied.

As Sheldon and Victor watched from the banks of Minnehaha Creek, Nan got into her car and headed to the Starbucks to meet Ian Rutter. She was thankful to be alive and that that man had not kidnapped Jenny. She wondered if she should go to the police and tell them about her ordeal. She decided that Sheldon was right—without evidence, they wouldn't believe her.

For now, she had to meet with Ian Rutter. But without the letters as proof, he probably wouldn't believe her either.

FIFTY-SIX

THE EARLY AFTERNOON FLIGHT from Minneapolis to Regan International Airport got Ian Rutter back to his office at the *Sentinel* at 3:35P.M., just in time for him to grab his notepad and pen and head across the mall to the White House. The president had called an emergency news conference at 4:00pm so it would make the evening news and Ian had to fill in for Silvia Mendoza until the paper hired someone to take her place. The White House communications office didn't say what the news conference was about—just that it was very important and he should not miss it. They'd issued no advance press release and Ian suspected it had something to do with an unpopular pardon or a controversial bill the president was trying to sneak through Congress during the last few weeks of his presidency.

As he hurried across the mall, he thought about his meeting with Nan Smith. His trip to Minneapolis had been a waste of time. Nan Smith had told him a fantastic story about a conspiracy to take over the government led by Senator Howard's billionaire campaign manager Sheldon Hanrahan and his cronies to pursue some vision they had of Utopia. There was also an elaborate cover-up by the White House to keep secret an affair President Dougherty had with one of Howard's interns and the transgressions of more than a dozen high-ranking government officials. Nan had even said that less than an hour before they met, she was almost killed for what she knew about the conspiracy.

When Ian asked to see the letters, she said she didn't have them because someone had taken them from her at gunpoint. "So," Ian had said, "you don't have proof of any of this? All you have is the accusation of a woman who has disappeared and some letters you don't have any more. I'm afraid it's not enough for a story."

Nan Smith had said she understood but could do nothing more than tell him her story. She apologized for bringing him to Minneapolis and said that if Ian wanted to investigate, she'd be glad to go on record. He said he'd call if he decided to go forward with the story. Then, he headed to the airport.

On the flight back to D.C., he decided he wouldn't pursue the story. Nan seemed like a credible source, but what she told him was unbelievable. And he didn't have the time or the staff or the approval from Bradley Schwartzman to do an investigation. He remembered how Bradley had first reprimanded, then fired Silvia for pursuing the conspiracy theory. Maybe Silvia was right and maybe Nan Smith was telling the truth, but without evidence, he would not risk his career on a fishing expedition.

Ian cleared White House security and settled into a chair in the pressroom. All the major press was there. They'd brought in extra chairs and still, reporters had to sit on the floor and stand in back. Apparently, the president was making a big deal of his announcement, whatever it was about.

At four o'clock, the television lights blinked on illuminating the lectern with its blue and gold presidential seal. Several of the president's staff came in. After a few minutes, President Phil Dougherty stepped into the room and up to the lectern. The president usually held a commanding presence when he addressed the press corps, but now he looked small and sad and the skin on the back of Ian's neck began to tingle. He could tell something big was about to happen.

"My fellow Americans," the president began, "It causes me great pain and embarrassment to have to confess something I've kept secret for over five years."

The pressroom sat in stunned silence as the president went on to describe his affair with Elizabeth Czerwinski. The air was thick with tension and the only sound in the room was the president's voice. The president explained that his affair was part of a grand conspiracy led by Sheldon Hanrahan to blackmail high-level government officials. He admitted he had organized a cover-up to protect his reputation and that he'd endorsed Senator William Howard to continue it. He apologized to all Americans for his weakness and lack of courage to act when the country needed him. He asked for forgiveness and said he would humbly accept any punishment congress and the courts saw fit for him.

At the end, he pulled himself straight and said, "My only hope is that my confession will help correct my mistakes and keep our great country strong." He walked out of the pressroom without taking questions.

Ian, along with the rest of the press corps, sat without moving as if what they had just heard was part of a great, misunderstood joke. Eventually, reporters rose from their chairs and scurried out of the pressroom.

Ian stayed seated. Nan Smith had indeed told him the truth. And Silvia was right about the conspiracy, too. Had the *Sentinel* let Silvia investigate, it would have had the scoop on the biggest story Washington, D.C. had seen since Watergate. But the newspaper management had been afraid of offending the D.C. establishment and the *Sentinel* didn't get the scoop.

Silvia was right about newspapers, too. They'd lost their edge. They had become nothing more than mouthpieces for the D.C. elite and had ignored their duty as the fourth estate.

Ian walked out of the White House, back across the mall to the *Sentinel.* He still had inside information from Nan Smith and from the research Silvia had done. Perhaps he could lure Silvia back to the newspaper to help conduct the investigation.

And this time Brad Schwartzman wouldn't stop them.

FIFTY-SEVEN

SHELDON HANRAHAN SAT ALONE in his office watching the news analysts try to make sense of the president's shocking confession. He couldn't believe what the president had just done. He thought he had Dougherty pegged—a proud, two-term president with an impeccable public record and a secret to conceal.

He had to admire Phil Dougherty. The president had made what was for him, the ultimate sacrifice—his reputation. Sheldon didn't think the president had the courage to do it. But there he was, on national television, destroying his reputation just to keep Sheldon and his inner circle from getting their hands on the White House. It was a bold move—the type he would have made.

Sheldon wasn't worried about what would happen to him. The accusations the president had made would be only a minor setback. He had the best legal advice money could buy and people in Washington on the payroll to help him. He'd escape prosecution and, with an effective counter attack, he might still get Howard to win the election.

Sheldon pressed the 'Off' button on the remote and the television went dark. He went to his desk, reached into a drawer and pulled out a small mirror. He removed his dark glasses and looked at himself. One handsome, perfectly formed eye and one horribly deformed, lidless eye stared back at him. He focused on the ghastly eye.

Things could have been different for him if not for his repulsive eye. He could have been the president himself. Maybe his beliefs would have been different, too. Perhaps if he hadn't had lost so much, he would have come to believe what Nan Smith had said about love being the key to the survival of the human race.

And maybe, with two good eyes, a woman—a woman like Nan Smith—would have loved him.

He slipped his glasses back on and put the mirror in the drawer. Yes, his life could have turned out differently, but it hadn't and he had learned how to survive.

And he would come back, stronger than ever.

FIFTY-EIGHT

Election Day

THE BEDROOM WAS DARK when Nan awoke from another nightmare about Frank Pierce. She got out of bed trembling and terrified. She tried to shake the nightmare away but knew she wouldn't be able to go back to sleep. She went to the bathroom and splashed cold water on her face. She looked at herself in the mirror. The circles around her eyes and lines on her face clearly showed the effects of her ordeal. It was going to take time, but she'd get over it. If only the nightmares would end.

Perhaps they'd end today. It was Election Day.

She pulled on her robe and slippers in the dark and went downstairs. The clock on the stove read 5:15. She brewed a pot of coffee and the aroma filled the kitchen. She poured herself a full mug, went to the den and turned on the television. Perhaps it would get her mind off the nightmare.

The news shows were already talking about the election. On a set with a huge map of the United States in the background, a female anchor interviewed a bearded Georgetown University professor. "This is the most dramatic election in the history of the United States," the professor said. "Even more dramatic than Bush vs. Gore in 2000. With all that happened leading up to the election, it's difficult to predict the outcome."

"Why is that?" asked the perky anchorwoman.

"The electorate is confused," he answered, looking professorial in his tweed jacket. "They're not sure what to make of the accusations that have been flying around the past few days—President Dougherty's allegations against Senator Howard and his campaign manager, and the surprise discovery of Governor Bloomfield's internal e-mail about his willingness to negotiate with terrorists. Of course, everyone is denying everything and none of it will get sorted out until after the election."

"So, professor, who do you think will win?"

"I wouldn't venture a guess but I believe it will come down to what happens in California."

The television flashed the latest poll numbers from California. Bloomfield and Howard were dead even.

All that happened leading up to the election. Three weeks earlier, Nan would've never imagined she would have been involved in one of the most controversial elections in the country's history. From the moment President Dougherty had announced his support of Senator Howard, her life had been turned upside down. In a few short weeks, she'd gone from being a state campaign manager to being offered the position of White House Communications Director to resigning her position with the Bloomfield campaign and almost being murdered. It seemed like a bizarre dream.

As she looked back, she wished she would have gone to the police right away when Mrs. Wilson accused Senator Howard of murdering her daughter, but it probably wouldn't have made a difference. When she made a report to the police after the incident with Frank Pierce, she could tell the detective who interviewed her didn't believe her. He said the police would investigate and if they uncovered anything, they'd get back to her. But what would they find? Frank Pierce was a professional killer and wouldn't have left evidence of his visit to Minneapolis. They'd certainly destroyed Elizabeth Czerwinski's letters and poor Mrs. Wilson was gone, too.

Nan also wondered if the authorities would ever get to the bottom of what Sheldon Hanrahan was up to. She doubted they would. Sheldon was too smart and had the resources to derail any investigation. There was still a real possibility that Howard would win the election and Sheldon and his cronies would get control of the White House. Nan prayed that Bloomfield would win and wondered if she had done the right thing by resigning from his campaign.

After Nan's third cup of coffee, Ben plodded into the den, yawning. "You're up early. You all right?"

"I couldn't sleep."

"Worried about the election?"

"They can't predict the outcome," Nan said. "They think it'll come down to California."

"Great," Ben said as he scratched his head messing up his hair even more. "Our country's future depends on the wackos in California. I gotta get some coffee."

As Ben disappeared down the hall toward the kitchen, Nan felt a pang of guilt for not telling him the whole story of her ordeal with Frank Pierce. She had told him Pierce had faked kidnapping Jenny and had threatened her at gunpoint to get the letters from her. She never told him he held a pistol to her head and had almost killed her or how terrified she had been.

She hated her Scandinavian stoicism. She wished she could have told him every detail and cursed and cried and screamed and gotten it all out. But that wasn't her way. She'd handle her emotions quietly, by herself, and not burden Ben with her problems. He had enough to worry about with his still-struggling agency.

She heard Jenny upstairs getting ready for school. Ever since she thought someone had kidnapped Jenny, Nan had clung to her daughter. She knew her fear wasn't rational. Jenny wasn't in any danger. But the thought of losing her had so terrified Nan that she worried whenever they weren't together. Over the weekend, she'd stopped Jenny from going to Marisa's house by taking her to the Mall of America to buy a new cell phone to replace the one Jenny thought she'd lost. And Nan insisted on taking her to school and picking her up after lacrosse practice.

Nan knew she'd have to get over her fear for Jenny. For the time being, however, she'd continue to cling.

*

After breakfast, Ben went to work and Nan took Jenny to school. Nan's anxiety returned as Jenny disappeared into the building. She tried to push it aside and headed off to vote.

The lines were already long when she arrived at the polling station in the neighborhood elementary school. The election official at the door of the gymnasium predicted it was going to be a record turnout. As Nan waited in line, an elderly man in front of her wearing a Twins baseball cap and leaning on a cane greeted her with a smile.

"Can you believe this election?" he asked. "I've been voting since 1944. I've never seen anything like it."

"Me neither," Nan said.

"I don't believe what they're saying about Senator Howard and Mr. Hanrahan," the man said with a wave. "Seems to me it's a bunch of political hooey."

"I wouldn't be so sure," Nan replied.

When Nan got to the front of the line, the election official handed her a ballot and pointed to an open booth. She marked her ballot for George Bloomfield and on the way out, they gave her a red, "I Voted!" sticker.

She drove back home. It was time to find a new job. She sat in her home office searching the Internet for groups advocating election reform. The groups she found focused on either campaign financing or balloting reform. None seemed to be concerned with the way candidates campaigned. *Wasn't anyone against campaign dishonesty and dirty tricks?* she wondered. *Wasn't anyone concerned about ending negative campaigns and attack ads? Didn't anyone want elections to be about issues?*

In the afternoon, she turned off her computer and lugged the television from the den into the kitchen to watch the news coverage while she cooked dinner. Ben had suggested that he pick up Jenny from lacrosse practice and take her with him when he voted. Nan had wanted to pick up Jenny herself but agreed to let Ben do it instead. Perhaps she was beginning to recover.

As Nan slid the apple pie in the oven, the back door crashed open followed by the clunk of lacrosse cleats hitting the floor. "Hi, Mom," Jenny said, "I'm home."

Thank God Jenny is home. Nan didn't let her relief show. "How was school, sweetie?"

"Good," Jenny answered. "I got an 'A' on my social studies paper. It was about elections."

"Wow! Congratulations. Come give me a hug. Did you go with your dad to vote?"

Jenny gave Nan a quick hug. "Yeah, there was a long line."

Ben stuck his head in the kitchen as he took off his coat. "I'll say," he said. "The longest I've ever seen."

"Well," Nan said, "I guess that's something good about this crazy election year. It got people out to vote."

"What's for dinner?" Jenny asked.

"Pork chops and apple pie. It'll be ready in an hour."

"Apple pie on Election Day," Ben said. "Perfect."

The family ate dinner at the kitchen table with the television on in the background. As the results came in, the news analysts called each state as they went for either Howard or Bloomfield. As predicted, Minnesota went to Howard, the native son. And, as the Georgetown professor had predicted, the entire election was coming down to California. The exit polls in California had the race too close to call. There was only a razor-thin edge for Governor Bloomfield.

*

After dinner, Nan and Ben moved to the den to watch the election returns while Jenny did her homework. Nan rested her head on Ben's shoulder as they watched. She was glad to be home with the man she loved. She was glad for the simple pleasure of just being alive.

Shortly before 9:00, Jenny came in, said good night and went to bed. An hour later, they still hadn't called California for either candidate. Ben yawned, and said he was heading to bed, too.

"You staying up?" he asked.

"Yep."

"You should go to Bloomfield's campaign headquarters and watch the returns there." Ben said.

Nan nodded. "Yeah. I've been thinking about that. I kinda want to."

"So go."

"May be I will."

Ben kissed Nan good night and disappeared down the hallway. Nan sat in the den for a few minutes, then grabbed her car keys, pulled on her coat and drove to Bloomfield's Minnesota campaign headquarters. News trucks and parked cars lined the street so she had to park a block away. She hadn't been there in over a week and it felt strange coming back, but it was exciting, too.

As she got close, she could see the place was packed. She pushed through the red, white and blue door. Stephanie was the first to see her. "Nan!" she said. "You're back!" She gave Nan a hug.

"Just to see the returns," Nan said, smiling.

"I'm glad," Stephanie said.

"How are you?" Nan asked.

"You know, I'm doing just great," Stephanie said with a smile.

Nan nodded toward the bullpen. "What's the latest?"

"Too close to call," Stephanie said. "They're still counting in California."

"I better check it out," Nan said. She walked into the bullpen. The big TVs that Bob Hilton had brought in were showing the election returns from several different networks. The anchors were interviewing pundits who kept shaking their heads. Frank, Lora, and Will saw Nan and others greeted her with waves and hellos. Off to the side was Hank. His arm was in a sling and his eye was a greenish yellow, but the knob on his head was gone. He grinned when he saw Nan.

"Well, well," he said.

"Hi, Hank," Nan said giving him a hug. "How are you?"

"Much better. Karen isn't too happy with me being here, but I couldn't stay away."

"Me neither," Nan said.

Hank pointed a chin at the TV. "What do you think of the election?"

"Crazy," Nan replied. "I have some things to tell you."

"Yeah, I want to hear it. But you have something to do first. We got a call from Bob Hilton. He left a message for you to call him if you came in."

"Hilton?"

"You have his number, right?"

Nan nodded. She patted Hank on the shoulder. "We'll talk after," she said.

She went to what was once her office. She sat at the desk and looked out at the people in the bullpen. These were her people. They were passionate about their candidate and what he stood for. They probably didn't know or even care that the election system was broken and needed to be fixed. They just wanted George Bloomfield in the White House so he could lead the country in the direction they believed was right.

She watched them stare at the TVs and talk to each other. Some looked worried. Some looked hopeful. They hugged, shook hands, gave each other pats on the back. And then she realized how much she wanted to be one of them. She wanted to feel the passion she'd first felt in college. But it would be a different passion. It wasn't just about winning and losing. It was a passion for her country, her family and doing the right thing.

She took out her cell phone. She pressed the number for Bob Hilton. He answered on the third ring.

"You're at the Minnesota office, aren't you?" he said without saying hello.

"Hello, Bob. Yes I am," Nan said. "Bloomfield's my man. I wanted to be here."

Bob chuckled. "Good," he said. "I'm glad you called. I wanted to say thank you for what you did for the governor."

"I quit, remember?"

"Yeah, I remember," Hilton said. "And Nan, it was the right thing for you to do."

"Yeah, well. Now I won't be the White House Communications Director."

"Probably not," Hilton said.

There was a long silence. Then Hilton said, "I gotta go. I just wanted to say thanks."

"I really hope George wins," Nan said.

"Yeah. Me too," Hilton replied.

*

A half hour later, Nan was telling Hank about the last crazy weeks of the campaign when someone yelled, "There's a winner!" The screen on one of the TVs flashed, "Winner Declared." Everyone stared at the TV and the bullpen went still.

Someone turned up the volume as the announcer said, "With 97% of the votes counted in California, NBC, along with the Associated Press, projects the winner of one of the most bizarre presidential elections in our history is Minnesota Senator William Howard."

ABOUT THE AUTHOR

FOR OVER THIRTY years, Bill Andrews was a marketing/brand
executive/copywriter with several Twin Cities ad agencies and
Fortune 500 companies. At night and on weekends (and
sometimes during the workday!) Bill wrote fiction.

Bill's novel, DAUGHTERS OF THE DRAGON—A Comfort
Woman's Story, won an IPPY for historical fiction and has made
several bestseller lists.

Today, Bill is retired and focused on his writing.

DAUGHTERS
OF THE
DRAGON

A COMFORT WOMAN'S STORY

BY WILLIAM ANDREWS

DAUGHTERS OF THE DRAGON
A Comfort Woman's Story

DURING WORLD WAR II, the Japanese forced 200,000 young Korean women to be sex slaves or "comfort women" for their soldiers. This is one woman's riveting story of strength, courage and promises kept.

The Japanese take Jae-hee, a 14-year-old Korean girl to be a sex slave, or "comfort woman" for the Imperial Army. Ja-hee suffers terribly at the hands of the Japanese. Now with Japanese gone, she must carry on an important family legacy.

Her terrible ordeal shapes the rest of her life as she finds and loses true love in the surreal communism of North Korea. After escaping to the south, she's forced to run a *kijichon* (brothel) for the American military in South Korea. Finally, she finds success in the cold capitalism of South Korea's economic boom until her coworkers discover that she was a comfort woman. But through courage and strength, she's able to fulfill her duty to her family. Set within the tumultuous backdrop of 20th century Korea, this book will make you cry and cheer for Ja-hee. In the end, you'll have a better understanding of the Land of the Morning Calm.

Set within the tumultuous backdrop of 20th century Korea, *Daughters of the Dragon* by award-winning author William Andrews will make you cry and cheer for Ja-hee. And in the end, you'll have a better understanding of the Land of the Morning Calm.

Praise for DAUGHTERS OF THE DRAGON

William Andrews has created a masterpiece of fiction.
- Midwest Book Reviews

This book is an easy 5/5 stars, with its passion swept across the pages. This book spoke to my very soul. EVERYONE should read this story and pass it on.
- Brittany McCann – Author and Reviewer

I finished reading "Daughters of the Dragon" and remained still in my chair with the book in my lap. I was enveloped in the characters and their stories. The author's descriptive passages made me sense the beauty of the country, the desperation of war, and the humanity, good and evil, of each character.
- AMiB: Amazon Power Reviewer

Very emotional story that is hard to put down. Well-developed characters and vivid descriptions bring the experience to life. Sad that it is based on historical truths, but definitely a story that needs to be told. Reading this book provides a poignant look into the Korean culture and a true sense of the strength it takes to be a survivor.
-KE Burke" Barnes and Noble reviewer

I have to admit, I was not sure about this book. A white man telling this story.... I just didn't know if he could pull it off. But he did. It was powerful, unsentimental, and not gratuitous. I am beyond impressed. The reality of this story is still VERY raw across Asia, and it is important that it be told in order to understand the current relations between Japan and its neighbors.
-Rosanne: GoodReads Reviewer

Have you ever read a book that you don't want to end because it is that good? That is how I felt about Daughters of the Dragon: A Comfort Woman's Story. The author handles this difficult subject with great care; the story is captivating and well-paced. I will look forward to reading the next book by William Andrews.
                    -Minty Mom: Amazon reviewer

This was an awesome book, about something that you never hear of. The devastation is impossible for anyone to comprehend, and yet the courage and strength that these women had is fantastic. I HIGHLY recommend this book. I read often, and many, and this book easily rates in my top 15. I can't wait to read more by this author.
                    -Ryan Ober: Amazon reviewer

This book is both a tragic and triumphant telling of the atrocities that over 200,000 Korean women had to endure at the hands of the Japanese soldiers during WWII. It is an unforgettable story that for too long has not been told. The author provides historical information that is easily read and powerful. I highly recommend this book to everyone who loves to read and shares a thirst for knowledge. I am looking forward to more from this author!
                    -Karen Rogers: Amazon reviewer

AVERAGE AMAZON REVIEW: 4.8 stars out of 5 from hundreds of reviews.

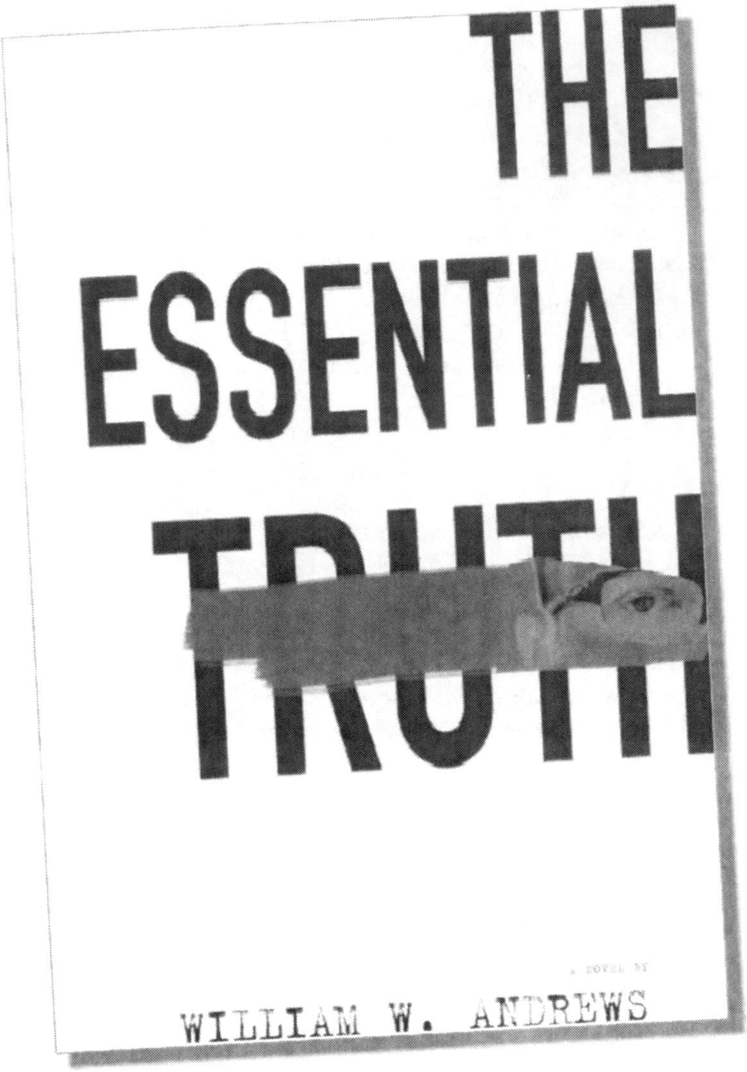
THE
ESSENTIAL
TRUTH
A NOVEL BY
WILLIAM W. ANDREWS

THE ESSENTIAL TRUTH
A Novel by William Andrews

WHEN THE FOUNDER OF Jacob and Marin Advertising mysteriously dies, Ben Smith must take over the agency just as their largest account comes up for review. He becomes the victim of Watergate-like dirty tricks because his agency does the campaign advertising for Congresswoman Janice Theilen who is running against Senator William Howard for his senate seat. Sheldon Hanrahan, the billionaire head of a rival advertising agency, controls Howard and needs the Senator to win big in the election so he can launch a presidential campaign. If Howard wins the presidency, Sheldon will impose his radical vision on America. To keep the agency afloat, and to keep Howard from winning reelection, Ben must confront not only Sheldon but also demons from his past. And, he must learn to become a leader. The stakes are high, and Sheldon is a powerful and cunning foe, but Ben has secret allies behind the scenes.

The Essential Truth is full of suspense, mystery and action as well as plot twists, a murder investigation and even a chase scene. And, *The Essential Truth* shows the reader the quirky personalities and workings of an advertising agency.

**WINNER OF THE MAYHAVEN AWARD
FOR FICTION**

CPSIA information can be obtained at www.ICGtesting.com
Printed in the USA
LVOW06s2134140116

470661LV00004B/487/P

9 780991 395835